CASTLE & KEY
A TWO MONARCHIES NOVEL

W.R. GINGELL

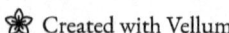

IN THE TWO MONARCHIES SEQUENCE

For everyone still caught in the little box they came in, desperately trying to escape.

PROLOGUE

"Well now, this *may* be my fault," said Susan.

Five horselords turned varied looks of gloom, incredulity, and annoyance on her. An elite force in the kingdom of Glause's mounted army, they were familiar with war, skirmish, and the odd bandit attack. They were also by now quite familiar with the vagaries of their New Civetan attaché, Susan Farrah, by whose aid they had gotten into—and often out of—a greater number of sticky situations than they might otherwise have encountered.

Overwhelmingly superior numbers and a breakdown of diplomatic processes had seen to their present position today. Miryum, her short-spear and buckler tossed carelessly atop the other confiscated weapons, had been tied in an uncomfortable curve. Her wrists were lashed tightly behind her, and a short length of rope connected her bound ankles to her bound wrists, a testament to her fighting prowess while tied the first time. Katrina and Curran were bound back-to-back and far too tightly to breathe with any comfort, and Brennan had been wrapped in a coil of rope as long as it was strong. Emmett, bound with a similar spiral of rope, had the additional discomfort of being strung by his ankles to the main support pole of the conical tent. He was looking slightly flushed, but as taciturn as ever.

Miryum asked, "What on *earth* did you do to these people, Susan?"

"It's more what I wouldn't do, actually. When we met, the chieftain decided that I'd make him a wonderful wife—he's been trying to convince me of as much every time we meet. I thought he'd have gotten over it by now."

"Got news for you," said Brennan. "He hasn't."

"No, he's pretty determined, isn't he? The first time, he only posted guards on the tent."

"The *first* time?" said Katrina, rather breathlessly.

Curran said, "Sit still, my darling: your exertions are making me light-headed."

"Well, yes," explained Susan. "He does this quite a lot; he's under the impression that my escaping is maidenly coyness. I must say, he does seem to have learned from our encounters, though."

"Not enough," said Emmett, flexing his shoulders. Susan hadn't seen him wriggling, but he'd managed to loosen the spiral of rope that sausaged him, and it uncurled in slow, lazy coils as he flexed. Her own bindings were quickly loosening due to a small knife that she'd pinched from the chieftain.

"If he had any sense, he would've spelled the ropes as well," agreed Brennan. "Go around kissing stray chieftains who want to marry you, do you?"

"Of course!" said Susan cheerfully, wriggling her shoulders free. "How else was I supposed to get his knife? Besides, he's a good kisser."

"We noticed," said Miryum dryly.

Emmett made an unimpressed sort of grunt as he curled up to unhook his feet and dropped lightly into the dirt. He silently approached Susan as she delicately flicked her stolen knife at the knots that bound her ankles, and she let him take the knife, watching without flinching as he wrenched it through rope a mere hairsbreadth from her skin.

"A bit raw, but nothing too bad," she said, observing her bare ankles. There was quite a bit of her bare at the moment: the chieftain was a firm believer in the traditional wedding garb of his people. That meant that Susan had been dressed in silky blue pantaloons that were distressingly thin and buttoned only just below her knees, leaving her calves quite bare. The bodice of the ensemble was scarcely better: her stomach was covered, true, but the neckline scooped low and wide, and her arms had also been left bare. Silky blue ribbons fluttered from her shoulders and tickled her calves when she walked, the exact colour of the desert sky if they could have seen it above them.

Emmett batted the ribbons away and lifted one of her feet for inspection.

"They're *fine*, lummox," said Susan.

He ignored her, but after running a thumb over the slight damage, he seemed to come to the same conclusion and released her. Susan grinned and resisted saying 'I told you, didn't I?' because she was well aware that she would have done the same for him regardless of assurances.

"We're fine too," said Brennan. "Thanks for asking. Just peachy."

Susan said amiably, "Oh, shut up," and untied him, which kindness he repaid by wriggling his eyebrows at her wedding garb.

"Very nice, Su!"

Emmett gave him a casual backhand in passing, with the immediate effect of laying him out in the dirt again, and went on to untie Miryum. Susan smirked and untied Curran and Katrina, and by the time everyone had gathered together in the centre of the tent, Brennan was also once more on his feet.

To Susan's amusement, Miryum and Emmett exchanged glances—one of their coded communications that always made them seem as though they shared a single brain—and then Miryum translated for the others.

"Do you want to try and sneak out, or hit hard and run fast? We could probably get out if we hit hard and run fast, but it won't do much for our diplomatic relations; the king will understand, but if we kill anyone—"

"I'm all for sneaking," said Susan, bright and sanguine.

She knew the chieftain rather better than any of her companions did, and if the group could only sneak away without anyone noticing for long enough, everything would come out exactly as it was meant to. As a matter of fact, Susan had counted on that when she brought the horselords to meet with this particular Lacunan chieftain on a mission from the Glausian King. She was quite sure that the king had also counted on it.

"Oh, sneaking without a doubt!" agreed Curran, and Katrina nodded.

Susan had seen the glance that passed between him and Katrina while Miryum spoke, but unlike Emmett and Miryum's unspoken communications, their secret language was opaque to her.

"Sneaking it is, then," said Miryum.

"What about the agreements?" Emmett asked briefly. "Won't they try to destroy them?"

"We'll have to pinch them, of course," Susan said. "And I'd like to see them *try* to destroy a sheaf of twenty double-spelled spellpapers in a single night!"

"No need for all of that," Brennan said. "And I'm not being shoved under a tent again, so—"

"You're the slenderest," pointed out Susan.

Miryum looked up from checking her weapons. "Don't complain, Brennan; if you don't want to be pushed through windows and holes in tents, you should eat a bit more."

"I'm naturally slender, you overgrown set of beanpoles!"

"My friend," said Curran, putting a hand on his shoulder, "resign yourself to being hefted through or under any necessary obstacles, and put on a happy smile!"

"I won't, you know," Brennan said.

Susan looked at him suspiciously. "What do you know that we don't know?"

Brennan flourished a set of papers at her. "Already got them," he said. "Figured it was a good idea if something went wrong. Knew that if we were working with you, something was *bound* to go wrong."

"How appallingly rude!" said Susan, grinning. "You know things only go wrong when I mean them to go wrong!"

Brennan eyed her gloomily. "Yes. Knew that too. It's why I pinched the perishing things!"

"Aren't we all working well together these days!" Susan said. "Won't the king be pleased! All right, if someone's got a good bit of muffle magic, I can make sure anyone who looks at us thinks we're just the breeze passing through camp and flapping the canvas."

"Be the first time any of you lot were mistaken for a zephyr," remarked Brennan, and expertly dodged two swings and one attempted kick. "Careful! You'll make me drop the papers, you perishing long-shanks."

"I'll muffle our steps," said Emmett, his eyes amused. "Weave your spell, stripling."

They found their horses waiting patiently exactly where they'd left them, half a day and a few decent struggles ago.

Susan, who had somehow never had her own horse and hadn't thought to ask for one in this case either, as usual travelled along pillion behind Emmett. She had asked for a horse the first time she went out with the horselords, of course: no horse had shown up for one reason or another, and Susan had scrambled up behind Emmett on his huge, grey horse with a cheerful, "Coming up, lummox!" at him.

Emmett had gone quite still, which made her think at first that she'd done something wrong, but the other horselords had only grinned and set off at a sprawling sort of jog-trot that settled into a more cohesive canter while Susan clapped Emmett on the shoulder and asked, "Are we stopping or going?"

"Going," he had said briefly, and urged his big, dappled grey after the other horselords.

After that, there hadn't ever been a question of Susan getting her own horse. It was taken for granted that her place was behind Emmett, and since she was more than happy to have her hands free while lacking the horsemanship to ride thus by herself, everyone was content. It was also pleasant to be able to rest her head against Emmett's broad back and yawn at the swiftly closing day around them as they moved steadily through the desert.

"I suppose we'll have to hustle home?" asked Miryum, when the patchy bushes began to show more often between stretches of red sand and the air itself began to feel less scorching. The horses, finding more solid ground, had begun to move more quickly despite the heat. "We can leave the horses to rest and feed in the closest town once we're back on solid ground, but—"

"Oh no!" said Suzan breezily. She was quite well aware of how close they were to safety. "No need to leave the horses! We're nearly on the border, and he won't come after us once we're past that: fair is fair, and I've gotten away again. He'll just refuse to treat with anyone but me—and he'll be better prepared next time."

Emmett's voice sounded for the first time since they'd set out. "He'll have to treat with someone else next time."

Susan said comfortingly, "No need for that, lummox: I'm not worried about having to marry any time soon. I'm quite sure the chieftain would regret it intensely if he did manage to marry me, and I have other ideas about marriage anyway."

"Marry anyone you want," said Brennan, squinting toward the reaching shadows of the approaching treeline in the last light of the highest sun. "Poor fellow! Point is, none of us like being tied up like sausages, so if you want to do this sort of lark, I'd rather you did it alone."

"A lie if ever I heard it," Curran said lightly. "None of us would let you do this alone, Su."

"Well, no," Brennan admitted. "But she ought to think of the rest of us."

"That's fair," said Susan. "Sorry, Brenners. I'll buy you an ice in the closest town, all right? And we'll talk to the king about all of this when we get back."

"Lights ahead," said Emmett, his back humming against Susan's cheek as she yawned.

She stretched to look around him and caught sight of a faint glow of colour toward the horizon. "How nice!" she said. "We can have a bath and something good to eat."

"Just in time," said Miryum. "I don't want to push the horses too much further."

"Especially not Emmett's horse," muttered Brennan.

"Anything nearer by? Or even a little further off?" enquired Curran. "I've a feeling that those lights are from a town by the name of Way Back Wells."

"Odd name," Brennan said suspiciously.

"A suspicious place, or so I've heard," said Curran lightly. "Just quietly, word is to stay away from the town—there are no explanations as to why."

"I vote to stay away," Brennan said. "Awful places, towns. Nasty little secrets lying around and popping up when you least expect 'em. People expecting you to eat potatoes."

Miryum and Emmett exchanged a glance and seemed to come to a silent agreement, which Miryum spoke. "The horses need rest and a rub-down, and we need food—and there's nothing else on the map for another half-day's journey in any direction. We'll stay for the night and keep going as soon as we breakfast."

"As you wish," said Curran mildly. "But if I'm murdered, I'll haunt you."

"I thought you were going to haunt me for the rest of my life," Katrina said, shooting him a meditative look.

"My love, undoubtedly you'll be slain attempting to save my wretched life; we'll haunt Miryum together."

"And if it makes you feel better, I doubt that you'll be made to eat potatoes," added Susan. "If I'm not wrong, the main food group around these parts is sheep, followed by beef. Probably not even a sniff of a potato. It's all the volcanic soil as soon as you get away from the desert—grass everywhere."

"There are always potatoes," Brennan said gloomily. "And if I get bitten by a small dog, I'm disowning the lot of you."

ONE

From the size of the town as they rode in—a reasonably sprawling and well-built town in the midst of a fertile valley that sat on the red, volcanic soil Susan had mentioned earlier —Susan had expected less staring. She was clothed in her normal tunic and riding breeches again by now, so her appearance shouldn't have been contributing to the staring, at least.

"Lambs to the slaughter, or amusement second only to the fair passing through?" wondered Brennan, with no lessening of gloom. "Never seen so many noses in m'life."

There *were* a lot of noses poking through curtains, thought Susan in amusement. She was shielded from the full extent of the staring by Emmett's immensely broad back, but she caught sight of enough shifting fabric, outright jaw-drops, and double-takes to be aware that whatever else this town was used to, it was not visitors.

She felt Emmett shift slightly in the saddle and said quietly in his ear, "Regretting it, lummox? Should we keep going?"

After a few moments of silent deliberation, he said, "No. We'll stay one night."

"That's the spirit!" Susan said bracingly. "What can happen in one night, after all?"

"Inn ahead!" called Curran gaily. "How delightful to know that dinner and beer are only a half-hour away!"

Much to their surprise, however, the innkeeper greeted them at the door with folded arms, an impassive face, and the news that there was no room for them.

"How appallingly unfortunate!" said Susan, letting her gaze linger on the windows, through which she could see the entirely empty taproom—and then the stables, which were likewise empty. "I suppose this is your busy time of year."

The innkeeper went very faintly red about the ears, but said stoutly, "Very busy. I doubt you'll find a room in the town."

"A bustling metropolis, in fact," said Curran, nodding.

"There'll be a procession passing through tonight; there's no room for visitors."

"We'll try further on," Miryum said shortly, but Susan was quite sure she didn't miss the raised brow of the innkeeper that seemed to say, *Aye, and we'll see about that.*

As they walked the horses sedately down the street, Curran said softly, "It's an odd procession that leaves an inn empty by passing through."

"Told you," said Brennan gloomily. "Secrets. Never stop in little towns."

"There's another inn further down," Katrina said. "Don't get too comfortable in your glooms just yet, Brennan!"

But the next inn, silent and sullen in the street with its lack of guests, also refused them. The only other two inns within fifteen minutes' walk also turned them away—the second innkeeper going so far as to peek at them from between his curtains without venturing out or even answering their calls. By the time Katrina and Curran had gone ahead to scout out any other possible places to stay in the deepening night, it was beginning to look as though they would have to sleep in the streets.

"At least we'll have a good view of the procession," said Susan, with a soupçon of cheerful sarcasm. "And you're nice and warm to curl up against, lummox. Otherwise, I'd freeze my bones this close to the desert."

"I'm interested to see this procession," Miryum said dryly. "It must be something if it puts the entire town at a standstill just to allow it to go through."

"I'll find us somewhere out of the way," said Emmett.

Miryum, despite her profession of wanting to see the procession, nodded. "Meet us back here when you've found somewhere. I'm inclined to move on again without either baths or food if there's much more nonsense."

As much by proximity as by habit, Susan accompanied Emmett, her gaze darting around the streets as they plodded sedately along the almost empty, red dirt-lined road, and her ears very faintly spell-lined to make the most of the echoes from the building-fronts while filtering out the sound of hooves.

Bad luck, said a whisper, with a flutter of fabric at a window. *Bad luck for a bride on her wedding day.*

It's all bad luck anyway.

Strangers? They'd best not linger.

They'll keep the castle folk waiting, at this rate.

We'll be starting soon; who's that in the street?

Focused on the whispers and snatches of conversation, it took a little while for Susan to notice that Emmett had glanced over his shoulder at her at least twice—something that was tantamount to a demand for attention when it came to Emmett.

"Whispers," she said. "I'm collecting. Go on looking: I'm sure we won't find anywhere, but I'd like to be sure."

"Someone's tampered with the road," he said, and faced forward again.

"Yes, I suppose so," said Susan. "Do what you want with it; I'm going to collect a few more whispers as we go."

She vaguely felt what he meant as they continued; a trickle of magic ran through the red dirt as a constant presence, but there was another magic there, strong and subtle and misleading. If Susan had had to guess, she would have expected that it was something to keep them away from important areas and steer them toward the outer edges of town. There was also a good amount of power pumping into the town toward various sources, though those sources all seemed to initiate from the same direction—up and out. Susan would have liked to have known what it was doing and where it was going, but she didn't have the attention to deal with it.

Emmett, on the other hand, was strong enough to deal with it, so she left him to do so and turned her attention back to listening. There wasn't much more to hear that she hadn't already heard, to her mounting surprise; everything seemed to circle around *the bride, the castle, the procession,* or *the strangers.* She even heard a *We'll have to do something about it if they linger,* and an unpleasant grumble very akin to *Outsiders shouldn't be in the way when there aren't enough jobs for us as it is.* Despite herself, Susan had to rub a hand over the back of her neck to settle the standing hairs there when Emmett finally turned his horse and took them back unerringly the way they'd come.

"Having fun?" she asked him, and saw the side of his cheek rise slightly in a smile.

Emmett enjoyed puzzles: he had a slow, methodical, and entirely exasperating way of pursuing a thing until he got it, unable to be hurried, worried, or deterred from his course until he got there. No doubt he'd enjoyed following the streets he wanted to follow while ignoring the magic that tried to lead him astray.

Susan found herself grinning, her spirits lifting again. Emmet was a delightful restorative.

They re-joined Miryum just in time to see Curran and Katrina walking their horses up a narrow side street toward them. From a distance, Curran waved brightly and managed to convey with one-handed gestures that they had found an inn and that there were hopeful signs of being able to lodge there.

Still, when they were closer, Katrina said anyway, "We found one. It's a ways off the main road, so we might have a better chance of not spooking the keeper. It's the only one we were able to find, so it's our last chance."

"Let me talk to them, this time," Susan said as she dismounted, cutting off Curran, who had probably opened his mouth to say the same thing.

In most cases, she would have deferred to Curran's superior

finagling skills, but in this case, she rather thought she might do better.

Emmett shot her a meditative look that suggested he was wondering what she was up to, but he didn't question her. He simply led the way back up the street from which Curran and Katrina had emerged and fell in beside them when they caught up with him, the horses' hooves echoing solidly against the buildings along the street. Miryum and Susan were left to bring up the rear with Brennan, to whose mumbled monologue they lent an amused ear.

The final inn, when they found it, had a new, shiny sort of look to it, like a newly bought top hat. Even the paint on the sign gave off the feeling that it had only just dried, and the innkeeper and his wife both bustled out at the first signs of movement.

They did, Susan noticed, stop suddenly when they saw that every one of the five people at present clustering around the front door was a stranger.

Susan flicked a look between the two of them and made sure to address the wife as well as the husband. "We'd like a few rooms," she said. "We noticed that you're off the main road, so we thought you'd be a bit quieter than the other inns—once we turn in, we don't like to be disturbed."

None of the horselords, Susan thought, missed the look that passed between the man and his wife.

Despite that, he said after a moment's hesitation, "We don't take in many guests. We're new-built, not even properly furnished —there's only a few pieces in the rooms from the estate sale last month to keep us over until we can do the thing properly."

"These good people don't care where we got our furniture!" scoffed the wife. "Look at them: they just want a meal and a hot bath."

Brennan visibly brightened, and even Susan felt cheered. "We don't much care about furnishings, so long as there are beds and baths," she said. "And a good, hot meal will be the first we've had since yesterday."

"I don't know," the innkeeper said, to the obvious disappointment of his wife. "It's the procession tonight, and we're full, so to speak."

"Looks like we'll have to sleep in the streets, then," Susan said, heaving a theatrically large sigh that seemed to wring the innkeeper's wife's heart. "I'm sure someone will sell us food, at least."

It wouldn't be the first time they'd slept in the streets—or a convenient park, if it came to that. The horselords slept with their horses more often than not when deployed, and Susan hadn't been speaking idly when she mentioned that Emmett was decidedly warm to sleep next to.

"You can't do that!" the innkeeper said, appalled. "It's not safe out there!"

"Dear me!" said Susan happily. She had wondered if she would get this reaction, and it was gratifying to find that her suspicion was correct. "But what can we do if there are no rooms for us? We've got to look after the horses, you know!"

"Of course we can't turn them away!" the innkeeper's wife said, scoldingly. "They've money to spend—you've money, haven't you, dears, yes, of course!—and they'll catch their deaths out there tonight!"

"It's not all that cold," muttered Brennan, who seemed to prefer sleeping on the open streets despite his obvious desire for a bath.

"We're not even on the main road," said the innkeeper's wife, as though making one last appeal. "They won't be in the way, and they'll keep to their rooms. The grand furniture won't bother them, I'm sure."

The innkeeper's jaw tightened, and Susan could have sworn that he pinched his wife's arm. Still, he appeared to hesitate.

"We'll keep to our rooms and be on our way first thing in the morning," Susan said, highly amused to discover that Brennan, in some way, had been absolutely right: there was certainly a secret here.

But although it might be amusing to discover what that secret was, it was far more important to get the horselords back to the king with the papers they held and thereby ensure that the Lacunan desert clans were given the navigation equipment and high-tensile metal parts that they needed to keep their airships scuttling across the red dirt desert's dunes. In return, the Lacunans would provide guides and equipment for Glausian miners who came to sift through the shifting red dirt for free magic.

That, thought Susan as she watched myriad emotions pass across the innkeeper's face like red dirt in front of a hefty breeze, was the important thing. Other interests would have to wait until later.

"Looks like the missus has decided," the innkeeper said at last, at just above a mumble. "Mind: you're not to open any doors that don't lead to your rooms once you're in the suite—leave the furniture alone. You'd best get your horses stabled and fed; we've an hour before the procession begins, and I won't have you out in the streets nearby to get into trouble."

"We wouldn't dream of getting into trouble!" said Susan earnestly, and followed the innkeeper around to the stables with the horselords.

There was hot food waiting when they got into the common room of their suite, and a small bath on either side behind a swinging door marked with a prim "gentlemen" or "ladies".

"You first," said Miryum to Susan, who cheerfully took her usual place in the bathing procedures when those procedures involved an actual bath.

Technically speaking, it ought to have been Katrina who went first—these days she was a half-inch shorter than Susan and therefore could be said to take up less space in the bath—but Katrina splashed more water than even Miryum with her truly formidable size, and preservation of water was the biggest concern.

Susan finished her bathing swiftly and efficiently, then retired to her own small room closest to the door while Curran was threatening to remove the slender Brennan from the bath by his hair. She gave Emmett a grin in passing, commiserating with him for having to wait until last for his bath, and shut the door behind her. The room was just big enough for a bed and a wardrobe, and a little space in which to dress or stretch, if she so chose: a delightful space that would keep her comfortably sleeping until their rising time. Susan couldn't help shooting a contemplative look at the wardrobe —which, she surmised, was one of the pieces of furniture that was new and to be left alone—but managed to restrain herself from opening it.

Since that time was still a decent way off, Susan threw herself on the bed in her cotton under-breeches and night shirt, and started up a commlink to talk to her sister until she could discuss the doings of the day with the other freshly washed horselords.

When the curving of the edges of the spell showed that it had connected with Isabella's hand mirror commlink, she wriggled happily and grinned.

A moment later, Isabella's face appeared, long and clever and stately, with a sprinkling of freckles across the queenly nose and extremely red hair braided over her shoulder and well past her waist, although that waist was at present somewhat extended with her second child.

"Hallo, Belle!" said Susan. "Shouldn't you be sitting down and drinking something cold with your feet up?"

"Susan," said her sister, in a contemplative sort of voice that made Susan feel rather small and sit up straighter, "I'm quite sure you told me that there had been a change of chieftain and that I needn't worry about you while you were away."

"Well, yes," Susan said guiltily, resisting the urge to clear her throat. "The thing is that there *had* been a change of chieftain; it's just that there had previously been another change that I didn't tell you about, so this change put the old chieftain back after the previous one. If I'd realised that you were overdue and that the worry might hurry the next kid along, I would have told you."

"I've a very good mind to name this child after you," Isabella said, an amused glint to her grey eyes that reflected a glow of lights and relieved Susan somewhat. "And for your information, Susan, I am indeed sitting down with my feet up! The last news we had of you was that you'd been taken prisoner by the chieftain I was quite sure you'd told me had been ousted, and the child showed no sign of taking your capture as the catastrophic event Delysia thought it to be. No doubt a very sensible child—I shall certainly name her after you."

"Don't do that, Belle! I'll feel as though I have to behave if I have a namesake!"

"I would be the last person to suggest that you need to learn how to behave," began Isabella, her mouth pious, "but it would be remiss of me to fail to mention that the horselords certainly can't be expected to teach you better manners than they possess, and as for Emmett—well, I'm quite certain you corrupted him at least a year since!"

"Oh, at least!" agreed Susan, as something soft thumped inside her wardrobe.

She might have thought it was from the main room, where the horselords were still scrumming for a bath, if it hadn't been for the fact that the wardrobe was right beside the bed and on the opposite wall to the wall her room shared with the main room.

Susan waited for another moment and was rewarded by a distinct slithering sound and a muffled exclamation from within the wardrobe.

"Good heavens!" she said happily. "I rather think there's someone in my wardrobe! I really do wonder if it's a coincidence, or if that's why they didn't want me to touch it. I can't help thinking that wardrobes aren't the best place to store living things, after all."

"How exciting for you!" Isabella said, with a pleasing lack of concern. "Shall you call in Emmett, or attempt violence by yourself? How did they get in there, by the by?"

"Well, the innkeeper did say they'd furnished with everything they got from an estate sale, so perhaps someone forgot to remove one of the estate children before selling," said Susan, shrugging. "I'm sure I don't need to bother the lummox at this time of day. Besides, I'm not sure he'd fit—I'd have to sit on his lap, and then what would Delysia think?"

"Nothing worse than you mean her to, I suspect," said Isabella, but her eyebrows rose when there came a thump loud enough to be heard over the commlink.

"I'd probably better see who it is before they knock the

wardrobe to pieces," said Susan. "Good night, Belle! Tell the kid it had better come out before I get home, won't you?"

Isabella gazed at her for a moment or two before she said thoughtfully, "I think I'd prefer it if you commlinked again when you're finished."

"All right, but if you see me with a black eye, it's your own fault," Susan said cheerfully, and ended the commlink.

The shifting and slithering continued from the wardrobe, as though the person within had been moving so much that the noise of their own movements had hidden from them the fact that someone else was in the room with them.

Susan flicked her legs over the edge of the bed and laid her bare feet silently on the floor, then rose and crossed the floor at a prowl. It would be nice to shake out her muscles in a fight after the half day of riding.

She reached out silently to the wardrobe knobs, and then, with a fizz of delighted excitement, flipped the doors open and found herself looking down into two frightened brown eyes that were surrounded by a massive puff of golden lace.

They stared at each other for a moment, Susan taking in the golden dress that had somehow been stuffed in a wardrobe that was by far too small for it, and the girl who was also far too small to have been stuffed into that dress gazing up at her in mute misery.

"Hallo," Susan said. "It looks a bit cramped in there; would you like to come out?"

The girl looked around in wonder as she removed herself from the wardrobe, her skirt expanding into the tiny room after her but not quite wholly escaping the wardrobe. Susan assisted her with a raised brow at the richness of gold lace between her fingers, and settled the skirt out of the way enough to lever the wardrobe doors shut again.

"I wasn't expecting visitors tonight," she said, as the girl turned a circle to fully appreciate her surroundings. "Everyone seemed a bit pent up about us being out on the streets, so I assumed there wouldn't be much chance of people running around."

Susan felt rather regretful when her words took away the wonder from the girl's face and replaced it with anxiety.

"I won't bother you," the young woman said, clutching her fingers together. "I just—can't I just sleep here tonight? I'll go away tomorrow before the sun comes up."

"If you need to," said Susan, now less amused and more concerned. "Look, what's your name?"

The young woman, her fingers closing around a small, ornate perfume pendant that hung from a long, golden chain about her neck, said, "I'm Janet."

No mention of station or rank there, thought Susan. Did that mean there was none? She couldn't be sure: Janet was certainly dressed in an ensemble far finer than anything that even the most influential ladies at court would wear, but the hands she was wringing looked faintly red and rougher than a lady's hands usually looked. Nor did she speak with what Susan was quite sure was the standard upper class Lacunan accent for this area; there was a broadness and nasality to Janet's voice that suggested she was middle or even working class.

"I'm Susan," she said, instead of asking any of the other questions she wanted to ask. She didn't want to frighten the girl any more than she was obviously already frightened. "You can sit on the bed if you'd like. Do you need something to eat? I suppose you've been in there for a while."

Janet sat on the bed but said, "Oh no! I couldn't eat anything!"

"You look as though you're ready for the procession tonight," said Susan, by way of changing the subject, since the girl really did look ill at the mention of food. "I haven't seen anything yet, but we've been hearing about it since we got into town."

Janet's brown eyes fastened on her again anxiously. "*We*? I thought—I thought it was just you!"

"You didn't hear the others bathing?" Susan asked, amused all over again.

She had heard Brennan being dragged out of the bath while she was on the commlink with Isabella; Curran would be bathing with more swiftness than his elegant appearance suggested, as usual, and there was an indistinct buzz of talk from the other room as he called out to Katrina and she answered him.

"I didn't—I didn't hear anything," said the girl, and she suddenly seemed almost terrified, her fingers white around her pendant. "Oh no. I shouldn't have run away. I didn't—I didn't mean to do it. I just suddenly couldn't bear to do it, and..."

Susan let the words sink away into silence without pushing, because Janet's eyes had welled with tears.

"Did you sneak out to see the procession?" she asked instead.

"No," Janet said in a small voice. "Actually, I *am* the procession."

"That's a wedding dress," Susan said in sudden realisation. So this was *the bride* she had heard being talked about in whispers behind curtains earlier! "It is, isn't it? It's a wedding procession?"

Janet nodded, her arms wrapping tightly around her upper arms and her fingers digging into the fabric of the sleeves. "Yes, they always have a procession for castle weddings."

"Castle weddings?"

"Didn't—you didn't see the castle on the hill?"

"Not even a pennant!" Susan said. "Is it a proper castle, then?"

Janet seemed to have sunk into anxious thought, but she roused herself to say, "Oh no. Not a real one; it's the estate that the town used to belong to. We've always called it *the castle* around here."

"You're passing through on your wedding processional, then," said Susan, thinking aloud. "I understand that. What I don't understand is why you're hiding in my wardrobe."

"I don't really understand it either," the bride said, biting her lip. "I don't think...I don't think I want to get married. I ran away, but I shouldn't have. I didn't mean to."

Susan kept her more personal thoughts to herself for the time being and merely said, "Yes, you said that before. Are you marrying the owner of the estate?"

"Yes. It's tradition: one of the townswomen has to marry the lord of the manor."

"Just because it's tradition doesn't mean that you have to be the

one to do it," Susan suggested gently. "It doesn't look like you're
terribly interested in being married."

The brown eyes filled with tears again. "I should be. Oh, I'm an
awful person!"

Susan had some quite firm convictions when it came to naming
the awful person between a party of two when one of those two was
hiding in a wardrobe because she was terrified to get married.

"I always make it a matter of course to say no to getting married
to someone when I'm hiding in a wardrobe to get away from them,"
she said. "But then, I make it a matter of course not to get married
to someone because it's tradition, too. Good heavens, what is that
noise?"

The bride, who had started violently and made a small, choked
protest at the battering sound coming from the door to their suite,
tottered to her feet as though in a dream.

"They've found me!" she said. "I suppose—I ought to go now."

"You don't have to go anywhere," Susan told her, but Janet was
already moving toward the interior door, still in that trance-like sort
of way that suggested she was going on instinct.

She followed Janet into the main room, where they were greeted
by perplexed horselords and an outer doorway fairly bristling with
soldiers, who were heavily enough armed to make Curran, who was
hanging over the top of the bathroom door and dripping on the
floor, raise an eyebrow at Susan.

"The bride needs to come with us," said the soldier foremost.

He wasn't wearing the official uniform of Lacuna, nor Lacunan
colours, though he did bear the insignia of a key on a background of
red, green, and blue that Susan had seen several times as they passed
through the town. Susan didn't doubt that every horselord in the
room had seen and realised as much: Miryum stood just a little back
from Emmett but on the right side of the door and in front of
Susan and Janet; her left hand was very close to the pommel of her
short sword, which she hadn't yet removed. Brennan lounged on a
chair that was turned away from the door with his lids dropped low
and his hand resting lightly on his small crossbow where it couldn't
be seen by the soldiers.

Curran, Susan was quite sure, was naked and unashamed, but she was also quite sure that he was hiding at least one weapon behind that bathroom door. Katrina openly leaned on her own crossbow, which was several times the size of Curran's.

Closest to the door, Emmett met Susan's eyes for a brief moment before he turned back to the soldiers and said, "That's up to the bride, I'd think."

"There are a few of us," said Susan softly, for the ears of the bride only. "I can easily get you out the window while my friends deal with this lot."

Janet straightened her shoulders and lifted her chin, and one of her hands dropped away from her pendant. "No," she said, and Susan felt her heart sink. "I can do it. I'll do it."

The bride turned her head, and Susan caught those brown eyes, glowing with determination. "I can't not do it. I'll make sure that no one else ever has to go up there again. You'll see."

"What's the answer?" asked Emmett, his eyes still on the guards but his ear turned toward the women.

"She says she'll go," Susan said, but the words felt bitter.

Janet was going of her own will, but Susan wasn't sure it was free will, and it grated at her that she could do nothing about it. Emmett had even given the girl a chance to think about it, and she'd still said she would go.

Miryum's elbow dropped a little; her hand came away from her short sword. She said shortly to the guards, "Stay where you are. She'll come out to you."

The bride went, her shoulders set and her chin high, but Susan saw how badly she was trembling. She followed Janet to the door, where one of the guards turned back to say warningly, "Don't follow, or you'll regret it. We have orders to see the bride safely to the castle."

"No need to be unpleasant," Susan said, smiling at him with what she hoped was terrifying friendliness.

She waited until she heard the last of the footsteps on the stairs and the outer door downstairs close for the last time before she stepped out of the room and turned back to the others to say, "I'll be back. That was the bride from the procession everyone was talking about earlier. I'll tell you what I know when I get back."

Emmett's eyes found hers. "I'll come with you."

"No, I think not, lummox. You'll scare the man."

"I think it would be a good idea if he were scared," Emmett said deliberately.

"Pleasant, but not useful," she said. "Let me do it my own way. I'll call if I need you."

To her relief, he nodded and simply closed the door after her. There would be time later to talk over what Susan knew—right now, she felt as though she wanted to know a little more before she discussed it with the horselords.

Susan prowled down the hall and downstairs, then straight into the kitchen, where she found the innkeeper sitting by the stove with a robe over his nightshirt and a haunted sort of look to his face.

She was pleased when her, "I thought I might find you here!" made him jump and spill the spirits he had been sipping over his robe.

"What are you—what are you doing down here?" he asked, putting his glass down with a shaking hand before he spilled any more. "You said you wouldn't leave the rooms!"

"That was before a bride hid in my wardrobe to escape being taken up to be married at the castle," Susan said. "I make it a rule to leave my room when someone hides in my wardrobe. I suppose the guards have gone now?"

"You shouldn't have seen that," he said. "Not any of it. Forget you did. You should have ignored anything you heard—I told you not to touch the furniture!"

"I'm not good at forgetting things unless there's a reason for it," Susan said pleasantly. "And right now, I don't have good reason to forget that I saw a young girl who didn't want to get married escorted out of an inn to go to a castle and get married anyway."

He picked up his glass again and took what looked like an unpleasant gulp from it. "You won't do any good asking questions about it. No one can help it: it's the way things are."

"What things?"

His eyes bored into hers. "If I tell you, you have to promise to leave the town at first sun's light."

"Oh, certainly!" she said affably.

The direction in which she went after leaving the town had nothing to do with the innkeeper, after all. Castle or Glause, it was all the same to him.

"There's a new bride every half-year," he said. "Sometimes it takes longer, sometimes it's shorter, but there's one roughly every half-year. The lord of the manor marries them after a procession through the village."

"Where does he keep them all?" demanded Susan in bafflement, unsure of whether to laugh or believe. "You can't tell me that he has them all sitting around his drawing room together! Where are the others?"

"Dead," he said simply. "Every one of them. Mostly he sends the bodies down for burial, but sometimes there's no body to send, or it's so badly burned that there's nothing left of it."

"You're telling me that every bride your town has sent up the hill to the castle has died within six months, and you keep sending them up there?"

"You don't understand," he said angrily. "No one could. No one from the outside understands that it's the natural flow of things —you go against it, and the entire town falls apart. For the sake— for the sake of the town...!"

"For the sake of the town, you sacrifice your young women," Susan said, with the clarity of searing anger. "Yes, I see. What sort of power does the lord of the manor have over you all that he can murder his wives with impunity and then send their bodies back to you?"

He muttered, "We don't know that he does kill them. It's accidents that happen—girls falling off horses, or falling downstairs. Some of them disappear. They say he's cursed, or the estate is; whatever it is, when we don't send someone, the town begins to fall apart."

"Yes, you said that," Susan said. "What do you mean, it begins to fall apart?"

"Parts of the outskirts sinking into the earth, magic running riot through the streets and confusing travellers—horses shying and killing people, kids turning odd and the old folk turning senile."

"And you believe that by sending a young woman in sacrifice to the lord of the manor every six months or so, you're stopping that?"

"I know we're stopping it!" he said furiously. "I've been here long enough to have seen the last time we tried to make an end of sending girls up there—my sister was the first one to go up to the castle after the village began to sink into the ground and run wild with magic. It stopped the next day."

"I see," said Susan. "Are the girls being killed to prevent that?"

"We don't do blood sacrifice here!" he said harshly.

"Oh, sorry," Susan said. "I assumed that sending girls up to a castle to die for the good of the town might figure as the same thing in your mind."

Bitterly, he said, "I suppose it must look the same to you. I don't have any more information for you—you'd best leave as soon and as fast as you can tomorrow. If they suspect I've told you anything, they won't let you leave."

"In that case, I appreciate you telling me," she said.

Although he smiled rather more bitterly at that as he stared into the stove's firelight, Susan had for once spoken entirely without sarcasm. She left him to his spirits and his memories, doubting that he would be able to say which of the two were more bitter, and went back upstairs to acquaint the horselords with exactly why this little town was on a suggested *do not visit* list.

TWO

"It's not a castle," said Brennan, slightly hoarse in the cool of the morning. "Not even a sniff of a moat."

As Susan had promised the innkeeper, they had left at the first sun's light; that first sun had barely risen as they left the town, glittering against windows and fence-tops while magic glittered amidst the red dirt, and as soon as they were out of the town, the castle was plain to see. In fact, as they ascended the hill toward it, Susan was left wondering how any of them had failed to see it from the town yesterday; even in the dusk, it should have been obvious, towering above the town as it did.

And as Brennan now mentioned, the structure wasn't exactly a castle. It had a grand appearance but that was mainly due to the fact that it was made from massive blocks of sandstone and from a front view was squarer in shape than a manor would normally have been even though, more correctly, it should have been called a manor. It also flew two flags: one on either side of the main, double-gated entrance they could see above them.

Those flags, Susan had noticed, were both emblemed with keys.

She wasn't sure whose horse stopped walking first, but certainly Emmett had drawn his to a halt very early.

"I hate to sound like Brennan, but I'm not sure that continuing to go up there is wise," said Miryum. She had also stopped. "After last night and the oddness of the town—not to mention the warning to stay away—it seems risky. And we already have our own responsibility."

"Look at it: proper windows, no arrow slits. Didn't even see it from town yesterday—you can't tell me that makes any kind of sense!"

"I had the impression that it's the town's grand estate," Susan said, ignoring Brennan's mutters. "She did call it the castle, though."

Emmett looked back at her briefly. "You still want to go?"

"I think we'd better," she said, feeling the frown between her brows. "Whatever else was happening, that girl didn't want to be taken off to get married—and we know that the girls who go up there are only lasting six months or so before they die. The rest of you can always go back to Glause while I'm having a poke about. Someone was saying in the bakery this morning as we passed that they're always looking for staff at the castle. I'm sure there'll be a way in for me."

"Not a good sign," said Brennan.

"I know, Brenners, but they can't just sweep young women off to get married—especially when none of the young women seem to survive longer than six months before they die."

"Delightfully useful things, curses," said Curran thoughtfully. "An excuse for any husband who's a bit too free with his fists or his magic."

"Or negligent estates that care more about what kind of magic and crops they get out of their lands than who it harms," agreed Katrina. "There's a lot of magic coming down the hill and into the town; I don't think it has to be a curse."

"No," said Susan thoughtfully. "But if the lord of the estate has been killing wives for the fun of it, he's been doing it for a long time while keeping people convinced that the town will fall apart unless they keep sending people."

"He's a strong magic user," Emmett said.

Susan saw his shoulders expand and then sink again in a silent sigh, and knew that he was making up his mind to come with her. "Yes, all right, lummox," she said. "No need to blow us away with your sighs. Of course you're coming in with me. Miryum, you can look after the agreements, can't you?"

"I'd prefer to come with you," Miryum said, treating Susan to a long, thoughtful look that made her feel delightfully warm and loved. "But magic is not my strong point, so I'd probably be very little use, and the agreements have priority."

"That's where it's so nice to be an attaché with the horselords instead of a horselord proper," Susan said happily. "I'm free to have other priorities when they turn up. I can't let that girl go up there to die without helping her out."

"What about the rest of us?" asked Curran. "I'm not prepared to talk about priorities when a girl's life is at stake, but—"

"The lummox and I will be perfectly fine by ourselves," Susan said. "The two of you and Brenners had best go back with Miryum; if there's any trouble, you can just say I went off on my own, as usual, and Emmett had to come save me from the consequences of my own actions."

"We'll see you to the top of the hill," said Miryum, over the top of Brennan's complaints of why *he* always seemed to have to bear the consequences of Susan's actions.

"Don't be like that, Brenners," said Susan cheerfully, kicking him gently in the leg in passing as Emmett urged his horse on. "Look at me, leaving you out of things. No consequences for you this time!"

"Just as well," he said, but he still seemed unhappy.

This, Susan knew as well as Miryum, who was smiling grimly, was because Brennan, despite his complaints, was rather sore at being left out of the fun. He had five sisters and was particularly sensitive when it came to women being treated badly.

"You're a darling, Brennan," she said, grinning back at him.

He looked distinctly worried. "Don't like it when you're nice to me. Always waiting for something nasty to be shoved down m'collar."

"Never mind, Brenners," said Katrina. "We'll rescue you. Ooof, there really is a bit of magic up here, isn't there?"

"It's been gathering since we left the town," Emmett said. "Threads of it from down there running all the way up here, as well as what's coming down. Stay to the right of the path, you four."

"And don't worry if we disappear suddenly," added Susan, feeling the softness to reality toward the left of the road along which she and Emmett were trotting. "There's an entrance spell here somewhere, but it doesn't seem as though it's trying to keep people out, just slow them down. It might be a bit much to plough back through to get home to Glause, though."

"No fear!" said Brennan, riding single-file behind the other three. "I'll stick to my side, and you stick to yours. No funny business."

"It will be a sad day when there's no funny business," Susan told him cheerfully.

Emmett snorted softly and added, "And if there's none to be had, you'll make it."

"It's delightful to be so well understood by one's friends," said Susan, and felt the words stretch out and go fluffy as the world around her also turned to a living version of cotton-wool.

Emmett might have said something in return—or perhaps the others on the far side of the road did—but Susan didn't seem to be capable of hearing or understanding or speaking for a few seconds.

That was a regrettable state of affairs, so Susan, flexing cotton-wool muscles and forcing cotton-wool brains to think, said aloud, quite clearly, "That's enough of that, thank you!" and put her arm on Emmett's huge forearm.

The warmth of his skin beneath her fingers made her heart jump in relief—he was alive and human, then, despite what the world felt like—and suddenly reality began to feel solid and present again. Susan kept her hand where it was, clutching at the firm reality of Emmett, and realised slowly that she could see the world around her again in all its sharp-edged nuance.

"Don't," said Emmett stiffly, his voice thick and choked, "Let. Go."

"I shouldn't dream of it, lummox," Susan said. "I rather fear the both of us would be lost if I did so. What a good thing the others were on the far side of the road. This is so much stronger than I expected from the outside!"

"Inside," he said, still slow and heavy.

"Yes, I think we are," Susan said, looking around as the horse beneath her seemed to grow solid once again.

Where there had been a road to their right just moments ago, there was now a wall: massive and high and repressive. The world around them was chilled with mist that clung to the trees of what seemed to be an overgrown orchard, and further up the dew-soaked hill was the foreboding aspect of the manor, rising out of the mist like an ancient god to tower over its domain.

The effect was beautiful, chilling, and not quite tangible—though when Susan stretched out with her free hand, balancing herself with her knees and the one hand that clung to Emmett's arm, the apple tree branch she touched was real, cool, and wet beneath her fingers.

"Just a moment, lummox," she said, and turned her head toward the massive wall beside them. Catching her breath, she yelled, "Miryum? Brenners! Anyone out there?"

The sound moved and expanded as it should toward her left and both before and behind her, but Susan couldn't convince herself it had penetrated the wall. What a good thing they had already discussed what would happen should she and Emmett disappear!

"Cold," said Emmett, with difficulty.

"You've got to let it know who's boss," Susan said, but she wrapped her arms around him anyway, because after all, his warmth and solidity had drawn her back from a mindless, cold world that had nearly swallowed her. And then, because she was worried, she pressed her cheek to his back as well, and added, "Concentrate on me, lummox."

He must have done so, and it must have helped, because in just a few moments, his arms dropped with less stiffness to cover her own around his waist. He detached them with all of his usual dexterity a few moments after that.

"I'm back," he said. "What was that? It felt like sand."

"I'm not sure," Susan said, still looking around with sharp eyes. "But it rather felt as though I were fodder for a moment or two, and I didn't really care for it. Shall we go on toward the castle?"

Emmett nodded, then said, "Wait. Get down. We'll walk."

"Probably safer," Susan agreed, much amused. "Can't be having an accident this soon after arriving, can we? We'll have to be careful until we know whether it's a cursed estate or a person that's doing the trick."

Emmett allowed her to use his arm to dismount smoothly and swung his leg over and down a moment later. He said, "There's too much magic here."

"That's not like you, lummox!" protested Susan. "Think what a lovely puzzle you'll have trying to sort it all out!"

"I prefer low-stakes puzzles," he said, and started up the hill toward the manor.

"You're going to be a lovely old man," Susan said, following him. "You'll sit in the park with your games in front of you and play anyone who walks past, and I'll never be able to drag you away until after the suns have set."

She found that Emmett was favouring her with an indeterminate sort of look. He asked, "*Are* you still going to be dragging me around in my old age?"

"You don't think you're going to get rid of me that easily, do you?"

"Only until the suns set, apparently," he said, but he was smiling faintly when he looked away, in that particularly Emmett way of his: lines by his eyes, the smallest crease upward of the lips, and an indent that was almost-but-not-quite a dimple in his left cheek.

"Speaking of suns setting," Susan said, relieved by that smile and looking around critically again now that she wasn't worried about him, "don't you think that the suns have gone back down a bit? Or is it just the general mood in here?"

"It's not dark," Emmett said, turning his own head to look around and then tilting it to look up. "But the mist is filtering more than it should."

"Exactly," said Susan darkly. "Very suspicious! I should be able to see the glow around the first sun at least, but all I see is a general lightness to the sky. If the fog is as thick as all that, it should be darker. Do you suppose we'd be able to see the triad if the mist was gone? Will the mist even leave?"

"You think we're in a pocket dimension?"

Susan hesitated. "I don't know. All I know is that it *feels* like a pocket dimension, and the idea of pocket dimensions is that you're not supposed to be able to feel that it is one. At any rate, it's good that the others are well out of it: I have the feeling that this is going to take a little longer than we were planning on being away."

This time, the look Emmett shot her was slightly apprehensive. "We'll see. Doors ahead."

Susan had already seen the doors—they were twice Emmett's height and about four times as wide each—so she interpreted the statement as a warning to be careful what they said from then on. It was a legitimate warning. After all, one never knew who was listening when doors and windows abounded, and they were in unknown territory.

"It's a good thing we met in the town," she said to him, stripping off her horselord overcoat and stuffing it into the saddlebag nearest her. "I would have been terrified to come through here alone, just to be a lady's maid!"

Emmett's eyebrow cocked. "Terrified?"

She continued blithely without acknowledging the challenge. "It's all right for you; you can apply for any of the vacancies that need strength or size. All I can do is help my lady in and out of her outfits and go to fetch tea."

"That's all, is it?" said Emmett, his cheek creasing slightly as a smaller door in the left-hand great door opened. "I'm sure your lady will be relieved."

Susan at first fancied she saw a woman in the shadows of the door—a strong, beakish woman with hollow cheeks and a ballerina's forehead—but when she blinked and looked again, although the face was still hollow and beakish, it was a man's face: hair neatly queued and tidy above a bottle-green overcoat that ought to have been two sizes smaller if it were meant for the wearer. Still, it was a good coat, with nothing pretentious or too furbelowed about it.

That face was set off by a second which appeared beside it a moment later—this one rounder but somehow harder, with blue eyes that stared sharply out of the shadows and seemed to suggest, without saying anything at all, that these circumstances were *highly irregular*.

The butler and the housekeeper, Susan rather thought. She climbed the stairs, leaving Emmett below, and gave a nod instead of a curtsey.

"I'm the new bride's maid," she said.

The butler looked sharply at her, as did the housekeeper, but it was the housekeeper who stepped out into the misty morning and said slowly, "Is that so? Well, I can't say that we weren't expecting someone, but what kept you?"

"I did hear," Susan said delicately, meeting the housekeeper's suspicious look with a limpid one of her own, "that there was some trouble with a wardrobe. I don't know exactly what happened, but I was told to wait until first light to set out, and so I did."

"Probably didn't want to confuse the master with two arriving at once," muttered someone, from somewhere inside. "There's always trouble with the furniture they take away."

Dear me! thought Susan. So all of those threads of magic that connected in the town and coalesced in one place did so *here*. No wonder she had found a confused bride in her wardrobe!

It didn't take the annoyed look that the housekeeper shot toward the interior of the manor to inform Susan that yet another someone had been within earshot until now, when hasty footsteps announced their departure. "You'd best come in," she said to Susan.

Evidently she had been speaking only to Susan, because when Emmett tied his horse to the lower colonnade to the right of the door and followed her up the stairs and into the house, the woman seemed both startled and discomfited to see him there.

So was the butler, who, with something of the shape and air of a budgerigar, made a pecking sort of movement in protest toward

Emmett, who was too busy looking around the grand hallway and either didn't see or ignored the movement.

The housekeeper's look turned sour, and she said rather more sharply than before to Susan, who had apparently moved a little too close to one of the massive and ancient pieces of furniture in the grand hallway, "Don't touch that, miss! It's worth more than your life's salary!"

Susan gave the grand old hall stand a frankly admiring look. "An antique, is it?"

"New as you are, miss, and I'll thank you not to scratch it!"

Much amused, Susan raised a brow very slightly at Emmett, who impassively refused to acknowledge that brow and continued to look around him.

The housekeeper, who seemed to be getting more suspicious by the minute, asked, "I suppose if we call the bride down here, she *will* know you?"

"I'm absolutely certain!" said Susan, with all of the bounce and verve of absolute truthfulness.

That bounciness seemed to assuage the housekeeper, even if the butler shivered a little. The suspicion in her demeanour vanished almost at once, but she said chidingly, "You shouldn't have brought someone with you, though. We don't typically take in matched pairs here. It makes things difficult."

"I came with him from the town below," said Susan. "He thought he might be able to get some work here and tagged along with me."

"We don't need anyone else," said the butler, picking at his chapped lips with fingers that trembled very slightly.

Susan wondered if he'd been drinking as deeply as his colour and mannerisms would seem to suggest, now that she saw him in the light of the massive chandelier that hung in a series of progressively larger waterfalls from the ceiling. Of course, Emmett's sheer size and bulk might have made him nervous enough to account for that colour and those twitches. She gazed at the butler a little longer, softening her eyes so that the attention wasn't as invasive, and wondered if the man always crossed his arms so tightly across his narrow chest, or habitually wore clothes that seemed to hang on him.

Mind you, if there was any truth at all to what she had heard in the town last night and this morning, Susan was quite sure that the stress of living in a house that routinely killed young women was sure to make anyone lose weight.

"That's a shame," she said. "He looks very useful, don't you think?"

"It doesn't matter," the butler said, gripping his upper arm more tightly with the hand that wasn't picking at his lower lip. "There are only a set amount of positions here, and not all of them have to be filled all the time. We make do. We always make do."

"Oh, I don't know," said the housekeeper, looking Emmett up and down in a way that made it very hard for Susan not to raise her brows again. "We lost another one last night, didn't we, Mr. Oswald?"

The butler seemed to flinch. "Yes, Mrs. Carmichael. The master's man had an accident, so to speak. But—"

"You know what will happen if we have to wait for the master to fetch another one. For all we know, it'll put him into a good mood to have it taken care of without the need to be dragging people around from the town. No one likes it when we have to do that, and not all of them manage to get through the protections. Whole, that is."

Susan managed to restrain herself from raising her brows a third time. So it wasn't just a procession with a not-so-willing bride: the lord of the manor also dragged off people to be his servants. Servants who, if what was now being said was true, were not guaranteed to live lives longer than the brides themselves.

"I'm already here," said Emmett, and the butler flinched once more, as if his sudden speech after a lengthy silence was startling. "There's no need to pull people out of their town."

"Any experience with dressing a lord?" asked Mrs. Carmichael. "I can see that you ride, at least—our master is an original and likes to have a valet who can ride out with him when the fancy takes him."

"Something happen to the stablemaster, too?" Susan asked irrepressibly.

Mrs. Carmichael's frosty eyes glanced off her and came to rest on Emmett instead. "The grounds can be dangerous," she said. "You'll need to make sure the master comes to no harm while riding, as well as keep him in proper style around the manor."

"I have experience in keeping people safe," said Emmett—and then, making Susan nearly choke, he asked, "What's the pay?"

"Five gold coveys each week," Mrs. Carmichael said, and Susan nearly choked once again.

If the people of the village were coming to the manor to die, they were certainly doing so at a very good price. Most valets would command a price of two silver coveys each week if they were very good at what they did; five gold coveys, Susan was rather certain, was the price of a lamb to the slaughter to sweeten the evidently sour deal that might otherwise stop people coming to the manor.

The butler, as if making one last attempt at reasoning with the housekeeper, said, "They're not townspeople—not really. We've got enough to spare from in the town without pulling in strangers, Mrs. Carmichael."

"You know as well as I do that the numbers need to match when we start," she said, in a reproving undertone. "The master is already on edge now that there's only four of us in the house; two more will round us out to the right number without having to wait to send to the town or see what comes through upstairs."

"No need to wait when you've got two people already here!" Susan said brightly, aware that she was pushing the bounds of believability but unable to stop herself from doing so. How fortunate that they had come just in time to forestall anyone from the town coming through what appeared to be the passage of furniture, whether willingly or not! "What a coincidence that we've arrived just in time!"

She and Emmett must present a very odd appearance—not to mention a distinctly suspicious one—and she was interested to see how much Mrs. Carmichael was prepared to blink at in order to fill the two positions. She had barely made a token resistance earlier

when it came to Susan's credentials, and she had since very deliberately tried to entice both Emmett and Susan with the idea of five
gold coveys each month.

"There are no coincidences at the manor," Mrs. Carmichael
said. "The master doesn't like them. You, miss—come up with me
and I'll take you to your mistress. Mr. Oswald will take you to your
master, young man."

Susan shot a grin at Emmett over her shoulder as she followed
the housekeeper down one step and out of the panelled and gold-
edged entryway into a vast, chequered-marble atrium that was
bounded on both sides by sweeping staircases. Her last sight of
Emmet was him dwarfing the entryway by his sheer size, the butler
leaning away very slightly to preserve some personal space, and a
half-quizzical, half-resigned look to his face that she knew very well.

There was no time to be looking back after that; there was far
too much to see and remember. They passed between and then
beneath the grand staircases, pushing through a double set of
carved, gold-tooled wooden doors beneath the landing and into a
dark, quiet hallway that had both sconces and the latest in gas
lighting fixtures—but only a single candle burning in every second
sconce.

"You've got gas lighting," she said, by way of asking without
asking about it.

"Those things have a mind of their own," Mrs. Carmichael said
comfortably. "They don't work—not steady-like, at any rate.
Ridiculous things; I'll never know why they were put in. I would
have said something about it if the master had asked. They'll be
turned on later tonight."

"I suppose the master doesn't come down here much, then?"
suggested Susan, straining her eyes to see the walls of the great hall
and uncomfortably aware of the yawning, shadowy space above her
head.

"Well, if you suppose so, you'd be wrong, miss," said the housekeeper. She seemed mildly pleased to be able to say so. "The master
doesn't care to see the portraits, so we don't bother to keep it well-lit
when the gas lights aren't on."

"Perfectly reasonable," said Susan, making a mental note to take a look along the hallway walls later, when she could do so by the light of her own magic.

She could see the vast, faintly gold-edged frames of what must be the portraits, but nothing beyond that other than the odd matte glow of candlelight against painted canvas every so often. What could be painted there that the master of the house kept the hall as dark as night to avoid seeing them? Susan had a suspicion that she knew what it could be, but after all, it was no good making assumptions when she'd only just arrived.

Susan took in the doorways along the hall: a music room on the left and a breakfast room on the right; then, further along to the right, a glass-doored room that opened out into a walled and glass-topped garden in the swift glance that Susan could spare it, while on the left, a closed door emanated the faint scent of something chemical.

Beyond that, the manor opened up into wings on either side of the grand hallway. Susan thought that Mrs. Carmichael seemed to speed up as they passed the yawning spaces, and she didn't blame the woman; the cavernous, shadowy wings were double the width of what they were now passing along, but just as shadowed, and a dusty breeze swept along the floor, chilling both her ankles and, somehow, her neck.

Some normalcy and brightness crept into the grand hall after the wings, though there wasn't much more to be seen. Now there was a butler's pantry on the right, well-lit and immaculately tidy, and what Susan assumed from the massive lock to be the porcelain and silver room on the left. Beyond that was only the kitchen, which opened through a final set of double doors to take up the entire end of the manor beyond, and a narrow staircase set back into the panelled wall on the right side of the hall.

"This is one of our staircases," Mrs. Carmichael said, gesturing at the cool, shadowed, wooden steps that bore very little similarity to the grand marble ones at the front of the manor. "I don't want to have to be telling you not to take the main staircases when you're not with your mistress, mind. They're not for the likes of us."

"I wouldn't dream of taking liberties," said Susan, in her best estimation of well-bred horror. "Which wing will I find my mistress in?"

"The left wing," said Mrs. Carmichael, leading the way up the staircase.

"How interesting!" Susan said, with utter truthfulness. She wasn't sure whether Mrs. Carmichael simply didn't observe cardinal directions or didn't know them, but the interest of calling the wing on the left of the house the "left" wing instead of the "west" wing, as it ought to be—if Susan's sense of direction had not misled her— paled under the consideration that the bride had been given a room in the side of the manor that could be expected to get the least sunlight and the most gloom.

She followed Mrs. Carmichael up the stairs and to the second story, emerging from a polite door to soft, sound-muffling carpet beneath her feet and the gentle glow of mist-softened sunlight through a series of windows directly across from the door. Susan took in a deeper breath and felt as though a weight had been lifted from her chest. She wasn't reliant upon sunshine for her cheerfulness the way that Curran was, but she also hadn't realised exactly how oppressive the air in the downstairs level had been.

What a good thing the lummox and I came alone! she thought to herself, continuing along by Mrs. Carmichael's side when they emerged from the staircase. She wondered briefly if Emmett and Mr. Oswald had already made it to the master's rooms, but there was no sign of either of them when she cast a surreptitious look over her shoulder to check the right wing as they proceeded down the left.

There were fewer windows along the left wing than there had been in the upper great hall, but there were enough so that Susan had a rather good idea of the layout of the left side by the time they reached an area of the left wing that smelt faintly of perfume, and where they might shortly, Susan thought, find Janet.

Her eyes lingered on the ornate garden which must be accessible from the music room on the first floor, and which was separated by a narrow hedge from the orchard beyond. It was still deep in fog and somehow disturbing to look at.

"I would have thought the fog would have begun to lift by now," she said aloud, throwing a glance out the windows of the other side of the wing.

There was fog there too, but not as much. The sandstone edges of the manor were crisply visible around the back of the kitchen and the gardens there were almost free of drifting cloud, too. No doubt being high on a hill made a difference, but Susan wouldn't have thought it would make that much difference.

Mrs. Carmichael shrugged one shoulder and stopped in front of an ornate door. "This time of year, the fog doesn't lift for most of the day."

"What time of the year?" asked Susan in interest.

She had been quite sure that it was summer when she and the horselords rode up the hill toward the manor—she was equally sure that they hadn't lost time in their dangerously woolly passage between outside and inside—and she could see the distant, blurry shape of the town through the mist toward the back gardens, so it was obvious that they were still where they had been this morning when they rode up the hill.

The housekeeper seemed to take a moment to process the question, as if she hadn't heard such a question before and didn't quite know what to make of it. At last, faintly puzzled, she said, "The fog doesn't lift much at this time of year," and knocked at the door in front of which she had stopped.

"So I hear," said Susan easily, and fell into place behind the woman like a proper lady's maid as Mrs. Carmichael opened the door.

Within the suite, with its great, high windows and stonework interior, massive wooden furniture had been effectively arranged to make the best advantage of the space; within that arrangement sat the slender young lady in golden lace, slumped back in one enormous red leather chair as though she'd fallen asleep there, entirely dwarfed by the room and its furniture. She was only just waking up, if her drowsy look toward the door was anything to judge by.

Mrs. Carmichael said to that startled and sleep-heavy look, "Your maid arrived just now, mistress."

Susan wondered if it was merely her imagination that made the word *mistress* sound sarcastic and even insulting. She curtseyed to Janet's startled face and said brightly, "Here I am again, mistress! I've just come from town this morning to catch up with you!"

It would have been amusing to see how Mrs. Carmichael would have reacted to Janet's obvious confusion if she hadn't made the effort, but Susan rather thought that she preferred to keep things as normal as they ought to appear—at least for a little while. Let Mrs. Carmichael at least pretend to think that—and act as if—Susan couldn't be anything other than mistress' maid.

"She'll help you into your new clothes," Mrs. Carmichael said, with something of a meaningful look. "Something suitable for breakfast, of course."

Janet jerked into something less of a supine position, disturbing her pendant and its chain and setting her gold rings clicking against the wooden arms of the chair as she grasped them. "Breakfast? Is he —is the master going to be there?"

"Good heavens, no!" said Mrs. Carmichael, laughing. "The idea! No, the master breakfasts first thing, mistress! The breakfast room below will be ready for you when you come downstairs."

"I see," Janet said slowly, and sank back into her chair a little. Susan couldn't decide if it was relief or disappointment on the other woman's face. "I'll be down in about half an hour, I should think."

Susan, who had a very good idea of exactly how long it would take to remove Janet from her intricate wedding dress and install her in a new, slightly less intricate ensemble, doubted it. She was quite certain that the housekeeper doubted it, too, but to her surprise, Mrs. Carmichael merely curtseyed and took herself off, shutting the door firmly and politely behind her.

Susan watched her go and then turned back around to find that Janet was watching her with deep and unfiltered suspicion. "What's wrong?" she asked. "You're looking at me as though you think I spat in your soup."

Janet flushed in confusion. "It's not—you don't have to take up so suddenly! It's just that—well, if you knew about all of this and were planning on coming here as a maid back at the inn, shouldn't you have told me?"

"I didn't know a thing," Susan said. "I've come here to pretend to be your maid and help you get away if you want to get away. Everything I seem to know is either a bluff or found out by pure chance."

"You came—" Janet stared at her for a long time before she said, flushing again, this time with tears, "You shouldn't have done that. You need to leave while you still can."

"Certainly not!" Susan said, crossing the room toward her new mistress. "There's a mystery to be had here, and I love mysteries. You'd best stand up so I can get you out of this thing—I don't suppose you got much sleep last night in all of this."

A note of indignation entered Janet's voice momentarily. "I couldn't get any of it off! Any of the bits that I could reach with my own hands were out of sight, and the bits that were in sight were fastened in ways I've never seen before!"

"Dressmakers are a plague," Susan told her cheerfully, chivvying Janet to her feet with a gentle but firm hand beneath her elbow. "I'm sure they get together in their little gaggles to snigger about how hard they made it for this bride or that bride to get out of her wedding dress, knowing full well that there's no man alive who could free his wife from their contraptions. My sister loves them, but that's because she's equally sinister."

Janet allowed herself to be turned this way and that as Susan took stock of the dress and then began on the laces at her back, but she said, "It's lovely of you to help, but I really do think you should leave as quickly as possible. There's nothing you can do about me, and I don't think it's very safe here."

"Yes, but it *is* very interesting," said Susan, loosening the laces at the top of Janet's arms as well. "And I do like an interesting life! Besides, I don't think whatever is around the manor will let me get out again."

"That's the protections," said Janet, threading the loose ends of her sleeve-laces through her fingers as if she needed to keep moving. "It's meant to stop the curse overspilling into the town."

"Is it?" asked Susan, who hadn't got the impression that the odd magics on the border of the estate were for keeping magic in so much as people. "Well, that's very thoughtful, I suppose. Have you seen your new husband yet?"

Janet's eyes grew luminous, but Susan wasn't sure if it was with tears or not. "Last night when we got married, but not since then. He didn't—he didn't come to my bedchamber afterward."

"Small mercies, I suppose," said Susan, ducking back behind to loosen the bodice.

"Yes, I suppose so," Janet agreed, in a small voice.

There was a tickle of amusement in Susan's chest as she enquired, "Good-looking, was he?"

Janet was looking very conscious when Susan began to unhook the myriad tiny fastenings at her wrists and the hidden buttons that made the elbows of the dress tight while puffing out the upper arm. "I thought he seemed sad," she said. "He only looked at me once."

"I daresay he feels guilty," said Susan. "One hopes so, at least. When one is responsible for the slaughter of innocents, whether wilfully or by mischance, I feel like one really ought to feel guilty."

"Yes," said Janet, looking down again. "I suppose one ought to."

THREE

S usan didn't see Emmett for the remainder of the day, much to her irritation. She accompanied Janet to the breakfast room and then was sent back to the suite upstairs when Janet discovered, in a panic, that she hadn't worn her apparently protection-charmed necklace that morning.

Susan went quickly and quietly, certain that there was very little that could befall a young woman in a breakfast room, and took the servants' stairs two at a time to make the most of the brief freedom she had. She did quickly venture down the right wing in hopes of coming across something useful or at least enlightening, but the only thing that shed any light was the triad, slinking across the glossy floorboards that the right wing had instead of the carpet in the left wing.

She hadn't seen a scrap of sunshine make its way into the manor on Janet's side, much as she'd suspected. Perhaps the master of the house liked to starve his brides of light and warmth to properly break their spirits before he killed them.

Susan stole back the way she'd come on swift, silent feet that were practised in sneaking, darted briefly into Janet's suite for the necklace—which was nothing like so strongly protected as she had expected from Janet's panic—and fairly sprinted back down the hall toward the servants' staircase to make up for lost time. When she got back to the breakfast room, she could hear the murmur of voices within, and the butler, who exited just as she arrived, closed the door behind him and shook his head silently.

"Are the happy couple at breakfast?" asked Susan softly, and was rather relieved than otherwise to see how the question made Mr. Oswald flinch.

"The master is within," he said, his face shuttering. "You should come back in an hour or two—or sooner, if you hear your bell."

"Very well," said Susan. "I suppose that means the master decided to keep that big fellow as a valet?"

"The master appeared to be adequately attired," said the butler. "I'm sure that's all I know."

"Of course!" Susan said affably. What an unpleasantly tight-lipped little man! "I'll go and acquaint myself with the manor so that I can direct my mistress later on, shall I?"

"Stay away from the right wing, and you may do as you please," said the butler, in hollow tones. "Good day, Miss Susan."

"Bother," said Susan softly to his back. "Now I want to go back into the right wing."

Comforting herself with the thought that there was still the night in which to explore any part of the manor in privacy, Susan went back to the main entrance instead and began a thorough reconnoitre of the manor from front to back. For now, it would be enough to familiarise herself with the areas she had already briefly explored when she walked through earlier.

She walked softly and slowly through the hallway and from thence into the vast foyer with its chequered floors, following the sweep of the stairs with her eyes and then craning her neck to look at the chandelier. She could barely see where it disappeared into the ceiling, which was so far above that it seemed to blend with the shadows that climbed the walls.

Susan gave up on trying to make out anything beyond the sparkling splendour of the chandelier and moved on to the ornate, gold-panelled entry chamber, where the massive hall stand she had seen earlier took up far too much space to the right of the doors and encroached upon the entryway itself.

"You're a bit ugly," she said to it. "What are you doing right there?"

She suspected that it was there simply for intimidation purposes; no one in their right mind would have put something so ugly and grand in a place where it could be so little use. The question was, who was the master of the house trying to intimidate, when no one but the bride and the servants seemed likely to be in the house at any time? The bride herself?

Rather uneasy at that thought—and the further one that she had left Janet alone with the master for quite some time now—Susan abandoned her reconnoitre of the inside of the house and climbed out the window beneath the stairs on the right side of the manor and into the garden. She stole softly through the trees on velvety grass with her eyes alert and swiftly moving to spot any gardeners before they saw her first. The garden was far too well taken care of not to have gardeners. One would as soon expect not to find a giant dog in the sitting room or a suit of armour in the library as not to have gardeners somewhere about the place.

Still, she was able to draw near to the double-doors that acted as windows for the breakfast room without being seen from either the garden or the breakfast room itself, feeling a kind of echo to her movements that confused her until she was startled by a flare of light and looked up with the belated remembrance that the garden was roofed in with panels of glass.

That explained the filtered quality to the light in the garden, not to mention the orchids that were growing closer to the doors of the breakfast room. It also, thought Susan, wrinkling her nose a little, explained the heavy scent of flowers that was permeating the air. She had passed a small patch of tiny, round tomatoes and cucumbers a little further back, too; it must be a proper hot-house built around the breakfast room, from which one could exit to bring in either fresh, delicate produce or the brightest flowers. The sunshine made the whole place warm and heavy around her, and provided no fresh air to waken the sleepy wanderer.

That seemed to suggest that there would only be sunshine here part of the day as the triad passed overhead and lit up the left wing with the last light—if the manor was placed precisely as Susan thought it to be placed, with the left wing corresponding roughly with the west. She would have put such a hot-house at the back of the manor, where it might enjoy sunshine all day—or whatever sunshine could get through the mist.

Still, there didn't seem to be a great deal of mist by now to obscure the suns, though the glass made it fuzzy enough to barely be able to make out the separate suns. Someone should really clean the glass, Susan thought critically, gazing upward with her hands on her hips.

No use pointing that out, of course: Susan was exceedingly well aware that to point out a job that needed doing was to volunteer to do it oneself, and in a manor where young women were said to die more often than was normal, it didn't strike her as wise to be sallying forth across a delicate glass roof.

To her satisfaction, the glass doors were already open when she drew carefully nearer to peep into the breakfast room. Susan took the longest way around to make best use of the shadows there, and by the time she had tucked herself in behind the soft purple and green fronds of a miniature wisteria, she had been hearing the two voices of those within the breakfast room for some minutes, clear and bright in the warm air. Moreover, she was well provided with a spot that left her shadowed, and the room into which she wished to see open to her gaze.

From here, she could even see the master quite clearly, though only from the back. The back was quite nice, as it went, Susan thought. The man was fairly slender but well-built, with good shoulders and a neat waist, and although his almost blueish black, longer-than-fashionable hair was tumbled, she was quite sure it was tumbled artfully, and that it had taken someone some time before the mirror to achieve. She rather doubted that Emmett had been the one to do it.

He had nothing like the presence that Emmett did, but if you liked the slender, broody type, he presented quite the picture.

Janet, thought Susan amusedly, *did* seem to like the slender, broody type. She could see the other woman far more clearly than she could see the master, sitting primly at the front of her chair and leaning forward very slightly in a way that was more interested than uncomfortable. If Susan was any judge, her eyes were also fixed on the master's face, remarkably wide and unshuttered for a girl who had been brought to a mysterious manor to die. Only her foot, tapping without rhythm beneath the breakfast table, betrayed any sign of the turmoil that one might have expected of a woman in such a position.

"What a shame," Susan murmured to herself.

Whether the master of the manor was murdering wives himself or merely facilitating that murder by being cursed and working along with the curse in hopes of breaking it, there was no scenario in which he could figure as a good man. He was certainly not a safe man to be gazing at with big eyes and caught breath. Otherwise, Susan fancied that the two people presently exchanging shy gazes in the breakfast room might have managed to get along quite well together. The master, she had noticed, was also leaning toward Janet, his hands clasped behind his back as if to keep himself back from the eagerness that his body otherwise displayed.

And that, thought Susan, was also interesting.

"You should try again," said Janet's voice.

Susan wasn't entirely sure what they were discussing, but she rather thought it was music. She'd been too busy trying to get into a good position unseen to pay attention to the substance of what the voices she could hear were saying.

"It's no good doing that," said the master, his voice almost petulant. "They'd never let me—it isn't allowed."

Janet, on the other hand sounded indignant. "What should it matter if no one else likes it? You can do as you please!"

"No one can do as they please," he said. "Not me, not you."

"I do as I please," Janet said quietly.

"You're here."

"I chose that," she said. "It wasn't an easy choice, but it was mine."

"You—you *chose* to be here?"

"We talked about it in the family," she said. "I chose to come here as the Bride. I thought I might be able to make something good out of it—you usually can, if you look at things in the right way."

"Do you think you made the right choice?"

Janet gazed at him for quite some time before she said unexpectedly, "I haven't decided yet. At any rate, I think you ought to do as you please when it comes to this sort of thing."

"No one uses the music room anymore," he said, but Susan fancied his voice was less dismissive and more longing now.

"I should like to hear it," Janet said wistfully.

Susan saw the master move as if he couldn't help it—saw the way his arms folded around his body as if hugging the words to himself.

In spite of that, he said roughly, "You don't know how it is here. Talk about something else."

"Oh," said Janet. "Then would you tell me about that little door along the hall upstairs? I tried to get in there because I thought it might give me a good view of the orchard, but it wouldn't open. I don't think it's locked, but—"

"You're not to go in there," the master said, sharp and furious. "Not even a step—not even a finger on the doorknob!"

Janet flinched back in her chair, her shoulders hitting velvet. "W-why?"

"You don't need to know why, you just need to do as you're told!"

"Now look what you've done," Susan said below her breath, chidingly.

Where Janet had been leaning forward and drinking in the conversation, now she had pushed herself as far back in her chair as possible, her fingers clutched white and her arms stiff.

Susan sighed and left them to it. Nothing she had seen led her to think that Janet was in any immediate danger from the master, though it looked as though he wasn't above trying to intimidate her, after all. Susan would have to see what was in the room that wasn't to be touched with so much as the bride's little finger; she wasn't at present inclined to believe that the master was a murderer, but that he was hiding something, there was no doubt.

She re-entered the manor by the same way she'd left and shut the window behind herself. There was still a lot of manor to explore downstairs, and barely any time in which to explore it now that she'd taken up so much time on the master and mistress. Still, it would be a good idea to do what she could, so Susan started with the music room with the idea that she would be close enough to hear any bell summoning her—as well as to potentially catch a peek at the master's face.

When Susan made it into the music room, she was at first startled and on her guard at the sound of someone's breathing; it took her only a moment to discover that the room's only other occupant was a massive dog that had curled itself up on the giant leather couch by the piano.

Susan caught her breath, then grinned and crossed the room to make a closer acquaintance with the dog. "You look just like my friend Emmett," she said to it, scruffing its ears.

She settled in the chair next to the dog, looking around the room as she stretched out the cramp from settling too long beneath the wisteria in the garden. It was a pleasant room to gaze around: dark but not oppressive, it was panelled in deep red cedar that had been oiled rather than polished, a decorative choice that took in light softly and didn't reflect it back like a lacquer might have done. The floorboards had been left bare and oiled, too, with a single rug beneath the couch upon which she sat and another over by the doors that led out into the decorative garden and the orchard beyond that. There was so much wood and warmth to the room that it took Susan some time to realise that there was also a violin at the other end of the room, sitting primly on a small stand and glowing faintly with reflected light from the glass doors that faced the garden.

Susan roused herself to cross the room and inspect it. When she touched a finger lightly across the strings, the fifths all sounded perfectly in tune, which surprised and amused her all at once. The only thing more fitting to the general melancholic splendour and reputation of the manor would have been an oboe, or perhaps a clarinet.

All of the books in the room had to do with music—sheet music or music theory—so Susan left those where they were and threw herself back onto the couch with the dog for another brief scratch behind its ears before she would have to move on to the next room.

She heard a faint scraping above her head as she did so, and cocked an eyebrow at the dog. "Shall I go explore that, too?"

The dog seemed to consider that, then gave a lazy sort of deep half-bark and shook its ears.

"You're right," said Susan. "It's more comfortable down here, anyway. If it's ghosties, they can wait decently until it's dark. It's not as if there's been much magic to chase after, anyway."

The dog looked at her with mournful eyes, then bumped its huge nose under her arm to precipitate more patting. Susan obeyed that silent demand and stayed as she was, still gazing around the room and wondering at the lack of any sort of strong magic around the place until, from the hallway, she heard muffled sounds of one raised voice and another protesting, and the slam of a door. Both her brows rose this time.

Goodness. Had the master lost his temper again?

She left the dog where it was and crossed the room softly, pausing by the door for a moment before she eased it open and put an eye to the crack she had made. She saw the blaze of light before she saw the source of it: the master, pulling Janet along the hallway behind him with one hand that dripped with magic glaring against the walls and the portraits there, one after the other.

"...Diana," he said, his voice suddenly clearer. He pulled her around to the other side of the hall, his back to Susan once again, while Janet's pale face was pulled around into view. "Frances, Jennifer, Mary-Anne, Thomasina, Charis—"

Susan would have gone to Janet's assistance, but just as she put her hand to the door to push through it, Janet wrenched her hand out of the master's, and Susan heard the hitch in her voice when she panted, "You don't have to tell me all of their names! I already know them! All of us do!"

"Then why don't you understand?" he snarled. "They came here, they thought they could do something, they put their noses into things they shouldn't have, and they died!"

"I'm not going to die," Janet said, reaching out one small hand to lay it tentatively on his arm. "You'll see."

The master seemed to stare at her for a long time; at last, he laughed a short laugh that was nearly a sob and said, "You or me, what's the difference?"

"Oh, very effective!" said Susan softly to herself as the master shook off Janet's hand and strode away down the hall toward the connecting wings.

She waited until he had turned down the right wing and was well out of sound as well as sight before she eased herself out of the music room and went to join Janet, who had turned to watch the master go and now seemed to be gazing forlornly down the hallway after him.

Susan bumped her arm against Janet's shoulder in a friendly sort of a way and put the bride's necklace in her hand as she said, "It seems like you found a bit of a sensitive subject."

Janet drew in a shuddering breath and clutched her fingers around the pendant of the necklace before she looked up rather blindly at Susan. "Oh, you're there. Yes, I don't think he liked me asking about that room upstairs. Or maybe he just didn't like me keeping on asking after he'd told me not to look in it."

"What room?"

"The one upstairs in the main hall as you go toward the ballroom."

"We have a ballroom?"

To her surprise, that made Janet giggle in a kind of suppressed relief. She lifted her necklace over her hair carefully and said, "That's right; you're not supposed to go there, are you? Mrs. Carmichael seems to be very strict about that. Do you want to see it?"

"Why not?" said Susan. "We might as well dance if we can't go poking our noses into more interesting rooms."

Janet laughed again, this one a little closer to a sob, and said, "Oh, I'm glad you came! Let's go and dance before we die, anyway."

Having failed to sight Emmett all day, Susan took to the halls that night. She didn't tend to be an anxious person, but she preferred to know where her companions in mischief were when they were sojourning in a location that was known occasionally to be bad for the health of its servants as well as its mistresses.

That mistress was at present sleeping soundly in her bed, her delicate face innocent in sleep and surrounded by curls from her recently coiffed hair. Susan, studying her face for a few moments in silence, made sure to ward the room before she left: rather like the master, she suspected, she felt a need to protect someone as small and soft and fragile as Janet.

The room warded as best she could do it, Susan hesitated briefly at the parting of ways in the grand hall, looking wistfully toward the front end of the manor where she might possibly be able to pick the lock on the door of the room that was not to be entered. She might, alternatively, climb through the window and try the window of the room instead, but there had been enough mist curling at the windows to discourage that notion. Not only would it be unpleasantly cold, it would be dangerously slippery, and visibility being so low, she couldn't guarantee being able to see well enough to avoid anything unpleasant that might be waiting for her in the dark.

She stopped briefly at the door, despite deciding that it would be better to move on to the right wing and explore it instead, and felt the torsion of the knob before applying a small brilliance of magic to the lock to see what she could see.

What she did see was that the door was unlocked. Susan huffed a sigh and said to the lock, "It's very hard to stay strong in the face of such temptation, but needs must!"

She left the delightfully tempting unlocked-yet-unopenable door behind her before she could change her mind, and continued on to find Emmett. She didn't think she would be able to rest comfortably before she saw that he was well and healthy, and she was just as certain that he wouldn't rest tonight until he had seen that she was likewise.

Susan was only a few steps down the hallway of the right wing before she realised, with something of a shock of surprise, that the moon was shining on her, clear and bright, through the windows along the hall. The mist-to-clear ratio was apparently the same both day and night when it came to where you stood in the manor.

"How terribly interesting!" she said.

She would have liked to have discussed the matter with Isabella via commlink: no doubt her sister would have had some useful advice to give—if there was advice to be given about a manor that seemed to keep its gloom on one side and its light on another.

The wing opened out a little way past the first set of windows, which was exactly what she remembered from the morning and which made her grin with the ridiculous thought that at least she knew she wasn't dealing with an enchanted manor that would change at will to confuse its inhabitants. Susan angled herself slightly more to the right on the assumption that a wing named the "right wing" would probably place its occupants toward the right of that wing, and nearly walked into a banisters that protected unwary occupants of the manor from the inky blackness beneath and behind it.

She caught herself up and fancied that she saw a huge shadow at the top of what must be stairs the banisters were protecting. The odd thing about that, she thought, as she ceased to move—and nearly to breathe—was that the figure seemed to have its back to the stairs.

And there was only one person she knew with shoulders so broad and a head so closely shorn. Emmett was also out and about —not very strange—and he was standing still in the velvety night with his back to a staircase and his face toward shadow and wall— which *was* strange.

What was he doing?

She made a very faint noise with her foot against the floor to alert him to her presence, and to her surprise received no response. Was he asleep? Surely not! Emmett had no other proclivities when he slept than to occasionally roll over and suffocate her in a hug, which vice she had learnt to deal with by poking him in the ribs until he woke, grunted at her, and rolled back over.

Still, he was not moving, and that made Susan distinctly uneasy. She rapped her knuckles against the closest part of the banisters, and the huge figure startled with an indrawn breath, head snapping around. His feet shifted, too: a quick, instinctive step forward and to the side that had him facing her in a moment, alert but unable, if Susan's estimation was accurate, to see her clearly.

"Lummox!" she hissed, and saw the stillness of recognition that fell over him. "What are you doing wandering around at night-time?"

He strode around the banisters and crossed the floor at a swift, grim-eyed stride that would have frightened her if she hadn't known him so well, and caught her by the shoulders.

"Well, lummox?" she asked him, gazing up at him. His fingers dug into her shoulders, and she wasn't entirely sure that he wasn't making sure she was real. She eyed him suspiciously. "Have you been seeing things?"

A faintly rueful look came to Emmett's eyes. "Seeing things—or dreaming."

He released her and breathed out at the same time—a breath of relief, it seemed.

Susan felt a happy little bubble of delight form in her chest. What a delightful puzzle they'd found!

"How interesting!" she said. "Perhaps there really are ghosts here! I take it you saw me—or a facsimile of me—while you were in your trance?"

Emmett passed a hand over his short-cut head of hair, and hesitated. "We...fought. You tried to kill me."

"How unpleasant of me," said Susan. "I hope that was your clue that it wasn't me."

"It wasn't the first, but it was the one that convinced me," he said grimly.

"I would hope so!" she said. "I can't imagine that Juniper would let me ride him if you weren't there holding him in place, and I can't be expected to do without my daily exercise, after all!"

A shade of laughter took away the grim look on his face. "I'm glad to know I have some value to you. Are you safe?"

"Safer than the bride, I should think," she said cheerfully. "No one has tried to kill me yet, and I haven't felt ghostly fingers down my neck, either. I've a feeling our bride is falling for the master, however."

Emmett's eyes dwelt thoughtfully on her. "That's quick."

"Isn't it! I don't know whether it's natural or curse-born, but they were getting along very well when I spied on them in the breakfast room this morning."

"He was in the breakfast room this morning?"

"Yes. They seemed to be discussing myriad different things, but the one thing that really got a reaction from the master was when Janet asked about the little room on the left side—good heavens, now I'm doing it!—and he told her very definitely that she wasn't to go near it."

Emmett nodded, eyes shadowed, and said quietly, "I'll have a look in there."

"Certainly not," Susan said. "I'm the one who's good with locks, if you'll remember!"

"Tonight?"

"No, I think not. I've a feeling there will be an alarm on it, and I've no intention of being kicked out of the manor *quite* so quickly, thank you very much!"

"Then why did you come out?"

"Just to see you, lummox; why else?"

That seemed to perplex him, much to her surprise. She didn't often see Emmett perplexed—not when it came to her, at any rate—and she wondered exactly what he'd gone through during the dreams in which a manifestation of her had tried to kill him.

"I didn't come out to kill you, if that's what you're worried about," she told him. "In fact, I didn't dream at all. I don't usually, you know. I wanted to know that you were alive and—"

"We need to establish a place and time to meet tomorrow," he finished for her, his face clearing.

"Exactly so," said Susan. "Tomorrow at three should work, I think. Mrs. Carmichael and Mr. Oswald seem to settle out in the back courtyard at that time of day with a cup of tea, and Janet will spare me if you think you won't be needed then."

"That's when the master goes into that little room he didn't want Janet going into," said Emmett.

"Hm," Susan said. "That's all very convenient, isn't it?"

"You think it's a trap?"

Susan took a moment to think about that. "I don't see how it can be—not yet. I'm just...suspicious. At any rate, I'll meet you tomorrow at three."

"Where?"

"The butler's pantry, I think," said Susan. "It has a nice little muffling spell on it to prevent the rattling of bottles disturbing anyone in the usable rooms, and has the added advantage that no one should see us sneaking off together from any windows."

Emmett asked warily, "Will I fit?"

"Oh yes, it's massive! You won't even hit your head. Sleep well, lummox; don't let the ghosties bite!"

"You." Emmett caught her sleeve as she turned, and Susan turned back around to face him. "Stop."

"Don't worry, lummox," she said, grinning at his concern. "If someone looking like you tries to tempt me out of my room and kill me, I'll be certain to know it's not you and stay inside instead of sleepwalking."

"They're cold, not warm," he said. "The one that tried to—that tried to kill me was cold."

"You're lucky it didn't try to shove you down the stairs instead," Susan said. "I don't know whether ghosts can kill you in your sleep or not, but I do know that a fall downstairs will do the trick. Take care, lummox."

"I'll walk you to the crossway," he said, and Susan wasn't sure if it was for her sake or his own.

They parted at the division of the wings; Susan turned down

the left wing and Emmett the right. She saw the tendrils of mist making pictures at the windows: voiceless faces and grimaces in the fitful light along the wing.

She said to them, "You go to sleep as well. Emmett doesn't bite, but I do."

FOUR

Susan woke early, alone, and in a bed that bore more resemblance to a series of boards than a mattress, if the effect on her back was anything to judge by. Rather pleased with herself for having risen in good time to make the best impression on the other servants and very slightly disgruntled at having woken alone for the first time in roughly a month, entirely bereft of the warmth of Emmett behind her and the soft, steady snore of Miryum not far away, Susan yawned. It was something of a comfort to see Janet across the room in her own bed.

"Goodness me!" she said to herself. "I'm becoming a pack animal, after all. Won't Belle be proud of me, becoming so socialised!"

She rose silently, used to being the first up and about, and stole downstairs after pulling a tunic over the breeches and undershirt she'd slept in. She wasn't sure if it was the morning light that made the tunic seem longer on her than it usually was—an inch or so of shadow that brought it nearly to her knees—or if she was simply misremembering which clothes she had brought with her.

There was already a kettle of tea being prepared in the kitchen. Susan said, "Good morning!" cheerfully to Mrs. Carmichael, and made that lady startle considerably.

"Good heavens, you're up at a good time!" she said approvingly, once she'd taken the hand away from her plump chest. "Then again, I suppose the manor is a good influence like that. Your mistress will want tea when she wakes, no doubt; you can get a tray from the silver cabinet and make it up. There's a hob over her fireplace upstairs."

"Yes, I saw that," said Susan. "Very convenient! The pump in the water-chamber seems to be in good working order...?"

"Leave it until after the ninth hour," advised Mrs. Carmichael. "Those pipes make a dreadful noise, and you'll have the master up betimes if you try to make up a bath or a wash-bowl before then."

"Delightful," Susan said. "Then I'll be back for the tea kettle once I've got my tray."

She took her time getting the tea tray; it was interesting to know that the silver cabinet was unlocked at this time of day—though not, perhaps, useful unless she were planning on robbing the manor —and more importantly, it gave Susan a chance to observe the spells on the butler's pantry again and at leisure. She did so, and returned to the kitchen to fill the tray with the pleased knowledge that the pantry would, indeed, make a very good meeting spot.

Susan met Mr. Oswald on the servants' stairs, and found herself wondering if she had a particularly villainous look to her this morning or if the butler usually clasped what she assumed to be his washing defensively to his chest when he passed others on the stairs. She had thought that she was looking very demure this morning: with her longer-than-usual tunic and a tea tray in her hands, Susan had been under the pleasing apprehension that she was the epitome of domestic propriety.

Maybe Belle was right—maybe Susan would always have a somewhat dubious look to her. She grinned to herself, hefted her tea tray a little higher, and took her disturbing visage back to the bride's suite.

Janet was sitting up in bed when Susan edged herself carefully into the room with a delicate shuffling of weight and tea tray. She shut the ponderous door behind her with one foot and threw an amused look at the bride, who appeared to be lost in her own thoughts, her shawl wrapped around her shoulders with loose curls spilling across the folds of knit and her eyes far away. Her fingers were wrapped around her golden pendant as if she were inhaling scent and memories all at once, and when the sound of the door closing fell heavily into the carpeted room, she startled.

"Pleasant thoughts?" enquired Susan.

She fancied there had been a small lift to the corners of Janet's mouth, even if there was a line between her brows.

The bride let go of her necklace and drew her shawl closer, wrapping her arms around her knees. "Yes—and no," she said, watching Susan settle the tray beside the bed.

"I presume you were thinking about the master, then," Susan said cheerfully. "Did you dream?"

Janet's eyes fastened on her face at once. "How did you know?"

"You're blushing," Susan told her, grinning. "Oh well, at least it looks like you had better dreams than my friend did."

"You know I had dreams because I'm blushing?" Janet said, her eyes surprised. "Oh! And what do you mean, your friend? You can't —people can't just walk into the manor!"

"We rode," said Susan. "And very unpleasant it was, too! If you need help and the big, short-haired gentleman's gentleman is about, just trust him, all right? And I suspected you had dreams because he had some nasty ones last night—dreams or ghosts, anyway. The blushing only told me that yours were more pleasant than his."

Janet gazed at her anxiously. "If your friend is a good one, you should really try to get him away from here. I heard that the last valet disappeared a little while ago."

"He's a very good one—and being such a good one, I doubt I could move him from the manor if I tried with a team of horses. He's also very good at not being killed or kidnapped, if it makes you feel better."

"I remember him from the inn," Janet said quietly. "He stood up for me when he didn't even know me—I didn't get a chance to say thank you. Why did he come here with you?"

"For the single purpose of keeping me from the consequences of my own folly, I suspect," Susan said. "He's all for investigating things that are wrong in the world, but he also tends to be protective. It's very hard on him."

"Yes, I suppose," said Janet, and began to pick at the biscuits on the tea tray while Susan hung the kettle on the hob and lit a small fire.

She was still nibbling crumbs when Susan went to fetch the day's clothes and pour a small amount of water into the wash-stand in the bedroom.

"You'd better wash up if you want to be ready in time to go down to breakfast," she said to Janet. "The kettle will be a little while yet: I'm not too bad at lighting fires, but the chimney seems to be blocked, so there isn't a lot of heat yet."

"There's *hours* yet!" Janet said in surprise.

"Well, yes; but I thought we might do a little bit of exploring and sneaking," said Susan. "And I really do find that it's best to be properly dressed for that. Nothing like so picturesque, of course, but much more comfortable!"

Janet looked as though she didn't know whether to be pleased or apprehensive. At last, slipping her feet down onto the carpet beneath her bed, she asked, "What are we going to explore?"

"Don't you want to have a bit of a poke around that little room the master didn't want you to poke around in?"

"That would be very rude," Janet said, her mouth as prim as the words. Despite that, she crossed the room toward the washstand with something of a spring in her step.

"Yes, but *very* satisfying!" Susan told her, and was pleased to hear the other woman giggle. "Have your wash while you decide whether you're going to come along and be rude with me, and I'll fetch out your clothes. Something warm, I should think, with all this beastly mist."

She'd barely crossed the room toward the closet and dresser when Janet shrieked. Susan turned at a cautious half-crouch, ready to find herself confronted with ghosts and mist-creatures—or perhaps assassins—at the window, and saw Janet staring out into the orchard in horror.

"They're burning a body!" she said, her voice choked.

Susan crossed the room at a very decent turn of speed and caught herself against the frame of the window, staring through the glass and mist and trees to the faint signs of a fire where either dead-wood or rubbish was being burned by two very tall gardeners who did, in fact, have a long bundle of something that looked very much like a human body wrapped up.

"Dear heavens! I wonder if that's the valet!" she said. "What a good chance to find out something about what's going on around here! I didn't know there was anybody outside the house."

She started back across the room toward the door, and Janet's voice, almost imploring, quavered, "Where are you going?"

"To see what they're doing, of course!" Susan said, surprised. "Are you coming?"

"But what if it really is a body?"

"Then we'll know for sure," said Susan, and made for the door again.

Rather to her surprise, Janet was behind her when she got to the main hall and even followed her down the servants' stairs; they both trod lightly by the kitchen doors and then scampered down the hallway toward the cross section that took them into the lower part of the left wing.

Much to Susan's satisfaction, there was another morning room further along the hallway, with a very large, low-silled window that opened easily and allowed both herself and Janet to climb out of the room and into the decorative garden that led into the orchard.

They stepped out into mist that curled around their ankles and added a sheen of cool moisture to their faces and arms as soon as they exited.

"Good grief!" said Susan. "It's heavier down here. This way!"

Whether she was determined to see what was happening or whether she was merely frightened to be left behind, Janet kept up with her, sweeping through the wet grass with her hair and her shawl streaming behind her.

Appearances, thought Susan, as she heard the crackle of a fire and saw the glow of it against the mist, were certainly deceiving when it came to Janet. It was all very pleasing. She would have to tell

Belle if she could figure out how to safely and securely make a comm-link in the manor.

The mist cleared away a little once they were between the trees of the orchard, and it became easier to see the fire—not to mention the two figures that Susan assumed, from their clothing and general demeanour, to be gardeners.

Close to, the gardeners looked decidedly suspicious. One was tall and straight, the other tall but hunched inward, with a pot belly that might have been from an illness but was more likely from drink. Both had warm, baggy hats and warm woollen coats with holey mittens protruding from the cuffs, with rough hands. Their faces were very nearly indistinguishable, but Susan couldn't quite figure out why: if she looked at their faces side by side, she could pick out the differences quite easily.

Both of the gardeners, as the two women approached, seemed to move as though to step in front of the fire and hide it from view— or perhaps just the bundle that was toward the front of the fire and still had a very wrapped sort of look to it.

Susan only caught a glimpse of it before it was covered, and it struck her that it was smaller than she had expected it to be from closer to—but then, the gardeners also seemed to be somewhat shorter than she had expected them to be now that they were nearer. And yet, when Susan measured them up against the height of the fire, they were no different than they had been from the window. Could it simply be that they were thinner than she'd expected?

The fire, too, was not merely a fire. What they had not been able to see from the window and through the mist was that the fire was bounded by a massive, curved sheet of metal that surrounded it from the back and to the sides, effectively making the fire a furnace, and distinctly hot to stand in front of, while allowing the mist to remain all around it.

"What ho!" said Susan cheerfully, her eyes running over every-thing that there was to be seen. "We saw you burning a body from the windows, so we came to see if we could help."

The two gardeners looked at each other wordlessly before one of them, the more bowed-inward of the two, said solemnly, "Aye, could look like that from the windows."

The straighter of the two touched his finger to the top of his hat-brim and said, "Mistress. Morning to you."

Janet, clutching her wrapper around herself uncertainly, shifted from foot to foot. "There's a lot in there," she said, tilting her chin toward the smoking, flaming hole in the furnace.

"There is, a bit," said Susan, impressed with the frightened girl. She evidently wanted to be anywhere but where she was, and she'd still spoken up. "It's smelling a bit, too. Does your furnace usually smell like that?"

"Thistle roots," said the hunched gardener, in a burst. "Nothing to worry yourself about, miss."

"What about the bundle you just threw in?" Susan enquired, in a friendly sort of way. "Was that all thistle roots, too?"

The gardeners exchanged a slow, ponderous look. "Aye, miss."

"I saw boots," Janet said. She was still clutching her arms around herself, but she had a determined light to her eyes. "Black, with a green trim around them."

The hunched gardener said, "Only master wears fine boots."

"Or perhaps a valet?" suggested Susan.

The gardeners once more seemed to look at each other.

"Could look like boots from the windows," said the straighter one cautiously. He added, as a clincher, "Mist."

"Yes, I suppose so," Janet said, her voice reluctant.

"Take very good care of our furnaces, we do: can't have people wandering into them."

"We didn't imagine for a moment that anyone had wandered into it," said Susan, in her friendliest tones yet. "Not with all that metal around the back, at any rate! I've not seen anything quite like this, as a matter of fact—"

And as she spoke, she manoeuvred herself around the taller gardener and nudged herself forward as if curious to see what there was to be seen. The gardener moved in what seemed to be sheer surprise, and Susan was able to get a very clear view of what lay within the curved embrace of the furnace's metal cover. That, of course, meant that she had an unobstructed view of the bundle she and Janet had seen from the windows.

Whatever material had been wrapped around it had begun to curl and fall away in peels of ash, and it was quite plain to see that it was indeed a bundle of some kind of thistle, wiry and thorny.

"Dear me!" she said, moving a little so that Janet could see around her and into the heart of the furnace. "That is rather a lot of thistle! We'll leave you to your work, then!"

Was she imagining the look of relief that passed across those two faces almost simultaneously? Susan didn't think so.

Janet lifted her chin just a little. She obviously didn't know how else to proceed—they had seen for themselves that there was nothing in the fire—and really, there was nothing more to be done.

"I should think the kettle has boiled by now for a nice cup of tea," said Susan. "Why don't we have a walk through the garden and go back up to get warm before breakfast?"

She put a light hand to Janet's elbow, and the other woman turned with her; together, they waded through the wet grass once again and re-entered the decorative garden through the hedge before either of them spoke.

Then, Janet said softly, "There were boots."

"Yes, I rather think there might have been," agreed Susan. "It's no use trying to find them now, however! Those two are either not quite right, or very much on their guard, I think, even if they're not used to getting rid of bodies."

"Do you suppose it's been the gardeners killing brides?"

"They look villainous enough," Susan said. "Perhaps I'll be able to scrabble through the ash heap at some point for some other signs of a body—there must be more traces of the man than a pair of boots, after all! I'll ask the lummox if the last valet left any clothing behind when he disappeared."

"The lummox is your...your valet friend?"

Susan opened the window for Janet to step back into the manor. "That's right. I've a suspicion that we'll find the valet liked to wear boots that were slightly above his station—heaven knows with what he would have been paid to work here, he could have afforded them easily enough!"

"What now?"

"Tea," said Susan, who could distantly hear the beginning overtures of a kettle starting to whistle from overhead. "And dressing. Then breakfast. I fancy that'll be enough to go on with at this stage."

"I don't know if I can stomach tea," Janet said doubtfully, passing ahead of her and down the hall.

"That's the good thing about tea," said Susan cheerfully, catching a glimpse of Mr. Oswald in the courtyard at the back of the manor through the open door of a room with a clear line of sight to the window and the courtyard beyond. "It's always easy to stomach, even after bodies."

She lingered just a little in the hall, watching the butler. Mr. Oswald seemed to be hanging out the clothing that he had been carrying when she met him earlier on the stairs, but if Susan was not mistaken, amongst the couple of male shirts and butler's cravats, there were two pairs of decidedly feminine underwear.

"I suppose so," said Janet. "Are you coming? I don't want to walk along here alone. It's too dark."

"Coming!" Susan said, leaving Mr. Oswald to peg a third pair of women's pantaloons to the courtyard line. "I rather think it's time for a little rest and some thought."

Janet must have thought the same. At any rate, when they returned to the suite and rescued the by-now wailing kettle from the fire, she sank into a meditative musing that left her absent and doll-like for Susan to dress and prepare, and only when she was dressed and ready, with nearly an hour before breakfast, did she seem to wake.

"Shall we go down and explore a little before breakfast?" suggested Susan, amused to see the change. "We might not have a chance for that little room, but there's enough to explore along the main hallway as it is."

"No, you go down first," said Janet, pulling her shawl around her again although it was quite warm in the room. "Have something to eat in the kitchen with the others. They won't eat in peace if I go down early—the servants, I mean. It's not fair to make them work too early."

"All right," said Susan. "But make sure you don't go doing anything too dangerous, all right? I'd stay in the suite, if I were you."

Janet nodded fervently. "Oh yes! I don't want to see anything else shocking this morning. You'll come back for me at breakfast time, won't you?"

"Of course," said Susan. "We can't have you going astray in the halls, can we?"

The kitchen was significantly fuller with people than Susan had expected when she returned. Emmett wasn't yet down, but the other servants had doubled—in other words, there were now four instead of two.

One was a curvy sort of girl at least a head shorter than Susan, with black, short-cut hair and almost purple eyes; the other was a tall boy with blue eyes, deeply tanned skin, and deep lines in his cheeks that served instead of dimples. They were both eating a hearty breakfast across the kitchen table from the housekeeper and the butler—a table which was exactly in proportion to the giant kitchen but ridiculously large for the four people who presently occupied a mere few feet of its thirty-foot length.

It was not a table, in other words, for a handful of servants— suggesting that at some point or other, the manor had been far better supplied with servants and, presumably, guests to serve. What had happened since those early days? Susan found herself wishing that she had been able to stop for a little longer in the town to do further research before they came.

On the other hand, there *was* a library just up the hall a little ways. Surely there would be some manner of family history there.

Susan tucked that thought away for later and fetched herself a plate under the curious gaze of the two younger servants before sitting down next to Mr. Oswald.

"Good morning!" she said. With any luck, the girl at present sitting across the table from her was not in fact the bride's real maid, but merely a housemaid. Otherwise, Susan was well and truly caught. "I would have come down sooner, but the mistress wanted to go out into the garden."

Mrs. Carmichael made a small sniff beside Susan, whether disapproval or pity, she wasn't sure. "They all do that at first," she said. "It doesn't help the poor lambs, of course, but they all like to do it."

Not pity, then, decided Susan, despite the epithet of *poor lambs*. Mrs. Carmichael's voice threaded contempt through a kind of carelessness, and the upward pinch of the left corner of her mouth clearly spoke contempt, too.

"They always think they can save him," said Mr. Oswald sombrely, with all the air of a man drinking away his sorrows despite the fact that he gazed down unseeingly into a cup of nothing stronger than coffee.

This time, the small sniff Mrs. Carmichael made was easily identifiable as a laugh. "Or change him!" she said. "You wouldn't catch me doing any such thing, if I were the mistress!"

The tall boy across the table gave a chuckle and said, carelessly insulting, "You as the mistress? He would never!"

"I haven't met the master since I got here," said Susan, in the interest of keeping the conversation in a useful place. Mrs. Carmichael looked as dark as a thundercloud. "What's he like? The mistress seems a bit nervous of him."

"The less you talk about your betters, the better," Mrs. Carmichael said repressively, turning her disapproval on Susan. "The master doesn't flaunt himself about for the eyes of you and me, I can tell you, Miss Susan."

"Not without a valet to get him ready, I suppose," Susan said, unsquashed.

So the mistress was free to be talked about, but the master was not to be touched? Interesting. Susan wondered, if she was very quick and clever about her eating, whether she might not get a chance at properly meeting the mysterious master as she came to escort Janet from her suite to the breakfast room—or wherever else around the manor she might be persuaded to explore along with Susan after breakfast.

She added, "Still, I thought I might have had a chance to greet him by now, at least."

"I shouldn't bother: master's a bit odd," said the black-haired girl. "All right, Mrs. Carmichael, there's no need to glare at me! It's the truth, after all! He's always wandering this pile at all hours and scowling at a body in the hallway."

"The master has worries on his mind that you've no understanding of," Mrs. Carmichael said repressively. "And a newly-wed, to boot."

"I wouldn't be scowling if I'd married a woman as beautiful as the mistress," said the tall boy frankly. "I'd be shining my boots and bringing her flowers every night."

Mrs. Carmichael made a threatening move toward him, and he sat back, grinning, as Emmett shouldered through the kitchen doors and dropped down silently at the table across from Susan.

He nodded at the others, which apparently charmed Mrs. Carmichael so much that she passed him a plate as she said reprovingly to the tall boy, "I'll thank you to stop pretending you're on equal with your betters, Mr. Helfer."

"I heard in the town that the master's had a few accidents with his wives," Susan said. "I think the mistress was a little worried until she got here, too."

"The mistress has no need to fear the master," Mr. Oswald said, and Susan fancied he was almost offended. "Even if a few of the girls have died, that's not the master's fault! He does his best, all things considered!"

"What things does he have to consider?" asked Susan at once, as Emmett helped himself to a mountain of food in very quick order.

Mrs. Carmichael, as swiftly, said, "None of your nevermind, Miss Susan! And try to stop your mistress from bothering the master outside of meal times, won't you? There's no need for her to be seeing him except at meals. I'm surprised he's breakfasting with her at all; it's not usual."

"I'll try to keep her where she ought to be," Susan said.

"Try to keep her safe, and that'll be enough," said the girl across the table.

Susan fancied there was pity in those nearly-purple eyes, so she grinned at the girl and said, "I'm Susan: new maid to the mistress, as you might have guessed."

"Regan—and that's Helfer. We come up from the bottom of the hill to help out every day."

"Do you?" Susan said thoughtfully, nodding a greeting at Helfer, who seemed to be dressed as a footman. "How convenient for you."

She met Emmett's eyes over the food and saw in them the same question that lingered in her own mind. The horselords had passed around nearly the entire base of the hill before they found the road that brought them up the hill to the manor: there had been no sign of habitation, poor and servile or otherwise.

Emmett shifted forward slightly on his elbows. "Do the gardeners go down the hill every night, too?"

Helfer and Regan looked at each other in what might have been surprise or confusion, or both.

Regan said, "I mean, they're gardeners, aren't they? If they're out there, they can't be allowed to come inside and get the manor dirty."

"They must live at the foot of the hill, too," agreed Helfer, rubbing his chin. "I don't remember seeing them go up and down, though."

"The gardeners get up much too early for the likes of you, you slack-a-bed," Mrs. Carmichael said. "And no doubt they have better things to do after a long day in the sun than to pass the time of day with you."

"I'll say hello to them next time, anyway," Helfer said. "No need to be rude, even if they are from outside."

"Be as polite as you like, so long as you don't bring them inside," the housekeeper warned him. "Miss Regan, if you're finished your breakfast, I'll thank you to get to your work and help me with the dishes for the breakfast room."

Once Mr. Oswald had departed for haunts unknown, Susan left

Emmett at the table with a carefully friendly nod and quickly ducked outside into the courtyard that nestled in the corner formed by the left wing and the kitchen to satisfy her curiosity.

She found exactly what she had seen from the manor's hall, though it took some searching to do so. Mr. Oswald, apparently in fear of being seen, had arranged the drying line behind one of the passionfruit vine-covered screens in the courtyard—a place that would also have been out of sight from anyone in the room, unless they were entering the room and chanced to look through the window at just the right time.

Susan gazed at the shirts, drawers, and cravats, and stuck her hands in her pockets to think about it all. Mr. Oswald was washing women's underthings in the laundry in secret: how very unexpected and interesting! Was there another, hidden occupant in the manor —those light, silky drawers would certainly never fit Mrs. Carmichael!—or had Mr. Oswald's immediate reaction of distrust and secrecy been the very real worry of a man who had nearly been caught pilfering women's underthings from elsewhere in the servants quarters?

But if he had been pilfering them, why was he washing them?

Susan wondered for the first time if, rather than a haunted house or a cursed (or murderous) master, it was possible that the troubles at the Castle on the Hill all came from its suspicious staff. For example, why had two of the servants said they came from outside the manor every day when there were no dwellings where they claimed to come from, and when all the information that she and Emmett had suggested that no one regularly came out of the manor?

The only problem with that suspicion, thought Susan, making her way back upstairs to find Janet, was that she was very good at spotting liars, and she would have sworn that both Helfer and Regan really believed what they had said.

The thought stayed with her as she walked Janet to the breakfast room later on, passing under a foreboding series of rafters that alternated dull red, green, and blue and were emblazoned with the same key that the manor's guards had worn. Susan had seen neither Helfer nor Regan on their walk down either upper or lower hall, which made her wonder exactly what they were up to. At this time of morning, either or both of them should have been in evidence stoking up fires, dusting the furniture, or polishing silverware. She did see Mrs. Carmichael as the housekeeper exited the breakfast room with an empty tray, which she pressed to her apron in order to curtsey to Janet in a manner perfectly befitting a housekeeper greeting her mistress.

The manner in which she said, "Good morning, mistress. The master is likely to be *very delicate* this morning and will require special care," however, didn't share that outward deference.

It sounded grim, accusatory, and very much like a warning.

"Dear me," said Susan quietly, as the housekeeper bustled down the hall. "I take it that you made quite the impression on the master. I wonder if he had bad dreams, too?"

And Janet, who had just raised her hand to the doorknob, seemed to hesitate for a moment. "Oh, I *wonder!*" she said, and then she opened the door with rather a decided motion, leaving Susan outside with her own wonderings.

She wondered even more when she returned to the breakfast room some hours later, curious at not hearing her bell, to find Janet glassy-eyed and on the point of walking into the breakfast room's massive stone fireplace, her right hand outstretched over the fire and slightly sooty.

Susan caught her left hand, sharply uttering, *"Janet!"*

Janet stumbled back, her horrified eyes taking in the leaping flames that were mere inches from her skirts, and the blackening of soot already on her fingers. She hastily wiped her hand on her skirts and allowed Susan to help her sit down in a nearby armchair, as if she was still somewhat numb.

Susan patted her on the back briskly once or twice, then went to check the tea things, which were not on the breakfast table but instead on a small table between two other armchairs that had been put together so snugly that the occupants thereof could scarcely have avoided brushing knees.

Susan sniffed at the teacups and fancied she smelt something faintly sweet and lingering on one of them—was it lilly-pilly oil? If so, that would have put Janet into enough of a stupor to lead her about as anybody wished; the problem was that there hadn't been anyone in the room when Susan entered.

She returned to perch on Janet's chair arm and asked, "What did you see? Didn't you know it was the fireplace?"

Janet seemed to hunch in on herself. "I saw *him*," she said. "As if he'd come back into the room and was trying to lead me away somewhere delightful. He said...he said that there were many secrets to the house, and it was time for me to see one of them. He smiled, as if he was sharing a real secret, and I didn't even think to stop."

"Hm," said Susan, her thoughts whirling. "I should probably try to avoid going off with insubstantial beings, if I were you. Even if they do smile at you and look exactly like someone you know."

"He wasn't insubstantial," said Janet, her chin very slightly crinkled as if to hold back tears. "I even felt his hand around mine. It was so cold, but I could feel it—I would have sworn it was real."

"My friend had a problem a bit like that," Susan said thoughtfully. "He came to the conclusion that if the skin is cold, he's not touching something living. He made sure to grab me and check the next time he saw me, too, so whatever ghost or phantom that tried to have a go at him certainly felt real enough to trick him at first."

Janet gazed down into her lap unseeingly. "We had such a good conversation before that. I really thought that...oh, but I shouldn't let myself think as though it was actually him. That's not fair."

"Who gave you the tea?" Susan asked gently. "The master?"

Swiftly, Janet said, "No! Of course not! He left a little while ago, and there was still tea in the pot when I came back in from walking through the glasshouse out there. More than I thought we'd left, actually. I started feeling...odd...a little while after I took a few sips."

And that, thought Susan, after walking Janet around the room a few times before returning her to her suite, didn't help clarify matters at all. Whether it was the master himself or one of the servants that had done it, someone had slipped a dose of lilly-pilly oil into Janet's final cup of tea.

. . .

Susan was still vacillating between the two ideas when she slipped into the butler's pantry to wait for Emmett. As she had told Emmett, the pantry was very large. Wider than her arms—or even Emmett's arms—could stretch on either side, it was lined with spelled shelves, bottle holders, and tobacco pouches. It had also been fitted with several different spells that coated the walls and the door to prevent excessive vibration from the outside, not to mention any unwelcome clinking or shuffling noises from inside the room that might upset the silent stoicism of the halls outside. There were some fermenting brews lower on the shelves, too, and the stains on the walls that had barely been scrubbed away made Susan grin. No wonder they'd soundproofed it from the inside, if they'd been having bottles of beer exploding in here.

She was still going over the various spells that lay around the pantry when the door was unceremoniously twitched open and Emmett's face appeared in the sudden crack of light.

"There you are, lummox!" Susan said happily. "I thought you weren't coming!"

With something of a put-upon look, Emmett shouldered his way into the pantry and pointedly around her, as if there was barely room for him to do so.

"Nonsense," Susan said at him. "There's plenty of room for both of us, and no matter how many times you huff at me and fold your arms, you've got to admit that there's room *to* fold your arms."

Emmett settled his shoulders against the opposite set of shelving and looked impassively at her.

"Don't admit it, then," she said. "We've got other things to talk about, anyway. No more ghosties this morning? Janet says they're cold, too, by the way."

"No more," he said. "The bride has seen one, too?"

"Just this morning in the breakfast room," Susan said, nodding. "Someone seems to have dosed her with a bit of lilly-pilly, and something that looked like the master tried to hand-lead her right into the fireplace—she said his hands were cold when he touched her."

He nodded. "The phantom version of you felt real, but cold. You're much warmer."

"All right, we'll have to make some rules, then," she said. "No going off at night or under the influence of anything without making sure the person we're with is warm. And apart from when she's in her suite and I'm down here with you, I'll try not to leave Janet alone, either. She seems to be very impressionable—though I do think she's frightened enough to keep to her suite if I put her there."

Emmett raised his brows at her. "Impressionable?"

Susan, musing about that regrettable impressionability, said, "Look, what *does* the master look like? If I'm not wrong, Janet is already fairly smitten, and I don't know why if it isn't part of the curse or someone's magic. He's quite nice to look at from behind, but that's all I was able to tell from the garden. *Is* he good-looking from the front?"

"Classically handsome," said Emmett, after consideration. "Very intense. He has a scar."

"Well, a lot of women like that sort of thing," Susan said. "And yesterday they did have some conversation about music or something like that; they seem to have bonded over tea this morning, at any rate—enough to have Janet going off with him when he offered. It could be natural inclination. I like to think I wouldn't be inclined to fall in love with a man who might be going to kill me after just two days in his company, but there's no accounting for temperament. On the other hand, it's also fairly likely that it's something cursed or magic doing the damage."

"I can't find a curse in the house," Emmett said. He was perturbed enough to uncross his arms, which amused Susan. "Nothing like the tangling threads that were through the town; nothing that I could trace back to anyone. I can't see that there's more human magic in the house than what you'd get in the Commander's manor."

"I wonder how much the ghosts have to do with it," Susan said, almost to herself. Then she asked, more sharply, "What do you think about the servants?"

Emmett's eyes met hers for a meditative moment. "Between them and him, who's most likely to be killing brides?"

"Either they're lying or he's got them so trapped in his spell that they think they go back to their houses every night," Susan said bluntly. "Or he's cursed, and it affects them, too; but it's an odd curse that affects the people around the cursed person rather than the person himself!"

"If he's a strong enough magic user to hide his workings from me—"

"Pride hurt?" enquired Susan, grinning a bit.

"If he's strong enough to do that, then we're going to need to take precautions while we find out what he's done."

"I always take precautions," said Susan. "And we'll have to take them regardless—we don't know if it's ghosts, a curse, or the master himself. Once we know that, I fancy it'll be easier to keep Janet safe and ourselves in one piece."

"I don't think the ghosts are killing people."

"You said one that looked like me tried to kill you," Susan reminded him.

"When I woke up, it disappeared: it wasn't really there. All it could do was make me think it was real and lead me somewhere I shouldn't go."

Susan, wondering if insubstantial ghosts could nevertheless manage to be dangerous enough to start up the rumour of a curse, asked, "Where did you wake up?"

Emmett drew in a breath through his nose before he asked, "The first time or the second time?"

Susan stared at him. "Goodness, lummox! You have been suffering! The second time, then."

"I was in the halls, just when you found me."

"Did you think you were in the hall before you woke up?"

Emmett paused before replying again. As if in acknowledgement, he said, "I didn't know I was in the hall."

"You could have gone over the banisters without knowing it," Susan pointed out, aware that she didn't need to belabour a point he had obviously already grasped. "Or backwards down the stairs.

I'm not going to have ghostly versions of myself throwing you over banisters; if it gets too much for you, we'll have to share a cupboard somewhere at nights so I can wake you up if you look like having that sort of dream."

"I tied a bell to my toe," Emmett said, folding his arms over his chest again.

"I take that to mean you don't want to share a cupboard with me," said Susan, well aware of the kind of obstinacy that lay behind that particular gesture. "I have to say that I'm offended, lummox."

"I don't want to wake up to find that I've strangled you."

"I'm sure you'd stop before you killed me," Susan said affably. "After all, there's a great deal of difference between an insubstantial woman in your dreams and one in real life that you're trying to squeeze the life out of."

"Not enough," he said.

"You can't imagine that I'd let you kill me, lummox!"

"I'm more afraid of what you'd do to me," he said, and shouldered past her toward the door.

"Wait," Susan said, grabbing at his arm. "We haven't made our plans yet!"

"We don't yet know what we're fighting."

"Fair. All right: you look after your master and I'll look after my mistress, and we'll work on the suspicion that there are a few too many ghosts in the manor for anyone's good. I'll see if I can get anyone inside to talk—why don't you try to have a word with any servants outside while the master's out for his ride?"

"Who are you going to try to talk to?"

"The maid or the footman," said Susan. "If I can find them. They seem a bit more willing to talk. I'll also try to keep a closer eye on Janet when she's with the master. They're a lot closer than I'm comfortable with."

FIVE

That night, Susan woke to the strains of a violin and a suite empty of anyone but herself. She saw a face at the window in her quick but comprehensive look around and recognised in the instant between sight and reaction that it was only the mist playing games again. Still, it felt like a bad omen after finding that Janet was gone, and Susan rose swiftly without taking time to put anything over her sleeping breeches and loose shirt. It wasn't until she was on her feet that she realised one of the windows was open, with fingers of mist curling around the edges of it and faint strains of music drifting in likewise. When Susan poked her head out into the morning, however, she didn't see more than the shifting of more mist.

She took to the hallway with the immediate thought that Janet was likely to have fallen prey to the same kind of dreams—or ghosts —that she had the previous day, sending a ribbon of light ahead of her to gently brighten the way. That brightness threw strange shadows on the walls, but Susan ignored them: like the mist, they were insubstantial and unlikely to do more than play tricks with her mind. She moved swiftly through the upper level and threw a quick look along the intersecting hallway as she met with it; then, thinking better of her first impression that Janet might be led places unknown by a ghostly figure, she concluded that it was more likely that Janet had been led places unknown by the ghostly music Susan could still hear. The window, after all, had probably been open to better hear that music.

That being the case, it seemed more useful to follow the sounds of the music than to waste time searching the hallways for Janet. Susan started up the hall toward the front of the manor, reflecting with a grin that Mrs. Carmichael was unlikely to meet her here anyway, and that if she found Janet, she would in fact be adhering to directions about the use of the grand staircase anyway.

She passed the forbidden room with barely a glance, and tranquilly ignored all of the shifting shadows and misty faces until a forcible rattling of the imposing doors of the ballroom on her right made her narrow her eyes and wriggle her shoulders a bit to shake out the night stiffness of them in preparation for what might happen. Not entirely to her surprise, however, nothing came through the doors at her approach, or even as she passed by. Susan couldn't help the way her hair stood up on the back of her neck as she continued toward the front of the manor with the doors behind her, but she also didn't try to stop the wry smile on her lips.

If she hadn't seen Janet walking blindly into the fireplace this morning—and if she hadn't heard the stories of disappearing and dying brides, in fact—Susan might have thought the movement of the walls and the ridiculous rattling of doors was a carefully implemented plan—not really to kill, but to frighten the metaphorical life out of anyone so unfortunate as to marry the master.

Susan threw a quick glance around the wide-open space of the vast front chamber as she entered it, and trod lightly down the first couple of stairs to her right, following the curve of the room. Breezes that shouldn't have been able to enter the house swept around the chequered marble floor in eddies as she reached the bottom of the stairs, chilling and vaguely menacing, and Susan sent a touch of magic out and about to stop them.

As yesterday, there was nothing she could see or grasp that would have told her that someone was working magic, but her own magic did seem to quiet the breeze. Susan sent her small flicker of ribbon light toward the front doors to see that they hadn't, in fact, been left open a crack, and saw that they were shut tight as the ribbon of light glanced off the hall stand and then the doors themselves.

She thought she heard someone say, "Ow!" softly and indignantly, but there was no one else in the room, and the hall stand's single door concealed nothing but dust when she took a few swift, light steps toward it in the raised entryway and softly tugged it open.

More tricks, she was inclined to think. And since she and Emmett were having so much trouble detecting magic of any kind, it occurred to her that it would be a good idea to check for tricks of a more physical kind when she was not otherwise engaged.

Susan followed the now-louder flow of stringed music down into the hall and found that the eyes of the portraits there seemed to follow her without the aid of magic. She ignored them: if portraits were going to play silly beggars in a badly-lit hallway, she felt as though they ought at least to do so with the aid of magic, and she didn't particularly want to feel the hair stand up on the back of her neck twice in one night.

That was the eerie thing about the manor, she decided—the truly eerie thing. She had come across both haunted houses and cursed houses in her life; she had also come across people who were cursed. None of those things or people had acted in quite the same fashion as the world around her now acted.

Ghosts ought by rights to be making a lot more noise around the manor than just some kerfuffle in the hallways and a rattling of doors—and they should certainly do more than make the eyes of portraits move.

Susan slowed her steps as she approached the music room; the door was open, and she didn't wish for her shadow or her ribbon of light to pass across that opening. She recalled her light to herself and spent a moment or two in the shadows of a massive epergne to readjust her eyes to the darkness.

When that was done, Susan pushed herself away from the wall, and was preparing to softly creep around the side of the epergne when the sound of footsteps impacting softly against carpet struck her ears. Susan crouched low and glanced carefully around the marble column.

She was too late: dashing down the hall in a great hurry, her tent-like nightgown blossoming around her like a sail, came Mrs. Carmichael. From the other wing, Mr. Oswald intercepted her and then followed along by her side, struggling with a light-stick in one hand and the fastening of his trousers in another, his face delicate and hollow-eyed with lack of sleep.

Susan drew back into the shadows of the epergne and its stand, feeling the tickle of ferns that ought to be stone but were remarkably feathery despite that fact. She resisted the urge to brush them away from her arm, since they shouldn't be able to be brushed and she didn't want to encourage them by being reactive. Heaven knew what those stony ferns would do if they thought they could get away with it.

And so, while Mrs. Carmichael and Mr. Oswald bustled with furious silence into the music room, the loose flap of a dressing gown slapping against the marble stand, Susan avoided thinking about marble ferns that soon became more solid than feathery.

If she had expected to hear an explosion of muttering, or perhaps even a scream or a yell from within the music room, she was mistaken. There was certainly a sudden scrape of bow against strings that was far less melodious than anything that had yet emitted from the room, and the snap of a window closing, then a furious figure stormed out and up the hall without troubling to quiet his steps.

Susan, with a sudden suspicion, swiftly turned back and sank quietly into the windowed alcove before the music room, keeping to the shadows. And there through the window, in the glitter of the moonlight, was Janet—nightgowned, with stars in her eyes and dew in her hair—just turning away from the window of the music room.

Susan said softly, "Good heavens," as the housekeeper and butler returned to the hallway, shutting the door to the music room behind them. She stole another look at them as they retreated toward the back end of the house, murmuring to one another.

She thought she heard one of them say, "...destroy that wretched fiddle tomorrow...!" and her brows rose. So the master wasn't quite above reproach, was he? What kind of power did the servants in this house have, to come and prevent the master from doing exactly as he chose at any time that he chose?

Susan let a small, thoughtful breath escape her and turned back to the window to try and make out if Janet seemed to be heading for the door—and, if so, whether she would need someone to open that door for her.

She fancied she saw a flutter of white through the mist and trees, then something stirred in the hall behind her, making the hairs on her neck stand up.

She said calmly enough without turning around, "Hallo, lummox."

A sigh gusted across the empty space. "Why are you wandering the halls again?"

"My mistress disappeared," Susan said with a touch of frivolity as Emmett's presence entered the alcove and stood beside her at the window. "I thought I'd better find out where she'd gone."

She would have reached out a hand to touch his arm, just to be sure, but Emmett did so first; a huge, warm hand wrapped briefly around her forearm and then released it.

He said, "Shouldn't you find her now, then?"

Susan tilted her chin toward the window, and even if he didn't quite see it, he must have felt the motion of it, because she saw the shadow that was his head turn to look out the window.

Both of them saw the last flutter of Janet's nightgown as she disappeared into the mist—heading, if Susan wasn't mistaken, toward where she might conveniently be able to climb back into the manor through the window that had been left open.

"She'll be all right so long as she doesn't fall," she said. "And it would take something to fall down from there: it's all solid trestles and foot-wide decorative ledge."

"One of them died by slipping on the front step on a frosty day and hitting her head on the colonnade."

"That's quite a trick," Susan said. The front stairs were roughened to prevent exactly that sort of incident—she had noticed it when they first entered the manor.

Emmett said with some significance, "Yes."

"Bother," said Susan, after a brief moment. "You're probably right. We'd better go out and bring her in another way."

Emmett was before her; he started toward the doors that opened back into the main atrium, and she hurried to catch up, aware of the coldness sweeping down the hall that felt as though it was terror but was probably just whatever enchantment had also swept the breeze in eddies around the marble-tiled atrium earlier.

They crossed the black-and-white chequered floor and stopped at the front doors together because although there wasn't any magic that Susan could see on the handles, there was a very impressively large lock on them that didn't contain the key that would have opened it.

"How awfully archaic!" said Susan, feeling instinctively for her pockets and the picks that would usually be there and remembering too late that she was in her sleep breeches. "Bother. You should have told me that I'd need pockets in all my sleepwear—Belle would have."

"I don't want picks sticking into my back in the middle of the night."

"Fair, I suppose," said Susan, lifting the lock with one hand and sending a little spark of light into it.

This close to the doors, it was even colder, and she shivered as she turned the lock to see as much as she could see inside the keyhole. Emmett waited patiently for her, leaning his shoulder into the hall stand, and it seemed to creak.

Then it said, "Hullo. Do you think you could *not* do that? You're a bit heavy, old man."

"Good heavens!" said Susan, jumping and dropping the lock with a clatter. "Talking furniture: just what I wanted to find next!"

"Pleasure t'meet you and all that," it said to her. "By the way, wouldn't stand there if I were you."

"Why wouldn't you stand here?" asked Emmett, gazing closely

at the stand. He seemed to be trying to ascertain where the voice was coming from, as if he expected to see a mouth, or perhaps eyes. "You are here."

"Well, that's where the will-o-wisps get in," said the hall stand. "They're a bit strong."

Susan felt the touch of bitter, biting cold against her leg, and hurriedly moved away from the door—and the finger of what looked like mist but must be will-o-wisp. "Ouch!" she said. "That is a bit much."

Emmett's eyes were still on the stand. "So is a talking hall stand."

"See if I help you again," said the hall stand. "Lack of gratitude, that's what it is!"

"Don't be like that," said Susan coaxingly. "You didn't talk the other day. Why start talking to us now?"

"Don't know," it said. "Seemed like a good idea at the time."

"All right," Susan said. She wasn't about to waste a good source of information, no matter how unconventional, and she had no way to know if the hall stand would speak again after tonight, moreover. "Well, now that you're talking, how about telling us a bit about what goes on in this house?"

"Mist for days, and then someone plummets through the glasshouse roof," said the hall stand promptly.

Emmett's brows quirked. He asked, "Who went through the roof?"

"*I* don't know. I'm just a hall stand."

"How do you know someone did go through it, then?"

"Very loud, glasshouse rooves," said the stand. "They carried him out through the front doors, too—against the rules, that is."

Susan couldn't help asking, "Did the body have on boots with green piping around the sole?"

"*Oh* no!" said the hall stand. "It's against the rules to answer questions."

Emmett flicked another look at it. "You've just been answering questions."

"I have, haven't I?" it said, in some surprise. "Why did I do that? Well, I'm not answering any more, and you can't make me."

"So I see," said Susan, rather amused than otherwise. If the hall stand was still talking tomorrow, it could possibly be tricked into answering just a few more questions if she came back suddenly and it forgot again that it wasn't to answer questions. "Well, if that's the case, we'd best be on our way."

"Must we?" asked Emmett, his eyes on her.

"This way, I think," Susan said, jerking her head toward the front doors and laying her hand on the huge handle of one. "I'm quite sure I can fiddle this open."

"No going outside at night," said the hall stand. "That's another rule."

"A person should always be free to go outside," Susan told it. "That's my rule. Let's go. I don't want to lose Janet."

"Just wait," the hall stand said threateningly. "You'll find yourself falling over the banisters or going through the glass roof out there. You won't be the first."

"I don't really like being threatened," Susan told it pleasantly, turning back briefly from the front doors.

"I'll burn it in the garden furnace," Emmett said, his voice very nearly as cold as the will-o-wisp. "It'll be hard to make threats from there."

The hall stand sounded distinctly unsettled. "You can't do that!"

"Not alone," said Emmett. "It'll take two of us."

"Lummox," it said uncertainly. "*Lummox*, you'd better not."

"I don't particularly like people copying what I say," Susan said warningly, but she didn't remove the restraining hand on Emmett's arm, and he didn't try to either move or remove the hand.

Then it occurred to her that she hadn't called Emmett *lummox* anywhere in the vicinity of the hall stand—or anywhere else but closed rooms, the closed-off hallway, and upstairs.

"Didn't copy you," it said. "Can't be throwing people into fires, you know."

"That's the thing," Susan said, with growing coldness. "You're not a person. You're a hall stand."

"Yes. Well," it said. "That's rude, but I suppose it's right. But I might have been a person if I'd tried a bit harder, mightn't I?"

Susan asked, with a frozen heart, "Brenners? Is that you?"

"Oh," he said, and seemed to sigh a deep, woody, creaking sigh. "So that's my name. Think I was looking for that."

Susan looked up somewhat blindly into Emmett's face and met his eyes. "That's torn it," she said. "Brenners must have been too close when we went through."

"What's my name, Brennan?" Emmett asked the hall stand.

It would have been impossible to confirm that the hall stand focused on him, but there was a moment of tense tightening in the air before the hall stand said, "You're Emmett. Ye gods, Su! Properly done it now, haven't you?"

"Don't worry, Brenners, we'll fix this," she said.

Brennan seemed to creak rather than say, "Can't be fixed, only completed."

Emmett's eyes found Susan's once again. "What do you mean?"

"Blest if I know, old thing. Just popped into my head. Whatever happens in this place gets into your head; I've spent half my days thinking I *am* a hall stand, you know."

"I suppose that's why you didn't talk until now," said Susan, remembering the *ow*! she had heard in the silence of the night as her flicker of magic touched the hall stand that was Brennan. Perhaps she'd done something for him after all. "Oh, by the way, Brenners—how do we turn you back?"

Brennan, as though without thinking, said readily, "Got to get the Perfect Result before I get out, old thing. Can't fix anything without the Perfect Result."

"Of course," said Susan lightly, pinching Emmett's arm to warn him to stop staring at the hall stand before he put Brennan off. "And what's the Perfect Result?"

"Beggared if I know, old thing," he said, after a pause. "Don't even know why I said it."

Susan met Emmett's gaze. "It must be the curse," she said softly. "This is more like it!"

"If it's really a curse—"

"Yes, it will make things quite hard."

"Wish you two wouldn't speak in code," Brennan said.

"I'm going to try something," Emmett told him. "See if I can get a sense for the magic on you."

Susan waited and watched in interest. She was better with locks, but Emmett was better with magic puzzles; he had a kind of sense about them, not unlike his sense for unravelling confusion spells. She saw his magic moving about him in subtle teal shades and even saw it shimmer along his hands for a brief moment, then there was a similar shimmer around the hall stand that was Brennan, though she couldn't see what it was doing.

Brennan seemed to gasp a little and then groaned, and the groan sounded suspiciously like a creak. When he spoke again, that was a creak, too. "Ouch. Hurt."

"I'll try again," Emmett said, his jaw flexing.

"I really wouldn't, lummox," Susan said thoughtfully. "I rather think Brenners finds it more difficult to talk when you do that."

"*Perishing* difficult!" said Brennan, and she could hear the effort in his voice. "Don't like it, old man. D'rather you wouldn't."

"I fancy we'd be far better off trying to find out more about *the Perfect Result* and get at the thing that way," Susan recommended. "Curses don't much like people trying to shorten the road with magic. We've got all the time in the world while we're here, after all."

"Shouldn't stay in a place like this," Brennan said, more seriously. "Best get going—take the bride with you before something happens. I'll be all right."

"Goodness me, no!" said Susan. "Once it's known that one will put up with one's friends being turned into household equipment, every man and his dog want to do it. Hold tight, Brenners; we'll figure it out. Not today, probably, but we've got time."

"All right," he said. "But while you're here, you should keep away from the master, at least."

"I'll look after the master," Emmett said. "Susan will focus on the bride."

"Good plan, old man," said Brennan, and there was a creak that seemed to suggest he was yawning.

He didn't speak again, even when Susan patted his side, and she said quietly, "I suppose we'll be able to talk to him again tomorrow. I fancy the magic took a bit out of him."

Emmett nodded, a line between his brows. "I'll ask the master about the Perfect Result."

"If he talks to you about it," Susan said sceptically. "If he *can* talk to you about it. I'll focus on the servants, then. Good night, lummox. I'd better find Janet before she has a chance to get winkled into someone's idea of a Perfect Result."

"I'll walk with you as far as the wing."

"No need," Susan assured him. "I can find my own way in the dark, you know. Off you go; I'll go up later."

Emmett, his jaw mulish, made one more attempt. "I'll wait."

"No, no, lummox," said Susan. "You go your way, and I'll go mine. I have something else I want to get before I go back to our suite. Unless she's gotten lost in the mist, Janet will be in bed by this time, I suspect. If not, we're already too late."

Emmett turned obediently toward one of the staircases, but he asked over his shoulder, "What if she has gotten lost in the mist?"

"Then what I have to fetch will be doubly useful, I should imagine," said Susan cheerfully. "Goodnight! Mind the ghosties, and I'll see you tomorrow at breakfast!"

She went back through the hall but didn't go further than the door to the music room, which she eased open and slipped through, with an odd little hope lingering in her mind. And just as she had hoped, the master's huge dog was there: a massive coil of shadows that took up nearly the entire length of the couch on which it was curled coalesced all of that darkness into two pools of inky, shiny blackness that were its eyes as it raised its head at her entrance.

"Good dog," said Susan softly, hearing the faintest of growls.

The master, whether in pretence or in all seriousness, seemed to have taken to Janet. Susan was hoping that his dog would do the same. Even if it was just drawn to her because of the curse, the dog would likely keep Janet safe at those times when Susan herself couldn't. Now that Brennan needed to be considered, her attention would necessarily be divided, and Susan had no intention of leaving the bride to die like other brides before her.

No, a guard dog would be the very thing. And just as Susan hoped that the dog being the master's dog would incline it to be friendly with Janet, did she hope that it would make Janet more likely to accept such a companion.

She didn't even have to call it: the dog rose in a smooth surge of fur and muscle and trotted toward her, then followed her straight out of the door as if it had been waiting for her to fetch it. Interesting and useful.

Much heartened, Susan strode swiftly up the hallway once again and said a quiet, "Night, Brenners!" in the direction of the hall stand as she loped up the stairs with the dog's ears brushing against her fingers as she went.

She felt rather than heard the constant growling that vibrated quietly from the dog's chest as they passed through the upstairs hall, and thought that the shadows and mist writhed more than they had earlier, though the ballroom doors didn't shake as she passed them this time. Susan was surprised at how much safer it felt with a dog the size of a small horse by her side and was comforted that she had made the right decision.

She found a wide-awake and slightly green-stained Janet waiting for her with one single light-stick aglow beside her on the table there, her arms clutched around her knees and a worried line between her brows.

That line vanished in astonishment when the hound entered the room behind Susan and swung its massive head from side to side as if taking in the potential dangers of the suite.

"Good heavens!" said Janet, her eyes wide. "Did you...did you mean to bring that in?"

"Of course!" Susan said briskly. "If you're going to be wandering about the manor or its grounds at all times of the night and day, you'd probably better have someone to take with you when you don't want to wake me up."

Janet blushed faintly and used the leap the hound made to her bed, and the subsequent padding and turning around and around to find a comfortable mess in which to rest, to recover her colour before she spoke again.

"You were downstairs, too?" she asked.

"Not at first," said Susan. "But when I woke up, you were gone. I thought something might have happened."

Janet wrapped her arms around the hound's neck and rested her chin on its head. "Nothing happened."

"Yes, I see that," Susan said, nodding at the stains on Janet's night gown. "We'd better wash that tonight so that no one else has to strain their belief muscles, if we're going with that story. Did you get those climbing out the window?"

Janet looked down in confusion, caught sight of the staining, and audibly gasped. "Oh no! I didn't think about that!"

"That's the delight in having more than one nightgown," Susan said bracingly. "Come along; we'd better take it off and get it washed. I'll get you another one."

Janet climbed meekly out of bed and allowed herself to be stripped of the nightgown, but when she was working her arms into a new one and Susan took the other over to the washstand, she said with an assumption of coldness, "I suppose you were very surprised to see me in the garden."

"Not surprised," said Susan, working a small bit of magic into the water and then into the stains as she rubbed the layers of fabric together. "A little worried, perhaps. Someone tried to kill you yesterday morning, and we still don't know whether it was your husband or not. I thought you would have felt safer keeping to your suite for now."

"He's not trying to hurt me," Janet said, putting her chin in the air. "He wouldn't do that."

"All right," said Susan easily. "So *he's* not trying to kill you. But there's something or someone about the manor that *is* trying to kill you, and wandering around at night in your nightgown doesn't seem like the most sensible idea."

"I know," Janet said, working her fingers in the folds of her new night dress. "But I don't seem to be able to help it. How can I, Susan? I feel like I'm only seeing the outside of him, and I can see him in there *trying* to get out, but he can't. Him playing the violin was the first time that I thought I could see him—really see him—and they wouldn't let him do it during the day."

Oh dear, thought Susan, turning back to the task at hand to hide her dismay. *She really is in love with him.*

It was far too soon for anyone to be in love with anyone, but it couldn't be helped.

"All right," she said once again, lifting the wet fabric to the light to check for remaining stains. "Just make sure that when you go out, you take me or the hound with you. Accidents might happen to one of us by ourselves, but the two of us together should be able to look after each other. The hound should be useful at a pinch."

"I'll be more careful," said Janet.

It sounded like she was agreeing, but Susan was well aware that she hadn't said she wouldn't go off alone, and that both worried and interested her.

She tucked that thought away for further consideration later, and asked, "How did you hear the violin, by the way? I could only hear it because you left the window open."

A happy flush came to Janet's face. "I think he was playing for me: the window to the music room was open into the garden as well."

"That doesn't explain how the sound got through our windows," pointed out Susan.

"I don't know about that. I just know that I was dreaming about him, and then I woke and opened the windows for some fresh air. I heard it as clear as a bell."

"Delightfully simple," said Susan, nodding. "That's very useful to know."

Janet's eyes widened a little. "Is it? Why?"

"I don't know yet," Susan said, wringing the nightgown out

gently and hanging it beside the fireplace, which was burning low but still there.

She didn't particularly want to stoke it up, given Janet's unfortunate incident yesterday morning: the nightgown could dry at its own pace without anyone belowstairs being the wiser, and the two of them could avoid another fireplace incident.

Susan was a little later rising the next morning, but Janet was still asleep when she left the room despite that. All for the best, Susan was inclined to think. The hound raised its head as she exited the room but showed no signs of following Susan, which was very satisfactory, too; there might be time after breakfast for a chat with Brennan, if he was still talking by then.

Mrs. Carmichael and Mr. Oswald had already eaten and abandoned the kitchen when she got there, and though Regan and Helfer were still there, they were both in the last stages of their meal. To Susan's satisfaction, Emmett was also at the breakfast table, though by no means so far advanced in his meal.

"You're down early," she said to him.

He sat beside Regan, methodically putting away enough bacon and eggs for a small platoon and patiently ignoring the way the housemaid frequently elbowed him, as well as the sardonic grin from across the table, where Helfer drank coffee.

"Isn't he ridiculous?" asked Regan of Susan. "I didn't know they made people this big."

Susan grinned and sat down next to Helfer, aware of the shade of amusement in Emmett's eyes across the table. "He does take up a bit of space, doesn't he? I'll have to remember not to sit across from him next time so that I'll have enough space for my legs."

"You'll be lucky if there's enough food for a next meal," said Helfer, rising with his plate in one hand and his coffee in the other. "Move your bones, Regan; Mrs. Carmichael said we're to do the rugs today."

Regan grumbled but gulped down the last of her tea and followed him to the sink, and then out of the kitchen, a half slice of toast still in one hand. That left Susan and Emmett alone at the table together. She grinned at him, then rose and trod across the room to make sure that there really was no one around in a hidden corner, or an open window that could be conveniently used to eavesdrop.

When she dropped back down into her seat after double-checking the light sound-proofing spell on the doors that kept in the clatter of dishes and cutlery, Emmett looked up from his breakfast and said with a full mouth, "Well, stripling?"

"We've got the room to ourselves," she said. "Isn't it nice? If you don't want more coffee, I'm going to finish it, by the way."

"Finish it," he said. "How's the bride?"

"Grass-stained," Susan told him. "She crawled back in through the window like a champion. Lummox, I'm a bit worried."

Emmett reached for the last slice of toast and began to mop up egg yolk with it. "Why?"

"Well, so far, we've got a curse *and* ghosts. One or the other would be enough to deal with, but two together is much more difficult. It's all right to be trying to break a curse, but it gets complicated when ghosts are trying to kill you as well—and then, of course, we still need to find out who laced Janet's drink. Villainous staff or master as *well* as ghosts and curse—well! It shouldn't be this complicated."

"There's only one thing that bothers me," Emmett said through a mouthful of bacon and eggs.

"Yes," Susan said thoughtfully. "What about the other horselords?"

"They were all on the other side of the road, nearly into the trees."

"And Brennan wasn't quite," agreed Susan. "Do you think that was enough, or are they adorning the manor as talking furniture, too?"

"I'll search the right wing," Emmett said. "In between times; top and bottom. You can handle the left wing and the stables, can't you?"

"Stables," said Susan, frowning a little. That was odd. Both she and Emmett spent most of their time with horses, and Juniper was Emmett's pride and joy; despite that, she hadn't thought of Juniper since Emmett had tied him up at the front of the manor. She didn't even remember if Emmett had taken him to the stables. "Bother. I'd forgotten about those."

She saw the answering worry in Emmett's eyes, and the line between his brows. "I forgot, too. I haven't thought of Juniper since yesterday's ride. The stables are self-feeding, but I'll check on him straight after breakfast; I don't like being made to forget things. Do you think you'll be able to manage the bride?"

"I should think so: Janet likes to have someone with her, but she's a biddable little thing. She'll come along with me if I ask her to. She'll probably even approve."

Still frowning, Emmett nodded. "Good. That will keep her safe at the same time."

"Make sure you let me know if *he*'s going to be getting too close to us, won't you? Things tend to get a little bit odd around the place when he gets too close to Janet."

"Odd in what way?"

"That's what I can't quite figure out," Susan said, frowning her perturbation at Emmett's arm as it rested on the table. "It's not magic. It's like the air gets thicker, and I start getting that little tickling feeling."

Emmett stopped eating and stared at her. "*That* feeling?"

Despite her own worries, Susan couldn't help grinning. "What, you're worried *now*?"

"Every time," he said. "When you get a tickle of excitement and possibility—that's when things get complicated."

"It's a bit different this time, though," she said. "It's like the start of an adventure, but instead of being light, it feels as though it weighs everything down. I don't know—expectation instead of excitement, perhaps?"

"You think it's the curse and the Perfect Result?"

"Could be," she said. "At any rate, I think things will be less complicated if we can keep the two of them apart as much as possible—at least until we figure out what the curse wants for its Perfect Result."

He nodded. "All right. Are you going?"

"I'd better," she said. "I'll have to dress Janet and walk her down to breakfast soon. Don't go falling over any banisters or following any ghosts, lummox. It'll take the two of us to carry Brenners out of here at the end of all this if it goes badly."

She went to see Brennan instead of going straight back to the wing she shared with Janet, despite that. Let Janet shake the cobwebs out of her mind before they spoke together; no doubt it would be the better for both of them. In the meantime, she could find out if Brennan was still capable of speech this morning.

"Hallo Brenners," she said softly as she approached the front doors. She heard the creak of Brennan stirring his timbers. "What ho!"

"Don't *what ho* me," he said. "Beastly business, this."

"It is, a bit," she said. "But I came to see if you're still talking, and here you are, talking. That's rather a good sign, don't you think?"

"*Good sign*," he repeated gloomily. "Maybe to you. I was a man and now I'm a hall stand."

"Yes, but you're still talking," said Susan. "You weren't even doing that until last night. And you know me, Brenners—I'm bound to be able to do *something* to help you, even if the something is only discovering the best place to take you once we manage to get out of here."

"Not much use getting out right now, though, is there?" Brennan pointed out. "Can't be trotting off and leaving the poor girl to die. Not to mention the next one that comes along."

"Remind me to set you up with some delightful girls of my acquaintance when we get back to Glause, Brenners," said Susan lovingly. "Have I told you that you're a darling before?"

"Yes, and I don't like it any more now," he said. "I won't have girls thrown at me, Su! Not ones that know people like you!"

"You're someone who knows people like me," she reminded him.

"Only because of m'work," said Brennan, and then added, "Yow! What was that! Stop it!"

Susan sighed. "Never mind. I was just trying something."

She had tried, briefly and without success, to pick at whatever enchantment or curse bound him, to see if she could piece out what it was. It felt as though she were picking at Brennan himself—felt, moreover, as if she were picking at wood grain and varnish. It was a distinctly unpleasant sensation.

"It'll never work," he said. "You'll have to carry me out of here on the big man's back."

"Now there's an idea!" Susan said pensively. "I wonder what the lummox will think of dragging you out into the mist tonight and throwing you back through the mess around the manor. If coming through it made you turn out like this, it might reverse it by going out."

"Can't get out," he said. "Got to know the right doors to get out, and I can't even walk." And then, "Don't ask me *why*, Su. I don't know. It's another one of those things that's just in my head. Rather think you had it last night when you said you'd best focus on the curse."

"Yes," she said regretfully. "All right then, Brenners. By the way, what do you think of the master?"

"Not right in the head," he said gloomily. "Same as everyone else in this house."

"Thank you very much, I'm sure. What do you mean, he's not right in the head?"

"Plays the violin," he pointed out. "At that time of day, too."

"What does the time of day matter to you?" asked Susan. "You're a hall stand! If someone plays a violin at three in the morning, shouldn't it thrill your woody little heart?"

"Might as well have stepped from out of a book," muttered Brennan. "I don't know why he can't behave like a normal person."

"I suppose a couple of decades or centuries in a house with ghosts and mysterious gardeners is liable to have you playing the violin at dead-early in the morning," Susan said excusingly. "What I don't understand is Mrs. Carmichael rushing down here to stop him—and Mr. Oswald, too. The two of them don't get along terribly well, but they both came running to stop the master playing his violin, and that's more interesting to me than the fact that he plays the violin at three in the morning."

"Wouldn't be if you had to listen to it from start to finish."

"Your problem is that you're too low-brow, Brenners," she told him. The master had played quite remarkably well, she thought; it was a shame not to encourage such a talent. It wasn't as if the violin wasn't a classical enough instrument to be playing. "No appreciation for the finer things in life."

"I'd appreciate a good full breakfast," Brennan said rather wistfully. "That'd be enough for me."

"Never mind," Susan said, patting him briskly on the side in what she hoped was a good mix of comfort and encouragement. "We're bound to get you out of here, you know—one way or the other."

"Don't scratch my varnish," he said, but Susan knew that he was comforted despite that—and in his comfort, she was made a little easier. "You'd better go look after your bride, hadn't you?"

"Yes, I suppose so," she said. But she couldn't help asking one last question. "By the way, Brenners: the footman and the maid— do you see them coming and going?"

A scream tore through his answer, sharp and ragged, and Susan heard a mad scuffle from the direction of the landing above the main hall. She was already on the run and leaping down onto the chequered marble floor of the foyer when something red flung itself over the banisters above and into the void below.

Susan froze between the two curving staircases and rocked back onto her heels, staring up uncomprehendingly at the rag of crimson that dangled from banisters of the upper landing directly ahead and far out of reach.

Then she dashed for the stairs once again, leaping up them three and four at a time while the hound howled unceasingly and scrabbled madly above, with the sickening thought that she was already too late stuck in her throat.

Susan heard distant yelling, but she ignored it, focused on that one point of need—that one point of horror with the bride as its core, hanging from the banisters by a cord as bloodily crimson as her dress, her head hitched to one side and her eyes shut, her feet dangling into the void between the landing and the marble floor below.

SIX

Susan remembered with great clarity every long, drawn-out moment of frantic stairclimbing, but the process of hauling Janet up and onto the landing passed by in a flash. The bride, a rag of red sprawled and lifeless on the floor, didn't breathe at all. With the howling of the hound in her ears and the sound of another, single set of footsteps thundering away down the hall, Susan tore at the silken scarf that had wound itself tightly around Janet's neck and arm. She had no time to see who it was who ran; Janet's face was so white that it was very nearly blue, and although the silk hadn't snapped her neck, it had restricted her breathing enough to prevent any kind of resuscitation until it was removed. Susan tugged at the scarf until it loosened away from the bulging flesh around it and then applied her doubled hands just below Janet's breastbone and pumped vigorously three or four times until the woman breathed again.

A looming warmth at her back made her say, "Carry her down, will you? We'll put her in a chair in the breakfast room and trickle a bit of brandy down her throat."

Emmett wordlessly did as he was told, and Susan at long last threw a look down the upper hallway. There was no one there by then, of course, but she saw the shuddering ballroom doors nearby and heard the constant, keening whine of the hound from behind it. Susan trod quickly and lightly across to the door and wrenched it open; the hound nearly bowled her over in its snarling haste to be up the hall and after the lingering shadow that was all that was left of the person she had heard earlier in the hall.

Susan let it go and swiftly descended the stairs after Emmett; if the hound managed to catch someone, she doubted it would let them go. There would be time to attend to Janet's attacker later, when there was less chance of Janet dying from her injuries.

Mr. Oswald met them below, wringing his hands as Emmett stepped down onto cold, chequered marble, and Mrs. Carmichael entered from the hall at a run with Regan just behind her, panting.

"Coming through," Susan said rather breathlessly, taking the lead from Emmett, who silently shouldered his way through the servants to follow her.

She opened the double doors of the hallway for him, and then the door to the breakfast room as well, and found the fire pleasantly warm. Susan turned a chair away from it, regardless; Janet was better off feeling a touch of cold than she was looking into a fire that had nearly welcomed her into its embrace not so long ago.

Regan grabbed the other side of the chair and helped her, a practical help in stark contrast to Mr. Oswald's hand-wringing. Mrs. Carmichael looked as though she wanted to help but didn't know what to do with her hands either, so she hovered too close, very nearly as useless as Mr. Oswald.

"Didn't I tell you it would do no good?" she said, but her voice was jerky, and Susan wondered if she had had to deal with one of the bodies before. "Try as they might, they all end up the same way."

"She's not dead," Susan said briskly, moving the woman aside by her shoulders so that Emmett could settle Janet in the chair. "She's breathing again, but we'll need to cut the scarf off and apply just a little brandy to help with recovery."

Susan thought Mrs. Carmichael said, "Now *there*'s a waste of good brandy," as she moved toward the door, but Janet moved in her chair, sharp and defensive, and needed to be attended to, so Susan didn't speak the scathing retort that sprang to her lips.

So she knelt at Janet's feet, pressing the woman's hands as Emmett unceremoniously tore the scarf around her neck into two drifting ribbons of silk and magic, and said soothingly, "It's all right; you're safe."

Janet opened her eyes and shrank toward Emmett who, hunkered beside her chair, allowed it with an impassiveness that didn't break even when she unconsciously moved her hands away from Susan and clutched them around his huge arm.

Susan watched, wondered, and when Janet's eyes cleared and focused on her, said again, "It's all right; you're safe."

Janet tried to speak, failed, then cleared her throat in a painful sort of way and tried again. "Where is she?"

Susan's brows twitched up. "She?"

"The hound," said Janet with luminous eyes. "She got caught when the door shut."

"The hound went after someone in the hall," Susan said. "Someone who ran away while we were getting you down."

Janet turned her tear-brightened eyes up at Emmett, still clinging to his arm, and asked, "Did you get me down from there? Thank you!"

Susan managed to control the sarcastic brow that tended to spring upward and ruin any chance of presenting an expressionless appearance, but had a harder time controlling the twitch of hands that wanted to firmly remove Janet's fingers from Emmett's arm.

"I got you down," she said, but couldn't help the spurt of truthfulness that forced her to add, "Emmett got the scarf off and carried you in here."

Janet couldn't have fallen in love with Emmett as well, could she? Susan hadn't thought her the sort to fall in love with anyone as quickly as she had fallen for the master, but she was quite certain the woman had. It would be beyond a joke if she'd just fallen for Emmett, too.

Susan bit the insides of her mouth, meditating on what best to say that wasn't, *Janet, must you cling to the closest male?* and met an open, inquisitorial sort of look from Emmett that asked a question she couldn't quite read. Perhaps it was a question he was asking himself, because it seemed to Susan that he was seeing her for the first time—and whatever answer he found seemed to content him, because she thought he nodded just slightly and dropped his gaze to Janet instead.

Susan found that her fingers were curled tightly in on themselves where they rested against the velvet of the chair seat and relaxed them. It was no good over-analysing the people around her; in a place under the thrall of a curse, it was as likely to lead to madness as it was to lead to wrong conclusions.

"What happened?" she asked Janet. "You said the hound got stuck behind the ballroom door—what happened after that?"

"There was no one there, but the door shut behind me," Janet said, through bloodless lips. Her eyes, distant and a little bit glazed, seemed to be seeing the events of the previous fifteen minutes again as her fingers tightened on Emmett's arm. "I tried to get the hound out, but the door wouldn't open for me. I thought it must have locked behind me. She was howling, so I hurried toward the landing to get the keys from Mrs. Carmichael, but when I got to the landing—"

She stopped, and Susan asked, "Did someone push you?"

"I can't remember," said Janet, her eyes still distant. "Too much happened all at once. Something got between my feet and then my scarf caught around my arm, and I think—yes, I think someone shoved my shoulders just as I tripped. Then I was somehow falling over the banisters and I don't remember anything after that."

A bustle near the door alerted them all to Mrs. Carmichael's return. She said as she brought in a glass of something amber, "You're not dead, then. That's a nasty bit of red around your neck, mistress."

She presented Janet with the glass of liquor, and Janet took it gingerly with one hand, as though it might be a snake. Susan didn't blame her.

"That was from her scarf," she said. "Luckily for her, it caught under her arm instead of just around her neck. It would have snapped her neck otherwise, I rather think."

"Oh well," said Mrs. Carmichael, more comfortably. "That would be an accident then, wouldn't it?"

"Only if she threw herself over the banisters as well," Susan said dryly, feeling as though she would quite like to take away Mrs. Carmichael's ability to self-soothe for a little while, at least.

It did seem to discomfit the woman; she moved back and stood with Mr. Oswald, who was pale-faced and anxious, wringing his hands. Susan heard him murmur in distress, "I knew it was too late when I heard him playing that cursed violin! We should have got rid of it, Mrs. Carmichael!"

"For all the good it would have done!" the housekeeper retorted, below her breath. "You've got your own irregularities to worry about, Mr. Oswald. If you want to end up like the master, I've no mind to join you. I'll be off about my duties if I'm not needed here."

Mr. Oswald hesitated but followed her, which Susan thought was for the best. She glanced up at Emmett, who was still stoically putting up with Janet's clinging hands, and met his eyes once again.

One of Emmett's brows rose a little bit as he tipped his head toward the door. The question, Susan knew, was, *Did you hear that?* She nodded.

"I'd probably better go and find the hound," she said to Janet. "It was after someone as soon as I let it out, so we might be lucky enough for it to catch whoever did this to you. Emmett will—"

Someone knocked at the door, and Helfer's apologetic voice said through the panels, "Incoming hound! She's a bit upset, so watch it."

Then the hound thundered into the room, forced itself between the arm of Janet's chair and Emmett's leg, and gave vent to a howling trill that expressed both the joy of being with its people and the sorrow of having suffered an unpleasant episode.

Both of them, thought Susan, gazed up at Emmett with much the same expression of adoration. Unlike the hound, who could step on his foot and lean heavily into his side with the evident desire of being patted and given attention, Janet could only gaze wistfully at Emmett and cling to his cuff—but Susan thought rather acerbically that Janet probably had the advantage when it came to soulful gazing.

"The master will be down soon," added Helfer, venturing further into the room with a tray that held a bottle of something spiritous.

More generous than Mrs. Carmichael, thought Susan, with a stab of amusement. She asked Janet, "Do you want to stay or go?"

Helfer put his tray down on the table beside Janet, who looked toward the door and said hurriedly, "I'll stay. Mrs. Carmichael has probably already told him what happened; he'll be worried."

"She won't need to tell him," said Susan, nodding at the red, angry marks still wrapping around Janet's neck. "Those will probably bruise before long, too."

"Mr. Oswald has some salve," Helfer said, lingering as if he hadn't managed to say everything he meant to say. "If you ask him for it, he'll give it to you."

"I've got the feeling that magic will do better," Susan said.

"Should we leave her alone?" asked Emmett, and although he was looking at Helfer, Susan knew he was asking her.

She heard the sound of footsteps and an irritable voice that she was coming to recognise, and said quickly, "Perhaps not."

"No, leave us alone," said Janet, sitting up a little straighter. "He won't hurt me. I'll be all right."

"Whatever you decide, you'd best be off yourself," Helfer said to Emmett, his voice low. Susan wasn't sure if he meant her to hear it or not, but he was certainly talking to her when he said, "He'll be in any second. If the two of you are going, you'd probably best go out by the glasshouse; he'll see you leaving, otherwise."

Susan, who had an instinctive grasp and nothing more of what he was trying to convey to her, caught Emmett by his free arm and pulled him toward the long windows, breaking Janet's hold on his other arm.

"I'll come back when you ring," she said to Janet, and carried Emmett off with her and out the long windows into the hot house.

She didn't let him go until they were far enough away to be

screened from sight of the breakfast room, then threw a look up and down the strip of grass that lay between the wall beside them and a series of passionfruit vines that grew over a half-wall. There was no way out that she could see, and the window by which she'd entered the hot house the first time she spied on the breakfast room was closed fast, without even the room to slide a fingernail beneath.

Susan sniffed a little bit and let go of Emmett, looking back the way they'd come for another possible method of egress. Emmett, his head cocked, didn't have to ask the question.

"I don't know," she told him. "I thought it would be best for us to stay out of sight of the master—particularly you. I got the feeling that Helfer was trying to tell us something without telling us. Perhaps the master is inclined to be jealous when it comes to his brides—perhaps he doesn't like the idea of anyone getting fond of women he's likely to kill, whether by intent or proxy."

Emmett nodded. "The footman was trying to protect her."

Susan was less sure about that. "We'll see, I suppose," she said. "I got the feeling that he was trying to protect something else; I just don't know what that is. At any rate, it felt wise to leave."

"What are you looking for?"

"A door," she said. "Or somewhere the glass is broken."

"They'll see us if we go that way."

Susan reluctantly moved away from a promising but far-too-low lane of trees and said, "Bother. Looks like we won't be getting out any time soon."

Emmett started toward a garden chair a little bit further back, but Susan caught his arm and pulled him on toward the next instead.

"Not there," she said. "If you think they won't see your ridiculously long legs *or* the top of your head, you're very much mistaken. Besides, we'll get some sunlight if we sit on this one."

Emmett stretched himself out on the bench much like the hound would have stretched itself out in the sun, wriggling his shoulders against the bending boards until he was comfortable, and leaned his head back into the bricks of the short wall behind him.

Susan dropped down beside him in the small amount of space

he had left and did much the same, then settled with her arms folded across her chest and her shoulder pressing familiarly against his and yawned up at the glass ceiling.

"You noticed?" she asked. "That there's only ever sunshine over this side of the manor?"

"I noticed," said Emmett, without opening his eyes. "The fog stays on your side, too."

"I'd like to know why that is."

"Is it important?"

"It's annoying," she said. "And it's not that it's important, it's that I don't know if it *is* important. Have you noticed how things around the house get sort of tighter when those two are in the same room, by the way?"

She'd felt it around her as the distant sound of a door closing filtered through to the garden: the distinct impression that threads were drawing tight around her in the way they were meant to draw tight. This time, however, she felt as though she and Emmett—or perhaps just Emmett—had been caught up a little tighter in the process as well.

"I noticed," he said again, and Susan thought there was something of a smile to his voice.

"I see," she said. "So you've been waiting for me to catch up, have you? Thanks."

"I only came to that conclusion today," Emmett said. "I would have told you this afternoon. You said yourself that you got something of the same feeling from them the other day."

"It's no good trying to pretend that you're not terribly brainy," Susan told him. "It might work with people who think that brawn means no brains, but it won't work on me."

"That's rich," said Emmett. "When you're constantly making people underestimate you and outwitting them."

"No, I'm just devastatingly honest, and that upsets people," said Susan cheerfully. "Either they think I'm bluffing and overplay themselves, or they're disarmed and want to help me; either way, things seem to work out very well for me."

Emmett gave a very soft huff of laughter and didn't reply. He seemed to be enjoying the sunshine and peace alike, though she didn't doubt that he could feel that odd tightening she had mentioned, pulling away at the garden around them.

She turned her head and let her gaze rest on Emmett's profile. His chest rose and fell rhythmically as his breath sent the motes dancing on the sunshine around him; he looked perfectly peaceful there in the warmth, and she felt the tension that had built up unknowingly in her shoulders ease itself out.

There was always a restful feeling to being around Emmett, and Susan had never been sure if that was because he emanated peace himself or caused it in others. None of the other horselords but Miryum seemed to feel any of that peace, however—Emmett didn't tend to sit down very often, so they might not have had the chance to judge properly—and Susan had wondered from time to time if she made up a part of what was restful about sitting with him.

Maybe it was synergy—a kind of inverse of what happened whenever Janet and the master met.

"No more nightmares?" she asked, and regretted it almost at once.

It was hard to say how he became any stiller, but she thought he did. Perhaps he stopped breathing for a moment and that was what made her think so.

"Nothing I can't handle," he said, without opening his eyes, his shoulder warm against hers.

"Oh well," said Susan, softly back-pedalling. "At least you shouldn't have to worry about them out in the sunshine. There's nothing like a sunshiny day for making the nightmares run away and the muscles relax. I don't feel like I get the chance to sit in the sunshine often enough."

"Is that why you cause so much trouble?" he asked. "Not enough sunshine days for you?"

Susan huffed out a breath that sent motes spiralling in the sunshine. "Nothing of the sort, lummox. It's just that it's hard to enjoy a sunny day when there are people being taken advantage of or hurt. I get into trouble in pursuance of more sunny days."

"I suppose that's what the report said when they booted you from Trenthams."

"'Student was expelled for being too headstrong in pursuance of sunny days'?" Susan felt a chuckle catch in her throat. "Well, I suppose it's not too far off, after all. Do you know what I like about you, lummox?"

Emmett turned his head, eyes cracking open, and gazed at her.

"You're nothing like Kit or Father, but you're nothing like Belle's Alexander, either," she explained.

After a moment, he asked, "The charm of novelty?"

"Nothing of the sort," she said. "That wouldn't make me like you. Curran is different, too, and most days I'd quite like to kick his feet out from under him."

"Most days you *do* kick—"

"Don't be like that when I'm trying to compliment you, lummox."

"Is that what you were doing?"

"I meant," she continued serenely, ignoring that remark, "that Kit is too clever for his own good and will help someone out if he loves them or feels interested in the problem. And Father is a dear who likes to gently encourage people to help themselves in the most useful way possible. You just wade in honestly and hit people on the head, and nine times out of ten, you hit the right person on the head."

Emmett sounded slightly pained. "You said you were trying to compliment me?"

"*Then*," she continued, "you stand there like a nice, strong bulwark while people pick themselves up and figure out what they want to do next. And if they ask, you give good advice. Alexander is a lot more tricky about who and how he helps, and he usually thinks a bit longer before he wades in."

"Nine times out of ten isn't good enough for the Commander of the Watch," Emmett observed.

"Exactly so," agreed Susan. "Aren't you glad you aren't Commander of the Watch? I am. You're much nicer as a horselord."

Emmett gazed at her for a little longer before he asked, "Am I supposed to tell you what I like about you?"

"I wasn't asking for reciprocation," she said. "I just like to tell people nice things sometimes. Is that paint over there? Or sunshine?"

Emmett sank his head back against the wall and closed his eyes once more. "Neither," he said. "It's sunlight against a doorframe: two magic kinds interacting, I think."

"That would mean that the suns here are—a *door*, did you say?"

Susan sprang to her feet and padded over to the dingy wall of the glasshouse. She ran her hands over the palely luminescent lines that were there and felt the faintest indent all the way around what was certainly a door. She tried what appeared to be the handle and felt it form beneath her fingers, ready to be turned.

"Good grief, how tricky!" she said admiringly. "I shall have to install something like this when I build my own estate."

Emmett's eyes cracked open again, his head jerking away from the wall. "*Are* you going to build an estate?"

"Not just yet, I should think," said Susan, observing the door up and down to see how it had done what it had done. "I have more sunshiny days to pursue yet, don't you think?"

"A lot more," he said. "Why are you thinking of setting up your estate? Sick of the roving life?"

"Nothing of the sort," Susan said. "I should very much dislike stopping roving—at the very least, I would have to make stables so that I'd have ample room for all the horselords. How did you know this was here, by the way?"

"I found it yesterday," he said.

Susan stared at him. "Lummox, do you mean to tell me that you knew that was there the entire time and didn't say anything?"

"The bride and the master are safe," he said. "For now. And no one expected us elsewhere."

"I see," she said, and threw herself back down on the bench. "Then I suppose we might as well enjoy a bit more sun before we have to go back into the cold."

．　．　．

Susan parted from Emmett on the other side of the glassy door—a state of affairs that may not have occurred if she hadn't caught sight of one of the gardeners striding along at a guilty sort of lope toward the back of the manor after, she was quite sure, turning from the window he had been earnestly peering into.

"Look there," she said, tilting her head toward the gardener. She couldn't tell which of the gardeners it was, but it was certainly one of them. "What's he doing, do you think?"

"Nothing good," Emmett said briefly, and took off after the man.

Bother, thought Susan. She couldn't really go traipsing after Emmett and the gardeners; the sound of the bell that had roused her and Emmett from their sunny rest signified that Janet was ready to be taken back to her room—or at least required Susan's presence. The hound was with her, but Susan preferred not to leave her alone too long after what had happened this morning. As it was, she reckoned that Janet had been alone with the master for a good two hours, which was probably just about long enough.

Susan passed a few words with Brennan as she entered the house —"Don't like it, old girl; there's a tighter buzz around the manor this morning. You did something, didn't you?"—and stepped lightly through the doors into the lower part of the grand hall just in time to see a male figure exiting from the breakfast room.

He wasn't so far away that she shouldn't have been able to see his face, at least in profile, but the darkness of the hall had her squinting to see despite that. She knew his figure, at least.

The master, thought Susan, with a frisson of excitement and interest. As with every other time, she could only see him from behind, and she was beginning to suspect that it was part of the curse, too—the mysterious lord of the manor, not to be seen or interacted with. Much of a well-made curse was about perception and Susan tended to think that if it *was* a curse they were dealing with, it was one that liked to make sure people saw things and other people exactly as it meant them to do.

In pursuance of finding out more about that possible curse, Susan affably offered to help Regan beat out the rugs after she returned a rather quiet and thoughtful Janet to her suite with the hound and extracted a promise from her that she would stay there until Susan returned.

That led to a good three hours of work, not the least of which was physical. Susan was used to physical work and mental exertion alike, but she preferred to keep the two separate when she could. She also preferred to deal in devastating honesty in order to get what she needed. Today, however, it was necessary to exercise her muscles and cunning all at once.

"Did you see what happened to the mistress this morning?" she asked as they collected the rugs from the first floor and made a pile of them in the courtyard beside the kitchen.

"I try not to see things I shouldn't see," Regan said, dropping her armful of rugs onto the pile and massaging the shoulder they'd been weighted against. "And I'd do the same if I were you, Miss Susan."

"It's a bit hard not to see the mistress dangling from the banisters by her neck," Susan said. "They pay me to keep her safe, after all."

Regan seized one of the rugs and threw it over the nearest rope line. "They pay you to be with her, not to save her. You should remember that if you don't want to end up falling from the banisters yourself."

"I've got the feeling it isn't likely to happen to me," said Susan, battering away at her own rug and panting a little. "It seems a bit too dramatic for a maid, don't you think?"

Regan shot her a look. "You're pretty well informed for someone who didn't come from the town."

"I get the feeling," Susan pursued, happy to be absolutely honest, "that everyone is sort of being *pushed* in one direction or another. And then when two paths cross—especially *those* two paths —things start getting rather tighter."

"That's a good way to describe it, I suppose. It's when things get looser that you have to worry."

Susan shook out her shoulders and removed her rug from the line to replace it with another. "It's the why that seems odd to me.

It's an odd sort of curse that keeps pulling people into it and growing tighter when paths converge."

"It's not a curse," Regan said. "It's just the way things are."

"Then why do Mrs. Carmichael and Mr. Oswald refuse to discuss it?"

"Oh, it's not much good trying to talk to the older ones about it," said Regan. "They know that talking about it makes it tighter."

"If it's not a curse, then what?" asked Susan, stopping to rest.

"Well, it's about the Perfect Result, isn't it?" said Regan. "Can't you feel it? They say it's a curse in town, and oh well! perhaps it is— but I get paid well, and all I have to do is keep things tidy. So long as we all do what we're supposed to do, we'll come out all right. Everyone just has to mind their *P*s and *Q*s. The sooner you learn that, the better off you'll be."

"What about when someone doesn't do what they're supposed to do?" enquired Susan. "Is that the sort of thing that needs to be made tidy?"

Regan didn't look at her; she beat the rug harder instead, focusing all of her attention on it. "That's when people start falling through the glasshouse roof and brides start knocking their brains out on the front step," she said. "That's why it's better if we stick to our own kind and they stick to theirs. I can't help them catching it, but I can help catching it myself."

"Catching it? *Can* you catch a Perfect Result?"

"No, but you catch it if you can't turn out the Perfect Result," Regan said, grinning. "And we'll catch it if we're not done in the next two hours, Miss Susan, so I'll save my breath for beating the rugs, if it's all the same to you."

SEVEN

Susan woke in the early hours of the morning to find that she was once again alone in the suite.

She huffed an exasperated sigh up at the ceiling and thought that if Janet had been as determined to explore the manor as Susan was, she couldn't have been oftener absent. At least the windows were all decently closed this time, which meant that Janet must have taken to the halls; it was also a comfort to see that she had taken the hound with her again. Susan suspected that the hound would press to Janet's side during the entire excursion after their last outing.

Since there was no telling where they might have got themselves to, Susan resolved not to worry and took herself out of bed and the suite alike to wander the halls alone. Her exploration throughout the day with Regan at her side hadn't done a great deal of good; she hadn't had enough unobserved time to search the rooms for anything so delicate as what had been done to Brennan, and had no more idea at the end of the day than she'd had at the beginning if the other horselords really did exist in furniture form around the manor.

The halls were dark and shifting with shadows when Susan left the suite. There was no sign of Janet or the hound in the hall, but that wasn't surprising: Susan rather thought that the other woman had slipped out some time ago. She would just have to hope that the hound would keep Janet safe enough while Susan checked the left wing for any other signs of sentient furniture. It was evidently necessary to find them as soon as possible if they really were in the manor: Susan had spoken to Brennan from time to time throughout the day, and each time she did so, it seemed to make him a little less fuzzy about who he was and where he had come from. She didn't like to think how easy it might be for him—or the others—to be lulled back into the stiff, woody certainty that they were just pieces of furniture.

She tried the doors along the hallway as she went and found only one of them unlocked. That was no issue, of course: Susan could pick locks with the best of housebreakers in the Two Monarchies—had, in fact done so for a good three months as a part of learning how to pick those locks. The first door she opened was a linen press with no space for any kind of furniture. Susan touched her fingers to the linens there despite that, alert to any kind of difference in the threads or the folds of the material. There was nothing to be discovered there, so she moved on to the small wooden plant stand between that door and the next. The plant stand was also merely itself, but Susan took a few minutes to talk persuasively to it anyway and moved on again regretfully when it didn't talk back.

She picked two locks in the hall before she turned into the upper grand hall. A crack of light met her eyes as she turned into the otherwise dark hall: someone was in the little room that Janet had been warned off, and that was fun and a little bit interesting. Susan didn't think it was Janet: Janet wouldn't have had the light on. She might be more reckless than Susan thought was sensible when it came to her position in the house, but Susan didn't think she was stupid.

Emmett certainly wouldn't have left the light on, either, which left the servants and the master to consider. Susan was inclined to think that it was the master, and regretfully decided against surprising the room's occupant with a confused, bumbling entrance to enquire why they were within. There would be time enough to meet with the master later.

It was quite early in the morning when Susan passed back along the grand hall. She had gotten as far as the ballroom in her search with absolutely nothing to show for it but a faint headache that reminded her she ought to get some sleep if she wanted to be functioning the next day.

The ballroom shouldn't take too long to go through; she would try again tomorrow night. It might be larger than the rooms she had passed through in the darkness, but there was bound to be less furniture to search through in there. There was also the chance that it was going to be distinctly more dangerous than the other rooms —Susan had yet to see exactly how a servant could absolutely disappear within the manor as she had heard they had, but she knew that there had been something in the ballroom that wanted to get out when she passed this way the other night.

When she came back the way she'd already passed, Susan turned, almost by instinct, down the right side of the manor rather than down the left. She wasn't quite sure exactly why she did, except that she thought she wanted to make sure Emmett was safely abed and not walking anywhere in his sleep.

It wasn't until she had gone to edge slightly to the left—another instinctive move, to allow for the angling of the hallway—and found herself nearly walking into the wall, that she realised something wasn't quite right.

When there wasn't an opening to allow a branching away to the left a little later on, Susan positively grinned. There should be an opening right about where she was. She stopped and put a hand to the wall, wondering at the solidity of it, and backtracked just a little with her hand resting against the wall. All of it was solid, sure, and entirely without the kind of moveable quality that would be required for a trick wall.

Now that, thought Susan, her mind sharpening as she moved down the hallway again, was *very* interesting! She was quite certain of her way, and she was even more certain of the shape of the manor from beneath. The hallway she was exploring tonight was not the same hallway along which she had wandered the night she met Emmett as he walked in his sleep.

She couldn't say for sure which was the correct configuration, either; she *could* say that they were different, and that neither iteration matched the lower configuration of the manor. She could also say with reasonable certitude that the walls were entirely solid and unmoveable, and that there was nothing of roughness or incompleteness to the carpeting that would have suggested a hidden door anywhere, either.

No; the manor itself seemed to have changed configuration between last night and tonight. More, it had done so without recourse to any spell that she was aware of. Susan wondered briefly, shivering a little, if it had changed after Janet passed through, or before. She began to walk a little more swiftly, eager to catch sight of some sign that the other woman had passed through the hallway ahead of her.

She found herself being directed toward the right by a hallway that seemed to be narrowing gradually via the left-hand wall angling itself inward, and for the first time caught sight of the marks on the carpet.

They were chalk marks: faint, small, and easily scuffed away by an unwary foot. By them, it was easy to see that the left-hand wall was indeed converging on Susan, and it struck her that the marks were exactly for that purpose.

Susan wondered for the first time, with crystal clear mind, exactly why the bride—or indeed, Janet herself—would be wandering down changeable hallways, clearly prepared for the changeability of them, when it was much safer to be abed.

"Have I been duped, I wonder?" she asked aloud, her voice falling softly in the heavy air. "But then, she wouldn't have thrown herself over the banisters like that. Whatever she is and whatever she's doing, she's clearly in danger."

And more than half in love with the master and Emmett alike, remarked a small, acerbic part of her mind. That was something that bothered her rather a lot, although she was honest enough to admit that not all of her irritation was strictly to do with the curse-related complications that Janet's shifting attention was likely to cause.

She wasn't sure how much of that irritation was personal, however—or exactly what she should be doing about it. It wasn't as though other women hadn't shown interest in Emmett in the past, so it shouldn't bother her so much now.

Mind you, Susan thought, incurably honest with herself, Emmett had never before shown the faintest sign of a returning interest in anyone else. She couldn't say he'd shown an interest in Janet, either; it was more that he hadn't repulsed her at all, and Emmett had never been afraid to kindly and gently detach potential interest.

Susan was still considering that troubling point with a frown when the vague fluttering of light and shadow at the end of the hallway caught her attention. If the first shadow moved past before she was able to see it properly, the second, half its height and considerably longer, was unmistakeable.

The hound—and undoubtedly Janet—had just passed along whatever part of the manor met with the end of this particular hallway. And now that Susan looked, she could see the faint luminescence of moonlight further down, dawning into the hallway where it certainly hadn't been before.

She hurried toward the light, as certain as she was that she didn't want to lose Janet, that if she didn't leave while the moonlight fell into the hallway, she might not be able to get out again. Susan didn't like the thought of continually walking down a hallway that never ended, walking ever onward as it gradually became narrower and narrower.

She found herself back in a part of the manor that she recognised: and as she had seen it the first time, there was Emmett standing in the shadows far ahead. This time, he stood as though in thought where Susan fancied there had been a staircase the first time she saw him here. There was no staircase there now, though there was a small, banister-bounded square of plants and decorative stands where it had been.

Impossible for someone to fall down there, thought Susan, suddenly amused again. Perhaps it was because the air felt lighter here than it had in the last section of the manor. Perhaps it was just nice to have visual confirmation that Emmett was alive and well and not in any immediate danger.

That feeling of well-being lasted for the few seconds before Janet's head jerked up as she saw Emmett.

"Emmet!" said her hushed voice. She sounded tremulous and relieved. She crossed the remaining space between them, and Susan saw her wipe chalky fingers on her skirt and then reach out to Emmett as she said, "I'm so glad to see someone! I thought I'd gotten lost!"

"You shouldn't be in the halls at night," Emmett said. He said it as if perplexed, and Susan noticed that he didn't remove Janet's hand from his arm. "It's dangerous."

"You're here," Janet said, gazing up at him.

Susan wondered if she was calling attention to the fact that Emmett himself had braved the dangers, or if she was, more simply, suggesting that the hallway was no longer dangerous now that she was with Emmett.

Either would have been equally true, but Susan couldn't help the twisting feeling of irascibility the statement caused. The girl who had spoken of the master with stars in her eyes had no business gazing up at Emmett with the exact same expression.

It was also, Susan thought, a dangerous thing to be doing when the master could be supposed to be sleeping not too far away from where his valet was, and could in fact, emerge at any time to see his bride passing the time of night with his servant in the moonlight.

More worryingly, the hallway around them shifted and softened around the edges as she watched—it seemed almost as if the whole place was thinking and reforming around them as they stood there.

"Bother," said Susan softly to herself, because she rather thought she knew what the curse was.

If it was what she thought it was, she and Emmett were in for a very delicate job. She had a little experience in such things, and

Emmett was very good about not being misled by magic, but this wasn't normal magic.

Susan nearly went forward and joined them but caught herself at the last moment and turned and slipped away in the darkness. If Janet was with Emmett as well as the hound, she was bound to be safe. Emmett would be safe, too; to think otherwise was ridiculous. There was also very little Susan could do about the way the air around the two of them seemed to thicken the longer they stood together—not while together with them, at any rate.

That was something for tomorrow's Susan to figure out. Today's Susan had some idea of what needed to be done, but a good night's sleep would undoubtedly help develop that idea.

Susan woke the next day with a heavy feeling she was quite sure Janet shared when she woke the other woman later.

"Some breakfast in bed might be better than going down to the breakfast room," she suggested to the pale, dark-circled eyes that gazed woefully up at her.

"Oh no!" Janet said. "I couldn't!"

"You could and you should," Susan said grimly. "You have dark circles—and a bit of mystery is good for budding romances, after all."

Janet bit her lip. "There's no time for that."

"I wasn't aware that you were in a hurry?" Susan allowed her voice to rise slightly, turning the statement into a question. "What with all the night-time wandering you've been doing, no one would suspect you to be a bride in danger of her life at all!"

Janet's eyes dropped.

"One would almost," pursued Susan, her eyes sharp as she remembered the chalk marks in the hallway, "suspect you of having an ulterior motive."

"I took the hound with me," Janet protested, lifting her chin a little. "I'm not entirely stupid, you know! And shouldn't I try to discover the secrets of the manor before the manor kills me?"

"Is that what you've been trying to do? Find out the secrets of the manor?" Susan didn't have to affect the tone of slight disbelief. "Walking through the fireplace and dangling from the banisters wasn't enough for you?"

"I didn't do that on purpose!"

"I didn't imagine so."

"I don't intend to sit back and die without doing something to stop it, anyway," Janet said defiantly.

Susan couldn't help smiling. "Janet," she said persuasively. "I really do think it would be better if you told me exactly why you came to the manor."

She said it on an instinct, without any reason other than chalk marks to think that there was anything to it, but Janet's face coloured at once, and although she said hastily, "I don't know what you mean!" Susan knew she'd struck a nerve.

She said briskly, "Nonsense. I don't know who made you do it or why you did it, but you came here on purpose and with a goal in mind."

"The only goal I had in mind was to stop the young women in my town from being sacrificed, one by one," Janet said fiercely. "I had no choice. One of us had to be the bride, and this time it was me."

"Yes, but you volunteered, didn't you?"

"I don't know why you'd think that, when I was hiding in a closet when you first saw me."

"Perfectly reasonable to get cold feet for a moment!" protested Susan. "I suppose I could have felt the same if I'd volunteered myself to do something that was almost certain to lead to my death. Besides, I've got a very good idea that it wasn't exactly *my* wardrobe when you climbed into it."

"You came here," Janet pointed out, climbing out of bed and removing a rather dusty night gown. "You knew the same as me."

"Don't think I don't see you changing the subject," Susan said cheerfully. She was already well-prepared with a soft, loose morning dress in delicate yellow. Her own tunic had been another couple of inches longer this morning, and the offerings in Janet's closet had all been of the same harmless, fluffy sort. The curse, it would seem, had very firm ideas about correct clothing for ladies and ladies maids. "It's no good, you know: I might look like a wolfhound, but I'm actually a terrier."

"I'm going to breakfast, anyway," Janet said. "You're not to try and stop me."

"Shouldn't dream of it," said Susan. "I have my own shenanigans to be getting on with, and if you want to run yourself ragged meeting with the master, I've nothing else to say."

It was by no means all that she wanted to say, of course; happily for Susan, she would be meeting with Emmett later that day and could then say all that she would like to. In pursuance of that happy end, she wiggled her eyebrows at Emmett across the breakfast table —noting, with concealed triumph, the distinct amusement in his eyes—and happily dragged him into the butler's pantry with her after a quick, gleeful look around the empty hallway once everyone else in the manor was off on other errands.

Emmett allowed himself to be dragged into the pantry and propped up against one of the walls while Susan shut the door, but he sent her a quizzical look.

She grinned at him and explained, "It's good policy to seize the day, lummox! I know it's not our usual meeting time, but I fancy we'll be quite busy later in the day—and Mrs. Carmichael and Mr. Oswald have sneaked away somewhere."

Emmett let the quizzical look rest on her for a few moments more before he said, "You've got an idea what's going on, don't you?"

"The curse," said Susan, her eyes sparkling, "—whatever it is, and whoever is doing it—I think it's pushing us toward a certain course of action."

"The Perfect Result," Emmett said, nodding. "The master mentioned it this morning, too."

"Did he tell you what it was?"

"No."

"Neither would any of the others," Susan muttered. "Not without pulling themselves up about it, anyway. Mrs. Carmichael and Mr. Oswald won't talk about it at all, and the younger two will only say as much as they think they can get away with. It's as if they think it's catching, and that by talking about it, they might catch it."

A light of consideration lit in Emmett's eyes, making Susan grin.

"Got an idea, have you, lummox?"

"A warning," he said, but Susan wasn't fooled; Emmett was obviously both appreciative and wary of whatever he had thought of. "If it's a sticky curse, it could come after us more quickly for talking about it. Very clever."

"That's all very well to say," she said. "But we have to talk about it to find out what it is and who's doing it. And it sounds like talking about it isn't the only thing that makes it stick to people."

"The household staff aren't dead," Emmett pointed out.

"Not all of them," she countered. "The previous valet is very dead, and I'm rather certain the gardeners disposed of him. And Brenners is a hall stand, so..."

"You said you know what it is."

"Well, I've got a good idea," Susan said. "Actually, it was Janet who made me think of it; I must thank her for that. I think it's a story curse: everyone in the manor and its grounds has a part they have to play, and the story it's trying to play out is their Perfect Result. Characters who go too far from the roles they're meant to play—"

"Die," Emmett said, nodding. He leaned his shoulders into the shelves, sinking into a brief few moments of thought that culminated in the remark: "And some of them are meant to die as part of their character."

Susan looked up at him approvingly. It was always so satisfying working on a problem with Emmett: his thoughts picked up where hers ended, and added to her thoughts. "Yes, I think so. The Bride is a reoccurring role, obviously. The servants seem to remain the same —except for the ones who die. And even people who come into the radius of the curse with ulterior motives seem to conform, either knowingly or otherwise."

Emmett gazed at her silently for a moment or two before he asked, "Even us?"

"Even us," said Susan, nodding. "My clothing changes a little every day toward something more suitable to a lady's maid, and you can't tell me that you don't get anxious about the master when he's not in your sight, because I won't believe you. I feel the same way about Janet."

"You came here to rescue Janet."

"Yes, but that doesn't explain why it's so hard to call her *Janet* instead of *the mistress*, or the fact that I'm just within reach every time something interesting happens," argued Susan. She couldn't help the faintly conscious look she shot up at Emmett before she added, "You must have noticed that it's the same with you."

"I haven't had to rescue the master yet," he pointed out.

"Yes, but you've had to rescue the mistress," she said, refraining from mentioning that the master seemed to be the last person they would really need to worry about. "And you must have noticed that you're always within reach of her when she needs help—"

"Only since yesterday," said Emmett, frowning. "Since I helped you rescue her."

"Exactly," Susan said. "And the bride didn't come here to die. Janet didn't, at any rate. She's filling a role in the curse, but she came here for another purpose entirely, and until I find out what that was, I rather think it's going to be harder to keep her safe."

"The hound will help."

"Yes, but how much?" Susan said. "And that's without accounting for what the curse may do to the hound in retaliation."

"A story curse can only do so much," said Emmett. "So long as I stay near the master and you stay near the mistress—"

"Yes, but that's not the thing that worries me," Susan interrupted. "The thing that worries me is that Regan told me *tidying up* is part of the servants' job."

Emmett's eyes dwelt on her for another long moment, whether in consideration or frustration, she wasn't sure. "The valet in the fire."

"Exactly," Susan agreed. "Which means that if we're going to go against the Perfect Result, we need to be aware that we're probably going to run into trouble from the servants as well as the curse."

"Then we conform to the roles," Emmett said. "At least for now."

"We only need to conform enough to stay hidden. And to keep the servants happy. They run around at night when they need to—when they're trying to stop the master from scuppering the Result, for example. I'd like to know how violin playing threatens the Perfect Result, but I suppose we shouldn't focus on that for now. Should we try to stop the bride from wandering, do you think?"

Emmett thought about that for a few minutes that were dense in silence, and said at last, "It's part of the story. Mysterious manor, mysterious lord—she has to keep wandering."

"I was afraid of that," Susan said gloomily. "All right; we'd probably better make rules, then. Now that the hound has taken a liking to Janet, the first should be easy: Never leave the Bride alone. She's the only one I can see who is actually *meant* to die when it comes to the story."

"Two," said Emmett in some deliberation, "we check in on each other every night as well as during the day."

"That's probably a good idea," Susan said, with a sudden, unwelcome flash of memory that included Janet gripping Emmett's arm. "If we're going to be wandering the halls one way or another, we might as well nod when we meet."

"Number three," he said. "Always be in character—or at least enough in character that we don't get tidied up."

"Number four," said Susan severely. "Don't lose yourself in the character."

Emmett's eyes rested on her thoughtfully. "We know that we're playing roles."

"I don't think everything is quite so cut and dried, lummox. I told you, my tunics have been growing by an inch or two every day since I've been here, and I've only just realised it. It's as if I'm being slowly changed into a more proper version of myself."

"What else isn't cut and dried? Something that isn't your clothing."

"Well, I hate to say it, lummox, but it seems as though you've been cast as the Secondary Love Interest. Something got twisted up when you rescued Janet—"

"I didn't—I didn't rescue her," said Emmett, shifting away from the shelves and uncrossing his arms. "I only carried her into the breakfast room and took the scarf away from her neck."

"Yes, but something went twisty right after you did it, and now you're meeting her in the bowels of the house at all hours of the morning," Susan pointed out. She didn't miss the conscious look that flashed across his face; it twisted at that Something in her stomach that she had only just begun to be aware was there. "So. Rule #4: *Don't Lose Yourself in the Character.*"

"I didn't go out to meet her."

"That's exactly the point," she said. "You didn't go out to meet her, but a chance meeting happened. I'm almost certain that a lot more chance meetings are going to happen."

Emmett took in a deep breath through his nose and let it out slowly. "I don't like this."

"She won't bite, I'm sure," Susan said comfortingly, and was aware of a prickle of guilty relief that had a lot to do with the thought that Janet's soft, clinging hands would have to cling to the master instead.

"I can look after myself," he said. "I'm more worried about what the curse has in store for your character."

"Well, if I don't like it, I'll just try to change it a bit," said Susan, patting his arm and then pulling her hand back with the sudden consciousness that it looked awfully like the way Janet touched the master. "So long as I'm clever about it, the curse will probably just find another way to get the result it wants by turning me into another character."

"Or get rid of you altogether," Emmett said grimly. Two lines, with a half-line above them, made creases in his forehead, but Susan had the impression that he was looking at the hand she'd drawn back. "Through the nearest glass surface."

Lightly, she said, "If you're wondering if I can be convinced to cut and run, lummox, I'd like you to know that I can't be."

"I didn't think you could," he said.

"Then you were wondering if you could hit me on the head and carry me out insensible," she retorted. "And I won't have it."

"What do you plan on doing that's better than leaving?"

"I think I'd better try to have a word with the master," she said thoughtfully. "I'd like to try and figure out if he's the one doing it or if he's suffering from it as well. If he's a part of the curse, we're going to need to try and rescue him; if he's doing it, I really do think we'd be justified in putting him out of commission long enough to get everyone else out of the manor—and whatever else we're inside of. I've got an idea about how to do it, too."

"I could knock him out straight away," Emmett offered.

"That would be delightfully simple," Susan said regretfully. "No, lummox; I think we'd better not. As much as I'd like to think it's the master and only the master, Mrs. Carmichael and Mr. Oswald are very concerned and very much more than just house-keeper and butler. They told the master what to do the other night, and he did it. I'd like to know how much they have to do with the curse."

"The violin," nodded Emmett. "All right. I'll have a word with the master myself."

Susan considered that but shook her head. "I don't think it will be as effective as me doing it."

That brought back two of the lines across his forehead; Emmett absently rubbed a hand over his arm and said, "Effective how?"

"You're probably already too close to him. Too close, and too far away." Reluctantly, she added, "If it was Janet, I'd get you to do it. We're close enough that she tells me nearly everything, but we're close enough that there are things she knows how to hide from me."

"Does that mean there's something you want me to find out from Janet?"

Susan would have opened her mouth to say that there *was* something he could ask about, but she didn't seem to be able to bring herself to say it. She hesitated just a moment too long, and the next moment, with a shock of unpleasant coldness up her spine, she heard two voices approaching along the hallway.

"That's all very well, but there's no wine for lunch, Mr.

Oswald," said Mrs. Carmichael's sharp voice. "And you know how the master feels about wine at lunch. We can pick out something now and get it to the kitchen in time for preparation."

"That's torn it," Susan said, meeting Emmett's startled eyes. "It will take them a little while to get through the bit of befuddlement I laid on the lock to make it hard to put the key in, but it won't be more than a minute or two."

"There's no other way out," Emmett said, looking swiftly around the small room despite that.

"I know that, lummox," she said. "I didn't do it to give us time to escape; I did it to give us time to think of something. They can't hear us, at least."

"There's nothing to be done," he said.

"Of course there is," Susan said cheerfully. "I can think of at least two ways to spin this situation so that no one figures out we came here together to save the bride."

Emmett flicked a look over at the lock as a series of scratching began. "Do we need to spin it?"

"I really don't think they ought to know we knew each other before arrival—or that we're working together," she said seriously. "I've got a feeling that will be more dangerous for us than anything. They seem very set on their Perfect Result, and I'd rather not be tidied up along with you because we're threatening that Perfect Result."

"Tell me *clearly* what you want me to do."

"I'm afraid you're going to have to kiss me, lummox," she said.

She looked up to find that Emmett's blue gaze was on her. His left hand closed around her right forearm as if to catch his balance or hers; then he blinked and said, "No."

"How distressingly rude of you," said Susan.

"What's the other option?"

"The other option is being taken for thieves and trying to wriggle our way out of it," she said. "And I don't much like our chances of getting out whole—or of getting Brenners out with us if we do get out."

"At least we'll be out," he said. "And we can come back again, better prepared."

"Yes, but will the bride still be alive?" Susan said, more insistently. "I realise that it's an unpleasant thought, lummox, but it really would be much better if you just kissed me."

Emmett, surprising and delighting her all at once, asked, "Better for *who*?"

"I can at least promise that it won't be an unpleasant experience!" she protested, with a chuckle deep in her throat. "Lummox, don't be a spoil-sport! I don't believe you're going to hove me out of the manor against my will."

"Don't you?" There was something of a grimness to Emmett's voice as well as his jaw that worried Susan out of her desire to laugh.

Had she been wrong about the one-sidedness of Janet's interest in Emmett? Surely not! She couldn't be. And yet, Susan couldn't help the cold piercing of anxiety that Emmett really was about to get them both kicked out of the manor because he had a pressing reason to not want to kiss her.

He released her arm and said below his breath, "Maybe I haven't made myself clear enough—"

The key slotted precisely into the lock, slid with a rattle to the length of its shank, and made the smallest *snick* against the back of the lock. Then it turned, and in that blank moment of oiled cogs clicking softly before the bit completed its circle, Susan said despairingly, "*Emmett!*"

The name had barely passed her lips when the key bit clicked into place and Susan found herself ruthlessly crushed against the shelves behind her with an arm of iron around her waist and Emmett's lips pressed against her own.

Susan had, in her assignment to the horselords, spent a great deal of time in close proximity with Emmett: she had fallen asleep against his broad back, been carted limply to safety against his chest when her sense of adventure outran her luck, and used him as a ladder to escape more than one inconvenient imprisonment.

She hadn't expected the act of being clasped to Emmett's chest to be either as intimate or as electrifying as it was—or perhaps she just hadn't expected him to do the job of kissing as thoroughly as he was presently doing it. She hadn't counted on her own instinctive response, either; she regained her senses just in time to find that she had slid her arm along his and then curled her fingers around his neck.

Then daylight dawned on them, and Mrs. Carmichael's voice gasped, "The very idea!"

Susan was briefly aware of Emmett reaching out and casually wrenching the door shut again, as well as the shocked clucking from outside that his actions provoked, but she was far too occupied with the hand that now cupped her face and drew her forward to kiss her again—a kiss that was this time so soft and persuasive that she couldn't help following that warmth—to take any notice of it.

This time, she became aware of what she was doing far more quickly and stopped that dangerous forward motion. Emmett nudged her back into the shelves but pulled away softly and slowly, one arm braced against the shelves instead of around her waist.

"Good heavens, lummox!" Susan said, shaken but approving. "Who would have thought you were capable of *that!*"

Emmett lowered his head again with a purpose that was unmistakeable, and Susan had the rather faint thought that he was actually about to kiss her again when the door was snatched open again and she turned a genuinely flustered face toward Mrs. Carmichael's outraged one.

"*What?*" growled Emmett, with no trace of embarrassment.

Susan cleared her throat and managed, though she wasn't sure how, to wriggle away from Emmett; Mrs. Carmichael watched that in outrage too, and said coldly, "I'll thank you not to take advantage of the butler's pantry for this sort of meeting!"

"It wasn't supposed to be that sort of meeting!" said Susan frankly, allowing her very real flush to make itself useful. "I only came down to make up the mistress' afternoon tea tray."

Mr. Oswald said plaintively, "There ought to be no fraternisation of staff!"

"Oh," said Susan. "Sorry about that. The master's man started it."

"That," Emmett said, ducking his head to set the words thrumming pleasantly through her ear, "is not how I remember it."

Susan caught a brief glimpse of his face; his eyes danced before her, his lips just a little too red from kissing, and she knew that her own must look the same.

She looked away at once, both fascinated and worried to find herself blushing again.

"Come out of there at once, both of you," Mrs. Carmichael said grimly. "Heaven help you if the master sees!"

"Will he throw us out?" asked Susan. "It was only a kiss!"

"You'd be so lucky!" said Mrs. Carmichael, and bustled away down the hall.

Emmett slipped up the hall in his usual soft-footed way at the same time and disappeared up the servants' stairs—or so Susan, who hadn't seen him go, assumed—leaving Susan alone with Mr. Oswald, who locked the butler's pantry rather pointedly.

"Don't be like that," Susan said reproachfully. "You must have had your moments with a girl in the pantry."

Mr. Oswald stiffened. "I never did! I'm not that—I mean, I obey the rules!"

"What are the rules?" asked Susan agreeably. "No one told me about rules when I started work here."

"They should have told you in the town," Mr. Oswald said. He looked as though he didn't quite believe her. "Everybody knows not to kiss in the pantry!"

"Isn't it better than kissing in the halls? What *are* the rules, by the way, Mr. Oswald? You can't have me running around the house and breaking rules!"

He hesitated, and it seemed to Susan as if he were on the knife edge of indecision.

She touched his arm lightly and said encouragingly, "Just think what a good job I'll do looking after the mistress if I'm not kissing men in the pantry!"

She had undoubtedly said the wrong thing: Mr. Oswald's face stiffened immediately.

"It's too late now, anyway," he said, hunching his shoulders.

"Don't touch me. I don't want to interfere with the way things ought to run around here. We only just cleaned up from last time."

And he bustled away nearly as furiously as Mrs. Carmichael before Susan could either bring up the matter of cleaning up and what that entailed, or mention that no one had managed to get the bottle of wine they had meant to collect.

She lingered by the pantry for quite some time, thinking her thoughts, and before long became aware that most of those thoughts involved Emmett, his lips, or both. That wouldn't do at all, so she started herself into motion, banishing the thoughts at the same time.

It was well past time, she decided, to see the master.

EIGHT

J anet seemed more weary after her late breakfast with the master than Susan had yet seen her, so it wasn't hard to get her to promise to keep to her suite and take lunch there instead. Since Susan herself wasn't planning on going too far from the suite, she had no compunction in taking the hound with her when the hound seemed insistent on accompanying her out of the room, either.

She had a good deal of time in which to explore the manor for any signs of the other horselords in furniture form, but without any success. The hound followed her patiently up and down the halls and into every room that she could get into via a combination of lockpicking and magic use.

Remembering the opening high above the main foyer, with its small remnants of balcony, Susan even nosed around the manor's second floor for any signs of a staircase that might lead further up into the rafters and ceilings. A manor of this size ought by rights to have some sort of attic system, and what she saw from the foyer seemed to bear that out, but she didn't find a single staircase that led up rather than down, and after she had been walking for several hours, Susan admitted defeat and went down to the kitchen to fetch dinner for Janet.

When she entered the room, Susan would have sworn that Janet had just been hiding something. There was nothing in her motions to suggest it, thought Susan, taking her time to close the door after the hound with one foot and carrying her tray to the table in the middle of the suite. In fact, Janet was sitting very straight in bed; the indications that alerted Susan to something not quite right were that very stillness—and the very faint flush of red that had brightened Janet's cheeks.

Susan made a mental note to search the room for anything interesting when she next had the chance, and roused Janet out of bed with a bluff sort of heartiness that seemed to dispel the bride's uneasiness. Although that uneasiness faded, Susan didn't think that the thoughtfulness or slightly crushed look had disappeared from Janet's face, and when the other woman finished dinner by listlessly declaring her intention of going to bed early, she chivvied Janet into her night dress and off to bed with fully as much bluff heartiness as she had chivvied her out of it.

Susan didn't bother to undress herself. It was early yet, and what she had in mind would be more likely to be effective if she went out earlier: she was far more likely to find the master out and about, for instance. She waited until Janet seemed to sleep, and then for a little bit longer until the bride really did fall asleep, and then left the suite with the hound once more at her heels.

It was past dinner time, but there was still the faintest light from the suns glimmering along the floor from the right wing's windows as Susan approached the main hall from the left wing. The hound followed without hesitation when Susan took the right-hand turn at the meeting of the halls—stopped obediently without a word from Susan when she paused in front of the mysterious door. It also waited patiently as she tried the handle of the door to again find it unlocked but unmoving.

"Bother you!" said Susan softly, because she could still sense no magic that should be stopping the door from moving. The hound looked up at her and whined, and she added, "Not you. This. You're lovely and solid; nothing ethereal about you."

That made her think again and, having done so, to drop to her stomach on the carpet of the hallway to look through the crack under the door. She couldn't help the deep chuckle of appreciation that came out: there was a thick, dark shadow at the rightmost side of the door, and if Susan wasn't very much mistaken, that meant that someone had shoved a chock of something beneath the door to prevent it opening no matter who had or didn't have the key to the lock of the door.

She leapt to her feet and darted a few steps down the hallway to the suit of armour that leaned drunkenly on its stand, and pinched its blunt axe. That popped the chock out from beneath the door in a single, smart tap, and Susan returned it with the sparkling feeling of having accomplished something.

The hound, as appreciative as Susan could have hoped, gave a soft trill when she opened the door, and preceded her inside to curl up on a couch: evidently the hound had no misapprehensions upon the score of this being a quick meeting. Susan grinned and replaced the chock of unpolished wood, then crossed the room after the hound. She didn't expect it to be terribly quick, either—it was one of the reasons she had chosen to use this particular room for her meeting.

There would always be ways of forcing a meeting, but in this case, Susan thought she preferred waiting for the master to approach rather than seeking him out wherever he was. It wasn't that she expected people to run away upon meeting her, but the master seemed distinctly flighty to her, and she had the impression that he would be less likely to fly at once if it appeared that he was the one who had brought about the meeting.

It was also far more private and comfortable to be sitting in padded chairs than trying to converse in the hallways where any of the servants could overhear.

All in all, thought Susan, throwing herself down beside the hound and stuffing her hands into the pockets of her breeches around considerably more material than she usually had to deal with due to a growing skirt, it was a happy circumstance and bound to produce happy results. She had to wriggle a little to fit both herself and the hound on the couch, after which, panting, she was free to look around the room and try to figure out exactly why the master had wanted to keep Janet from being in here—or exactly why Janet had so much wanted to get in.

It appeared to be a library of sorts, but it also held a great many ferns and other potted plants, some of them with flowers, some without. It also, Susan noticed, with sharp eyes, held a violin that she suspected to be the same violin she had heard a few nights ago— it sat out of reach but not out of sight, shut in a glass box that was probably as soundproof as it looked.

Had the master rescued it himself, or had it been put here as a sop to him?

Susan wasn't sure, but she was even surer than before that the master would come to her without any trouble if she remained where she was.

She was confident enough in her assessment that she snoozed a little as she waited. Luckily, she had remembered to put the chock back under the door when she closed it, and it was the soft *snick* of the chock of wood being smartly tapped out from beneath the door that woke her from her sleep.

Susan kept her eyes closed until the door shut behind the intruder, a soft light threw across the room, and a cold, haughty voice said, "What is *that*?"

She opened her eyes to find herself being stared at in well-bred, disdainful surprise by the master. His dark eyes were heavy with lashes, and his lips had been pulled slightly awry by a scar that ran upward toward his cheekbone on the left side. She could also, despite the shadows in the room, see the same distinctly blue sheen to the deep blackness of his hair that she had seen earlier.

He purposefully slid his gaze sideways to indicate the subject of his questions, and Susan patted the hound reflexively.

"It's your dog," she said. She didn't have a lot of patience for class as a weapon, and she had an idea that the master was trying to intimidate her. "Or so I presumed."

One side of his mouth made a small expression of irritation. "What is it doing on the *couch*?"

"Sleeping, by the looks of it. I shouldn't try to get it off, if I were you; I got back strain just trying to make space enough to sit down."

The master made a brief little choke of laughter and then tried to look as though he had never dreamt of laughing in his life to cover the slip.

"It's too late," Susan told him. "I heard you laugh. Do you want an apple? I pinched some of those tiny ones from the garden; they're delightfully sweet, and a couple of them fit in my pockets pretty easily."

"Those are my apples anyway," he said, his nose tilting upward very slightly. "Why did you come in here?"

"I heard you being rude to Janet about this room, and I thought that you'd only be very cranky about it if you spent a bit of time here and didn't want to be interrupted when you feel like being alone."

"I'm surprised you didn't consider that I might be annoyed at finding you here when I wanted to be alone, then."

"Oh, I considered it!" said Susan, bluntly honest. "But I thought you'd be a lot more annoyed if I collared you in the hallways."

Now that she had a chance to see him from the front, Susan could understand what Janet had found so immediately appealing. She herself didn't care for the very faint tinge of blue to the man's hair—she preferred hair of a lighter colour that had caramel tints to it—but there was an intensity and raw magnetism to the master's eyes that would have interested Susan herself if she had seen him as a free man.

Those eyes currently displayed a fresher pain than she would have expected. Adding that to Janet's rather crushed appearance when she'd walked the other woman back to her suite from the breakfast room, it seemed evident that something akin to a lover's quarrel must have happened earlier that day.

The master's eyes shuttered briefly, whether in surprise or protection, Susan wasn't sure. He said, "You couldn't have collared me in the hallway, anyway."

"It wouldn't have been easy, but you always have your back to me, so I expect I'd be able to manage the thing."

The master stared at her. "You're not allowed to do that!"

"I expect that's in the rules, too," Susan said. "Well, if it is, the rules should say something about you always having your back to me, shouldn't they?"

"It's got to be that way!" he said, perplexed. "Otherwise, we'd have too many problems with maids falling in love with the master!"

Susan eyed him in some wonder. "Are the maids you've had so far particularly impressionable?"

"I'm quite good-looking, you know," he said, rather stiffly.

"Of course you are!" she said soothingly. "There's no need to be defensive. I suppose you're just a bit raw after quarrelling with Janet this morning."

"I'm not—I'm not raw!"

"You can't tell me that the two of you didn't quarrel," Susan said. "Well, you can, but I won't believe you. Not after you were serenading her on your violin and the two of you were gazing at each other through windows in the wee hours of the morning. Now she's down the hall, crushed, and you're in here, crushed."

"I couldn't help liking her," he said. "But that's all it is."

It sounded defiant, and that amused Susan a little.

"You're allowed to like someone," she said. "I'm not going to tell anyone."

"You won't have to," he said. This time his voice was grim. "It doesn't help to talk about things. Things come out without talking about them, anyway."

"What a pleasant outlook on life that must be. I can assure you that I won't be talking out of turn."

"You're already talking out of turn," he said.

"Yes, but only to you," she pointed out.

"There are ears everywhere in the manor."

Susan laid her hand on the hound's head. "Only if we talk too loudly, I fancy."

He shrugged listlessly. "It's too late now, anyway. We've started, and we'll have to see how it all turns out."

"The story, do you mean?"

The master looked at her sharply. "If you want to look after your mistress, you ought to be a bit more careful about the things you talk about."

"I'm concerned about everyone," Susan said. "Nobody in this house seems to be terribly safe. Did you know that Janet has nearly died twice already?"

He looked away. "There's nothing I can do about that."

"Is there not?" Susan let the question linger in the air as the hound woke and stretched briefly, then closed its eyes again. "It's eating you up, though, I rather suspect."

"How do you know what I feel?" The master's eyes, dark and angry, met hers. "You're just one of the servants."

"People are pretty similar, upstairs or downstairs," Susan said, shrugging. "And here you are, brooding, so you might as well get it off your chest, mightn't you?"

The master stared at her for a moment longer, then laughed suddenly.

"I didn't expect her to care," he said, and Susan didn't think he was affecting the candour with which he said it. "They don't, usually. Most of the girls who come here are frightened out of their minds and just trying to survive."

"Understandably, I suppose," she said, with something of a dry voice. "They do tend to die pretty quickly, don't they?"

He muttered, "It's not my fault. I do my best, but none of them really do what they're supposed to do."

That, thought Susan coldly, wasn't exactly promising. She hoped she hadn't misread the situation; if she had, it was likely to be as dangerous for herself as it was for Janet. If the master was actually controlling the story curse, she had been far too open with him.

"I find that no one is very communicative about what the rules are," she said to him. "Perhaps making sure your brides and servants know what not to do would help matters."

"She won't be here for long," he said. "It's better not to get attached to them. I forgot that for a little while with this one, but I won't forget again."

"Janet isn't a cog in your machinery," Susan said tartly. "She's a woman who nearly walked through fire and was hung over the front banisters while trying to stay alive after marrying you."

The master reddened. "I wasn't—I wasn't always like this," he said, his eyes meeting hers briefly. "I was different, once. But there have been so many in and out that I can't take a chance on this one being the right one."

Susan, remembering the set of Janet's shoulders as she told Susan and the horselords that she would go with the soldiers, and the look of fierce delight and determination in the woman's eyes when she climbed back into the suite after listening to the master play the violin, asked, "Are you sure about that? She hasn't died yet, and she's pretty resilient."

"That's the problem!" he burst out. "I *don't* know! And anything other than perfect assurance and perfect matching is not good enough!"

"The Perfect Result," said Susan, nodding. Her heart felt quite light suddenly. So the master *wasn't* directing the story curse! "I know it's dangerous to say too much, but you might try to give Janet a nudge or two in the right direction if you want her to live."

"She already knows more than most of them," he said, surprised. "I haven't had to tell her anything that she didn't already know: I think that's why we bonded so quickly. She was trying to get me to push back, too."

"The violin," Susan said slowly. She had been right, then: Janet knew a lot more than she had given the woman credit for. "I thought that turned out rather well, actually."

"It bound us together," he said. "But it came at a cost: there are other threads now, and it's the other threads that do the damage."

"Other threads like your valet?" Susan suggested. "I shouldn't worry about that, if I were you. I'll take care of that particular thread."

The master stared at her in something very like awe. "That'll pull you in pretty tight. Are you sure you want to do that?"

"I'm already in tight enough," said Susan. "And if you think it gives me any pleasure to see Janet gazing up at my friend, you're very much mistaken. I've seen the threads that bind them together, and I'm not too pleased about it either."

He sat down opposite her, his face the most open she'd seen it since he walked into the room, and leaned forward on his knees to gaze at her over the table. "Are you in love with him?"

"I'm not sure," Susan said. "But I'd like the chance to find that out without having to fight off a curse and a rival at the same time. The curse isn't playing fair, and when I can see how I could play dirty too, it makes it hard for me to resist. And then there's another problem—"

The master said grimly, "You don't know how many of your own feelings are real and how many of them are from this cursed place itself."

"Exactly," said Susan. "The most I can do while I'm here is try to keep everyone's feelings at bay and sort them out later."

"I wish I could do that," he said, the dissatisfaction plain in his face. "But everything I do is bound up in feelings and making sure they're the right ones at the right time."

"You might try to be a bit more proactive with your bride," Susan suggested. "She already likes you, and I can't imagine she'd object to a bit more in the way of direct encouragement from you."

The master, much like the hound, flopped bonelessly against the seat of his chair and rested his chin on his arms. "Yes, but I'll have to give it to her soon, and then things will start falling apart," he said miserably. "They always do."

"Give her *what*, exactly?" asked Susan.

The master eyed her blankly over his arms. "The key, of course. It's always about the key—that's how any of us can escape this nightmare."

"Why not use it yourself, then?"

"Because it won't work for me," he muttered. "Not that way, anyway. I have to trust her enough to give it to her, and she has to trust me enough not to use it."

"And I suppose that telling her as much is quite out of the question...?"

"Of course. I've tried with a few of them, and they died the next day—the ones who did understand what I was trying to tell them didn't care enough about me to try and trust me, and the ones who didn't understand died just the same. It isn't allowed."

"There are those rules again," said Susan speculatively, wondering exactly what the key was supposed to unlock and how the using of it could possibly be construed as an assault against the Perfect Result. Rules were, of course, inevitable; but in Susan's experience, there were a great many ways in which one could take rules, and a great many shapes one could make with even the most rigid of them. "I wonder how far we can get away with bending them before they come around to bite us? Are they written anywhere, or are they inherent to the system?"

"Inherent," he said. "And as much as I think I'm bending the rules, I always end up following them without realising it. I'm supposed to fall in love with the brides, you know."

"Yes, I gathered as much," Susan said. "That doesn't mean you're not allowed to fall in love with one properly. Just because you're doing what the rules say doesn't mean that you're obeying the rules."

"A natural Perfect Result? I don't think that exists."

"Perhaps not, but a nearly-Perfect Result is probably good enough if it adheres to the rules, I should think," said Susan. "I don't suppose any of you know exactly what the Perfect Result is?"

"That's inherent, too. But we know it has to do with the key and trust. Any time the brides get too far away from me or the guidelines, they start to die."

"I'm surprised you haven't had Janet sleeping in your suite, in that case," Susan said, making the master cough in surprise and pretend that he wasn't hiding a blush behind his curls. "I've got a feeling that she'd say yes if you asked."

The master met her eyes for a brief moment before his own dropped.

"I wish," he said softly, "that it had been you as the bride. I might have had a chance, then."

"That's just the curse confusing you: I probably would have hit you over the head and taken the key the first night," Susan said bracingly. "You would have hated it."

"Yes, but you would have taken me with you," he said. "Carried me over your shoulder or dragged me by the hair, or something like that. You wouldn't have left me."

"You don't know that," Susan said, worried by the faint edge of hero-worship to his voice. It brought a faint sense of tightening threads with it, and she had the rueful thought that she may have made a misstep. "And if it comes to that, you don't know that Janet won't do the same thing that I would have done. I rather fancy she has a few tricks up her sleeve."

"I suppose so," he said. "But that's the problem—I don't know. I know that I care about her, but I also know she isn't honest with me."

"You haven't been terribly honest with her, either, have you?"

The master made a muffled noise of irritation into his arms. "All right, you don't have to be *that* honest."

"Can't help it, sorry," said Susan insincerely. "It's not a party favour for you in particular."

"I gathered that," he said, and this time he sounded nearly as dry as Susan herself. "Are you—are you going to stay here all night?"

"No, you evidently need a little more time to brood," Susan said cheerfully. "And there are a few parts of the manor I'd like to have a look at."

"Don't—don't spend too long in the ballroom," the master said. "It's not safe. I mean, none of it's safe, but that's where things have been a bit more active lately."

"I noticed," said Susan, without making any promises. She rose, and the hound lifted its head. "I'll keep an eye out."

"Aren't you going to take the hound with you?"

Susan paused, and to her surprise, the hound left the couch and came with her. "Looks like it," she said, and left him alone in the room.

She had enough to be thinking of without adding the ballroom to her list of things to do tonight, so Susan merely wandered from one end of the hall to the other, and then went downstairs to briefly visit Brennan. According to her pact with Emmett, she ought to have been actively trying to establish that he was still well and alive, and allow him to do the same with her, but Susan hadn't seen hide nor hair of him since emerging from the butler's pantry with him, and she felt as though she couldn't face him alone and in the dark. Not tonight. The thought left her worried and nervous and anticipatory all at once, and since Susan hadn't yet been able to work out any way of ascertaining which of those feelings—if any—were legitimately her own, she thought she would like to put off that meeting until she could at least regain some semblance of control over her feelings.

So instead, she exchanged a few words with Brennan to help keep his spirits up, then sank back into the shadows of his hall stand shape when a figure in velvet green shadows slipped down the right side of the grand staircase and passed silently across the chequered floor to vanish through the double doors and into the yawning dark of the lower main hallway.

That was Helfer, Susan was rather sure. She hadn't seen either of the younger servants upstairs before, let alone at this time of day. This particular circumstance caused her to say quietly, "Off I go, Brenners! Keep a look out for odd things, won't you?"

She ignored his mutter of "It's all odd, every part!" and stole across the room to follow Helfer with the hound at her heels. Unhappily for her, he had disappeared by the time she pushed through the doors, and Susan was left alone and perplexed under the gaze of far too many portraits with eyes that seemed to move in the darkness of the hall.

He couldn't have gotten to the end of the hall in the time she had taken to cross the room; nor could he have entered any of the rooms without Susan seeing or hearing the doors close. The hound was no use, either: she sniffed to the walls, turned in a circle, and then sat down and whined by the left side of the hallway.

Susan turned in a similar circle, her eyes falling over every surface that she could make out in the darkness, and then passed down the hall herself, looking briefly at and behind each stand that lined the walls. She had only gotten halfway down the corridor before she heard a sticky sort of movement high in the darkness of the rafters, and a frowning look upward toward where the roof met the walls showed her that the walls were dripping with something thick and dark red from the red, green, and blue shadows of the rafters.

Blood, Susan realised, with a very sudden, heavy heartbeat in her throat. Thick and heavy and far too abundant, it seeped down and through portraits and plopped heavily on the carpet in giant drops that pooled together and didn't sink into the carpet quickly enough.

The hound whined and pressed closer to her, and Susan said disapprovingly, "Nasty! Stop that!"

She turned her eyes away from the dripping blood as much from a sense that it would cease to happen if she didn't pay attention to it as from a desire to avoid the sight. This particular curse seemed to be inclined to performative displays, and although she would have preferred not to be able to hear as well as see this particular display, she hadn't long begun walking again before the drip-drip of blood ceased and the squishing in the rafters faded into silence.

Susan had to force herself to walk at her usual pace despite that: the silence was very nearly as nerve-wracking as the sound of blood dribbling down the walls had been. It yawned threateningly at the cross-section of hallway that led left and right, cold breeze tearing through and taking her breath away, and remained as she took the servant's staircase at the end of the hallway, the hound a shadow to her steps.

It wasn't until she was on the top floor of the manor that Susan felt as though the air regained some of its former normalcy and the hound stopped pressing quite so close to her as she walked. Out of that relief—or instinct—Susan paused at the turning to the suite she shared with Janet, and took a quick peek from the window on the left-hand side, her eyes gliding from window to window of the lower level, as far as her vision would hold through the fog. It wasn't until her gaze passed the third lower window that she saw, with a shock, the twin shadows of the gardeners—motionless, together, and staring through the glass of one of the bigger windows that gave into the sitting room.

They would certainly have been able to see her sitting on the marbled floor to—as it must have seemed—talk to herself. She hoped, with a cold heart, that the gardeners were not aware of anything so ridiculous as talking furniture; otherwise, they undoubtedly knew exactly what she was doing.

The idea of those twin sets of eyes on her as she talked with Brennan left her feeling uncomfortably crawly, and Susan returned to the suite with the unpleasant feeling that although she had found out rather a lot tonight, she had also given away rather a lot.

The morning came slowly, and in fits and starts. Susan dreamt, and woke, and shifted uncomfortably, then slept again. She felt lips pressed against hers and woke to see Emmett's face above her, but when she reached for him to see if he was real, he faded away at once, and Susan thought there was a mocking light to his eyes that she had never seen from the real Emmett. That did away with the tickle of excitement that had sprung up in her stomach, and she sat up, rubbing her mouth with the back of her hand, to find that Janet was already awake and watching her.

"You were out last night," said the other woman, vaguely reproachful.

"Yes," Susan said, deciding that complete honesty was likely to be as effective with Janet as it was with the master. "I thought that it was about time that I went to meet the master. I also thought it would be a good idea to meet him in the room he's a bit sensitive about."

Janet's hands clasped together in her lap, and Susan didn't miss the very slight biting of the lower lip that happened in an instant. So Janet didn't like Susan going to see the master at odd hours of the night? Understandable—and frustrating at the same time. If it frustrated her, why did she still cling to Emmett? Was the curse that strong?

"You really went to see him?"

"I thought it was a good idea at the time," she said. "He talked about you most of the time, if you wanted to know."

Was Susan mistaken, or did those little hands twist together more tightly in the bedclothes? "About me? Why?"

"I got the impression that he'd quarrelled with you and regretted it," Susan said. "I also got the impression that he's worried about you."

Janet coloured a little, but only asked, "What was the room like?"

"I'm not sure exactly what you would be looking for, but there wasn't anything special about the room that I could tell. There were plants, books, and a few couches."

Janet frowned. "Plants? And books? What kind?"

"If you mean the plants, they were little ferny things with purple flowers, and grassy looking things without. If you're talking about books, they looked as though they were for study: big, fat spines with titles a mile long and colons galore."

"Oh." Janet seemed to sink into thought, and Susan had the impression that she was refiguring a few things in her mind. "Well, that's not exactly what I would have expected when he warned me away from it."

"People often warn away from things that are more important to them than to anyone else," Susan said. "Or things that are more important to be hidden than they are important once they're out in plain sight."

"Yes, I suppose so." Janet didn't sound entirely convinced. Susan didn't blame her: it was just as likely, given the situation, that the master had given the orders based on prompting from the curse. "I'd like to look in it, regardless."

"If you knock and wait for an invitation, I imagine it will work much better than just barging in," Susan suggested. "Some people like being asked permission before having things taken from them."

Janet reddened a little. "I suppose that's fair. Do you think he'd let me in if I did?"

"About as sure as I am that he'll be in the breakfast parlour soon," Susan said. "The master seems to be the kind of person who likes to be able to trust someone before he opens up to them."

"I have to be able to trust him, too," Janet said, with some dignity. "I'm the one who will end up dead if things go wrong."

"Yes, that's the tricky part," said Susan. "Both of you don't trust each other but want the other to trust you first. Someone is going to have to go first."

"I hate this place," said Janet, with quiet vehemence. "Every time I try to think something through, it gets tangled with all the threads of everything else. I don't even trust myself here."

"I fancy you need a bit of sunshine," said Susan. "I'm sure the master would take you out for a walk after breakfast. Maybe the two of you can figure out who to trust over a stroll in the sunlight."

"We didn't—we didn't part well yesterday."

"Without knowing anything about it other than that you've both been miserable all night, I'm sure it's nothing that can't be solved by an apology—or two."

"It's like there are two people inside him," Janet said, as if to herself. "The one that knows how to apologise, and the one that only knows how to do things to apologise for."

"That's not a terribly good sign," admitted Susan. However, she was quite well acquainted by now with how sneaky the curse was, and she wondered how much of the master's duality was caused by the curse fighting against the man within—or perhaps the man within fighting the curse. "But there is a curse clogging up the manor, and—"

Someone screamed in the hallway.

"Here we go!" said Susan gleefully, as Janet scrambled out of bed with the hound at her side and threw on a cotton wrapper.

The two women left the room together at a run, and as they approached the meeting of the hallways, they saw two other figures dash past toward the front of the manor.

"Best be quick!" Susan said quietly. "They'll try to clean up anything before we can see it."

"I don't know if I want to see it!" said Janet, but she lengthened her stride despite that.

They rounded the corner of the hallway at a run, with Mrs. Carmichael and Mr. Oswald barely half the length of the hallway ahead; and Susan glimpsed something prone and unmoving on the floor in front of the ballroom doors, with Regan some way closer to the front of the manor and pressed against the further wall.

A body! she realised at once, bright with speculation. The question was, *whose* body?

She and Janet were quick enough along the hall to catch up with the two senior servants very shortly after they stopped at the body—quick enough to considerably startle the three servants when they realised they weren't alone. When they did realise as much, Mr. Oswald looked worried, and Regan tearful. Mrs. Carmichael alone seemed annoyed to see them.

"There's nothing you can do here, miss—that is, mistress," she said to Janet, while Susan surveyed the body. "You might as well return to your suite until breakfast is ready. It's just the master's old man."

Susan stared at Mrs. Carmichael. "*This* is the master's man?"

"*Was* the master's man," said the other woman grimly. "Of course he *would* turn up today, when he can only cause mischief! He's been nothing but trouble from the start."

It was useless to say, "I thought he was dead", because Mrs. Carmichael and Mr. Oswald had said, quite plainly, that he had gone missing, and it would have looked rather odd to have said that Susan and Janet were quite sure his body had already been disposed of in the garden fire by two very suspicious gardeners.

Susan met Janet's eyes, seeing in them the same bewilderment she felt, then turned her gaze back on the dead man. He was nothing like as large as Emmett, but he was tall enough to make a fine figure if that figure hadn't been sprawled on the carpet, face-first. It looked as though he'd been running as he exited the ballroom and had fallen flat at the very doorframe. Oddly enough, the doors were shut fast behind him—if he had fallen after opening them.

Who had done that? wondered Susan. Instead of either of the

questions she wanted to ask, however, she asked, "Are we sure he's dead? I don't see any blood."

"Heart attack, I'll be bound," said Mrs. Carmichael, with one hand pressed to her ample bosom. "That's what it usually is when we find them in the halls."

Susan knelt and felt for the man's pulse despite that; and, having ascertained that he was indeed without a pulse and breath alike, allowed Mr. Oswald's flutterings and Mrs. Carmichael's far stronger representations that they would *deal with it themselves like they always had done* to hasten her departure with Janet. It was a shame to leave Regan shaking like that—would they force the girl to help them carry the body to wherever they were planning on carrying it? —but Janet was enough to worry about right now.

Janet, much to Susan's interest and grudging approval, had something of a light of interrogation to her eyes as they turned back down the hall toward the suite.

She wasn't surprised when the bride said softly, "I have *so many* questions."

"I have only one question," Susan returned, as quietly.

"Where was he all this time?"

"No," said Susan. That was a question for another day—along with the question of whether it had been the valet battering at the ballroom doors at ridiculous hours of the morning when she first passed that room in the dark. "If that's the master's old man, I want to know whose body it was that the gardeners were burning when we first got here."

"Oh," Janet said, and her pointed little jaw firmed. "Do you think it's the curse playing with us?"

"Probably," Susan said. "Or there have been more bodies lately than Mrs. Carmichael and Mr. Oswald were admitting to. Did you notice his boots?"

Janet's brows twitched together, and Susan was sure that her lips pressed together for a brief moment as well—was that irritation or rue? "No," she said. "I suppose they were black with green piping."

"Exactly so," said Susan.

NINE

Susan didn't realise that she was so very on edge about seeing Emmett for the first time since their escape from the butler's pantry until she entered the kitchen later that morning and found only Regan. Mingled disappointment and relief stirred in her chest and made her too restless to do more than make a quick breakfast of the last of the porridge that was rapidly congealing on the table. It was ridiculous to be so discomposed at the thought of seeing Emmett when she had just felt for the pulse of a dead man in the hallway above-stairs a bare hour or two earlier.

She asked Regan, who was still looking faintly tearstained, "Are you all right?"

Regan shrugged—a miserable, half-hearted thing. "I hate finding the ones that have got lost. They're always so starey and limp and bloodless!"

Susan had a sudden, inescapable memory of blood seeping down the walls and into the carpet, and had to clear her throat before she could ask properly, "Have there been a lot of those?"

"More than enough," Regan said, and added with a sudden burst of energetic asperity, "And they're always left there for *me* to find! No one else is expected to find bodies before breakfast!"

"I suppose Mrs. Carmichael and Mr. Oswald just clean them up," Susan said bracingly.

"That'll be the gardeners," Regan said bitterly. "Can you see Mrs. C picking up a dead man? No fear!"

If it came to that, Susan couldn't really picture Mr. Oswald picking up a dead body with his delicate hands and shuddering looks. So the gardeners would make it into the house after all? Susan felt that she wasn't quite sure she appreciated that. It was one thing to know that the gardeners hadn't been burning the body she'd thought they'd been burning. It was quite another to trust that they hadn't been burning a body at all—especially when they'd spent a significant amount of time over the last few days and nights peering through the windows of the manor without moving.

"Isn't there anyone else who can do it? Someone from the town, for example."

It wasn't that she thought there might be—it was more that Susan wanted to know how much connection the manor had with the town below, apart from pillaging it periodically for women of a marriageable age or servants willing to bet their lives for a very decent amount of money.

To her surprise, Regan said, echoing what the master had said last night, "They can't get in once everything starts. No one can. No one comes in, and no one goes out. We have to make up for any lack by changing positions."

"How very practical!" said Susan, hoping for more.

Unfortunately, Regan seemed to have remembered that she wasn't supposed to talk about any of the things she had just talked about, and her eyes dropped. "Never mind that," she said. "I shouldn't be talking about things like this. You'll find out soon enough on your own without me telling you things, and I don't want to end up like the master's valet."

"No," agreed Susan. "We wouldn't want anything like that to happen."

But she couldn't help thinking about the fact that Regan, by withholding information that was obviously dangerous to speak, but equally dangerous to live in the manor without, was

condemning Susan to the very danger she refused to encounter by
speaking of it.

It was, she considered, as she paced down the hallway and past
the breakfast room, whence she could hear the murmur of voices, an
unhealthy sort of way to live: the options were to either speak up
and help someone while putting your own life at risk, or to keep
quiet and just wait for the inevitable drop over the balcony when
that person did something a little too risky or outside the Perfect
Result.

She said as much to Brennan, after scanning the room for
servants and the windows alike for gardeners, and found him as
lackadaisical about it as she had expected.

"Can't talk to anyone m'self, old girl," he said. "Not much use
wondering if I'd do something I can't do."

"Yes, but you could," pointed out Susan. "You'd run the risk of
the person thinking they were mad—although I'm inclined to think
they're used to that sort of thing in this place—or of someone
having you carted off to the furnace outside because they thought
you were possessed, but you could do it."

"Don't want to be carted off to the furnace, old thing."

"Exactly," said Susan. "And that's the problem: no one wants to
be carted off to the furnace, so they keep quiet—or even do a little
silencing of their own, I suspect."

"Cut-throat place, this," Brennan said gloomily.

"Yes," said Susan. "And I'd give a great deal to know how much
of that the curse is responsible for. It certainly alters people's percep-
tions and their natural desires, but I don't know how far that goes."

She was thinking particularly of Mr. Oswald—delicate Mr.
Oswald, who washed women's clothes secretively and was offended
at people speculating that he might have kissed women in the
butler's pantry—and it occurred to her that as little as she knew
what happened to Helfer and Regan of a night, did she know where
Mr. Oswald and Mrs. Carmichael slept.

That was certainly something to be thinking about. She was still
leaning against Brennan's conveniently sturdy frame and thinking
about it, in fact, when Emmett's voice said in her ear, "There you

are!" and for the first time in her life with the horselords, Susan startled utterly and comprehensively, without any artifice.

"Good heavens, lummox!" she said, gasping. "You might give me some warning before you do that!"

There was amusement in his eyes, Susan was well aware; she couldn't tell if it was from the fact that he had at last made her jump, or if he knew how fast her heart beat as he stood so close to her.

Susan turned a little so that she was facing him directly, with the hall stand at her back. Anyone observing them from this position could have assumed Emmett to be closing in for a kiss; Susan welcoming it. She wasn't quite sure, for a moment of madness—or perhaps the curse meddling with her mind—that it wasn't so.

Emmett, considering her, asked unexpectedly, "Are you avoiding me?"

"Good heavens, why would I be?" Susan asked, happy to have a question she could answer so unexceptionally.

When Emmett stared at one with that considering, faintly puzzled look, one could usually depend upon him asking uncomfortable, unfortunate, or downright inconvenient questions. Since Susan liked to be strictly truthful—especially with her friends—this habit of his had sometimes led to some inconvenience—especially since Emmett was terrifyingly good at following tricky things to their end instead of being decently befuddled like others.

This time, however, he seemed disinclined to follow any line of questioning. He merely rubbed the back of his neck as though he didn't quite know how to proceed and said, "I don't know. I didn't see you last night or at breakfast this morning."

"Last night, I was with the master," Susan said. "And this morning, I was looking at a body in the hall."

"Kill the fellow, did you?" asked Brennan, blithely unaware of Emmett's deeper frown.

"Of course not!" Susan said indignantly. "So there's no need to glare at me, lummox!"

"I didn't think you had," Emmett said, his colour just slightly heightened; and for the first time since he had startled her, he moved back a little.

Oh dear! thought Susan, caught between dismay and the intoxicating thought that she had been right last night when she spoke with the master, and that if she wanted to—and she really did want to at that moment—she could cheat just as effectively as the curse was cheating by tickling up Janet's feelings to interest her in Emmett. Emmett was certainly as unhappy as Janet had been about Susan meeting with the master.

Playing on that wouldn't do any good to either herself or Emmett in the long run, but it was tempting for the heart-beating now, when Susan would very much have liked to make sure that Emmett didn't look in Janet's direction again.

She said, "It was the master's previous valet, which I think makes a problem."

"Who did you see the gardeners burning," said Emmett, grasping the problem at once. "Or were they actually not burning a body at all?"

"Yes," said Susan. "I would have sworn to what I saw, but that was before I knew we were dealing with a story curse, amongst other things. Do you think you'll be going outside with the master today?"

"I can't go poking around in the ashes while he's with me," pointed out Emmett.

"I have to say, I find that very disappointing," Susan said. "It shows a lack of enterprise."

"I used up all of my enterprise yesterday," said Emmett, his brown eyes deliberately meeting hers with what Susan felt to be a distinct fizz. "In one shot."

She tried desperately not to cough on her own intake of breath, and hoped that her cheeks weren't as red as they felt. Oh well; as Belle said, no way forward but to attack. She said indignantly, "I told you that I wouldn't make it unpleasant for you! You can't tell me that it was unpleasant!"

"In my experience, it's always unpleasant," interposed Brennan.

Emmett, with even greater deliberation, said, "I didn't say it was unpleasant."

Susan had a startled, faint moment to grasp that he seemed to be teasing her before she rallied with, "Then what are you saying?"

It took him much longer to reply to that. His eyes dropped, and he thought for a few moments before he seemed to smile and said, "I don't know."

Later, Susan couldn't decide if the smile or the teasing had been more disturbing. She spent quite some time that day trying not to wonder about it, and quite some sleepless time that night in the same useless endeavour.

It wasn't as though she'd never kissed Emmett before, thought Susan rather wildly, as she lay sleepless and exasperated, staring at shadows that moved a bit too much on the ceiling. She had kissed him on the first day that they met. Granted, that kiss had been a very different thing: she had done it, as a girl barely twenty years old, in the absolute assurance that the years-older Emmett, who had captured her fairly in a fight, would immediately release her in horror. She hadn't looked her twenty years, and the act had been spectacularly effective. It was entirely another thing to have demanded for Emmett to kiss her in an act of subterfuge and to find that, when a willing party to the kiss, he was thoroughly consummate in the act.

Susan had been aware for quite some days now that it bothered her immensely that Janet seemed to be wavering between the man she was married to—and had obviously forged a connection with—and the man who had helped to rescue her from almost certain death. Until she knew how much of Janet's interest was the curse's doing and how much was genuinely from Janet herself, it was worse than useless to pursue any of her own bothersome feelings with regards to Emmett. For all she knew, Emmett had no more real interest in Susan than Brennan did, and by taking advantage of a situation where the curse would be likely to try to convince him that he was in love with her, just to gratify her own—perhaps momentary—feelings, she would be utterly unfair to Emmett. For her own part, it would be absolutely gut-wrenching to find out that she had fooled herself into thinking that Emmett really cared about her once the confusion of feelings was obliterated at their escape from the curse.

And perhaps, thought Susan hopefully, there would be no lingering feelings that remained at all, on either side.

No, far better to let the curse weave its toils and go along with it carefully and quietly, playing the part as far as she needed to and no further. As for the prickly, anxious, delicious little feelings that insisted on wrapping themselves around her heart—well, there was no harm in experiencing what it was like to be in love for the first time, was there? It was just a matter of making sure that those feelings didn't prompt her into doing anything to hurt Emmett.

Janet showed no sign of stirring, so Susan eventually gave in to the inevitable and got herself out of bed and out of the suite to touch base with Emmett and have a brief reconnoitre through the top half of the manor. She didn't particularly want to visit the bottom half of the manor, uninterested in seeing any more bloody walls; but when she left the suite and found the night far less advanced than she'd thought, she wavered. She could still hear vague noises from the lower level of the house, so when she heard Regan's voice from the general direction of the ballroom, it was no real surprise.

"Helfer! Come back here!"

"Do as you please, Miss Regan," said Helfer's voice softly. "I'm not taking the long way around just to please Mrs. Carmichael! I've been cleaning the ballroom for the last four hours, and it's not even my job; I'm taking the short road to bed."

"It's all of our jobs," said Regan, annoyance plain in her voice.

Susan—who had a very good idea that Helfer was about to pass down the main staircase and into the lower hall, as she had seen him do the night previous—darted forward and across the hall into the shadows on the other side, then skirted closely by the wall to duck down the servants' staircase before either of the younger servants could see her. Although she would much prefer not to encounter bloody walls again, it would have been a great shame to give up the chance to see where Helfer went when he was ostensibly going home.

She took the stairs three at a time, as silently as she could, then bounded lightly into the lower half of the manor and darted down the hallway to the plant-topped stand roughly halfway down. If she was very lucky, the place where Helfer had disappeared last night would be before he got to her hiding place. If she was not, well—there were a great many shadows in the hallway, and Susan would just have to hope that she looked enough like another of those shadows to pass notice.

She was, as it turned out, entirely correct. No Regan came up behind her to give away her hiding place, but the double doors that opened into the hallway from the front of the manor fluttered briefly and admitted Helfer, who strode up the carpet toward her, outlined in the slightly brighter room he had come from before the doors closed behind him. He walked quickly, but not quite steadily, and Susan had the impression that he walked more and more slowly as he came, until at last he stopped and turned to face the wall with his face turned up to gaze at it almost blankly.

Susan allowed herself to lean out further from cover than was strictly wise—and was repaid for that risk by the sight of the wall in front of which Helfer stood slowly collapsing from top to bottom, in an inward-turning scroll of vanishment.

The breath hissed silently between her teeth. Helfer hadn't pressed anything or activated anything, Susan was quite certain. He had simply stood there, swaying and gazing at the wall as if drunk, and the wall itself had rolled inward to allow him to enter. And Helfer did enter, myriad threads of magic tangling from within the new hallway that seemed to writhe and withdraw at the touch of neutral air that was in the original hallway.

Susan hesitated, but only for a moment. She knew, suddenly and coldly, exactly how someone had been alive and out of sight in the manor for so long; she also knew in that moment that this was an opportunity that might not be offered to her again.

She darted out from behind the plant stand and followed Helfer softly into the darkness of that hallway that ran with magic, and it felt as though the darkness closed around until there was only soft, woolly night behind her instead of an open hallway. She didn't dare to look back because she had a rather nasty idea that she would only see darkness behind, anyway. Now that she had ventured into suspended reality, there was no way out but to follow the person who had led her here.

Luckily for her, Helfer no longer seemed as if he was in full control of his body, let alone his mental processes; he walked slowly, stumblingly, and even though Susan let him draw further ahead, just in case, she was certain he wouldn't be capable of hearing her footsteps behind him.

As she walked, the hallway grew longer and wider; it never changed fast enough for her to notice it changing, but it was gradually so wide that it was hard to see the walls on either side in the indistinctness of darkness. A chill breeze swept along the hall, whispering around her ankles and her ears, and Susan thought she heard Brennan creak uneasily, although that was impossible.

She would have considered turning around and going back if she'd thought there was anything still behind her into which she could retreat. A glance over her shoulder showed only more shifting indistinctness—a swirling nothingness of empty space that was somehow as closed off as it was empty.

Ahead were shadows that still moved in Helfer's now-clumsy long-legged stride; Susan hurried onward again, then slowed down as the shadow of the footman seemed to stop and turn to face the wall to his left, once more swaying.

Susan stopped likewise. Then, frozen with horror in the darkness, saw a byplay of shadows that almost defied her imagination: Helfer in shadow, long-legged and fluid, swallowed up into the wall and dangling.

She didn't think she breathed. She didn't quite dare. Susan stole out of cover and approached the muddle of black, red, and green shadows, and saw that it was indeed Helfer suspended within the wall, his chin dropped down onto his chest and his arms and legs hanging bonelessly into the darkness.

He looked utterly white, as if there was no blood in him at all.

Susan, dazed and sick, had only a moment to take in the sight before something hit her on the head from behind, and she sank onto her knees on the carpet, and thence into a fuzzy blackness.

Light and feeling came back gradually, but for Susan, the first sense to return was smell: she scented rosemary and lemon and dust. She was staring at a section of green ceiling so far above her head that it made unpleasant shadows move amongst the rafters, and when her head turned sideways, a jagged edge of pain tore through it, dividing her sight for a moment.

Susan took a moment to settle her stomach and, in the midst of so doing came to the inescapable conclusion that she had been hit on the head and left lying on the carpet in a hallway by person or persons unknown.

Regan was the most likely of those persons, she supposed, lurching into a sitting position and clutching her aching head. If Helfer had been going to whatever ghastly version of *sleep* the curse had conjured for him, it was likely that Regan had been on her way there, too. If she had seen Susan gawking at Helfer's captured form, would she have hidden or hit Susan on the head? On the other hand, there was that lingering scent of rosemary and lemon that Susan rather thought she had smelt on Mrs. Carmichael the day she washed her hair.

Either or both of them were sufficiently motivated to do it, too —a lowering thought that also left her wondering if Janet would ever change to that extent.

Susan considered that, gazing around at the hallway as she did so. Now that she was sitting up with most of her wits recovered, it was plain to see that she was in the main lower hallway again, instead of parts unknown in the manor. The world around her had lost its moving, terrifyingly busy feeling of live magic.

Whoever had hit her must have been strong enough to carry her here: Susan could feel the tightness of dried blood on the back of her head, but there was nothing on the carpet when she conjured a small light to check. Wherever her head had fallen after being hit, it wasn't here, even allowing for an unexpected elasticity in the reality of the manor.

Susan sat where she was for a few minutes longer, wondering first if she was going to be sick and then if Emmett was likely to come along at any stage so that she could prevail upon him to carry her back up the stairs.

Since she hadn't thrown up after those few minutes and it seemed unlikely that Emmett was going to happen along the hallway, Susan staggered to her feet and wended a wavering path toward the front of the manor to see what Brennan might have seen. It was probably a good thing that no one was lingering around the grand entrance when she entered, because Susan wasn't sure she would have seen anyone in time to prevent a second blow to the head, should that outcome have been likely.

She was still unsteady enough on her feet that when she got to the hall stand that was Brennan and tucked herself out of sight between him and the front wall of the entrance, his timbers seemed to hum.

"All right, old thing?" he asked.

"Just a bit of a bash on the head," she said, leaning her aching head against the wood. "I don't suppose you saw anyone going into the hallway or coming out after the footman?"

"Not a bean," said Brennan. "Sorry."

"Not to worry," Susan said. "I didn't really think there would have been. It would have been a bit too much to ask for."

"I suppose you're the one who's been making a mess around here the last two days, then," Brennan said morosely. "The whole place is already sitting so tight that I can barely tell where my timbers end and the floorboards begin, and it just got tighter again! You might have left me space to breathe!"

"Yes," said Susan ruefully. "Tonight was a bit more than I expected. And I'm afraid I drew attention to myself by meeting with the master last night and being devastatingly honest. I was trying to get the curse to loosen from the bride and Emmett a little bit, but I have the feeling I've tangled it worse."

"What's wrong with the big man?"

"The curse seems to be making a story between him and Janet to tempt her away from the Perfect Result with the master," Susan said. It wasn't entirely guesswork, after all; her talk with the master had confirmed a lot of her suspicions, even if it had confirmed them by making things rather worse. "A sort of sub-plot romance between Emmett and Janet. I suspected it, so I tried to do something unexpected and draw away attention from that, and it looks as though the curse is trying to make two love triangles now. It probably didn't help that Emmett kissed me in the pantry a couple of days ago."

"Knew it!" Brennan said triumphantly. "You've been attacking people and stirring pots."

Susan couldn't help grinning. "All right Brenners, that's a bit much, isn't it? Are you calling my kisses an attack or pot-stirring?"

"Both, belike," he muttered.

"I'll have you know that I was the one who was being attacked," she said. "So watch it or I'll start sobbing at the unfairness of it."

"A likely story," he said, and that made Susan grin again. "When you just admitted that you'd been playing with the curse and the big man too."

Susan found that her head hurt a little less now, that and she had entirely lost the feeling that she was about to be sick every time she moved a bit too quickly. It gave her enough energy to retort, "Consider yourself lucky that I didn't kiss you. What else have you got to complain about?"

"Being a hall stand," he returned at once. "Look, Su—do you think you can stop those long-shanked tweed-twiddlers from peering in through the windows all the time? Gives me a nasty shock every time I look up and see them pressing their blank little faces to the glass, even if I'm made of wood."

"Yes, they've been a bit clingy, haven't they? Did you see them come in to get the body yesterday morning?"

"I saw them," he said gloomily. "It's nothing but bodies around here, isn't it?"

"Just not the ones I was expecting," Susan remarked. "Look, I don't suppose you see blood dripping from the walls every so often, do you?"

If a hall stand could have been said to stare in horror at anything, Brennan did so. "*Blood* dripping from the *walls*?"

"Just a bit of it," Susan said placatingly, as a vast shadow passed around the edges of the main entrance hall to meet them. "No need to worry, Brenners! You haven't got any blood to drip, just now."

"You didn't mention blood last time I saw you," said Emmett's voice, a murmur of shadows; then he was right there next to her, far too warm and big and close.

He settled himself on the floor, too: his back to the front wall and his arms laid comfortably across his bent knees.

"Nobody was dying," Susan said, rather too aware for comfort that she would have to manoeuvre around him to remove herself from her current position. She had always been aware, in some way, of how very large Emmett was as a companion-at-arms; it was another thing entirely to be aware of the extent of his height and breadth as a man. She corrected herself, "That is, I don't know if anyone was dying at the time. I was just strolling through the halls and then blood was rolling down the walls. I'd quite like to know if it was the previous valet's blood, actually."

"I've never seen a curse do that before," Emmett said.

"No, it's very interesting," said Susan. "I suspect that it was just to frighten me, but then, I wasn't quick enough to preserve any of the blood—that was very thoughtless of me."

She saw that Emmett was looking quizzically at her and explained, "At the time I thought it best to ignore the nonsense if the curse was trying to frighten me."

Emmett shrugged, the movement of it brushing against her legs via his arm. "It probably isn't the best idea to stay too long in the halls alone. I doubt we could have learned much from the blood that would have made it worthwhile."

"I was with the hound," Susan said, by way of offsetting what she would have to say next. "Still, I agree about not staying too long in the halls; it might stop people hitting me on the head, at any rate."

Emmett's eyes fixed on her. "*What* happened in the halls?"

"Never mind, lummox; it was just someone who wanted to convince me that I hadn't seen something I'd seen."

Emmett stared at her in massive silence, crossing his arms, until she gave in.

"Let's just say that I discovered exactly why the footman and the maid think they go home and where they go when they think they go home. I thought that the walls had swallowed that leggy footman, so *obviously* I followed him—"

"Obviously."

"No need to be snide, lummox; I got hit on the head for my pains, remember?"

"That's what I'm remembering," he explained, leaning forward to seize her head in huge, gentle hands.

"I doubt that there's anything but blood to be seen," she told him, but stayed as she was, uncomfortably bent forward, until he had examined the wound and set a trickle of magic tickling through her hair. "The important thing is that those two young ones don't go home: the curse or something else gets them to wander down into parts of the manor that don't exist during the day, and then—"

"And then?" prompted Emmett as she leant back against Brennan's woody side, feeling rather better.

She hesitated. "They sort of get sucked up into the wall and drop their heads down. If I didn't know better, I'd think they were giant clockwork or steam-work dolls."

"I don't know any story curses that do that, either."

"That's what I thought just before someone hit me on the head," agreed Susan. "What do you think it gets out of it? I would have expected it to drain the story of its magic and make it less effective."

"It should do," Emmett said, and he looked at her and then away again. "It's supposed to work in small things—implications and suggestions and dreams. It shouldn't be wasting power holding people prisoner physically."

"I'm quite sure it's not the master doing it, too," Susan said. "There was far more magic when I went into the walls last night than anything I've found in the normal parts of the manor—including anything from the master. It feels as though he's as caught up and scared as any of us."

"Did he tell you that?"

Emmett wasn't looking at her now, but Susan thought that he was listening very carefully.

"No," she said. "But he talks as though he's almost given up, and as if he had a bit of hope briefly from Janet. I think we'd best try to keep them together and happy if we want to get out of this alive. Apparently he has to trust her enough to give her a key that could get her out of the manor or some such thing—and she has to trust him enough to not use it."

Emmett's laugh rumbled across the shadows. "He should have picked you instead."

"That's what he said," Susan said, before she could quite stop herself. Hastily, she added, "He seemed to think I would have hit him over the head, taken the key, and carried him out with me."

There was the briefest of moments before Brennan's voice said, "Knows you very well, old thing, doesn't he?" and Emmett and Susan, chancing to meet each others' gazes, sputtered into a laugh at the same time.

Susan was still trying not to laugh when she said, "All right, we'll see what happens when we try to keep the two of them together more often. At the very least, it should be easier to keep them safe than it was trying to look after them singly—*if* the curse doesn't try to put a spanner in the works."

"I think the curse will let us do that much," Emmett said, sobering. "It's connected to them first and foremost, after all. It wants them together for the Perfect Result. The rest of us are just side-players."

"Oh well," said Susan. "At least it will be easier to connive from now on: we don't have to meet in the pantry, and we won't be suspected if Mrs. Carmichael or Mr. Oswald see us lingering in corners or putting our heads together."

She added hastily, "To talk, I mean!" because Emmett's gaze, slightly questioning, had met hers.

"Suspected of what, old thing?"

"Anything other than Proper Behaviour Befitting Staff," Susan said promptly, breaking that gaze with some relief to look over her shoulder at Brennan. "I mean, they'll think we're walking out together, which is scandalous, but it's not against the rules as such. The curse is very good at trying to thread itself through what it's already got going."

"Always thought you two already had something going," said Brennan dispassionately. "Surprised it's taken you this long."

Susan stared at him. "You thought *what*?"

"Shut up, Brennan," said Emmett.

"No need to be rude, big man. Well, it was obvious. Joined at the hip, both of you; you've even got a shared spell going, and if you don't know that horselords don't share their—don't try to bean me, old man. Can't bean a hall stand, for a start—haven't got a bean."

"There's nothing that you need to comment on," Emmett said, with one last threatening rattle of the hall stand.

He reached down to grip Susan' forearms and lift her up as she gathered herself to rise more slowly than he had done.

Brennan objected, "Yes, but if the two of you have been canoodling in cupboards—"

"I told you, Brenners," said Susan hastily, freeing herself from Emmett as soon as she was upright, "it wasn't canoodling, and it wasn't in a cupboard. It was in the butler's pantry, and it was entirely subterfuge."

"Odd sort of subterfuge, if you ask me," muttered Brennan.

"Nobody asked you," Emmett said, with finality.

Susan felt his eyes on her and forced herself to look up at him, but by then he was glancing away again. "Never mind, Brenners," she said, with rather too much heartiness. "We'll probably only confuse you until we get out of the manor. We can't do much about it until then, so just hold tight, all right?"

Brennan seemed to mutter something along the lines that *he* wasn't the one who was confused, but Emmett only asked, "No sign of the others?"

"Don't know, old man—haven't seen them walk through my

room, and the vibrations of the place say there should be a couple hundred people in the manor."

"No sign of them from my searching," Susan agreed. "Brenners, what do you mean, "the vibrations of the place"?"

Brennan said simply, "That's all I've got, now that I'm wooden: vibrations and footfalls and voices for a couple hundred people who never come out to play. They're all in the walls."

"Delightful," said Susan dryly. "Maybe it was one of those people who hit me on the head."

"I doubt it," Emmett said. When Susan looked at him enquiringly, he added, "I don't think they're capable of more than malevolence and trickery of the mind."

"Ghosts?"

Emmett shrugged. "Ghosts, or dreams."

Susan couldn't help thinking of lips pressed against her own, and of waking to a ghostly Emmett above her. She took in a thoughtful breath and asked Emmett, "How are the dreams, by the by?"

"Still there," he said shortly. His gaze dropped to hers, and there was something of a tentativeness there when he asked, "You haven't had dreams?"

And Susan, who couldn't think of any way to explain the dream she had had that morning that wouldn't cause more trouble than it was worth, could only look away, shrug, and ask, "Should I have?"

"No, I suppose not," said Emmett; but he was thoughtful, and that worried Susan.

It was one thing for her to be understanding things and making connections—it was quite another for Emmett to be doing the same thing when it came to inconvenient truths that were a little too close to home.

That didn't stop her from grinning at him and saying a somewhat malicious, "Sweet dreams!" up at him when he had walked her to the division of the halls and they were about to part. Perhaps she said it to test her fledgling theory; perhaps she said it to provoke the exact reaction it brought out: Emmett, speculation and uncertainty in his eyes, stepping toward her with the vaguest motion forward of one hand.

Susan wasn't sure, but she was certainly a little bit breathless when she turned and took her own path to bed, pretending not to see that step forward.

"Goodnight, lummox," she called softly over her shoulder. "Don't do any more wandering, will you?"

"Not while I know you're abed," he said, and Susan fancied that the ghost of a laugh followed her to the suite while her cheeks heated in the darkness.

TEN

Susan woke into an early half-light the next day, with fog at the windows that was golden around the edges as if there really were suns behind it and a weight beside her in the bed. It was so familiar a weight that it took her a moment to realise that, familiar or not, it wasn't supposed to be in *this* bed with her. When she did realise as much, Susan turned her head and found another resting on the same pillow with her.

She had never seen Emmett from just such an angle before, face-to-face and lying beside her. Confusingly, she could feel the faint tickle of his breath against her face, and as Susan was trying to recover from that particular life-like circumstance, Emmett's eyes opened.

She would have asked, "Lost your way in the dark?" but she was wary of giving the situation a more dangerous legitimacy than it had already established. It was also at that point that Emmett smiled at her, warm and close, and nudged his head closer.

"Absolutely not," Susan said firmly, turning her head away again.

He rolled over her easily, resting his weight on his forearms to either side of her, and bent his head until his nose touched hers, then pulled away playfully. Susan had exchanged many a playful

look with Emmett, but never in such a context and never in such a
way that set her heart beating in her throat. She felt bare toes brush
coolly against her calves and could only think *oh dear* as Emmett's
gaze drifted down to her lips. Reverting to *no way forward but to
attack* in her loss for what to do, Susan had a sudden, brilliant
epiphany.

She reached up and grabbed Emmett by his ears—and, pulling
him down toward her, said, "You're going to have to come down
here."

Susan saw the brief flash of confusion and then anger before the
ghost dissipated above her; then she took in a deep breath to begin
slowing her uncomfortably fast heartbeat.

"Yes, I didn't think you'd like that," she said to the empty space
above her, then rolled up into a sitting position to find that Janet
was staring at her from across the room. "Just a dream," she
explained. "They seem to get confused when you're proactive with
them; I fancy they like to be the ones doing the leading."

Janet seemed to think about that. Then she said, quite seriously,
"Thank you. That's very useful to know."

"Yes, I thought it might be," Susan said. "I wouldn't like to
forget that they can lead right over the banisters or through the fireplace, after all."

She felt light and happy for the first time in some days—probably because she thought she had really begun to grasp what was
going on and how to work with it. Feeling around in the dark to
winkle out secrets and conspiracies was its own kind of enjoyment,
but when lives were on the line, she preferred to unravel things more
quickly.

"What did you find out last night?" asked Janet. She was already
dressed and, from the look of her damp face, washed. "I saw that
you'd gone out, but the hound didn't want me to leave."

"I found out that the day servants don't go home at night,
and that someone doesn't want me to know as much. I also
learned that it's probably better for you to spend as much time
with the master as possible," Susan said. She swept a look up and
down Janet and made a pleasing discovery. "You've made up with

him, I see. You must have been out and about early this morning."

Janet went faintly pinker. "I'm not stupid," she said. "And I don't fall in love easily. So—"

"All right, so you're on a campaign," Susan said, delighted to be getting closer to a real acknowledgement of something she had begun to suspect some days ago. "I didn't actually think you were stupid; that's why it was such a surprise to see you falling for the master. And for—never mind that. What's your campaign?"

"You already know I'm trying to save my town," Janet said. "From the curse—from the master. And that's the thing: I don't seem to be able to stop liking him despite what I'm trying to do, and I don't think all of it is the curse working on me."

Susan wasn't so sure of that, but she also had enough confusion in her own feelings to be sympathetic to the position in which Janet found herself. "What is it that makes it hard to stop liking him?"

Janet looked away through the window, her eyes distant, and thought for some time. At length, she said, "I can see him fighting." She looked down at her fingers and added with some difficulty, "I see him fighting as hard as I fought to get here when I was still in town. And that's what makes things so hard."

"I'm not sure why that would make things difficult," said Susan. "You might even find that you're both on the same side."

"Because I can't be in love with him," she flashed. "I *can't*. We can't be on the same side after everything he's done."

She darted out the door with the hound behind her before Susan could protest.

When she did catch up with Janet, she said, "It's a little late to be saying that now, isn't it?"

Janet's jaw firmed. "It can't be too late," she said. "It's one thing to have feelings; it's another to let them take over and dictate what I do. You don't know how many women have come up here to die."

"All right," Susan said. "But don't be afraid to go along with the curse where you can—if we're right, it's a story curse, and things are more difficult when you go directly opposite to what it wants you to do."

"I thought it would be something like that," she said. "If that's the case, I suppose we're due for another complication very soon."

Susan thought of the master and his key, and said, "Yes, probably. In the meantime, I don't think it would hurt to be as friendly as we can to the master."

She didn't miss the look that Janet sent her from beneath lowered eyelashes. "Me, or you?"

"You, of course!" she said promptly. "You're the one the master was playing the violin to just a few nights after we were here: you've got a connection, and it would be a shame to waste that."

"Is that what it is?" Janet asked quietly, looking down at her hands. "A connection?"

"As close as you can get in this place, I shouldn't wonder," Susan said. "I'm not saying to pretend anything, mind—he's obviously already smitten with you, and there's no harm in going along with your feelings if it'll keep the curse happy for a while."

Janet's voice sounded hollow as she repeated, "No harm."

Janet, it would seem, had her own concerns when it came to pursuing romantic notions while under the influence of a story curse. Susan would have liked to have known whether those scruples were for her own or for the master's sake, but since she wouldn't have been prepared to answer the same question, she didn't ask it of Janet, either.

"That reminds me," she added. "Let me know if he gives you anything, all right?"

Janet's eyes met hers, almost convulsively. "Do you think that's the next complication?"

"I shouldn't wonder," Susan said, and paused by the grand staircase to allow Janet to proceed ahead of her as any good maid should do.

That brought about a silence that lasted until Susan opened the door to the breakfast room and left Janet there. She was grateful for the silence, because she had her own thoughts to think—and her own worries to concern her.

She could clearly see the romance line that had begun with Janet's entrance to the manor, but the sticky threads that had begun to wind around Emmett and Janet—and then Susan and Emmett—had been of a later creation, Susan was sure.

Perhaps the curse had been programmed with the possibility—or even the necessity—of a love triangle for its main storyline to proceed to the Perfect Result that everyone was so concerned about preserving. There could be no Perfect Result in the love storyline it had made for its main characters unless there was some form of testing and temptation to prove that it was real.

Good heavens! thought Susan, dismay creeping across her shoulders like an unpleasant spider's web. Of course it was the curse directing it all, from the start. And last night, when she had suspected that Emmett was having exactly the same sort of ghostly dreams as she was, she had teased him about it. Teased him about it and enjoyed it at his expense, when all of the feelings he had been experiencing were from the curse and the curse alone.

She would have to be far more careful in the future. While Emmett seemed to have had to be worked on by the curse to winkle out those feelings from the beginning, Susan had had them in advance of whatever dreams she would afterward get—and the curse had known as much. It hadn't had to work on her for as long because at least a part of the feelings she had were already present when she entered the manor.

That was unfortunate.

She had told the master that she would have liked to have had the time and freedom to examine her feelings; the dangerous truth was that she didn't have such time or leisure. And if she gratified her own budding feelings at the expense of Emmett, who could be said to be under duress, she would be the very worst—both of friends and potential lovers.

The problem was, with the newness of her realisations and what must also be the working of the curse, that it was very difficult to think of anything but Emmett—and even more difficult to prevent herself from repeating the same kind of conscious, delightful teasing that she had engaged in last night, when the only consideration seemed to have been that she was sure, in some indefinable sense, that Emmett was only waiting for her to speak.

That being the case, it seemed dangerous to go in search of Emmett—or to go wherever there was the possibility of running into him—and Susan eschewed the breakfast table to pick a couple of plums before she went in search of Helfer. She fancied that it might be useful to talk to the footman. And if not useful, at least she could have the fun of making a nuisance of herself without causing the same sort of damage that she might cause if she went to have her fun with Emmett. It might also help to get her thoughts back into line with the very real problem they were trying to solve, instead of caught in the web of that problem.

Susan found Helfer polishing silver in the courtyard on the sunny side of the manor, his legs propped against the angled trestle that held up the table and a polishing cloth on his knee while his hands moved rapidly across a fork with another cloth.

He squinted against the sun to see who it was and gave her a suspicious look as she sat down. That suspicion faded somewhat when Susan picked up another cloth, propped one of her own legs against the trestle of the table, and began to polish in a practised manner.

They polished together in a somewhat companionable silence for some minutes until one of the gardeners passed by them from around the sunny side of the manor, looked surprised to find them both there, and hurried away.

Susan mused, as if to herself, "Gardener One or Two, I wonder?"

Helfer grinned. "Blessed if *I* can tell! All the gardeners look alike from inside."

"I wonder if they think the same of us?" Susan mused, picking up another spoon. She explained, "They keep peering through the windows, so I suppose they must be looking at something."

"They're a bit nosy," agreed Helfer. "I caught one of them in the courtyard on the other side just yesterday. I thought they were going through Mr. Oswald's laundry, but they must have been staring through the windows then, too."

"Have you had problems with the gardeners before?" asked

Susan. "I've never seen gardeners do as little gardening and as much window-gazing as this pair in my life."

Helfer's lips quirked. "Not previously, no. You seem to have stirred up the house a bit."

"The idea!" Susan said promptly. "To blame it on me!"

"You're the only one who's been going around kissing valets in the butler's pantry and wandering the halls at night," he pointed out. "The gardeners are probably just waiting to see what happens to you—or anyone unfortunate enough to get caught up with you."

"That's a fair consideration," said Susan, allowing the implication that Helfer knew of her late-night rambles to pass without pulling him up on it. "Though in that case, I'm surprised they don't come inside to get a better look instead of hovering around the windows all the time. None of the windows are locked during the day."

"They aren't allowed *in*," Helfer said. "They're the gardeners. Strictly outdoors servants unless in an emergency."

"What counts as an emergency?" asked Susan, amused in spite of herself. What a nonsense this manor was!

"Too many people dying after the story starts, I suppose," said Helfer, as though he hadn't thought about it; then he froze. "Forget I said that!"

"Only if you explain yourself!" she said promptly.

The teasing note to her voice should have made him respond in some way; instead, he only said hurriedly, "I can't do that; I've said enough already to get myself in trouble."

"All right," said Susan affably. "Don't panic. I wouldn't dream of blabbing about the things people say in the sunshine."

She grabbed another spoon as she spoke, polishing it in long, slow strokes with no attention to anything else until Helfer seemed to have calmed down. As much as she told herself that she had come out here to have fun, it wouldn't be very useful if she frightened him out of any sort of talking.

So instead of pushing her previous line of questioning, Susan asked, "How long have you been working here? You seem to have a pretty good grasp on what happens around the manor."

"I mind my own business, that's all," he said swiftly; then he seemed to relent. "I haven't been here more than a year. I started a bit lower in the food chain, but the footman who was here before me died a few months after I arrived."

"How did he die?"

Helfer shot a look at her across his knee. "He wandered around in the halls a bit too often at night."

Susan grinned at him. "Really? I've still got some fuzzy memories from one night in the hallway, myself. I'll remember that."

Whoever had hit her on the head, Helfer had certainly been told about it.

He seemed to study her for a while as he polished a knife, then nodded as if satisfied. "It's no good being too curious, around here," he said. "You take the good things as they come and make sure you're not sticking your nose out too much. And when you need to, you do a bit of dirty work."

"Not much dirty work to be seen in the hallways, I should think," Susan said.

"There was another body the other day."

"True," said Susan, rather more soberly. She wasn't one to shriek and shudder over dead bodies, but she found herself uncomfortable with how very cavalierly they were treated at the manor. She supposed that if there were enough bodies, one would soon get used to them—that was fair enough. Perhaps it was the way that two people at the manor now had equated bodies with dirty work that grated at her. She added, "I got the impression that he disappeared into the walls and just now appeared again."

"That happens sometimes," Helfer said. He didn't bother reinforcing his words with another look, but he did say, "That's why it's better not to wander the halls at night. It's not so bad during the day, but at night..."

"...the ghosts come out to play?" suggested Susan.

He shrugged. "That's close enough, I suppose. Seen some in the halls at night, have you?"

"Early in the morning," Susan said, neglecting to mention that the ghost—or ghosts—she had seen were in her bed and not in the halls. "They prefer wandering around at night, then?"

"Don't ghosts all?" Helfer asked; then he added, lowering his voice, "They say that's how the first master perished."

He didn't seem frightened now—merely ghoulish—which gave Susan a very good idea of exactly how useful this particular story would probably be to her. Still, she had already given him a few nasty moments, so it was only fair to let him harrow her with whatever story he wanted to tell.

"The first master?" she enquired good-naturedly.

"The one who built this old pile," explained Helfer, gesturing with a butter knife at the manor around them. "Won it in a game of chance and then knocked down the ancestral pile that was already there against the old owner's wishes. He married a girl half his age— they said it was a love match, and maybe it was on his side, but what girl marries a man twice her age without the amount of money the old man had?"

Susan, who knew several women who had done just such a thing, kept her opinions to herself and merely asked, "What was the fly in the ointment?"

Helfer shrugged one shoulder. "Some say it was because he was a stickler and she was flighty. Some say it was because he was faithful and she wasn't—whatever the story was, she was thrown out with their son, and he disappeared into the walls, cursing."

Well now, thought Susan, her mind matching and discarding possibilities in a flutter of thoughts, this was more interesting and potentially more useful than she had expected. Did Helfer not know how pertinent his information was, or did the curse simply not care about the information being given?

"They say he's the one who cursed the first master of the house —his son," added Helfer. "Though I don't know how he could have done it after he disappeared."

"Sounds like he didn't think the child was his," Susan said.

"That's exactly it," agreed Helfer. "It was proved otherwise by magic when the kid inherited, but his father was long gone by then. The mother refused to come back and live at the manor, but the heir took it up regardless—him and his new wife. The day she died was the day the castle on the hill started sending out magic and connections into the town."

"The furniture?"

He stared at her. "You know about that too? Yes—anything down there that originally came out of the manor or the one before it turned into a sort of conduit. It's how we get more servants when we need them."

"How long ago did the first bride die?"

"Oh, well before I was born!" Helfer said carelessly. "Girls have been coming up here every year since."

"I'm surprised no one moved away from the town," Susan remarked. "If there were so many girls being killed."

"Some did," said Helfer. "But we give a lot to the town, you know: the ones who stay get rich. You have to give up a daughter every ten years or so, but your whole family can live well if you do."

Susan wondered if she felt sicker at the idea of that or at the entirely matter-of-fact way in which Helfer said it.

"You make a goodly enough amount from working here," he added. "And if you're clever, you can get away and live well afterward, too."

"Yes, I see that," said Susan, with her thoughts on the rich amount of money she had been promised for working at the manor. She hadn't yet seen a penny of that money, and she wondered if Helfer had—but she suspected that the question would send him into a confused, worried tailspin if she asked it, so instead she asked, "Couldn't the master just...not marry another woman? After the first few died just like his first wife, I mean?"

Helfer's eyes failed to meet hers for the first time in a little while. "Best not to talk about the master," he told her. "That's where it gets dangerous to be too curious or know too much. Just keep your nose clean, that's all you need to do. Follow the rules and the manor will look after you. It'll look after him, too, if he can manage the thing."

"Yes, so I hear," Susan murmured. As far as she could see, following the rules didn't look after the women who came here as brides; the rules only protected the surrounding people in town and manor who kept those rules. The women who were sent as tribute brides to keep up the town's prosperity were sacrificed to the rules twice: once when they were sent to the manor by those obeying the rules, and then again when they obeyed the rules themselves in the hope of surviving.

Since it wouldn't have been useful to express as much to Helfer —it seemed unlikely that he would even understand what she was saying—Susan exercised the greatest restraint she had yet exercised in the manor and held her tongue.

It was in the process of so doing that she noticed a shadow in one of the windows of the manor directly behind and above Helfer. No, not a shadow: a person. If Susan wasn't very mistaken, Mr. Oswald was looking down at them through a window somewhere in the right wing of the manor—had, perhaps, been watching them for some time.

She must have looked for just a fraction too long: Helfer turned to follow her gaze and immediately his shoulders stiffened. He turned back to the table, grabbed the few remaining forks and threw them in with the polished silver, and began rolling up the large polishing mat that he'd laid down, with all the silverware in it.

"I'll be in for it if I take any longer on this," he said. "You'd better get back to your own work, too, before Mrs. Carmichael comes along and boxes your ears."

"I'd like to see her reach," Susan said cheerfully, but it was too late.

Helfer, spooked and skittish, was already hurrying back toward the kitchen, leaving her alone in the sunshine with the spoon she'd been polishing and the distinct inclination to sit a little longer in the sunshine to collect her thoughts.

Since the shadow of Mr. Oswald vanished from the window a moment later and there was no sign of far-too-broad shoulders or spiky, close-cut hair to warn her of Emmett's imminent approach, Susan allowed herself to follow her inclinations and remained where she was to bask in the warmth and think.

What principally worried her right now was the gardeners. She already had reason to believe that not only were staff members not entirely safe from the dangers of the curse, but they were in an actively upward trajectory if another staff member died while the story curse was in course with a particular story.

Which meant that if the gardeners wanted to get into the house badly enough...

Susan shook her head. What a ridiculous thought! The curse might prompt people to do quite a lot of things, but most of the suggestions were light, insidious ones. And despite the significant sins of omission and greed that the townspeople and the manor people alike seemed willing to commit in pursuit of the prosperity of the town—or personal prosperity—she didn't yet have any reason to think that they were willing to commit sins of commission and actually murder others in the manor in order to move up the ranks. There was also no reason to suspect that the gardeners wanted to get into the house badly enough that they would kill anyone, despite their disturbing habit of peering through windows.

As a matter of fact, she might have thought Helfer was joking if he hadn't reacted so strongly after what he'd said. Hopefully, she would be able to think of some way to get him to talk about it again later—outside of the manor, where ghosts and curses attached to the master couldn't overhear.

Perhaps the thought was still nibbling away at her consciousness when Susan, sighting Emmett through the kitchen windows, hastily ducked around the sunny side of the manor to avoid him and returned to the breakfast room through the glasshouse entrance.

She said, "Don't mind me, I'm just passing through!" to Janet and the master—who were far closer to each other than would have been proper if they weren't married—and made Janet giggle. At the door, Susan added, "Don't worry, I won't come back soon," and that made the master choke with laughter, too.

Certainly the idea was in her mind when she passed swiftly down the length of the lower hallway, ducking her head into each doorway as she passed, because when she caught sight of the gardeners both standing at the window of the music room, one close enough to fog the glass with his breath and the other far enough away to look as though he was a good head shorter than the first, Susan stopped short with a feeling of satisfaction.

She wheeled and turned into the room, shutting the door behind her, and crossed the room while Gardener One, who was closest to the glass, watched her dumbly. He was still staring at her when she swung the long window inward and left only fresh air and mist between the two of them.

Susan leaned casually on the side of the window and said in a friendly sort of way to the closest tweed-surmounted face, "You might as well come in. I won't tell anyone."

Gardener One stared at her as if she had two heads, and Gardener Two slowly sank behind the hedge as if she couldn't see his booted ankles from where she was, or as if she hadn't *seen* him making his exit.

She added encouragingly, a little bit louder, "Your other half can come in, too. It's not much use him hiding behind the hedge when it doesn't go all the way to the ground, you know."

The other gardener slowly straightened from behind the hedge, once more adding torso and arms to the ankles.

"Can't come in," said Gardener One. "Why did you open the window?"

"Because you're always pressing your nose up against them. I thought you might like to get in and have it over with," she said pleasantly. "If it's your boots you're worried about, you can leave those outside, after all."

Seemingly perplexed, he said, "We're not worried about our boots."

"Well then!" said Susan, pushing the window open wide and stepping aside.

For a moment, she thought the gardener, hesitating on the outside, might actually step through.

Then, an irate voice from the door demanded, "What's the meaning of this? Miss Susan, what *are* you doing, consorting with the outside staff?"

"Exactly that," Susan said, with what she hoped was disarming honesty.

Almost in synch, the gardeners both took a step back as Mrs. Carmichael stormed across the room and flapped her apron at them. "Out! Out, you dreadful people! I won't have you trying to get into the house with your big boots and dirty fingernails!"

The gardeners beat a quick retreat, thoroughly browbeaten, and Mrs. Carmichael made a flurry of closing the windows before she turned on Susan and said severely, "I'll thank you not to encourage the outside staff to think themselves good enough to enter the house, Miss Susan!"

"They seemed interested in being inside," Susan said innocently. "I thought they must have had some business here."

Mrs. Carmichael sniffed. "Wanting to live like their betters, I should think. Once they get a taste for being inside, you can't get them back out again. They're carriers and diggers, and that's all they'll ever be."

"What if one of us dies and upsets the numbers inside?" suggested Susan.

She didn't miss the odd, secretive look that flitted briefly across Mrs. Carmichael's face. "That's another thing entirely," the woman said, and left the room.

ELEVEN

S usan threw herself into one of the couches to think and rest her tired eyes after last night's sleeplessness, and must have fallen asleep mid-thought, because she woke to the sound of a bell and the lingering remnants of the same thought.

"Bother you," she said to that thought, which was large with Emmett.

It took her a few minutes to shake her head and stretch out her limbs, and another few to make sure her mind was as empty of Emmett as the hall, before Susan crossed the carpet and sauntered toward the breakfast room once again. By her reckoning, it was close to mid-day, and while she slept, the sky had darkened on both sides of the manor, casting a faintly green shadow through the entire place.

Thunderstorm, thought Susan, with her hand on the doorknob of the breakfast room door. And a thunderstorm meant earlier dark, which probably also meant ghosts darting around the manor earlier than usual. She grimaced a little and entered the room, then stopped short two steps into the room, because instead of seeing Janet and the master together, or Janet alone, she saw Emmett and Janet standing together by the fire.

They weren't as close together as Janet had been with the master earlier, but they were still, in Susan's opinion, far too close to one another. And, she noticed with exasperation, Janet had her hand on Emmett's forearm once more, leaning forward to speak confidingly.

More annoyingly still, that hand didn't leave Emmett's arm when she looked around to see Susan standing there—it didn't move, in fact, until Emmett drew away from the fireplace.

"Shall I take you up to your room?" enquired Susan, her voice light.

"No, I'm to go for a ride with the master," Janet said. "You might as well...make yourself useful around the manor."

Her tone was as light as Susan's, but Susan caught the implication in it. She nodded and asked, "Are you taking the hound?"

"I think so. She seems to want to come; I think she likes the horses."

And she wafted out in a queenly sort of way that Susan knew she would never be able to pull off, leaving Susan alone with Emmett and unsure whether to be annoyed by that or simply relieved that Janet was no longer with him alone. She turned back to Emmett and found that he'd moved nearer to her and further away from the fireplace, which only had a small fire in it in deference to the sunshine that was presently streaming into the room through the windows.

"I wouldn't stand too close to that," she said, tipping her head toward it. "That's the one Janet nearly walked through the other day."

"I'm not asleep now," Emmett said, but he continued toward her and away from the fire. "I won't be led around by the nose when I'm awake."

For a moment, Susan was dreadfully tempted to seize Emmett by the ears as she had done to the ghostly representation of him that morning—and this time kiss him properly, if only to see how the real Emmett would respond to any such thing.

It could even be seen as an experiment of sorts—something like Emmett had done in the darkness of the left wing after following a ghost very nearly to his death. A touch to see if the skin was warm, so to speak.

But since Susan was very well aware that she would only be gratifying her own wishes by doing so, she stuffed her hands into her pockets to help resist the temptation and asked, "Do you really think so?"

It wasn't until he leaned down with mesmerising slowness to speak in her ear that Susan became aware how very near Emmett had drawn.

"It wasn't a challenge," he said softly. And then, into her suddenly buzzing ears, he added, "And don't look around at the window, but I fancy there are two gardeners out there watching us."

Susan felt as though the air stilled around her. She had suspected that there was someone in the glasshouse outside, and it only made sense for it to be the gardeners, who had evidently circled the manor to peer through some more useful windows.

It was not the information that the gardeners were once more staring at her that seemed to make the room stop moving. No, it was the fact that although Emmett's voice *said* he hadn't been making a challenge, both his tone and the bright light of his eyes said something diametrically opposed. And for the first time since they had arrived in the manor, Susan was genuinely uncertain as to whether she was experiencing reality or dream. She didn't have to think—or perhaps simply *didn't* think—she narrowed her eyes and took her hands out of her pockets.

"We'll see about that," she said, pulling Emmett's face down toward hers by his ears.

Dream Emmett had been startled and then angry at the loss of control; Real Emmett—and he could only be real, with the warmth of his ears and cheeks—was certainly startled, but he didn't resist the pull of her hands. He might even, thought Susan in the brief moment before she kissed him, have stepped forward with it.

Emmett's arms closed around her waist as she lifted her chin to press her lips against his, drawing her close against himself, but was otherwise gentle today where he had been forceful the other day. He was there, pressure for pressure and delightfully practised in the art of kissing, but there was no pushing her back against a wall or even a step backward; he simply held her in place and made the most of everything she gave.

And Susan, who had quite some moments ago in this exercise answered every theory and question for which she had desired an answer, found it very difficult to do what she should have done immediately upon having those answers, and break the kiss. Happily for her, a log shifted and fell in the fire; soft and unmistakeable at the same time, that noise seemed to break the spell. Susan turned her face a little to stop the kiss while it still seemed possible, and caught at whatever little sanity she still possessed while Emmett turned his head into her neck and settled there, his heartbeat mingling with hers.

She breathed into his ear, "Are they still out there?"

Emmett shifted a little, and for a moment Susan was quite certain that the embrace tightened rather than loosened; then she felt his head lift slightly and deliberately, and after a few, lingering moments, he said, "No."

He let her go as soon as she pulled away, but one of her hands was inexplicably in one of his, and Emmett used that connection to pull her back toward the fireplace and the fat, padded chairs there. She sat down in one of them, very conscious of Emmett's eyes on her face. She could have sworn that there was a sliver of concern in those eyes; mostly, she saw a certain wariness as he sat down opposite her, and she didn't really blame him for that. It wasn't the first time that she could be said to have attacked him, but it was the first time she had done so without warning.

"It's all right," she said. "I'm not going to go for you again."

Genuine amusement swept over his face. "Are you going to do that every time we're caught alone with someone watching us?"

"No," said Susan, heartily regretting what she'd done. It was so unfair to Emmett when he was labouring under the curse, and she could have effectively done the same thing in a far less invasive manner, even if she couldn't have confirmed her theory from the morning's adventures. "But I needed to check a theory, and this was the easiest way to do that."

Emmett's eyes fixed on her face. "You were checking that I wasn't a dream?"

"I could have done that just by touching your arm," Susan said, giving only that half-answer.

She wasn't sure if he would catch her in the omission, and it was a relief when he said instead, "I looked for you all morning."

"I was polishing silver," she said, relaxing a little. "And learning about the first owner of the manor, who apparently cursed the current one."

Emmett, who seemed to have opened his mouth with another question, closed it again and then asked, "Someone was willing to talk openly about that?"

"Yes, I fancy he didn't think it was important enough to worry about. Very interesting, that."

"He?"

"The little footman," said Susan. "And I don't think he was trying to be helpful, either; I think he was trying to warn me. In fact, I'm pretty sure the little blighter threatened me at one point."

"Is he the one who hit you on the head?"

"Not unless he was in two places at once. I've got my money on Mrs. Carmichael for the act, but I wouldn't put it past Mr. Oswald, either. I'm still not sure about Regan."

"All right. What did the footman tell you about the first master and this one? All of it."

"I'll tell you, but only if you tell me what you know about what the master usually does after dinner—and don't say *brood*, because I already know that."

When Susan had finished filling Emmett in on what she had learned from Helfer, and he had done the same with the scant information he had about the master, they both reluctantly decided that it wasn't wise to spend any longer together alone with the manor as highly strung as it presently was, and made for the door.

They returned to the hallway to find Regan dusting the closest planter, shooting a distrustful look up at the portrait above her and then at them as they exited the room. Susan managed a delightfully convincing giggle that made Regan roll her eyes and look away, and felt the huff of air that was Emmett silently laughing behind her. Emmett vanished with his usual quietness toward the front of the manor—perhaps for a brief word with Brennan—leaving Susan to meet Regan's meaningful look.

"You'd best get to the kitchen," she said to Susan. "Mrs. C is in a bate: the master wants the gaslight on for tonight, so of course it's off and on as usual—it always fails when we're already having an unsettled day! We'll be lucky if we get through the day without someone's ears being boxed, at this rate."

"Sounds absolutely delightful," Susan said, and turned reluctantly toward the kitchen.

"Of course, you won't have to do half as much as we will," Regan added as she walked away. "Being the mistress' maid."

"It's the joy of my life," Susan said over her shoulder.

She would have gone right on to the kitchen if she hadn't heard Mrs. Carmichael's voice wafting up from the left wing of the manor as she passed the turning; Susan took the left-hand turn and found the housekeeper in a room she had not yet seen the inside of. Wide and dark, and glittering with golden embellishments on every wall, golden ceiling roses curving around the lights in the shadowy ceiling, it was a room for elegant dinners and rich company.

Not, Susan would have thought, the sort of place to enjoy a quiet dinner in the presence of a woman you were being gently teased into caring for by a ruthless and far-too-powerful curse, in order to cement your goodwill and interest. A twinge of unease pulled at Susan. Was the master planning on using this dinner as a catalyst for giving Janet the key? Surely he would know that Janet would much prefer a warm, peaceful dinner in one of the smaller rooms—or, scandalous thought!—his suite.

Ah. Susan tapped a finger against her upper leg as she stepped into the room, catching sight of Mrs. Carmichael and Mr. Oswald by the windows and deep in discussion. It could be exactly what the master was counting on. In fact, if he framed it exactly right, giving Janet the key in this sort of a setting could only weigh it down with a feeling of expectation and cool formality. Exactly the sort of thing that might make her view it as less of a boon and more of a danger.

The question was, was the master that clever? Susan was inclined to think so.

"There you are!" said Mrs. Carmichael, turning sharply away from Mr. Oswald and taking Susan by surprise. "You can do light magic, can't you?"

"Enough to avoid getting lost in the hallways," she said pleasantly.

"Light won't stop you getting lost in these halls, Miss Susan," said the housekeeper. "So if that's what you're counting on to keep you safe, I'd suggest you think again. We'll need about a dozen lights in here, all along the ceiling; make it bright and glittering, the master says. The gaslight is unreliable today, and heaven help us all if we don't give him what he wants!"

"Of course," said Susan, greatly amused.

So the master *was* planning on loading the key as heavily as he could to help prevent Janet from using it. It was an exercise in which she could undoubtedly help him, so she would do her best: in this marriage at least, it seemed as though the master was going to great lengths to keep his bride safe. She wondered if that would extend to letting go of the white-knuckled grip he had on the rules and their place in keeping them safe, and found that she couldn't answer that question as easily.

Emmett, of course, would have done so without a second thought—and why she was thinking of Emmett, Susan realised in some irritation, was anyone's guess! If they had been in the same situation as the bride and the master, no doubt they would have been loyal and dead. She pushed the thought away, looking around the room for the best ways to lay the kind of light spells that would continue without her presence, and noticed belatedly that the table hadn't even been set.

"Where's Helfer? Shouldn't he be laying the table by—"

"You don't need to worry about Helfer," Mrs. Carmichael said. "He'll worry about himself. The master wants a proper dinner here in the dining room, and we're going to be busy enough with that without worrying about what everyone else is doing. You'll have enough to do in making sure that all the candles don't go out until it's time for your lights, what with the horrid draughts we get around this place."

"You don't believe in ghosts, then, I see," Susan said, following a natural grain in the wood that ran through the rafters above and could be used as a conduit.

Mrs. Carmichael huffed. "A lot of nonsense to distract the nervous ones. Just do as you're told and nothing will harm you in this place."

"So I hear," said Susan, and went on with her work.

It was tricky work, and Susan had lost track of both Mrs. Carmichael and Mr. Oswald by the time she was more than halfway through the job. To the greenish darkness of a stormy evening was eventually added a growling darkness of night, split occasionally by lightning and cracks of thunder. She was very nearly finished when someone in green velvet walked by the door and sent a wave of relief through her.

Helfer—no doubt going about his duties—was not lost in the manor or hit on the head and left somewhere for someone to find. She had been letting her imagination run away with her, and while that might be sometimes useful in the way of solving puzzles, it had done nothing but cause unfounded anxiety in this case.

Susan finished her magic rather hastily, laying a less-than-straight trail of magic down by one of the rafters to keep it out of sight and easily accessible for repowering the lighting magic, and darted out of the room in hopes of catching Helfer before he disappeared again. Imagination or no, she wanted to see his face with her two eyes and make sure that he was quite well.

When she jogged lightly to the division of the hall and looked first toward the kitchen and then toward the front of the manor, Helfer was just disappearing between the double doors that led to the grand entrance of the house. The lighting around her quivered and fluttered, and thunder growled. Susan muttered beneath her breath and darted after Helfer as the doors swung shut on the black-and-white harlequin tiling of the foyer, glad for the patch of light that the doors left when the lights went out completely in the lower half of the manor.

The tiles seemed to glow in darkness as Susan emerged into the foyer, and even through rolls of thunder, she thought she heard Helfer's feet on the stairs above as she came out beneath the landing. Exasperated at playing catch, she called his name as she jogged across the room and started up the stairs. She saw the brief movement of bottle-green velvet at the top of the stairs in a flash of lightning, but it vanished before she was two steps up the main staircase, taking two at a time.

By the time Susan was at the top of the stairs, the lighting there flickered at regular intervals as well, making a confusing nonsense of the patterned carpeting on the landing and forcing her to slow down. Despite that, she grinned: her quarry was in sight, just down the hallway and alternately appearing and disappearing as the lights flickered.

"Helfer!" she called, in the lull between two rolls of thunder.

This time, she was sure he heard her. He turned to face Susan, and she thought she saw for, a brief moment, the blankness of almost doll-like eyes and the loose jaw of a person sleepwalking. She narrowed her eyes against the alternating lightning and darkness, trying to see if he really was awake and if the cold whiteness of his cheeks was anything other than the blanching from sudden flashes of lightning through the open door to his left.

"Miss Susan!" called a sharp voice from below, while Susan, a soft glow of magic light beginning to emanate from her fingers, was still trying to make out what it was about Helfer that was so uncanny.

Helfer turned and went on. She would have tried to dart down the hallway too, but it was too late: at the top of the landing, Susan was in plain sight of that gimlet eye. She regretfully took her eyes off the retreating figure of Helfer and faced the housekeeper, leaning over the banisters to display an innocent face to the greenish shadows of the stormy evening below.

"Yes, Mrs. Carmichael?"

"I've told you before about going up those stairs! Get down here at once!"

"Yes, but if I do that, I'll have to come back down them," Susan said reasonably. "Shouldn't I go back by the servants'—"

"The master," said Mrs. Carmichael in murderous tones, "is coming down the *hall*! Come down here immediately!"

Susan did as she was told. As little as she was sure that Mrs. Carmichael could have her thrown out at this stage in the curse, she didn't want to make waves when she ought to be blending in as much as possible. Mrs. Carmichael didn't seize her by the ear at the bottom of the stairs as she had done with Regan earlier that week— she couldn't, as Susan had earlier pointed out to Helfer, reach as high—but she managed to pinch a fold of Susan's sleeve in something of the same manner and towed her grimly toward the lower hallway, with very nearly the same effect.

Through the glass partitions of the doors, Susan could already see the master approaching with Janet on his arm. The lights had steadied somewhat down on the lower level, leaving a mere flicker or two between grumbles of thunder, and she could also see Regan and Emmett trailing along in the wake of the couple of the house. Janet threw a worried sort of look over her shoulder at Emmett, and Susan felt her jaw tighten just slightly as the doors opened to admit the master, the bride, and Emmett and Regan in close proximity.

For a moment, nobody seemed to quite know what to say, or why it was that everybody was gathered here. The master, it was sure, knew Something Was Up, but didn't seem to know quite how to broach the subject, which Susan found amusing and slightly irritating. She would have liked to have thought his presence was because he did know something was wrong and had a desire to help, but that was probably a bit too much—unless Janet had prompted him to it by her urging or her presence. From the way she was standing just a little bit in front of him, Susan would have guessed that the bride had been leading the way.

"An interesting place to hold a meeting," said the master at last. "I suppose you're trying to figure out what to do about the lights."

"Although I don't know why you find it necessary to be manhandling my maid," Janet said, with a coolness that made Mrs. Carmichael drop her hand and even move away, much to Susan's approval.

The housekeeper was made of stern enough stuff, however, to address only the master. "It's not a meeting, sir; we were just discussing the Rules of the House so that Miss Susan knows not to go up the main staircase."

"I must have lost my way in the dark," Susan added helpfully.

"Yes, I do think I'd rather have the gaslight fixed than worry about the stairs right now," the master said, his beard gleaming almost blue in the half light. "Mrs. Carmichael, I trust that the dining hall—"

"You know, sir," said Mrs. Carmichael, very meaningfully and far too forcefully, "that I always recommend punishment for solecisms of this sort. I would hate to see the household in disarray, and you don't know how pert the maids can be."

"After finding this one in my private sitting room, I've got a pretty good idea," the master said, meeting Susan's eyes briefly. "I won't have you punishing her."

Susan was uncomfortably aware that every eye in the room was upon her, and that not many of them bore a felicitous sort of expression. Janet's gaze left her first; she was stiff and cool in a way that both worried and comforted Susan. Emmett's eyes remained on her, a frown between his brows and a slight flare to his nostrils that Susan would have liked to have soothed a great deal more than she at present wished to soothe Janet. Mrs. Carmichael's look was pure poison, and Regan's was speculative.

The master alone was cautiously, optimistically playful.

Susan couldn't quite help responding in kind. She explained gravely, "I thought it my duty to remove the hound, since you seemed to be disturbed at finding her there."

She lifted her eyes to the ceiling with perfectly timed saintliness; the hound, with just as well-timed accuracy, whined and pawed at the floor. Susan heard the master coughing a split-second later and, pleased, allowed her gaze to return limpidly to his face. He was trying to hide a grin. Emmett had folded his arms across his chest in massive, silent disapproval.

"Sorry about the dust," she said solicitously to the master. "We must have missed a few spots when we dusted this afternoon. It does get in one's throat, doesn't it?"

"Yes, it does," he agreed.

Mrs. Carmichael sent another nasty look in Susan's direction, and Regan turned her face away, presumably so that the house-keeper couldn't see that she was grinning.

"I do try to keep order in the household for your convenience, master," she said.

"I see," said the master, looking around the room. It was obvious that he couldn't see anything wrong and didn't know what else he might do. "Carry on, then. I've a few things to prepare in the dining room, so I won't want anyone in there for half an hour or so. My valet will help with anything else you need."

Susan exchanged a glance with Janet and was pleased to see the unaffected smile of gratitude that she bestowed on the master. He might not know what was going on, but the master was making sure his bride was safe.

While the master was talking to Janet in a low voice—presumably to tell her when to come to him—she asked Regan softly, "What's wrong with Helfer? I saw him going upstairs, and he didn't look right."

Regan may have turned her face even further toward the inky windows, but Susan could see the motion of her hands below her apron and knew the other girl was wringing those hands.

"I don't know," the maid said. "I wish I did! People not being where they ought to be and going off alone is bad news around here."

Susan said, "I can cover for you if you want to see if you can find him."

Regan's tone grew stiffer. "It's no use doing things like that," she said. "Either he's doing what he should be, or doing what he shouldn't be—either way, we can't help him."

She marched away to stand by Mrs. Carmichael and the doors,

waiting until the master got far enough up the hallway to follow him at a respectful distance. Susan knew that she would have no opportunity to do anything else.

Perhaps she could get a moment to whisper in Emmett's ear and—

The lights went out on the lower floor, this time with finality.

"Oh, whatever *now*?" demanded Mrs. Carmichael's put-out voice.

Thunder rolled, and a moment later, lightning tore through the room, glaring off every surface for a few seconds longer than should have been possible, and Susan saw a gash of dark green above the banisters.

She made a wordless protest and stepped forward, arms outstretched as if she could really do anything to stop the inevitable, and sensed rather than saw Emmett start across the room toward her.

It was too late, in so many ways. The rumble of thunder overlaid the sound of Helfer's body hitting the marble, but it couldn't disguise the fact that he was there, his body crumpled into a nonsense of limbs from the fall and his head split open.

Mrs. Carmichael gave a short, startled shriek and clutched the ruffles on her bodice in a convulsive grip, and Regan made a small, wailing noise and sank to the floor with her face averted. Susan, closest to the body, sent out a flicker of light to gleam off the chandelier crystals and crouched down to make sure Helfer was really dead. She could find no pulse.

There was very little blood; Helfer had possibly already been dead when he fell. He had been since just after she saw him last, Susan rather suspected. She wasn't even sure he hadn't been dead then—dead and walking, ready to slump over the banisters and make his final appearance in the manor with what the curse felt to be the best effect.

Silence, sticky with storm and fear, filled the room and curled around the marble floor in a cold breeze. Then the bell on the door tolled with crashing violence, splitting the sudden silence, and was followed by a tremendous clap of thunder.

Janet made a small, shrieking noise and caught at Emmett's arm. Susan fancied that he angled himself so that he was facing the doors and between Janet and them—which left her, she noticed crankily, to go and see who was at the front doors in this sort of weather, just as they had a dead body on the floor to see to.

She rose and crossed the floor, aware of Brennan's grumbling humming alongside the thunder, and threw open the smaller, inner door.

Thunder crashed; lightning lit the rectangle of cold, rainy outside and created a momentary silhouette of the two figures that filled the doorway, rain dripping in dark, inky drops from their tweed hats and glimmering on their boots.

"We're here about the empty position," said Gardener One triumphantly.

TWELVE

"How did they know he was dead?"

It didn't take the panicked quality of Janet's voice in her ear to let Susan know that the other woman was completely rattled: she also grasped Susan's arm with enough strength to leave nail marks through the wool of the tunic sleeve. Neither of them had left the suite for very long last night, and even now that the storm was over and the light of a new day had once again dawned on the manor, it felt more than ever like an unchancy and unsafe place.

"They've been watching through the windows for a while now," Susan said in a low voice, and stopped outside the breakfast room. "Did you speak with the master last night?"

"I'll tell him this morning," Janet said, avoiding her eyes.

Susan only nodded. She had a different worry on her mind—one of several, actually, but it was the one uppermost at the moment. It was one thing for the gardeners to have arrived at exactly the time of Helfer's death—or the discovery of the same. It was quite another for them to have arrived in the full expectation of a place within the house being vacant for them to assume. It didn't help that the two of them had been up before anyone else in the manor, dressed exactly alike in boots and uniforms that didn't fit anything like as well as they ought to have, stalking around the halls in tandem and dusting in slow, clumsy strokes.

"They make me shiver," Janet said, vehemently.

Susan couldn't disagree; out of all the uncomfortable things about the manor that ranged from mildly unnerving to utterly discomposing, the twin footmen-who-had-been-gardeners were a solid mid-of-the-range unpleasantness that had much the same effect as seeing a spider crawl sedately across the ceiling above the bed.

But that wasn't Susan's biggest concern.

It wasn't even the fact that the master had disappeared just minutes before Helfer plunged over the banisters—thereby making it impossible for Susan to rule him out as the person who had either killed or tossed the boy over. The thought left her torn between what she really wanted to believe, but it wasn't the worst of her thoughts.

No, the worst of her thoughts revolved around the one-in-three odds that had occurred to her shortly after Helfer's death—the one-in-three odds that she was responsible for Helfer's death.

Mr. Oswald had been watching when she talked with Helfer in the courtyard by the kitchen, drawing out information from him about the original owner of the manor. Mrs. Carmichael had possibly hit Susan on the head—and had certainly stopped her from going after Helfer when it might have prevented his death—when Susan discovered Helfer's night-time sleeping arrangements. Then there was the master, who had been out of sight, and might possibly have murdered Helfer. It was the only option by which Susan couldn't assign any blame to herself, and it was something of a relief when it occurred to her.

That relief wasn't enough to have allowed her to sleep well last night. Whatever the case may be, there was a two out of three chance that Susan had been indirectly or directly responsible for Helfer's death. That was something that bothered her more than her inability to assure Janet that the master wasn't responsible for Helfer's death.

"Keep the hound about you," was all she was able to say to Janet before the other woman entered the breakfast room. "And call me when you're finished breakfast. We'll take a walk and get away from the manor."

"Yes," agreed Janet fervently, shooting a look down the hallway to where the twin footmen were methodically yet uselessly sweeping at cobwebs on the portraits that lined the walls. "A *long* walk."

Susan could have gone further down the hall to talk with Brennan and see what he had to say about both footmen and Helfer, but it seemed expedient instead to see what there was to see around the suite she shared with Janet. There had been just enough of evasion in Janet's manner earlier that Susan wouldn't have been prepared to swear that the master hadn't already given her the key. If he had, Susan was quite determined to steal it. Janet would have quite some problem in running afoul of the Perfect Result if she didn't have the key with which—Susan could only assume—she could escape the castle. There was little other use for a key than a lock within which to put it, after all, and despite the fact that escape was a sensible plan, Susan was quite sure that a simple escape didn't feature in the curse's plans for the bride.

And since Susan had a sneaking suspicion that her actions could be considered in the light of a Jealous Rival—both searching and stealing—she felt that she could do it without too much concern about the curse striking back. A delightful case of killing two birds with one stone: prevent Janet from falling afoul of the curse and secure her own part in one blow. Belle, thought Susan, with a slight pang, would have been very proud of her.

She slipped into the suite with what felt like a comfortable few hours while the master and the bride conversed and flirted and wafted back and forth in the same dangerous sort of way that the curse seemed to enjoy. At any rate, there would be time to go through the suite to see what Janet may have hidden in plain, or not so plain, sight—not to mention the privy, which was much easier to visit without being seen and therefore more likely to have secrets hidden within.

She went to the privy first, impatient to see what could be hidden within its walls, and spent quite some time rapping on tiles along the wall, tapping her foot on floorboards, and inserting a tiny silver knife she'd pinched from the kitchen in between surfaces that might give to open any hidden door. Susan even stood on the porcelain frame of the privy itself to see if she could reach the vent that was above it. She could reach it, but barely, and she couldn't picture Janet, who was roughly a head shorter than herself, being able to do anything useful there. There were no signs it had been tampered with, either.

Her final area for search finally gave results; Susan, casting about for any other place that might be used to hide anything, called to mind the outside of this particular part of the manor, then grinned and opened the tiny window behind the privy.

It looked old and stiff but opened with hopeful ease, and Susan grinned more widely. This window, along with all the others at this level, had a framework that protruded a little from the window and scalloped inwards, leaving a space of an inch or so that was shielded from sight of anyone level with or below the window.

And there, in that little space of an inch, running the length of the window, were four little vials that were each stoppered with glass and perhaps rubber, and contained a clear liquid of roughly the same amount each.

Touched with the cold finger of sudden fear, Susan unstoppered them one at a time, sniffing the contents. Each of them had the smell of anise, to her surprise and relief. If Janet was having the kind of thoughts that involved imbibing hidden liquids in secret places as an answer to the slow, lingering threat of death before an inevitably horrible death, it would not be via the use of star anise. It was far more likely to be a tonic of some sort, though Susan didn't lose sight of the fact that it was hidden and likely to be something more.

There was nothing more she could gain from the privy, so Susan put everything back exactly as it had been and returned to the main suite for a more thorough look around. There was not too much to be seen, but Susan did discover a small, hand-written book beneath Janet's pillow. She turned it over in her hands, but like a diary would have been, it was absent a title and needed to be opened to provide any clarity. There Susan found written, in a clear, bold, almost type-faced hand, the heading *Early History of the Castle on the Hill: Master and Mistress.*

"Good heavens!" she murmured to herself, flipping through pages. So Janet had had the same idea that Susan had. She couldn't help grinning to herself, despite the ridiculousness of the situation. "We're going to have to be a bit more open with each other, I think."

It was all very well saying that, of course: there were some things that Susan certainly wasn't going to tell Janet, and no doubt there were things the other woman would still keep back. But they could at least try to come to some collusion as regarded the curse that was on the master of the manor—and sharing the information that they both obviously had regarding the first master of the manor.

Susan settled herself on her bed and read a good chunk of the first half of the little book, encouraged by the ease of reading the handwriting. She found the information to be almost exactly what she had already learned from Helfer the previous day, and made a mental note to warn Janet about being too free either reading the book near the master or mentioning it where the curse was likely to realise she knew about it. The information might not have been what got Helfer killed, but Susan wasn't sure enough of that to risk Janet's life on it.

She went on with her reading until a flutter of movement teased in her peripheral, and she found Emmett sitting next to the bed and gazing at her, his head on one side to watch her.

"I know you're not real," she said, turning her head. "Go away or I'll kiss you again."

Ghost-Emmett's face darkened with anger, and Susan fancied that she caught a glimpse of its real face for just an instant before it vanished again. It wasn't a pleasant face.

"That's what you get for popping out when it's not dark and I'm not half asleep," she said to the space that it had left beside her.

Still, it seemed unwise to be lolling on the bed when a lack of sleep might see her dropping off at any moment, so Susan sat up again with her finger between the pages of the book. She took another quick glance at it as she crossed the room to place it noticeably in the centre of the table beside Janet's bed, and caught sight of a final paragraph.

When it comes to love, the castle eats first. Our women are the property of the castle first, themselves second. Our prosperity is bound up in women; they are our saviours and our riches—too important to risk to their own devices or to our wishes.

Susan found herself wiping her hands on her tunic in something akin to disgust, and looked around the room one more time. Janet would undoubtedly be calling for her quite soon, and she wanted to try one last thing before she went back down.

It wasn't so much the thought of home that made her set up a commlink spell; home, for quite some years now, had been wherever she set up camp with Emmett and the horselords. Susan loved her family—and particularly Belle—but she had no plans of being maudlin. Nor did she have any illusions about the likelihood of being successful in her commlink: there was next to no chance at all that it would work. No, Susan had begun to set up her commlink because she wanted to find out what *would* happen.

So she attached the commlink to Janet's washstand with the fleeting thought that if things went wrong, it would be easier to break the link in water than in glass, and settled herself in front of the washstand. Palms propped on the marble top and her fingers curled around the edges, Susan linked the last bit of magic and gazed down into the water to see what would happen.

What happened was a muddy swirl of colour that had nothing to do with the water moving, exactly as she would have expected from using a liquid source of reflection instead of a solid one. Susan felt her spirits rise just slightly and reminded herself that hope was premature as the muddiness subsided to show the subtly shifting visage of her sister.

"Hallo, Belle," she said cautiously.

Isabella's grey eyes brightened with delight at the sight of her. "Su! I've been hoping to hear from you for far too long! Where have you vanished to?"

"Nowhere," Susan said promptly. "As you can see. Have we been gone long?"

"No one has had sight of you or Emmett or Brennan for the last four months! What happened?"

"Four months, eh?" Susan said thoughtfully. She would have given a great deal to know whether or not that was true. She was already further into this particular adventure than she'd thought to have gotten, and she was well aware that everything this version of Isabella said should be taken with a grain of salt. The real Isabella— if this were she—would forgive her for so doing and would not forgive any lack thereof. "I suppose that means the kid has popped out and you're pregnant again by now?"

Isabella made the sort of face that she usually reserved for tea that had been allowed to over-brew. "Good heavens, no! I've barely enough time for myself as it is, and between Alexander and the children, I'm likely to be driven mad by the chatter."

"You could always talk back?" suggested Susan.

"Oh, I rather think not! Children and spouses don't have much to say that's interesting. Susan, where have you been? What's happening? The last I heard of you, you were leaving a town somewhere near the Lacunan border."

"I've been having a bit of fun with a curse near that town," Susan said. "What do you know about story curses?"

"Enough to know that you ought to make sure you're not going to end up dead by doing anything you shouldn't," said Belle. "There isn't much leeway when it comes to story curses, and curses don't care for it when you try to get around them, either."

"They don't much like it when you talk about them, either," said Susan.

Her sister's eyes flitted over her. "They don't."

"Who are you, by the way?" Susan enquired amiably. "I know you're not my sister, but that's as far as I've got."

It got Belle's arch look exactly, terrifyingly right. "Am I not?"

"You're really good at expressions—where do you get them from, by the way? My mind?—but you're really not very good at emotions. You're not much good at relationships, either, I should think. I don't know what your experience of marriage has been like, but Belle and Alexander are about as tight and happy as any couple

I've ever seen, and they love their children. I know for a fact that they spend every night together and that there's trouble if they can't."

The reflected Isabella shrugged and lifted her chin. "All couples fight and need to take time apart to recover from the toxicity of the other. You should know that—you and Emmett have been teetering on the brink of disaster for several days now."

"Have we been?" inquired Susan. "How interesting! I had no idea."

"Liar," said the reflection, and now it changed with a faint ripple until Susan was looking at her own face. "You've been looking at him like this for the last few days."

It was disorienting to see the swift, vulnerable longing in her own face.

"Goodness me," Susan said, buffering herself with a few seconds to make sure her voice didn't shake. "You really are very good at that. We're not a couple, by the way."

"You will be," said her own face. "Consider it my gift to you. It comes with a warning: make sure that you do everything to win him, because I won't do all the work."

Was it possible, wondered Susan, that she was speaking to the personification of the curse rather than a ghost? She asked, "What do you mean, it's a gift?"

"Everyone here is given a gift: a sort of promise that if they do everything right and the story goes as it ought, they'll get something out of it."

"I see," said Susan. "And what exactly was the footman Helfer's prize? Because he didn't look too happy last night."

"I don't discuss other players," her face said. "And you'd better stop poking around in your mistress' things, hadn't you? That's the sort of thing that gets maids into trouble."

Susan didn't think she mistook the gloating look it wore incongruously with her own features. "Well, that's my job, isn't it?" she said. "And it's also my job to go and fetch my mistress safely from the breakfast room, so I think I'll go and do that."

She slapped her fingers down on the surface of the water,

breaking the commlink, but she thought she saw another face there in the split second before the spell broke completely. She had no time to take in the features, but she carried away with her the impression of black, malicious eyes, and Susan shivered as she let herself back out into the hall.

Janet met her in the servants' stairwell, sneaking up with the hound by the shortest way and, for a moment before she realised that it was Susan she'd run into, looked faintly guilty.

"It's all right, it's just me," said Susan, but her own teasing voice from the commlink version of herself whispered in her head that she needed to be careful, careful, because this was a rival, not a friend. "Where are you going?"

"I need something a bit warmer to wrap around me," said Janet. "Why don't you try to find my boots and an umbrella in case we get rained on. I've got the hound, so I'll be all right."

"Shocking," Susan said with a grin, although she thought that there was still a bit of that guilty look on Janet's face, as if the girl had hoped to meet accidentally with Emmett on the stairs. "A mistress, fetching her own wrap!"

She pushed away those thoughts and went down to look for Janet's boots while the bride fetched her shawl. It seemed likely that they would be at the front of the house with the umbrellas, so she narrowly managed to avoid meeting Mrs. Carmichael, who passed through to the kitchen just as she was rounding the turn in the stairs, and hurried on toward the foyer.

Fortunately for her peace of mind, the footmen were nowhere to be seen, and she made it all the way to the foyer without being accosted by anyone she particularly didn't want to talk to.

"Finally!" said Brennan, as she stepped up onto the entrance area. "Look, old girl, I know you've been busy with dead bodies and wotnot, but you haven't been to see me all day and I want to talk to you."

"I'm afraid I'm not here to see you this time, either," Susan said. "I'm supposed to be getting the bride's boots and an umbrella ready for us to take a walk."

"This is a bit more important than a walk, old thing."

Susan found the boots with a huff of relief, and threw a look down toward the double doors, through which she saw the vaguest flutter of movement that meant someone had just come out of the kitchen at the end of the hall. "Perhaps so, but there are people everywhere this morning; I'll have to come back tonight. I'll bring Emmett."

"It's all very well to say you'll bring the old man, but—"

"He'll bring himself, I should think," said Susan, with one eye on the hallway. It was certainly Mrs. Carmichael approaching, and that was trouble. "Good grief, she's really on the warpath; Janet had better come down before Mrs. Carmichael gets here."

"Ignore the old buzzard."

"You can't ignore someone when they have you by the ear," Susan told him. "I can't stop now, Brenners."

Brennan said indignantly, "You can't go; I have something to tell you! There's perishing little use being in this rattly form, but if there's one use for it, it's people thinking you're just a piece of the furniture."

"You are a piece of the furniture, and I hear footsteps on the landing upstairs. I have to go."

"Look, old thing—"

"I *would*, Brenners, but Mrs. Carmichael is coming, and I'm supposed to be escorting my mistress out on a walk."

"All right, but you'd better come and talk to me when you get back," Brennan said obstinately. "And don't go drinking anything without having that perishing hound have a lick at it first."

Susan stared at him. "Good heavens! All right, Brenners; will do. And I'll come and see you just as soon as I know I'm not going to be snabbled by the ear by the housekeeper."

She would have stayed if she could—Brennan so rarely insisted on anything that when he did, it was notable—but having already been caught once by Mrs. Carmichael doing what she was not supposed to do, Susan was unwilling to be caught again in a compromising position that didn't involve Emmett standing by silently and passively-aggressively in order to stare at the housekeeper.

It wasn't as though Brennan could get up and walk away, after all, she told herself. He would still be there when she got back. The thought didn't comfort her as much as it ought to have, and Susan still felt the lingering feeling of anxiety when she saw Janet descending the grand stairs, just in time to force Mrs. Carmichael to pinch in her lips and the words that seemed to be waiting to tumble over them as she entered the foyer and saw Susan, doing apparently nothing.

"Sorry, mistress," Susan said promptly, just in case Janet hadn't already seen the housekeeper and said something unfortunate. "I've got your walking boots here—there's still a bit of mud on them from last time. I don't think the footmen got to them yet."

"Oh yes, that's all right," said Janet hastily, darting down the last couple of steps. "I don't think there's any need to bother the footmen with my boots. They'll only get muddy again, after all."

Susan, who agreed on principal with leaving muddy boots to their own devices unless they were carrying their own weight in dried mud, said cheerfully, "Exactly so. I've got the umbrella, mistress. Shall we go?"

She opened the door for Janet and followed after the bride to find that although the air wasn't as cold as it could have been, there were still threads of mist clinging to the trees further away from the manor.

"You arrived just in time," she said to Janet in a low voice, once the door was closed. "Mrs. Carmichael was just coming in to see what she could snap at me for."

"I don't know why he keeps her around," Janet said as she slipped her boots on, and then winced a little. "Oh, that sounds awful! If she wasn't here, someone else from the town would have to be here."

"I didn't fancy you were wishing death on her," said Susan soothingly. "And speaking of death, if there's anything good about what happened yesterday, it's not having to worry where the gardeners are or what they're going to be up to in the mist now that they're being footmen inside the house."

She heard the little sigh that Janet let out. "Oh, I forgot about that! What a relief not to have to worry about them for a little while at least! I don't think it would be so bad if they didn't just *stare* at one."

"Even if they didn't, they'd still be doing everything in concert," Susan said gloomily. "And answering as though they've had to process everything through ten layers of fog themselves."

"At least we won't have to worry about anyone else coming in now," Janet said, and Susan had the idea it was more to herself than to Susan. The bride's fingers tangled with her long, gold necklace, and Susan wondered if she knew that now the story was begun, no one else would be replaced from the town until she had escaped or was dead and the story curse reset itself or was fulfilled.

"You're always wearing that," Susan said, to take the bride's mind off the unpleasant thoughts that were no doubt flowing fast through her brain. "I wondered why. Did someone special give it to you? The protection spell on it isn't very strong, you know."

Janet's small hands closed around the pendant, and her eyes darted to Susan. "This? Yes; my older sister gave it to me a long time ago. I promised her that I'd always wear it."

That was something of a relief: if it had been a memento from a lover, Susan wouldn't have been surprised to find the curse using it against Janet when it came to the master. Seeing how much it had already figured out—or known outright—when it came to herself and Emmett, she wouldn't have been surprised to find the curse using that against Janet. It was more than enough that the curse had set her up against Janet, and Emmett against the master.

That tickled up a small curiosity within her, and she asked, "Did you tell the master so?"

"Yes; he said he'd get me some oil of rose and violet to put in it," said Janet, her eyes dropping to the pendant with a small frown between her eyebrows.

"Did he ask first, or did you...?" Susan let the question drop delicately.

Janet seemed to pull in a breath and recollect herself. She let go of the pendant and said, "Oh, he asked. I think he thought—"

"I can imagine what he might have thought," Susan said, with a wry smile. A stray, unkind thought suggested that she ask Janet what she thought the master might say about her clinging to Emmett's arm and gazing up at him with trusting eyes, but she already knew enough of what she thought about it to answer the question herself. So she asked again the question she had already asked that morning. "Did you talk to him about Helfer and the new footmen last night?"

One of Janet's shoulders went up and down very slightly. "We didn't have time to discuss it. We talked about it this morning, though: he says he had no idea that something like that was going to happen, but that it's happened many times before. If a main character in the curse is killed and that part is more important than the part they were playing, they have to move up."

"I wonder if the gardeners knew that."

"So do I," Janet said, her shoulders hunching a little. "Susan— about the book—"

"I thought you might see that," Susan said cheerfully. "I left it out so that you would, at any rate. When did you find it for the first time?"

"Only yesterday—I really was going to tell you!"

"I'm delighted to hear it," said Susan. Since she didn't know any better, perhaps it was just as well to believe Janet—it was too easy to disbelieve others in this cursed manor. "Where did you find it, by the way?"

Janet's eyes met hers briefly and then dropped again. "The master very carefully told me where I shouldn't be looking and what I shouldn't be looking at."

"Did he so?" Susan said, much amused. "What a clever boy! So he made it clear that it was something you shouldn't be looking into and also clarified in which direction you *shouldn't* be looking. You think it's true that the first owner was the one who began the curse?"

Janet nodded. "I'm sure of it. I don't know how it helps me to know, and maybe I'm just grasping at straws, but—"

"Maybe we both are," Susan said, and this time she heard the grimness in her own voice. "But Helfer died the day after he told me about the original master and the current one, so I think it's more important than we suspect. Be careful about reading it or talking about it, all right?"

"He said that, too," Janet said. "I think we're safer talking about things when we're away from him, but—"

"—but there are the servants," agreed Susan. "Yes. I'd say to watch out for Mrs. Carmichael in particular, but it was Mr. Oswald that I saw watching Helfer and me the other day, and even Regan—"

"Talking outside feels safer, anyway."

Susan glanced over at the bride. "Yes, that worries me a little, I have to say! I don't trust things that feel safer. Do you think we should be putting the book away somewhere hidden, by the way?"

"No," said Janet. "I think we ought to read it as quickly and thoroughly as possible. I have the feeling that it's the key to getting out of here. It wasn't easy to find, even with the master's help, and I don't think it was meant for me to find. I mean, I think he put himself in danger by telling me—or not telling me, I suppose."

Susan's sharp eyes didn't miss the movement of Janet's wrist as she pinched her fingers around her pendant and twisted it back and forth. "Someone told you where to find the book before you got here, didn't they?"

Janet's shoulders stiffened. "You might as well know," she said at last, letting out a faint sigh. "We get...information every now and then. Sometimes the servants make it through one whole storyline and get away free—not many, just one or two. Someone who knew my sister made it in with her, but he was the only one who came back out."

"I see," Susan said. "And he told you everything he knew to make sure you could beat the curse and make it out alive?"

Janet's eyes didn't meet hers. "Yes," she said. "That's also why I need to get into that little room the master didn't want me in— really didn't want me in, not just pretending for effect. There's something for me in there. I can't...I can't tell you what it is, but I need to get in there."

"That's another thing I don't understand," Susan said thoughtfully. "I know you're here for your own reasons, but I don't see how finding things within the manor is going to get you out safely. If playing the game the curse wants you to play is what gets you out alive, then all the information in the world on how to escape won't help, will it?"

"Oh!" Janet said, her gaze lighting on Susan's face. "There's meant to be a way to escape the manor, once everything and everyone is where they're meant to be. Didn't you see the notes in the margin of the book?"

"Not a one."

"Some of the other brides must have found it before me; I found notes all the way through from the part where the writer starts to talk about the original owner's disappearance—there are at least two different types of handwriting."

Susan felt a little bubble of delight form in her throat. "I don't suppose any of them mention what sort of things might need to be done to push the curse into a certain direction?"

Janet gazed at her in astonishment. "How did you know?"

"Well, it's a story curse," Susan said, gesturing back toward the manor. "And by now we've passed through nearly two parts, I should suppose. If something is needed to happen before we can get to the next part, or if something needs to happen to open up a way to escape, we need to move the story on to that part. If any of the brides think like me, I'm certain they would have been wondering how to go on to the next section of the story, or how to push it on. I've got the feeling that the brides are each given a chance to escape —or maybe just a chance to make the story go along the Perfect Result lines—but the story changes based on decisions. If it was me, I would want to know what decision to make to bring about the best chance to escape the manor."

Janet, with bright eyes, said eagerly, "One of them mentions *the key*, and it does talk about trying to find the right way to push the right storyline."

"Dear me!" said Susan. "Perhaps you could show me those notes when we get back to the manor. We'd probably better be careful talking about it within the manor, but I shouldn't think the curse will know if we're simply reading it."

"I remember one," Janet said promptly. "*The heart of the manor doesn't reveal itself until the key is with the bride, nor will the doors open. There's no way out without the key. At all costs keep the key.*"

"Yes," said Susan thoughtfully. She still remembered the raw magic that ran through what must be the inner manor, and the sprawling confusion of it. Something like a key that had been pre-set for an escape door would do a lot of good there. "A lot of it does seem to come back to the key."

Janet's eyes fastened on her. "You've heard about it before, haven't you? What do you know about it?"

"The master said something about a key a day or so ago," Susan admitted. "I wasn't sure if you knew about it or not, and I didn't know how much of what the master told me would be useful and how much would be dangerous."

"He doesn't lie," said Janet, and her voice was very slightly resentful. "He can't help it if the curse pulls what he says out of shape or does odd things with it."

"I daresay he can't," said Susan. The ridiculousness of Janet being annoyed at Susan speaking in anything but glowing tones of her husband while at the same time clinging to Emmett's arm should have amused her, but it seared her heart with annoyance instead.

Janet lifted her chin a little as if Susan had said outright that she didn't trust the master. "He probably didn't tell me yet because it wasn't the right time."

"You said you didn't have time to discuss Helfer or the gardeners with the master when you met last night—what *did* you discuss?" Susan glanced sideways at Janet and added, "Since he didn't give you anything like a key, I mean."

"I was—I was too busy doing something else, so we only had a few minutes together to make sure that we were both alive and well."

Something else, Susan was rather sure, was meeting with

Emmett. "I see," she said stiffly. "You were busy in the halls on your own business."

Janet, her fingers tightly clasped around her pendant, seemed to have deflated. She said unhappily, "Yes, I suppose that's about it."

"Yes, I rather thought so."

"I don't—" Janet stopped, her fingers white and tight, and finished jerkily, "I don't want to do it. I didn't know it would be like this, and I don't know how to get through it all."

"I suppose not," Susan said, and she found that she couldn't help the coldness to her voice. "But it's a little bit late to be worrying about that at this stage, I'm afraid. You came here, and now you're stuck here, just like me."

"Yes, it looks like it," said Janet quietly. "I just thought there might be another way."

"There's always another way," Susan said. "It just depends on whether you want to pay the price for going that way."

She was short with Janet's subsequent sallies and replies, and when the other woman reluctantly suggested returning to the manor not half an hour later, Susan was glad to go. Perhaps Brennan would have some insight into what Janet had been doing last night, and with whom.

A vague echo of the malicious commlink entity's words, *Teetering on the brink of disaster* came to her mind, along with, *Make sure that you do everything to win him.*

THIRTEEN

S usan would have gone straight to Brennan when she returned to the manor, but she didn't get the chance. Immediately when she returned, she was set upon by Mrs. Carmichael, who didn't know where Mr. Oswald had gone and didn't seem to care, so long as Susan did the jobs she had prepared for him to do instead.

When she was finally free of selecting wines and setting tables, Susan found that she still couldn't get back into the main foyer without being observed: the footmen, dogged and slow, had gone back to dusting the portraits along the hall and were slowly making their way into the foyer to dust the suits of armour there, as though it was their default setting. Much to her irritation, she had still not been able to get back to see Brennan by the time the suns set, and when she and Janet finally returned to their suite, she stopped only long enough to suggest very strongly that Janet and the hound should both remain in the suite and left to find Emmett.

It wasn't until Susan was well into the right wing that she realised she had left the suite far earlier than usual. Softly stalking around the corner was Mr. Oswald, who was looking around nervously, but not, fortunately for Susan, in the right direction to see her. She ducked quickly behind a suit of armour that she was quite certain had been in a different part of the wing last time she had visited, and waited.

Mr. Oswald, still looking around like a particularly nervous pigeon, dodged and darted his way down the hallways, and took a left-hand turn that Susan had never seen before. The manor had begun to open out again.

Rather more carefully this time, Susan followed Mr. Oswald down a shadowy and tile-lined passage that seemed to swim with shadows that made sense when she finally caught up and found herself in an elaborate bathing chamber. Lined with potted plants and decorated with milky pillars, it was an easy room to slip into without being seen by the person she was following.

She was no longer sure that there was any reason to be following Mr. Oswald who, after all, had every right to come and bathe late at night, in secret or otherwise. Even the fact that he had come to a part of the manor that was running with a bit too much magic to be part of the regular manor wasn't necessarily pertinent.

Susan took a moment to feel the magic that ran beneath her feet, and reflected that it was only ever here, in the secret parts of the manor, that she felt as if the manor was a magical something existing in the real world. The outer part of the manor was more akin to a stage that was presented to the audience, with nothing that could be seen or grasped that wasn't meant to be seen and grasped—with all the mechanisms and practical magic hidden away out of sight to enhance the effect of the magic on stage.

This was the truly meaty part of the manor, and could she and Emmett bring Janet safely into it while possessing the key the master was supposed to give to Janet, Susan rather thought that there was a good chance of all three of them escaping the manor whole. It would do very little to help the master, however, who likely couldn't leave without his Perfect Result.

Treading lightly across the tiles, Susan heard a light splashing, as if someone had dipped a toe into the water to check the temperature. She peeked around the edge of a colonnade and saw a barefoot Mr. Oswald stripping off his shirt.

Susan, who had no pretensions to becoming a peeping tom, was about to make a swift and silent about-face to leave the bathing room as silently as she might, when she realised that Mr. Oswald, far from being completely bare-torsoed, was wrapped from the upper waist to just below the armpits in a few layers of what looked like bandage.

It was something she had worn often enough herself to recognise instantly: Mr. Oswald had been banding himself about the breast, and as he unwrapped himself, she could see that it was in order to flatten a chest that was absolutely not that of a man.

Mr. Oswald was, in fact, obviously a woman.

Susan, wide-eyed, saw the last of the bandages drop and let out a breath that mingled understanding with surprise. It didn't seem much better to be peeping on a woman unawares than a man, so she took the swiftest way around the potted palms she had been behind and came out slightly behind Mr. Oswald in order to give her the chance to do any covering she might want to do when Susan said amiably, "Nice night to bathe, I suppose!"

Mr. Oswald didn't even try to cover herself in the moment. She simply turned, and there was a hopelessness to the set of her shoulders that Susan couldn't miss.

"You shouldn't be here," said Mr. Oswald, her voice flat and emotionless. Despite that, there was a flush of colour in her cheeks. "And you should learn how to forget things you shouldn't have seen."

"I suppose the old butler died," Susan said thoughtfully, sitting down slowly on the edge of the bathing pool to dip her feet into the water and give the butler a chance to recover herself. "But I don't understand why you had to pretend to be a man to take over. Couldn't there have been two housekeepers? At the very least, I've seen more than one woman buttle!"

Mr. Oswald sat down on the tiled floor as if too numb to stand. "There's only ever one housekeeper, and there needs to be a butler. The butler is always a man."

"That's all very well to say, but you're obviously a woman."

"I always liked trousers and queued hair," said Mr. Oswald. Her eyes flickered to Susan and away again. "You can't like that sort of thing if you're a woman. It's not fitting. The story just helped me to understand what I really am. If I was meant to be a woman, it wouldn't have done that. I'm happier now that I know what I am."

Susan, whose sharp eyes had taken in the various lotions, soaps, and clothes that were carefully—almost ritualistically—laid beside the bathing pool, drew in a long, thoughtful breath through her nose.

"Not so much that you don't like your bathing time and your women's underwear," she said. "I did the same when dressing as a boy, by the way. Men's underwear isn't as comfortable as ours, and it was a nice way of still holding on to that part of me."

"I am a man," said Mr. Oswald, her face taut and despairing. "I am a man! Why else would the story have chosen me? What woman dresses in trousers and doesn't care for jewellery and prefers to be out and doing instead of sitting and sewing?"

"Well," said Susan apologetically, "ones like me. There are quite a few of us, you know. We're not a monolithic structure—and it's not as though wearing trousers makes you a man, after all!"

"I can't cook—I can't even be beautiful!"

"All right, all right," protested Susan. "I had no idea that I was so manly! You might care to know that my sister Isabella has also had occasion to dress as a boy from time to time—not to mention the height to pull it off—and that she sews better than any seamstress I know! Being a woman isn't what she does, it's what she is."

"The story knows what it's doing," Mr. Oswald said, turning her face away. "I'm content this way. I only come here from time to time when I don't seem to be able to bear it any more."

"Yes," said Susan. "That's the bit that sticks with me now that I know: the fact that you don't seem to be able to bear it without a break. I don't see why you can't wear your hair queued and keep your trousers and be free to be a woman anyway."

"I did so once," Mr. Oswald said, as if she couldn't help herself. "And there was someone who loved me as I was. But no one stays here long, and if you want the Perfect Result, you have to look and act the part. You'll learn that before long—I did, in the end."

"Yes," Susan said thoughtfully. "The curse really is very

concerned about the way things look and how people act. I don't suppose you'll believe me if I say that there never is a Perfect Result?"

"There has to be," Mr. Oswald said, and the despair was back in her eyes. "There has to be. It can't be so cruel as to refuse us the Perfect Result after everything I've given up."

Susan took in a breath that caught in her chest, sharp and sorrowful, and let it out more gently. "I see. If it helps, I think Janet is doing a very good job as the bride."

"Quite a few of them do, at first. But the story knows people, and it knows that they always choose wrongly."

"That happens quite often when the deck is stacked," Susan said, but she said it beneath her breath. She took her feet out of the water and rose carefully; she still had Emmett and Brennan to see, and she couldn't see them if the curse had caused her to knock her brains out on slippery tiled floors now that she knew a little more about it than she should. "Will you be all right?"

"As well as I usually am," Mr. Oswald said, and Susan saw in her shoulders the familiar pinch of fear that she had taken for stiff demeanour the first time she met the woman. "You can't—you won't tell anyone, will you? You can't tell anyone."

"Don't worry," she said, because she knew exactly what it was Mr. Oswald was asking. "I won't tell Mrs. Carmichael or the master that I saw you."

She had made no promises not to tell Emmett or Janet, though Susan saw no need to tell anyone other than Emmett if absolutely necessary. They both already knew that the curse was inclined to push on people feelings and roles that they had no desire to play, and Susan, softly padding through the halls to find her way back out of the maze she'd found herself in, didn't particularly want to think too deeply about this new reminder.

The problem, she was very well aware, was that she hadn't yet been presented with such a heavy and unmistakeable proof of the best reason to be more careful in her dealings with Emmett. It was all very well to say that she was simply going along with the story of the curse and that she had to do everything she could to keep herself and Emmett safe, but there was a difference between gliding along beneath notice in a magic system and subsuming oneself in the system for whatever temporal gains could be had. Susan wasn't sure which she was doing, and she didn't like that feeling.

When this curse was undone and they were safely out, it was going to be very hard to readjust to the fact that Emmett's feelings would dissolve along with it. In the meantime, and in the light of her own swiftly growing feelings, Susan found it very difficult to prevent herself from taking advantage of those feelings being there.

"This is what happens when you repress feelings for too many years," she muttered to herself as she passed down the lower hallway and toward Brennan's little nook in the front foyer.

It wasn't until she was well across the moonlit floor that she saw the bizarrely empty shadows that occupied the corner that should have been warmly full of wood and grumblings.

"Brenners!" she said sharply, darting across the last of the chequered floor, but he wasn't there.

He wasn't anywhere in the foyer, either. Susan threw a look around the entire place, even lifting her eyes as high as the chandelier and the remnants of a balcony so high up in the recesses of the ceiling that she couldn't see it properly. It wouldn't have surprised her at this point to see that the hall stand had been propped up on one of the ledges that ran around the walls higher up as a continuous sort of sconce around the room.

Failing to see him there, Susan took a swift lap around the room, checking into the recessed windows and back down the hallway again. She went as far down the right wing as she could go, ignoring the heaviness of her heart that told her there was no chance of finding him again, and couldn't stop herself from searching as much of the left wing as she could access as well. Night was pitch black by the time she got to the upper level of the manor, but Susan didn't hesitate; she darted straight down the right wing of the manor in search of Brennan or Emmett—or perhaps both.

With her heart in her throat, she jogged silently along the hallway, daring it to change while she was running, and heard the soft sounds of someone else approaching just in time to dart sideways and behind one of the suits of armour.

Janet swept past a moment later, and Susan could have called out to her, but she had no patience for talking with the bride when her mind was so full of Brennan, so she waited in the shadows, perfectly still, until Janet turned the corner. Then she stepped out again softly, her bare feet noiseless against the carpet, and went after Emmett. There was a coldness in her heart that had as much to do with Brennan being missing as it did with seeing Janet coming from the direction of Emmett's quarters; it was unsurprising but equally unpleasant to catch sight of Emmett mere moments after she started out again. Janet and Emmett had been meeting by either design or accident, but they had certainly met—they wouldn't have been able to avoid it.

That bitterness was in the back of Susan's throat, but all she could ask Emmett was, without preamble, "Have you seen Brenners?"

Emmett's brow lined at once. "I thought you'd know where he was! I couldn't find him earlier tonight, either."

"Someone's moved him, and I don't know who," Susan said, biting her lip. "I can't even see that they've moved him with magic, and you know how little magic there is in the outer parts of the manor!"

"I've been along the top hall and down as far as I could on the left side."

"I went through the bottom half of the manor, and not a hall moved out of place. If he's still in the manor, he's somewhere I can't get to."

Emmett nodded, his brows still pinched up in worry. "We'll have to ask the footmen."

"They won't be out and about," muttered Susan. "Not if they're like Helfer: they'll be caught up in the walls somewhere, being dribble-fed an idea the entire night that they've gone home and come to work the next day."

"We'll have to wait until tomorrow, then," said Emmett, but

Susan was under no misapprehensions that he liked the idea any more than she did.

"I'll go after the footmen early," she warned him, and he only nodded.

She had no doubt that he would want to be right there with her, asking.

Emmett walked her silently back to the hallway that ran toward the front of the house, and Susan couldn't quite decide if he was busy with thoughts of Brennan or thoughts of a recent meeting with Janet in the shadowy halls. She didn't ask, but Susan couldn't decide if that was because she was worried about Brennan or worried about the answer to her question—and she wasn't sure which made her feel more wretched, either. She went to bed still wretched.

Susan slept badly and woke early the next morning. She was up early enough to leave Janet sleeping with the hound stirring gently on the bed as she left the room, and made it back down to the lower half of the manor before anyone but the footmen were up.

Defying Mrs. Carmichael, she darted down the grand staircase at the front of the manor and nearly collided with one of the footmen, who was dusting something beneath the staircase.

"You, whichever one you are!" she said at once. "Where's the hall stand?"

The footman looked at her moonishly. "The hall stand is gone," he said. "We carried it out yesterday."

"You carried it out?" Susan felt the air leave her lungs in a slow suffocation. "Where? *Why?*"

"The master ordered it burned," said the footman.

"I *beg* your pardon?"

"Ordered it burned," repeated Footman Two, coming up behind her.

With the sound of those words in her ears, Susan left the manor at a run, ignoring the danger of being alone anywhere around the manor, ignoring the protracted stares of the footmen as the door slammed behind her and cut off their vision. She had only one thought in her mind, and that was to get to the fire pit as quickly as possible.

It felt as though she had to fight through the mist—as though it clung to her and weighed her down—and Susan barely knew where she was or how she had gotten there until she was stumbling into the slightly warmer ambience of the furnace with its metal shell.

The fire was low and small. Susan, panting and very nearly sobbing, stared at it wildly and tried to convince herself that it was too small and cool to have been burning something as large as a hall stand so recently as last night without anything to show for it. She couldn't convince herself, but neither could she say it wasn't likely that a hallstand could have been burned. And after she had sifted through what she could of the ashes to find any remnant that might clear up the matter one way or another, and found nothing, Susan could only return to the manor. There was still a little hope, but it was very little indeed.

She took the stairs of the servants' staircase three at a time and tumbled back into the suite to find the bride surprised and then flushed and pleased to see her. That would have tugged at Susan's heart if she had had the wherewithal to feel anything other than dread.

"The hall stand," she said, her words tumbling over themselves to get out. "Have you seen it?"

"The hall stand?"

"The one in the entryway. *Have you seen it*?"

"Oh yes, the talking hall stand," said Janet.

"I *beg* your pardon?"

Janet looked at her in surprise. "The hall stand that talks! You must have heard it muttering to itself when the mist creeps in! Lately, I sit there and talk to it; it helps to clear my mind and unburden myself."

"Yes, that's the one," Susan said, wondering rather wildly why Brennan would have talked with anyone when he knew it could be dangerous, and who else he might have spoken with.

Whoever it was, whatever he had learned in talking with them was likely to be the reason that he had been summarily carted off. Had it really been the master who had ordered it to be done? Why? What did he know, and had Susan been so wrong about his character as to have imagined him a good person when he wasn't?

"I saw the gardeners carrying it across the foyer last night," Janet said. "I thought it was odd, but I suppose it was needed somewhere else in the house."

"I don't think so," Susan said, her throat very tight. "They said they were told to burn it."

This time, Janet's gaze was horrified. "*Burn* it? But it's sentient!"

"Exactly," Susan said grimly. "And they said it was the master who told them to do it."

There was only a slight pause before Janet said, "You want me to ask him about it, don't you?"

"I think you're the only one who could get anything out of him about it," Susan said, dropping to the floor and resting her back against the wall with her head dropped over her knees. Her throat still felt tight, because no matter what she did, or what information Janet got out of the master about Brennan, it would already be too late. Brennan was gone—gone and burned, or broken apart for firewood.

She had promised to keep him safe and to undo what she had caused to happen to him, and she hadn't been able to do it.

Susan felt rather than heard or saw Janet leave the suite, and she was wearily glad for it. She had no strength to talk with the bride at that moment, and when the hound's claws tapped over the threshold as it followed Janet out, another care was taken from her. She stayed as she was, in a convoluted mess of despair and occasional, thready hope, until the door softly opened again and Emmett dropped down beside her.

Susan automatically laid a hand on his arm to feel the warmth of his skin before she spoke. Then, when she did speak, she didn't seem to have the energy or desire to remove it, so it simply stayed there, soaking in warmth.

"They said they burned him," she said wretchedly. "Those two moonstruck footmen. He said he had something to tell me—something he overheard—and I told him I'd come back last night. He was already gone by then; you saw it too."

"We don't know that he's dead," Emmett said. "We'll check the manor again, top to bottom. Even if he's not here, the curse could have changed him to something else."

"Could have," said Susan, laughing bitterly. "Do you think it has?"

His silence was enough to tell her that he believed it as little as she did. "I don't feel the kind of movement around the place that I did when Helfer died," he said, after a moment. "There's more of a pulling tighter, but nothing severed and joining together again."

"There's that, I suppose," Susan said, sitting up a little bit straighter. "Brenners said—he warned me not to drink anything without getting the hound to have a bit of it first."

"He thought someone was trying to poison you?"

"I suppose so. Someone must have known that he knew—and they had to know that Brennan wasn't just a hall stand, too."

"These people—" Emmett started, then stopped in frustration. "They know so much, and not enough."

"Yes," said Susan, feeling awfully numb. A thought occurred to her, and she asked, "Did Janet send you?"

"She said something had happened and told me where to find you."

Susan took in a deep, silent breath through her nose and said, "I'll have to find a way to talk to her again."

"Did you quarrel?"

"Nothing like so easy, lummox," Susan said tiredly. "Let's not worry about that right now, shall we? I've a feeling I'll need to do something about it later, but I don't know that I can do it well right now."

"I'll see what else the footmen have to say about Brennan, then," said Emmett, rising.

Susan wondered if he knew exactly how threatening he looked at that moment and thought that perhaps he did. He probably meant it, too.

"They were pretty open about it," she said reluctantly, but she rose with him. "They said the master gave orders to burn it, and that they burned it. Janet says she'll ask him about it, but she doesn't believe he'd do something like that."

"Do you think she will ask?"

"Oh yes," Susan said tiredly. "That's one thing I think she will ask. That's what makes it so hard to—"

She stopped, and briefly met Emmett's eyes.

He asked, "What's hard?"

"Oh, everything, right now," she said. "Let's not talk about the bride just now, lummox. We've more important things to worry about."

A kind of darkness lingered over the next day from breakfast through until well after dinner. Susan would have put it down to her own heaviness of heart if Janet hadn't remarked on that darkness as well; apart from that passing remark, however, she saw little enough of the bride, who seemed content to spend as much time as possible that day with the master. Susan didn't regret it.

Adding another layer of discomfort to the day, Mr. Oswald still wasn't in evidence at all, and that worried Susan in a numb sort of way. It didn't seem to worry Mrs. Carmichael.

Regan had said rather grimly at the breakfast table that morning, "We're losing a lot this time, aren't we, Mrs. C?"

Mrs. Carmichael didn't so much as look at the breakfast table. "Mind your own Ps and Qs, or you'll find yourself going the same way, Miss Regan."

"No fear!" said Regan, getting up. "I know what's what. I'll go do the fireplaces, shall I? We'll need the warmth today."

She had given Susan a grin on the way out, jerking her thumb at the footmen who had just bumbled their way into the kitchen in step. That had chilled Susan more than the footmen themselves, who, if unpleasantly unsettling, at least seemed to be unaware of their own oddness.

Regan, fresh from the death of her closest co-worker, merely seemed to find the threat laughable instead of awful. Was she so used to death that the feeling faded quickly, or was that something else that the curse seemed to do as well? Susan wasn't sure, but she found that the thought made her colder than the dense frigidity of the day.

If the day was frigid, however, at least it seemed to go by quickly. It went by so very quickly, as a matter of fact, that if Susan had had a watch, she would have been consulting it often throughout the day. She was never able to catch any of the clocks doing anything unto-ward, but she would have sworn that the time that passed was considerably less than they claimed it to be. Nobody in the manor seemed able to settle to one thing happily or consistently, either; the footmen were always on the move, Mrs. Carmichael was best avoided unless Susan wanted to be given tasks that weren't her job and took up more of her time than she was willing to spend on useless endeavours, and Regan was hard to sight altogether.

She could have made a concerted effort to find the master alone and work out exactly what he had done to make the footmen make off with Brennan—not to mention see about getting the key that would now save one less life if they managed to use it as it ought to be used—but Susan found one thought buzzing in her mind as the day drew quickly on, and that was that she needed to confer with Emmett. She could have waited until night, with how quickly the day seemed to be passing, but there was a sense of urgency she couldn't displace, and when Susan caught sight of Emmett passing along the hall and turning down the right-hand side of the manor, she went after him. She wasn't as familiar with the sunny side of the manor as she was the misty left, but at least there was sufficient light by which to keep sight of Emmett. There would also, if she were not mistaken, be a room somewhere along the hallway that she could conveniently drag him into.

She wasn't able to catch up with him: Emmett, with his long legs and silent stride, could cover a significant amount of ground when he so chose to, and Susan didn't dare call out to him on what was ostensibly the master's side of the manor. It was probably bad enough to be discussing things relating to the curse closer to him.

Sunlight sparkled through the windows as Susan passed them, spangling the inside of the manor. She didn't remember seeing these particular windows from the outside of the manor: she was sure she would have remembered the height and the gorgeously bevelled edges of them. Light danced off her vision when she glanced ahead again, and she nearly lost sight of Emmett.

She was curious now. Where was he going, and why was he so concerned about getting there that he hadn't noticed that she was following him? Or had he noticed and simply wanted a quiet place in which to talk to her? If that was the case, she thought, grinning, he would get his wish.

Still, Susan wasn't quite convinced that he was fully aware of what he was doing or where he was going—she was also quite certain that the manor itself was opening up new space that hadn't been around in the right side of the manor before. The hallway and the windows were vaguely familiar, but she had never seen the staircase that Emmett was now headed toward, and there was a feeling of magic and possibility to the hallway that suggested the manor was opening again.

It was possible that Emmett had explored this area so thoroughly that he had discovered the narrow set of stairs all but hidden behind a large, potted palm, but Susan was more inclined to think that they had once been a series of coloured lights playing on the wall opposite a stained-glass window and had now been made three dimensional by whatever type of magic—or curse—that was currently running through the manor. Moreover, he moved up those stairs in more of a dreamlike fashion than she cared for, and she had no compunction in hurrying after him and taking the stairs after he had gone a mere flight up, though she matched her footsteps to his.

After that were more stairs than Susan felt should have been able to fit into the manor without coming out on the roof, and she fell into the routine of step after step, still keeping in time with Emmett's steps above her. By now she was certain that he was asleep, and when she began to be aware that she could hear only her own footsteps instead of hers overlaid by his, she hurried to catch up with him. A thin door with a line of light around it stood at the top of the stairs, and Susan opened it gently, letting herself into an attic that was vast, draughty, and far dimmer than she had expected it to be, given the light that had shone around the crack of the door.

It lent a nightmarish quality to the air around her as she moved through the attic, passing heaps of trunks and drunkenly leaning furniture, feeling her way forward more than seeing it. Passing by a cluttered trunk in the gloom, Susan touched one of a group of dusty toy wooden horses atop it that made her think achingly of the horselords in general and Brennan in particular. They had no feeling of magic to them, so she left them behind with a pang and went on through the darkness, finding that the floorboards moved beneath her feet a little too much for comfort.

She took care to keep a single, more solid board beneath her feet moving forward, wary of plummeting through the floor, but that one still moved enough to feel as though the edges were cutting into her feet.

Then she caught sight of Emmett again, outlined in light from somewhere outside of the attic—perhaps another window?—and Susan felt enlivened again. In fact, she felt enlivened enough that it now seemed to her that she had been walking in something of a dream herself, as caught up as she had been in following Emmett. Without quite thinking about it, her feet slowed as she moved across the boards.

Someone, quite distinctly, said, "Susan!"

Ahead of her, Emmett had turned around, and Susan saw his eyes focus on her without any trace of sleepiness.

"Ah," she said, relief washing over her. "So you are awake."

"Did you think you could sneak up on me?"

"I've managed it once or twice," Susan said, grinning. Later, she would probably be annoyed at how easily Emmett had duped her; for now, she was simply happy not to find him standing at the top of a staircase with a single step between him and a bad fall. "How did you find that staircase, by the way?"

"It's always been there," he said, backing away from her. "Just like this."

Susan took one step forward, the floorboards hard-edged beneath her feet, and felt the coolness of too much air all around her. She took another step forward before her brain caught up with the sensation that she had passed through an opening a few steps ago without being able to see any such thing around her, and froze. She closed her eyes against Emmett's curious, quizzical look, and focused on the feeling of what was around her rather than the sight of it.

"Susan," said his voice.

Susan opened her eyes and saw truly.

She had stopped just short of a very long drop, unfamiliarly long skirts weighing down all around her and the air dusty and perilous with floating motes. With the length of her skirt, she couldn't see what solid thing was beneath her feet, but she knew that it wasn't big enough to extend past those skirts; she could see, with disastrous clarity, the marbled black and white floor of the foyer far below her. If she had a guess, she would have said that she had walked out on a balcony that had once existed in some sort of attic in a floor she had never visited before, and that now only consisted of a few protruding boards as the others rotted away around them.

Susan felt a hard edge of something toward the side of her left foot, felt another hard edge cutting into the ball of her right foot. Her arms came out instinctively for balance, sweeping through sunlight and dust motes, and the Emmett in front of her—the Emmett who stood on nothing and consisted of nothing—smiled mockingly and then disappeared.

FOURTEEN

"**B**other you!" Susan said quietly, though she wasn't sure if she said it to herself or to the ghostly version of Emmett that she had evidently been following. She added ruefully, "Or bother me, I suppose."

Time was certainly shortening, and Susan herself, not Mr. Oswald, was manifestly the next target of the curse. She hadn't expected as much, but she probably should have guessed when she wasn't able to catch up with ghostly Emmett.

She said again, "Bother," and then, "Emmett will never let me live this down."

It was no use considering the fact that she might not live long enough for Emmett to reproach her about anything; Susan simply considered the weight of her half-skirts, the almost empty space in front of her, and the distinct crackling that she could hear somewhere around the region of her feet.

Whatever was beneath her feet, it was breaking, and even if she could turn around without losing her precarious balance, a swift, careful look over her shoulder showed her that she was a good eight feet away from the opening into the attic area. So Susan took a brief moment to centre herself, another to focus on the corded line that emerged from the massive ceiling-rose above and supported the monstrous edifice of the chandelier below, and launched herself into space.

She was barely in time; as Susan sprang outward and a little upward, the brittle support beneath her feet fell away. She saw it fluttering away toward the floor in a brief, jerky flash of movement that was torn from her as her fingers closed around the cord of the chandelier and jolted her to a stop.

Braided cord slipped and burned her fingers, but Susan grimly held on. She felt the tautness of it tremble and vibrate as the three drop-levels of sparkling lights below her tinkled and swayed at the motion. When that motion had abated enough to allow her to safely descend, Susan let herself down hand over hand until she was at the highest, smallest level of the chandelier.

It only took a little bit of wriggling to lower herself over the edge of that sharp and metallic circle. Susan did so, clinging for a terrifying moment to thin metal that dipped terrifyingly with her weight, and was glad to reach safely for the corded mainstay of the chandelier once again.

At the second level, which was too big to lower herself over while still clinging to the braided cord but still too small for Susan to slip through the struts of the Catherine-wheel of a setting, she took a moment to look down. She saw Emmett standing just out of the cover of the landing, as if his feet were rooted to the black-and-white marbled floor, staring up at her, and felt a flush of relief that was as ridiculous as it was useless.

She was still too far from the floor; if any part of the chandelier broke, both it and Susan would be dashed to the floor as comprehensively and effectively as Helfer had been a few days ago. Still, it was somehow nice to have Emmett there, and Susan felt the warmth of that presence as she edged toward the curving metal edge of the second chandelier level and lowered herself over it.

She allowed herself to swing gently for a few moments before she released her hold and again caught at the central rope of the chandelier, her fingers burning and aching all at once. It was by no means easy work from here, but she rather thought she'd got through the worst of it. Fortunately, the lowest level of the chandelier was so large that the struts were both big enough to slip through and well enough girded to make her sure that they wouldn't easily break beneath her fingers and send her plummeting to the hard floor below.

On the other hand, as she lowered herself through the struts with her legs following carefully, Susan could feel the quivering of the entire structure. A few flakes of ceiling plaster fluttered down and into her eyes, and she had to stop where she was to blink them out, aware of what they meant and how little time she had to do what she needed to do.

When her eyes were clear, Susan risked a glance at Emmett: he hadn't moved, and his expression hadn't changed. His eyes were still fixed on her, in fact. She had a brief, desperately amused thought that at last she had broken him, but there was no time to allow herself to think it because there was an ominous creaking from above that suggested the chandelier would not long put up with the kind of usage to which she was subjecting it.

She let her legs down easily and tightly and said a sharp, "Out of the way!" to Emmett, who had at last moved, as though he wanted to stand below for her to drop into his arms. It was still too far from the floor to risk, though Susan would have risked anything else but the chandelier dropping on Emmett.

She moved herself gently back and forth, swinging the chandelier as she went, and the creaking increased. Susan felt the entire chandelier drop by a couple of centimetres, and began to swing more vigorously. No time for taking it easy; she would have to get as good of a pendulum as she could and catch hold of the moulding above the entryway box that had once housed Brennan.

Susan released her hold on the chandelier as soon as she thought she had enough height, and snatched wildly at the moulding as her fingers punched into the wall. She had it, but not for long. Her right hand lost its grasp a moment later, and Susan let herself fall in rather more disorder than she'd hoped for. It was a matter of a mere few feet; Susan landed well enough and rose from the crouch she'd fallen in, clutching her stinging right hand to her chest as she turned, apprehensive about the chandelier.

As she watched, the chandelier swung once more in a graceful arc, quivered, and detached from the ceiling. It seemed to float for a moment before it descended in serried ranks of lights to cascade all over the floor, flinging crystals into Susan's shins and chest. She instinctively covered her face with the crook of her arm, and when the sharp tinkle of crystals ceased, took that arm away to see Emmett striding across the floor through the wreckage.

Susan began, "Before you get annoyed at me, lummox—" but didn't have the opportunity to finish the sentence before he whisked her off the step and into an almost painfully crushing hug.

She made a small, inadvertent squeak in his ear and managed to breathe out, "You'll never guess what I found, lummox!" before Emmett pulled back, allowing her to take in a breath, then promptly stole that breath again by kissing her soundly.

Susan momentarily forgot about ghosts and news alike, and it wasn't until Emmett reluctantly drew back once again that she caught sight of an open-mouthed Regan over his shoulder.

Regan smirked and said only, "Lucky!" before she sauntered away, leaving Susan to wonder whether her luck was counted in being thoroughly kissed in the foyer after a near-death escape or if the escape itself merited such an appellation.

She pulled Emmett back up onto the small receiving area by the double front doors, where it could look as though they were passing the time as lovers if any of the other staff members passed through, then opened her mouth to tell him exactly what she had discovered while chasing ghosts. She was too late.

"You said you weren't going to fling yourself into the void again any time soon," Emmett murmured, resting one hand against the wall behind her and ducking his head just enough to speak in her ear.

Susan would have been distracted by this delightful nearness if it hadn't been for the news that had been waiting to tumble over her lips. As it was, she managed to look up at him before she quite realised how close he really was, and finding his face closer than expected, found herself saying, "I wasn't planning on it, but I didn't have a lot of choice. It wasn't too far of a leap, after all!"

"From below, it looked pretty far," he said grimly.

"Oh well, it was a close thing," Susan admitted, chuckling at the remembrance of that shock of pure electricity when she caught the centre rope of the chandelier after she'd thought she'd missed it. "At any rate, I wasn't doing it out of anything other than pure necessity this time, and that's not the important thing, anyway."

Emmett's jaw flexed and relaxed, but all he said was, "What is the important thing?" and there was amusement on his face, too.

"The important thing is that there's a part of the manor that neither of us have ever been in," she said. "An attic sort of place—you know, stuffed with old trunks and clothing and creepy old toys."

"The sort of place that might have spare furniture lying around from people who were caught up in a curse without knowing it."

"Exactly!" Susan said triumphantly. "If we can make our way back up there somehow, we might be able to find Miryum, Curran, and Katrina."

"Did you see—"

"No," said Susan, the twin frisson of adrenaline and discovery losing somewhat of their brightness. "I didn't see Brennan there; I was concentrating on not losing you."

"Me?"

"The ghosties apparently knew I wanted a word with you," Susan said. "One of them did such a good job of striding along the halls that I followed with all the guile of a lamb. Terribly embarrassing!"

"Why were you trying to find me?"

"The days are getting shorter."

Emmett stared at her. "What do you mean by that?"

"Exactly what I say," she said. "I think the curse is speeding up toward the end of the story. I was probably meant to be a nice little chapter ending for it."

"How do you know the days are getting shorter?"

"First, it was just a feeling—from yesterday, as a matter of fact," admitted Susan. "But did you notice that while we've been here talking, the suns have gone down from the upper window to the lower one?"

Emmett looked sharply to his left and made a small sound of frustration. "It's already nearly dinner time."

"Exactly," said Susan. "And it's only just been lunch. The story has begun to move more quickly, and so has time. We have all the information it thinks we should have, I suppose."

"The curse must be looking for another chapter heading," Emmett said slowly.

"Yes, that's what I thought. I think we'd better give it one, since this one didn't work out."

His eyes lit with an amused glow. "What did you have in mind?"

"Something I'd probably better not talk too much about," Susan said slowly. "But I suspect I need another word with the master."

"Any particular reason?" Emmett's voice was particularly expressionless, but his shoulders were stiff.

"None in particular, no—just a lot of little things that don't make sense. I'd like to make sense of them if I can, and I tend to think that whatever I learn will push the curse onward a bit."

Emmett opened his mouth to reply—and Susan rather thought it was open in protest—but before he could do so, Mrs. Carmichael's voice said in tones of outrage, "Miss Susan, are you responsible for this mess?"

"I don't really think I can be held accountable for chandeliers falling down!" Susan protested, peering out from behind Emmett, who had turned to face the housekeeper. That was nonsense, of course, since she had in fact been responsible for it; but unless Regan had told the whole of the tale, Mrs. Carmichael should have no reason for thinking any such thing.

The woman made a small noise of irritation and swept back around toward the still-swinging doors of the lower hallway. "The footmen will deal with it! Kindly don't make any more mess throughout the day!"

"Do you know, I'm quite certain she knows everything, but she's not willing to admit it?" Susan said softly to Emmett. "Because then she'd probably have to admit that she could do something about the deaths in the manor. She's the one who stopped me going after Helfer when I might have done a bit of good, at any rate; I don't think she likes to think about the things she doesn't do. It's easier to snap about messes and things in places they shouldn't be."

"I don't like thinking about it either," Emmett said, with some finality. "Try not to die as you keep the bride safe. I'll do the same for the master until the next chapter comes about."

"I'd rather you didn't die, either, lummox," Susan told him, with an undercurrent of bitterness for the empty space in the entryway behind them that should have held Brennan, no matter his form.

"I'll take care," he said, gripping her arm in firm assurance and then releasing her. "You don't have to go to the master tonight. You can just come to me; that would be enough to rattle the curse."

"I've got the feeling that it won't quite do," said Susan, her thoughts far away and moving swiftly. "Not to worry, lummox; we'll be out of it before we know it. Then everything will go back to normal."

And Emmett, with his eyes on her face, simply asked, "Will it?"

Susan didn't quite remember the rest of the day in detail, but she did remember that it seemed to move very swiftly, and when she found herself in the suite with Janet after dinner, she wasn't surprised. Janet seemed to have withdrawn into herself even more than she had the day previous, as if withering from the silent force of Susan's mistrust of her.

Susan might have tried to mend the discomfort if it wasn't for the niggling thoughts of annoyance whenever she remembered Janet turning the subject away from what she'd been doing in the halls when she ought to have been meeting with the master. Or perhaps it was because she had a very good idea of what the bride had really been up to.

Janet didn't seem to be in any mood for reconciliation, at any rate. After she had washed and climbed into bed in her underthings with the hound padding around on the bed to get comfortable, she turned her face to the wall, reading her little book. Susan, who hadn't had to help the bride, suspected that the other woman had gone to bed in her underthings instead of her night things in order to be able to more easily roam the halls after slipping on an overdress.

That being the case, Susan didn't sleep, though she thought that Janet might have done. She was still watching dancing shadows on the walls through her eyelashes when Janet sat up in bed as though still asleep and then seemed to shake herself awake. She climbed stealthily from her bed, casting more than one look toward the recumbent Susan, and redressed herself as quietly as possible.

She lingered by the dressing table for longer than Susan would have expected, while the hound waited at the door, then seemed to hesitate for a moment longer before she picked up her necklace and threw it over her head as well. She left with the hound while Susan remained, still watching the shadows on the walls.

"I wonder," said Susan to those shadows. "I really do wonder!"

She had neglected to consider how much more quickly time was passing than it had been a couple of days ago, and consequently, when she rose and padded out into the hallway in bare feet and her sleep breeches with a tunic over the top for warmth, the moon was well and truly out, and most of the fog had cleared away from the right side of the manor.

There was a light around the door of the master's room when she passed it, but Susan rather thought that she would like to see Emmett first—if only to tell him that she had come to see him first. As much as she disliked the uncomfortable feeling of being at odds that lay between herself and Janet, Susan couldn't help remembering the commlinked version of her own face telling her that she and Emmett were teetering on the brink of disaster and misunderstanding, and she found that she had more energy to fix the one than the other.

She found herself moving more swiftly than quietly along the right wing; she slowed down, cautious of what might be found in the manor now that it seemed to be getting more lively by the night, and had just moved past one of the suits of armour that lined this particular part of the hallway when she caught sight of the open section ahead, bathed in moonlight and perfectly beautiful. She froze with a breath caught in her throat, the image imprinting itself on her eyes: Emmett with one arm around Janet as if he'd caught her, and Janet on tiptoes, stretching as high as she could, to kiss him on the cheek.

She had been punched in the stomach several times in her career, but Susan felt that she had never been so thoroughly deprived of her breath as she was now. She wheeled about before she was aware of what she was doing, and started back down the hall, making for she knew not where, so long as it wasn't there. She didn't stop walking until she was back at the intersection of the hallway between the left and right wings, and there Susan hesitated, regret deep within her.

She could have walked forward coolly and said good evening to them both, just to see how they reacted. She could have made it obvious that she was there, or at least tried to let Emmett know she was safe, and about her work—as he ought to be about his instead of putting his arm around Janet and letting her kiss him.

Instead, she'd run away like a child.

"Bother," muttered Susan to herself. It was no good turning around and going back now—no good doing anything but going to find the master in order to bring about some good from this quickly-shortening night.

She was so distracted by her thoughts of Emmett and the necessity of finding the master that it took some time for her to notice, as she hesitated on the cusp of the left wing of the manor, that the master's brooding room still had a faint light outlining its door. There was a momentary lull to the dull misery of her mind, because here was something she knew how to do. Susan put her hand to the doorknob and entered the room. The master's eyes were fixed on the door when she slipped into the room, and Susan saw the hope that had flared in them disappear again.

"Oh, it's you," he said, his head dropping so that his sigh whispered into his chest along with his pointed blue-black beard. "I thought you were Janet."

"I'd like to know what you mean by quarrelling with her all the time!" Susan said, in some exasperation, understanding all at once. Janet must have come to Emmett directly from the master, and in need of comfort. "What's she doing out there in the hallways when she could be in here with you?"

"I never say the right thing," the master said morosely. He seemed more weary than she had seen him before. "And it was going so well at the start! Then I tried to warn her without warning her, and everything went sort of sideways."

"It's probably the curse, not you," Susan said, giving in to pity. She felt rather tired suddenly, but neither her tiredness nor her misery were the master's fault, and it wouldn't help to take things out on him. "We're having a bit of trouble with that ourselves."

The master's eyes fixed on her. "You're not going to—you're going to keep her safe, aren't you?"

"Of course," said Susan, though she added decidedly, "I'm going to keep everyone safe. All the ones that are left, at any rate."

The master smiled as though he couldn't help it, and Susan came to the realisation that he'd taken her comment as a comfort— or perhaps even as a promise. "Thank you," he said. "No one usually cares if I'm safe or not."

"That was probably bound to happen after the first couple of wives died around you," she pointed out.

"Oh," said the master, his mouth drooping just slightly. "Yes, that's fair."

Susan surveyed him for a moment or two before she said, "You seem to be more downhearted than usual tonight. Will it cheer you up if I'm very honest with you?"

The look he directed at her pierced her heart with its familiarity. It could have been Brennan there looking at her with mingled suspicion and hope. "I don't know yet," he said.

"Don't worry, it won't hurt you," she said, through the ache in her heart. "I want you to give me the key."

He stared at her as if he hadn't quite heard. "You want the key?"

"Yes. I have people I'd like to get out of here. I'd take you, too."

He sat in thought for longer than Susan expected, and when he looked up, she thought his eyes glittered with tears. "I can't," he said. "I wish I could, but I can't."

"Don't tell me that you actually gave her the key?"

"I had to," he said, shrugging and settling back against the leather couch back. "There was nothing else for it after the footman died."

"That's unfortunate."

The master said unexpectedly, "I wouldn't have given it to you anyway. At least, I don't think I would have. We'll see how well it turns out, I suppose."

"Yes, I suppose so," Susan said, her mind bright and angry. If that was the case, she'd better pinch the key as soon as possible: Janet was kissing Emmett in the hallways, which meant that there was a very great risk of her betraying the master as far as the curse was considering things. "Now was probably not the best time."

"It wasn't now, it was last night," the master said, tilting his head back in weary surprise. "After she asked me about the footmen. Tonight, I was just trying to...well, warn her, I suppose."

"That is very...unexpected," said Susan, sitting down next to him. "Last night, you say?"

"Time doesn't really matter anymore," the master said through a yawn; then his head seemed to slide helplessly across the leather and rested against her shoulder. "Nothing matters. No way out but death anyway."

"Goodness!" said Susan blankly, staring down at that tousled head. "What are you doing?"

If she had had to guess, she would have said he'd been dosed with lilly-pilly oil—and perhaps he had, but she couldn't see Janet doing any such thing if she had gotten into a quarrel with the master. Susan stared at him for an incredulous few moments longer before she prodded him firmly in the shoulder.

"You can't sleep there," she said. "That's reserved for a very large lummox."

"Oh," he said thickly, trying to raise his head. "I fell asleep again.

Have to get back to work before...before the master notices. You... distract him. Won't tell him we didn't sleep in the walls tonight."

"Oh no," said Susan, her brain bright and buzzing and wild with sudden realisation as several things all made sense at once. "*I wasn't always like this*", he had told her a few days ago, and she had taken it as a lament for how he had eventually ceased to care for people or deaths. She said again, "Oh no! You're not the original master, are you? The original one who was cursed by his father, I mean."

"Master isn't supposed to die," he said, as though he were trying to figure out why his tongue didn't work. "Safest place. That's what they told me."

Susan moved away, and the master slid bonelessly to the seat of the couch and blinked drowsily up at the ceiling. He laughed in a bitter, mumbling sort of way. "Safest place to watch people die."

"So I gather," she said, far too breathless with her own sudden knowledge and worries to be very much concerned about his state. "You're one of the original servants, aren't you?"

"I wasn't..." he licked his lips. "I wasn't always like this. Once, my hair was red and I had...I had a violin."

"Yes," she said patiently. There was too much at stake to rush over this. "You were a footman? Or maybe the butler?"

"I was a good footman," he said, his eyes fluttering shut. "Shouldn't have...agreed to be anything else."

Susan shook him, but he wouldn't wake again. There was a constant, deep movement to his chest that comforted her that he wasn't in any danger of overdose—just a good, long sleep—and there was nothing good to be done by sitting in the room with him, so she left him there. She didn't like the thought of Janet coming back in to see her with the master's head on her shoulder—or, worse, Emmett.

Susan didn't stop to catch her breath until she was back in the suite she shared with Janet. Then she let that breath out in a small, shaky huff and removed the handwritten book from beneath Janet's pillow and sat down on one of the small, spindly chairs that accompanied the small table.

She skimmed through the pages she hadn't yet looked at, fingers moving gently and constantly through the pages. She had a very good idea of what was going on now, but she felt that she would like to confirm it before she went too far in what she did. There was a time for swift action, but that time had not yet come; now was time to compare what she thought she knew with the only form of confirmation she had.

And so Susan read. She read until she reached the last page of the little hand-written book, and then right down to the last paragraph.

It was no use. The master had gone, his rage and bitterness sinking into the walls and the floor and the ceiling until the entire manor seemed to vibrate with his malice. Some say that he sold his soul to curse his son; others that he haunts the manor still. All that is certain is that whenever the master of the manor takes a wife, there's only one story to be told, and that story always ends in death. There is no aging here, and no true passage of time. There is only life and death; promises broken, trust unkept. Mistrust and infidelity. And so the same circle repeats itself, over and over.

Susan put down the book again, her hands shaking slightly. Then it was true. Everything she had understood in an instant when she knew that the master was not the master, and only a recurring character in his own right, was true.

She couldn't tell Emmett, of course—not unless she wanted him to fall into the same kind of danger as she had no doubt already brought upon herself. In fact, she would probably be lucky if she made it down the hallway again without being tricked into falling over or through something.

"I'm going to have to watch those suits of armour tomorrow," she muttered to herself, and grinned something of a sickly grin. "And the servants."

The master would soon forget again—if he had even been aware of what he was saying in the first place—and out of all of the characters in the curse, he was probably the safest. Nor had Susan made him say aloud anything that would compromise him to the manor —for the manor itself must be the source of the curse.

There had never been a master cursed by his father, who then went on to live for centuries, going through bride after bride as each one died, a sop to the curse. No, once upon a time, there had been an angry and insecure man, who had been so irrationally fearful that his wife was unfaithful that he had thrown her out of the manor with their son. Over the years he had become as much of a ghost as the ones that no doubt resided there already, whispering temptations and manipulations and lies into the ears of the new master— his son—and mistress until they, too, played out the same inevitable cycle of mistrust, betrayal, and death. And when that son had died by the curse, the story had simply picked a new master and begun again, and again, and again.

It was possible that the father hadn't even died; it was possible that he had simply mouldered away in body and mind until his body was what could be called dead, and his spirit of rank bitterness infected the entire manor. Susan had in her time seen chairs burned and carriages broken apart because the malice of their owners had seeped in until they were corrupted and dangerous, but she had never heard of an entire manor growing itself into a curse.

The manor itself, engorged with the hate of its first master who never seemed to die, must have grown in around itself as it played out the same story over and over again with new players as each died. And with each death, the manor must have grown stronger. It fed itself on magic and death until the manor and the curse were one and the same—or the one was merely a means of growth to the other.

The manor was now, in short, an amalgamation of magic and malice that had grown rules and regulations that could never be kept to the satisfaction of its spirit, and that could only be undone, Susan feared, by working within those rules until it was too late for the manor to discover that it had been undone.

The curse, she was convinced—and, by extension, the manor— was close to mindless.

The staff who upheld all of its rules, on the other hand, were not, and Susan was quite certain that the difficulty would be with them. She had no desire to harm anyone or prevent anyone from escaping the cursed manor, but she would also have no qualms about preventing them from harming anyone who was with her when she tried to get out.

Susan woke into a bright, cool morning with an almost terrifyingly clear view from the windows of the suite. When she approached the windows to take it in, she saw distant mist around trees that faded into an indistinct miasma.

"How terrifyingly apropos," she murmured to herself. "The appearance of clarity, but no real use to be had of it."

Luckily for Susan, however, she knew exactly what it was she was supposed to do. The first thing she needed to do was steal the key that the master had given to Janet to prevent the manor opening itself up before she was ready for it. Then she needed to find Emmett and do something she would very much rather not do in order to give him the best chance of understanding exactly what was going on. At the very least, she could make sure that even if he didn't understand, he was safe long enough for everyone to get out of the manor.

Janet woke as Susan was laying out her clothes, and seemed to stare at the ceiling for quite some time in an aimless sort of way before she sat up. Susan waited for her to do so before she passed her a cup of tea and enquired placidly, "Any news on the key?"

"Oh, that," said Janet, shrugging one shoulder and looking away. "I don't think that's a real thing after all. The comments in the book must have been talking about a meeting of several different circumstances that open up the manor for everyone to escape."

Susan said, "Ah. The master didn't give you anything over the last few nights, then?"

"The master," Janet said fiercely, "is an idiot and a madman."

"Undoubtedly. But that wouldn't necessarily prevent him giving you a key."

"I told you that the key isn't real!" said Janet, hunching her shoulders. "He can't give me something that's not real."

"I see," said Susan, with a small but growing dread. "I wonder what would be the key to opening up the manor, in that case? If the notes are correct, there's no way out of the manor without going through it with the key."

Janet's eyes met hers, briefly. "I suppose it would have to be something like trust, or faithfulness. Something to make the curse think we're worthy of escape before it opens up to let us in."

"There is that," Susan said, nodding.

She didn't for a moment believe Janet, and she wasn't sure if the feelings she was struggling with were disappointment or a certain sour, vindicated certainty. One thing she was certain of was that when the manor opened, it was for no good purpose. She was quite certain that she had been in what the book referred to as the "heart of the manor", and it had always been a bad situation when it did happen. If the manor opened to them while pretending it was a way out, Susan had no doubt it was merely in order to test—or perhaps break—the bride. And it seemed that Janet had already made her decision.

That decision, at present, seemed to be to exclude both Susan and the master from any part in her plans; if last night's tableau with Emmett was any indicator, Janet was now making plans of quite a different kind of escape.

Janet, it would seem, was not a terribly good liar—and that, thought Susan suddenly, was very interesting.

"Trust as the key to escape really would be a novel idea," she said meditatively. She had no real desire to trust Janet, and no real reason to, either. But if it came to a choice between trusting Janet and trusting the manor, there was really no other choice to be made. "That gets everyone together in the same place and working together, even if not everyone knows the right way through the situation. Then if there's only a few minutes to get out once the manor opens, everyone is all together and ready."

"Not everyone likes to work together," Janet said, rather sombrely. "No matter how hard you try—even if one of you knows the right doors to go through to get where you're going."

"Well," said Susan, with a voice that couldn't have been sharper if she'd tried to make it so, "I suppose you'll just have to make sure that you're with the right person when the manor opens up, won't you?"

Janet's eyes dropped, and Susan wondered if she'd mistaken the sudden glow of understanding that lit them. She hoped not.

"I see," the bride said quietly. "I suppose I will."

FIFTEEN

The key was exactly where Susan expected it to be—wedged between two of the little phials that Janet had hidden outside the window of the water chamber and wrapped in a handkerchief to prevent the shininess of it being too attractive to a passing bird. She stole it that morning while Janet was with the master in the breakfast room, and found herself hoping that Janet had left it where it was for the very purpose of being pinched. That was probably too much to hope for, even if Janet had understood her this morning, but the manor was certainly feeling loose and somewhat unravelled that morning as she took the servants stairway back down to the lower level.

Whether or not Janet had left the key for her, the giving of it a couple of nights ago and the stealing of it this morning had evidently had an effect on both the story and the condition of the manor. The hallways felt soft and pliable around her, and as Susan walked, she could hear the rustling of things—or ghosts—within the walls. Even the light seemed to have dimmed into a soft patina over the façade that the manor presented to its players.

All Susan had to do today was survive—and tip the fluid uncertainty of the manor over into the last part of the story: the escape attempt. At the very least, Emmett should be safe. Janet would be sure to bring him along with her when she knew that it was time. Susan was less sure about the master, but there would be time, she thought anxiously, to let him know that he needed to be with the others when everything began. At least, she hoped there would be time—time, in fact, would have to be made. Since he was also a victim of the curse and not its perpetrator, he shouldn't be left behind to his fate any more than Janet ought to be.

The ticklish question was, was the master just as likely to try and keep the status quo as the staff were? Susan didn't think so, but she had no guarantee that he wasn't. That meant that she would have to keep him in the dark until the actual moment of escape. Emmett, on the other hand, undoubtedly needed to be given as much of a warning as could be given without informing the manor that he had been given it. And since the manor, so obviously intent on offering the most damaging solutions to the problems it presented, was unlikely to be satisfied with something so benign as a simple conversation, Susan would have to offer something more sensational.

In furtherance of that goal, Susan was particularly wary of both stairs and being too close to Emmett for the entire morning. She narrowly escaped falling down the stairs when one of the boards was unaccountably loose, and narrowly avoided being alone in the kitchen with Emmett by the simple expedient of popping her head through the door and, finding him there, immediately withdrawing it and swiftly making herself scarce. By the time the bell rang for her to attend Janet back to her suite—or to wherever it was that she wished to go—Susan had successfully avoided an increasingly dogged Emmett a number of times and avoided disaster several more times.

She wended her way carefully back down the hallways, avoiding suits of armour with far-too-sharp weapons and anything that could possibly fall down and injure her as she walked, and arrived at the breakfast room just in time to see Mrs. Carmichael removing herself from that room with an empty tray tucked tidily against her apron.

She nodded a small curtsey, and the housekeeper sniffed and bustled away, leaving Susan to enter the room alone. She found

Janet within, looking rather small and frozen, her hands clutched in her lap around the pendant of her necklace.

"It's all gotten quite messy, hasn't it?" said Janet, as she approached.

"Night time roamings will do that," Susan said, for the benefit of the manor and anyone else listening. "Sometimes it's better to stay in your suite to avoid the mess—not to mention people you shouldn't be meeting with when you're married."

Janet gazed up at her with enough blankness to make Susan feel distinctly uncomfortable. "Is it?"

"Yes," she said. "In fact, I should think it's going to get very messy as soon as you get back to the suite."

"It's not as...messy as it needs to be," Janet said. She seemed to have woken up now, her eyes sharp and present.

"Not yet," Susan agreed.

She had the key instead of Janet, and no doubt that was what had stopped the manor from opening entirely, but as soon as she allowed Emmett to catch up with her again, she suspected that things would begin to move very swiftly indeed.

"I really do think that it'll be best if you're in your suite today," she added. Carefully malicious, she added, "You'll only be in the way down here. Oh, and be careful what doors you go through on the way back up, if the hound isn't with you. You never know how messy things are going to get."

"If things get messier, I'll come and find you," Janet said. She hesitated, and added, "I'll bring the others. Later; when it's messier. We should probably stay together if it's going to get more dangerous."

"All right," said Susan. If she was going to play the part of the jealous maid, she might as well do it whole hog. "But don't expect me to dance attendance to you there and back. You seem to have enough people escorting you through the hallways as it is."

"Oh," said Janet, in a small voice. "Yes, I suppose so."

She rose as she spoke, and although she didn't quite meet Susan's eyes, she didn't seem to be able to stop herself looking over her shoulder as the hound followed her out of the room.

Dear me! thought Susan, irritated and impressed in equal measure. It was almost terrifying how easily the manor still prompted her to care for the bride, and how easy it would have been to fall back into that. Perhaps being the jealous maid was just as necessary for her own performance as it was for subterfuge.

She left the room shortly after Janet and fancied that the door to the morning room across the hall was slightly ajar, as if someone had been in the process of exiting and had pushed the door nearly shut once again to escape notice. She didn't allow her eyes to linger, and when Emmett's voice said, "Susan!" from very near by, she felt the delightful prickle of the world coming into the right place around her.

Susan turned her face toward the sound of his voice, and was caught by the arms as Emmett sighed out a breath of either satisfaction or relief. She heard the door to the morning room move just slightly behind her, and caught the faint scent of rosemary and lemon. How delightful! The manor was certainly paying attention —and so, it would seem, was Mrs. Carmichael.

She looked enquiringly up at Emmett, and this time he didn't ask the question; he simply said, "You've been avoiding me." The line between his brows was more curious than it was sorrowful, and as the silence drew out and Susan failed to reply, a certain determination seemed to settle over his face.

Susan would have liked to have replied at once, but she had just then, while looking up into his face, discovered the exact reason she had been putting off this particular part of her day's work until the last moment. Once she did what she had to do here, that would be the end of it. One way or another, everything after this moment wasn't her and Emmett together as a possibility. Whether they lived or died, escaped or were lost within the manor, there was no more *us*, no more disturbingly heart-fluttering kisses in corners. There was no more of the lover Emmett, only the friend Emmett.

The Emmett that she didn't want to lose gazed down at her for just a moment longer and then drew her toward himself.

Susan, breaking herself out of the spell in sheer desperation, said, "I suppose the manor has been playing tricks again."

"Likely," said Emmett, his eyes searching her face. He couldn't have missed the way the manor felt this morning; it was probably why he had been so determined to find her again. "But why now? I don't think I did anything to make it happen."

"Perhaps the curse doesn't like you sneaking around the halls and kissing girls at midnight?" suggested Susan, removing herself from a grip that had suddenly loosened.

Emmett, his colour heightened, rubbed a hand over the back of his neck. "I didn't see you last night."

"Yes, that much was very obvious," Susan said, and she found that she didn't have to act out any of the dryness in her voice. "I was coming to tell you that I was still alive, by the by; you were a bit preoccupied at the time, so I went away again and had a word with the master instead."

Emmett looked up swiftly. "What did he say?"

"Nothing that you need to worry about," Susan said. "He just fell asleep on me."

"Don't let other men fall asleep on your shoulder," said Emmett, as though he couldn't help it.

"Don't go kissing other girls in the hallways," she said to him.

Emmett's breath drew in and out swiftly. "I didn't...I didn't kiss her."

"Don't let other girls kiss you in the hallways, either," she said, with a flash of anger that was far too real for comfort. "I didn't think I'd have to say it, but if you're free enough to tell me what to do, you might like to think about what you've allowed yourself to do!"

"Susan—" He caught at her arm, pulling her gently back toward himself

She hadn't expected to be shaking when it happened. That was the problem about really caring for people who should only ever be fairytale loves—it made things much harder when it came to ending things, because one really cared.

"Don't touch me," she said, pulling away. "You said—we said that we wouldn't get too deep into our parts. That was rule number four. You can't tell me you're not getting too deep into the part when you're taking kisses from the bride in the hallways!"

"It's the manor," he said, the bewilderment in his voice far too raw. "It gets into my head and I find myself doing things and allowing things I shouldn't allow."

Some of those things, thought Susan with a pang, were certainly things she had done.

"I'm tired," she said, and she didn't have to pretend to that, either. "I'm tired, and I don't want to do this anymore. Meet whoever you like in the hallways at night—just make sure you're with them when everything falls apart and it's time to get out, because I won't be coming for you."

She pushed past him and left him where he was without daring to look at his face or listen to anything that he might have said below his breath. Mrs. Carmichael—and hopefully the manor—had heard their fill.

There was a mere blink between pushing past Emmett and another step through the hall, much later in the day. The manor, dark and dangerous around her, seemed to spiral away in all directions with loose threads, and Susan wasn't sure if it was terrifying or exciting. She looked around her and found that she was still in much the same place she had been earlier, but now she was no longer alone in the hall: ahead of her, Mrs. Carmichael stood and watched as the footmen carried trays of plate and utensils into the formal dining room in the left wing.

Susan wasn't sure where the housekeeper had come from—but then, she had only the slightest of recollections of how she herself had come to be exactly here. Time had again started moving more swiftly within the manor. She felt as though the housekeeper, in some indefinable way, was just waiting for her. Never one to step back from a challenge, Susan continued down the hall and stopped beside the woman.

"It will be a big dinner tonight," said Mrs. Carmichael significantly, nodding toward the left wing of the manor and the footmen with their trays.

"So I see," she said. "The master must have something planned."

"There's always a plan," said Mrs. Carmichael, with an unpleasant smile. "We'll see what happens."

"If you're out here, who's cooking the dinner?" enquired Susan, reacting instinctively to the smile. "Shouldn't you be watching your pots?"

"My pots are none of your concern," the housekeeper said. "And I *could* ask what you're doing out and about the manor at this time of day, when you should be helping your mistress to dress, but I'll save myself the trouble. You'd best come and sit down with me for a cup of tea, Miss Susan; there are some things you need to hear."

"How delightful!" said Susan promptly. The manor seemed to move and groan around her, and the halls, which had once been entirely absent of magic, now seemed to be threaded with it.

She expected the housekeeper to lead the way into the kitchen; instead, she turned on her heel and headed back into the morning room that looked out on the orchard on the left side of the manor.

A pre-prepared meeting, then, thought Susan, now very much awake and aware. She would have to be very careful. Still, she followed Mrs. Carmichael into the room willingly enough, throwing a glance over at the long windows, which were cloudy and white with far too much mist. The sight of it gave her a chill that the swirling uncertainty of the manor hadn't, and when she sat down at the small table that was set with a tea tray, there was a prickle of exhilaration to her skin.

"Tea?" asked the housekeeper, sitting down firmly opposite her.

It was a question, but it was said with such heavy finality that Susan didn't think it really was one; nor was the teacup that was thrust in her direction given in a way that suggested she was allowed to refuse it.

Susan took it and, without so much as moving her hands, used the teeming threads of magic about the place and promptly switched teacups with Mrs. Carmichael while the woman was cutting cake.

There was no saying that Mrs. Carmichael would try to drug her, of course, but Susan wasn't one to forget the master falling asleep on her with the suggestion of lilly-pilly oil on his breath. She had no desire to end up the same way, especially since the use of such oil was also well-known to be a truth-producing serum in smaller doses.

She accepted a piece of cake from Mrs. Carmichael as well, and fancied that the cake, as much as it had been a screen for Susan in swapping the teacups, had also been a screen for Mrs. Carmichael to try and formulate what she would like to say.

"You'd probably better just come out and say it," she advised, into the heavy silence that fell. "I always do; it's so much better for the digestion!"

"You're making trouble here, and you need to stop before you break things," said Mrs. Carmichael, pleasingly obedient to the challenge. "If you want me to be as honest as that."

"Breaking seems to be the right thing to do with a curse," Susan said, setting her cake down primly and sipping her tea. "Wouldn't you say?"

"You're not breaking the curse; you're ruining the Perfect Result!" the housekeeper snapped. "Meddling with the valet was one thing, but you've been putting your nose into the master's business too, and I won't have it. The Perfect Result is hard enough to get when I only have to worry about the mistress—"

"That's still up for the taking," Susan said. "The mistress hasn't betrayed the master, and they're both still together."

Mrs. Carmichael gave a very faint snort. "Long *that* will last! That little baggage is just waiting for her moment! It's best to nip it in the bud now, while the rest of us are still alive."

Susan gazed at the housekeeper for long enough that the woman began to fidget. "I wonder why you think that."

"She'll do the master harm yet, you'll see." And then, rather contradictorily, Mrs. Carmichael added, "I won't allow it to happen! We've been through this before, and we'll get through it again; if I have to get rid of a few messy pieces, it won't be the end of the world."

"Not for you, at any rate," said Susan, nodding. "That little knock on the head you gave me was pretty close to it, though, and Helfer isn't around any longer."

"I never laid a finger on him," Mrs. Carmichael said resentfully. She didn't, Susan noticed, object to the charge that she had hit Susan over the head. She sipped her tea resentfully, too, and at last added balefully, "I just didn't do anything to save him from the consequences of his own behaviour."

"You stopped me from doing so," said Susan. "And here we are together in the morning room again. It's terribly lowering: I really thought I had you fooled with my byplay with Emmett this morning. I'd guarantee that the manor took it as truth, however, even if you didn't."

"The manor," said Mrs. Carmichael, with a gimlet eye on Susan over the top of her teacup, "doesn't always pick up on these little subtleties. They're for us to look after."

"Yes, the manor wouldn't be able to run anything like as well if it didn't have a steady supply of obedient and driven little minions for one reason and another. I can't for the life of me understand why you'd sell yourselves into slavery of this kind, but no doubt you have your reasons."

"It's not slavery, it's freedom," Mrs. Carmichael said, her cheeks flushed. She looked as young and earnest as Susan had ever seen her. "It's freedom to give up the foolish things that we think we want and let the manor give us what we really need. If you weren't such a little fool, you'd see that it's been trying to give you exactly what you want all along. So long as the bride is here, she can only stop you from getting that."

"Oh yes?" Susan couldn't help the amusement in her voice. "And exactly what is it that I want?"

"I'm not such a fool that I can't see what's happening in my own manor," the housekeeper said. "You've been pining for the master's valet since you came here—I've seen the way you look at him. I've seen the way you kiss him, too, if it comes to that."

"If you know the manor that well, you should also know that it likes to make side-romances with its characters," Susan said. "I can't help it if the manor is trying to push me into things."

"Push you into it, my eye! You've been his shadow since you arrived together—and you've been in love with him for a goodly long time before ever you set foot in the manor, I'll be bound."

"That might be true," Susan said agreeably. "But I don't really know, do I? All I know is that the manor likes to encourage people in my position to fall in love with others with similar positions."

It wasn't quite true: Susan had known—had possibly known since she kamikaze-kissed Emmett the first day they met—that there was something more between them. Or, at the very least, that she would have liked it if there could be something between them. She would never have allowed Emmett into her protective spell or shared a horse with him if she hadn't already been aware of the connection they had. She had simply, for as long as she'd been with the horselords, categorised it as friendship. Perhaps it had been, at the start. And there was still friendship there—it was the biggest reason that Susan had never pursued those intermittent thoughts that had occurred over the years. Her friendship with Emmett was precious, and she hadn't dared to risk losing it by entertaining thoughts that would have made him uncomfortable. While she was able, she had simply enjoyed his company and his warmth.

"He's never going to want you that way once you're out of the manor. You'd best get your fill of kisses in corners now, because that all goes away once you're out of here."

Susan couldn't help the pang of sorrow that shot through her, as much as she disliked it. "We'll have to see once we get out," she said.

She already knew that there would be nothing left of Emmett's feelings once they were out of the manor, but she was far less sure about herself, and there was enough of that traitorous feeling to make Mrs. Carmichael's words cling to the edges of her mind, sticky with desire and longing.

"You can't get out, anyway," added Mrs. Carmichael. "Once the manor has you—once you're a main character—there's no escape but death or producing the Perfect Result."

"Yes, so I've heard," Susan said. "But I'm very good at playing with rules."

"You're not as good as me," Mrs. Carmichael said, with finality. "I've been here since the first few lots of servants, and I know how this place works. If we can't bring about a Perfect Result, we have to wait out the story and try again next time—no one blames us for moving the story along a bit quicker, and you'd best remember that, Miss Susan. Stand against us and the manor, and we'll have to tidy up the edges of the story. If you stay here with us and help, you'll get everything you want and a chance to make the story come out well next time."

There was a fierce longing in her still—a longing that knew Mrs. Carmichael was telling the truth as best she knew it. But Susan also remembered Mr. Oswald, desperately trying to fit herself into the butler she was supposed to play, and she wondered what it would be like to allow herself to sink into the part and pull Emmett thoroughly into his part with her. Even if she could be sure that Janet wouldn't try to steal him, she wondered how long it would be before she and Emmett both were so far subsumed into the will of the house, so far sunk into the roles they were supposed to play, that they slowly forgot each other, themselves, and what love really was.

"And what's the price I'd have to pay for that?" she asked. "Will I have to kill someone? The bride herself?"

Mrs. Carmichael made a comfortable sort of scoffing noise. "What sort of a question is that! Killing people! The very idea!"

"You allowed Helfer to die to bring about your Perfect Result," Susan pointed out. "And you just told me that you'd have to *tidy me up* if I were to refuse you."

"You don't have to do anything," said Mrs. Carmichael, and there was an edge of irritation to her voice. "All you have to do is nothing—look the other way while those of us who know best take care of things."

"Ah," said Susan. "I don't much fancy doing that, if it's all the same to you."

"You'll have very little choice," Mrs. Carmichael said, with an odd light of victory in her eyes. "The bride has already made her choice, and one way or another, you'll not be leaving this room for a good while. If you know what's good for you, it'll be because you decided to help us."

"Do you mean because of what you put in the tea?" asked Susan politely, noting with some pleasure the frozen sort of expression that sank into Mrs. Carmichael's cheeks. "I suppose that would have made rather a difference—that's why I decided not to drink it."

"I saw you drink the tea," said the housekeeper, blinking rapidly. "You drank it all. If you didn't drink it, where did it go?"

"It didn't *go* anywhere," Susan said. "Well, not anywhere out of the room, anyway. I thought it might be better if you drank it instead of me. I swapped the cups with a little trick I learned while at finishing school—you'd be surprised how many well-bred people will try to make you drink things that aren't terribly good for you. By the way, whatever it was seems to be quite slow-working; you've only just started showing signs of the effects now."

This time, the expression passed across the housekeeper's face more slowly, and Susan felt a frisson of satisfaction. Whatever drug or poison Mrs. Carmichael had put in her tea was certainly beginning to take effect.

"I was—how did you know?"

"It seemed like something you'd do," Susan said. "So while you're fighting off the effects of whatever it is you tried to pour down my throat, I'll be off to make sure the bride and the master are safe from whatever it was you were going to do to them to stop the bride from working to the end of her own decisions. You'll excuse me if I lock you in, I'm sure."

She crossed the room, drawing the key she had stolen from Janet from her pocket as she went, and laid her hand on the doorknob as the housekeeper tried to follow her.

"It's too late!" Mrs. Carmichael said, staggering but still venomous. "He's already given her the key, and I guarantee you that the bride is harder-edged than you, Miss Susan!"

"Possibly so," agreed Susan, stopping at the door. "But I don't really think she'll be able to do much without the key, and I have the key."

She waved it happily at the housekeeper.

"That's the thing about Perfect Results and choices that are made by manipulation," she added. "As soon as people know what you're doing, they can fight back. Besides, Perfect Results in general are a lot easier to come by if you're sneaky about things that are supposed to bring out the best in people instead of the worst. You and the manor wanted the master to give the key to his bride after doing everything you could to make sure they distrusted one another; I just evened the field by stealing the key to make sure Janet couldn't do something silly while no one was there to help her see things in a more reasonable light."

"You can't—you can't *do* that!"

"Of course I can!" Susan said, slipping out of the room and speaking into the crack of the door. "That's what the jealous maid is supposed to do, isn't it? Steal things from the mistress and make life hard for her?"

She locked the door to the sounds of stumbling and falling, hardening her heart against going back in. If Mrs. Carmichael had intended to drug Susan, she would by now be unconscious. If she had tried to kill Susan, no doubt she was by now dead. There was nothing very much that Susan could do about that, but she could find and potentially save Emmett, the master, and Janet.

The manor felt cold and bare around her as she moved up the hallway, but Susan paid no attention to it: the manor wouldn't focus too much on her, so long as she was still the jealous maid. And Susan was still very much the jealous maid. So long as everything she did could be framed in those terms, she would be safe—and then perhaps Emmett and Janet and the master would be safe as well.

There was no sign of Mr. Oswald or Regan as she passed through the hallway that was longer than it ought to be. There was no sign of the gardeners, either. That should have been a comforting thing, but Susan, who knew the manor a little better by now, didn't find it comforting at all. She would have preferred to have found the staff moving about as usual—at least until she had found Emmett and Janet and gotten everyone into the changeable, malleable part of the manor that existed between the walls.

The hallway shifted around Susan, curving until it seemed to spiral in without ever meeting itself, and she followed it grimly. She had food in her pockets, along with a key to open whatever doors may present themselves to her, but that wouldn't do her much good if she couldn't find Janet and Emmett. On the other hand, the manor wasn't likely to allow her to die while she had the key on her —it wouldn't be able to guarantee that someone would find her body with the key on it to continue the story.

More, she had to make sure that she got safely out of the manor with both Emmett and Janet, and it would be hard to do that if they missed each other in the hallways and each became lost in the maze.

In other words, it was good to be in the hallways, but it was less useful to be in the hallways alone.

The lights seemed to flicker around her as she moved swiftly along the passageway, but Susan felt that it was a sense of various presences passing between her and the light more than a problem with the gas lighting.

Still, when the light grew momentarily brighter and Susan fancied that she saw ahead the play of shadowed wall against corners of a turning, she moved almost insensibly more quickly, as if the lights really could go out at any moment and that she needed to be within reach of the light source ahead before that happened.

Within a few feet of her goal, Susan saw the first signs, in the fluttering shadows of the wall ahead of her, that someone was approaching along the T-piece with which she was about to intersect. She slowed immediately, feeling the erratic beat of her heart that meant the manor had been urging her along by threading a series of uncomfortable fears through her consciousness.

"Bother you," Susan said aloud, and took a moment to compose herself before she edged toward the left-hand side of the hallway and listened intently.

She heard footsteps, and the faint sound of someone else's breath coming just a bit too quickly. Susan grinned; whoever it was, they were being pushed along by the manor just as quickly as they could walk, and they were in significantly worse condition than Susan was. Thus heartened, she pressed herself to the wall and took a quick look around the edge of the corner to see who it was that the manor had sent her way.

And there in the shifting hallway, dragging the master along by the hand, was Janet.

SIXTEEN

S usan would have laughed if she could have. The memory of Janet on tiptoes to kiss Emmett's cheek was still too fresh and raw in her memory to leave much goodwill, but as much goodwill as she had was pleased to see the master and the bride together as they ought to be. She hadn't quite been able to expect it, but she was glad to see it.

"Good timing," she said, emerging fully from her corridor. "I don't suppose either of you know how to make the manor go in the direction we want it to go?"

"We just got in here ourselves," said Janet. She was flushed and determined, and she hadn't let go of the master's hand. "Straight from the main hallway. I don't know anything about how to navigate in here: I only know what the door we're looking for looks like. Where are the servants?"

"Nowhere that I've been able to see," Susan said. "But Mrs. Carmichael is in the morning room in the outer manor, and she's likely to cause trouble if she wakes up too soon."

The master stared at her. "Wakes up? She's sleeping?"

"Drugged," admitted Susan. "Perhaps dead. She put something in my tea, so I swapped the cups."

Janet's eyes fixed sharply on Susan's face. "Why did she try to drug you?"

"I suppose so that she could do something while I was unconscious," Susan said. "I do think it would be a good idea to be away from the manor before whatever that is happens."

"We don't have far to go," Janet said. "The notes said that there are three doors; red, green, and blue. There will be a motif of a key on all of the ones that we need: I suppose it's a series of interjoined rooms."

"Oh good!" said Susan. "I was hoping that was what you meant this morning."

"And the key will work on all of the doors, from the first to the last," the master added breathlessly. "Once we get to the final door, we'll be out of the manor."

"I see that you both made your decisions," Susan said approvingly. She looked around at the other end of the hallway and saw the hound, which must have been slinking along behind, but no Emmett. Her heart sank. "Where's Emmett? Why isn't he with you?"

The master, his eyes glowing, said, "She came and dragged me out as soon as everything went fuzzy. She said we'd go together."

Janet, her face closed and sharp, said with the faintest whisper of anger, "I'm not going to leave you behind."

"I'm very happy for you, but *where is Emmett?*" demanded Susan. "If you've left him behind...!"

"I couldn't find him," Janet said, and her chin went up. "The manor started shifting and then closed around us as soon as I got the master."

"You mean the manor started changing and you chose to find the master instead."

Janet's eyes met hers and didn't fall. "Yes."

"Then," said Susan, with a white-hot anger that had as much to do with a feeling of vicarious betrayal for Emmett's sake as it did with the fury of being expected to simply leave him behind while the three of them escaped the manor together, "you'll have to wait here while I *go and get him.*"

She took the key from her pocket as she spoke, thrusting it into Janet's hands, and turned on her heel.

"We're not coming back for you!" Janet said sharply, from behind her. "And we can only wait for—bother you, Susan, come back here!"

"Don't follow me if you're not following me," Susan said, loping along the hallway from which Janet and the master had appeared. The hound came with her, as did Janet, her skirts bunched in her hands and panting, the master closer behind. Susan said to her, "Go and make yourself safe with the master if you're going."

"You know I can't get the two of us safely out without leaving you behind! There's only one key!"

"That's your decision," said Susan briefly, finding herself mercifully back out in the open hallway of the outer part of the manor. "I'm just telling you what decision I've made."

"That's not fair!"

Susan took the turning toward the right side of the manor without hesitation. "No, it's just not enjoyable," she said.

"I'm coming," the master said. "I'll help."

"Bother you, too!" Janet said, in the most exasperated tones that Susan had yet heard from her. "Where is he, do you think?"

"This way," said Susan, her heart in her throat. There was an intensely tight pulling of threads around where she was, along with the master and the bride, but the rest of the manor, halfway open and sprawling with magic, seemed to be loosening around the edges like a knot that had been teased apart at the edges to get at the tight core. Despite that, Susan knew where she was going. She was not the expert in following twisty threads that Emmett was, but the thread she was currently following through the manor was one that she would have been able to follow to the ends of the earth.

This thread twisted, wandered, and grew taut as they approached a door toward what Susan suspected to be the front of the manor—if a front existed in this odd, shifting part of the manor. The door itself was solid wood and banded with leather and magic, and it had a keyhole that was at once ridiculously large and entirely impossible to see inside of. It had been painted all over with a dark, light-swallowing red paint.

"Oh!" said Janet, staring at the door. "This is the first door! The first one we have to go through in order to escape, I mean. How is it the first door?"

"I don't suppose it's pure chance," said Susan, who was beginning to develop an amusing idea of how their escape was meant to be accomplished.

Janet might have suggested that the *key* was a right set of circumstances, rather than an actual key, in an attempt to distract Susan's attention from the fact that she had been given the key; but Susan had an idea that it wasn't completely wrong. Not when it came to finding the doors they needed, at least.

She wasn't surprised, therefore, when upon unlocking the door with the key that Janet silently handed back to her, she found Emmett sprawled on the floor halfway across the room with his back to the door.

Someone had hit him on the head, and although there was no blood on the carpet, there was enough clotting in his short hair to considerably worry Susan. It wasn't the only thing that worried her.

Dropping to her knees beside him, she said sharply to Janet and the master, "Get out—I'll bring him along as soon as he comes around."

"We can't go out, we have to go through!" protested Janet, while the master said at the same time, "Why? We have to keep passing through doors to get out."

"Stop there," said Mr. Oswald's voice, from the doorway. The hound growled as they all looked up to see the butler there with a short-barrelled shotgun pointing at them, her face taut. "This has gone far enough. Mrs. Carmichael wants you back in the outside manor so we can decide what to do with this cycle."

"That's why," said Susan, in exasperation, too late to be any good. It likely wouldn't matter where in the manor the doors were: if they kept doing the right things, the manor itself would bring the doors to them. Mr. Oswald with a gun, on the other hand, was quite another thing.

"Move back," said Mr. Oswald, her eyes wary.

"Mr. Oswald."

Both Susan and the bride said the butler's name, but it was Janet that Mr. Oswald looked at reproachfully.

"You shouldn't have done it, miss!"

Janet flushed. "I didn't do anything!"

That, thought Susan, her eyes flicking up from her ministrations to Emmett to look at the bride, was probably not entirely true. It hadn't stopped the manor from opening up, however, so whatever Janet had done, it wasn't an irretrievable step of betrayal.

Either that, she thought, her gaze dropping to Janet's bodice with the sudden realisation that the bride no longer wore her necklace, or it was the exact truth and had passed muster that way. She managed at last to turn Emmett's massive body over, and found that he was blinking at her dazedly.

"Oh good," she said. "You're not dead."

Emmett groaned, lifting a hand to his head, and tried to get up.

"Slowly, lummox," Susan said, helping him to sit. She pointed with her chin at Mr. Oswald and added, "You're making Mr. Oswald nervous."

Emmett's upper lip drew back briefly, causing Mr. Oswald to step back slightly. He said, "Going to kill us, are you?"

Mr. Oswald flinched, a brief tremor of movement across her transparent face. She licked her lips and said, "You brought it on yourselves. All you had to do was do the right thing, and everything would have been all right."

"I don't particularly like your way of doing the right thing," Janet said. "If it's the same as Mrs. Carmichael's way."

"You just had to resist temptation," Mr. Oswald protested. "Then everything might have been all right. But you always choose to save yourselves."

"I don't think you can really say that when Janet is there with the master," pointed out Susan. "It's not like she's betrayed him; she's trying to save him along with herself."

Was she mistaken, or did the gun barrel drop just a little?

"It would have been the same in the end," Mr. Oswald said, as if arguing with herself. "It always looks like it's going well, and then someone betrays someone else."

Susan looked meaningfully at Janet from across the room, tilting her head at the interior door that was just behind them, and saw Janet pinch the master's fingers. Then she ignited the protection spell that always clung to herself and Emmett in a single flicker of blue fire that flared and doused the both of them in an instant, and said very clearly to Janet, "Run!"

She wasn't sure whether the master dragged Janet through the door, or if she was the one pulling him away, but while Mr. Oswald jerked her shotgun back and forth in a flurry of paralysing hesitation and the hound darted behind Susan and Emmett, both bride and master appeared again, followed swiftly by Regan.

The housemaid bore a gun much larger than the one Mr. Oswald held, and the shiny determination in her purple eyes was unsettling. She said to Susan, "You can do what you want, but how well do you think a spell is going to stop a silver bullet?" She tilted her chin toward Janet and the master and added, "And if it doesn't work on you, I'll just shoot them."

Susan met Janet's apologetic look with a philosophic one.

Regan nodded at the blue fire. "Get rid of it."

Susan exchanged a glance with Emmett and then shrugged, releasing the enchantment. Blue fire flickered and vanished, and the manor around them became real and magic once again.

"I don't see how the manor is going to let you get away with this," she said. "I understand that it's malicious, but it does seem to be pretty caught up with rules, and I'm pretty sure you're breaking them."

"Don't you worry about that," said Regan. "We've done it before, and we'll do it again—and if the master tries to stop us, well, we've dealt with that before, too. You're not the only ones who have to live here, you know. You make it dangerous for the rest of us when you do stupid things."

Mr. Oswald's shoulders seemed to straighten, making Susan's heart sink. "Get out of the room," the butler said. "We're going back out into the main part of the manor."

There was nothing else for it but to do as they were told; it was no good trying to escape without half the people they had meant to take with them, and Janet and the master were obviously unable to protect themselves via magic. Susan and Emmett walked ahead of Mr. Oswald and her small blunderbuss while Janet and the master followed behind with the hound, Regan a few steps behind them.

"Where does she want them?" asked Regan after they had been walking for a few minutes. To Susan, it sounded as if the maid was worried—a suspicion that was borne out when the girl asked a moment later, "Where's the rest of it gone? It's never been this hard to get back out before! And where is Mrs. Carmichael?"

"I don't know where she is," said Mr. Oswald. The muffled quality to her voice suggested that she was biting her lip. "I haven't seen her since this morning. We were just supposed to find anyone who went missing and bring them back to the morning room."

"If we can *find* the morning room," Regan muttered.

Susan reckoned a further fifteen minutes passed before the girl stopped them all again.

"You and I both know we're not going to get anywhere with this lot right now," she said. "Let's just take the key and go. Mrs. Carmichael is the one who knows her way around the inside of the manor. Let's throw them in one of the rooms and leave them there."

"We can't just leave them free in the manor!"

"We're not leaving them free; we're locking them in a room with only one door," said Regan. "And you know as well as I do that it's far more dangerous wandering the halls than it is staying in the room."

"You should be coming with us to escape, not stopping us," said the master. "How long have we worked together?"

"That's what I'd like to ask you!" Regan said promptly. "We've been together longer than I like to say, and I never thought I'd see the day when the master would put his trust in one of the flighty little pieces that get sent up here!"

"Maybe that's why we've been here so long," the master said.

"This room will do," Regan said, ignoring the reply. She called ahead to Susan and Emmett, "Stop there! Turn around carefully and don't get too close to Mr. Oswald, or I might just get nervous enough to pull the trigger."

Susan turned, Emmett doing the same beside her, and saw the paleness to Janet's cheeks—the sudden glitter to her eyes. That made her look more carefully at the door they had just passed. Having done so, she tried not to grin, because it must be the second door. Just like the first it was leather-ornamented and carved in sections, the dull paint green instead of red.

"In you get," said Mr. Oswald.

"All right," Susan said. "But I think it's locked."

"You've got the key, I should think," said Regan, her eyes sharp and malicious. "Go on. Open it."

Susan flicked her gaze up and sideways to meet Emmett's curious eyes, and felt comforted. So Emmett was thinking the same as she was! How delightful!

Janet silently passed her the key, and Susan unlocked the door. No sooner was it open than Regan plucked the key from her hand and tossed it to Mr. Oswald. "We'll take that. It looks like there's only a few windows in there, but I wouldn't try to climb out of those: it's only mist outside when you're this far in the manor. Some of the mist isn't empty, either."

Mr. Oswald caught the key and clasped it against the barrel of her gun, as though unsure of where to put it now that she had it, and motioned for Janet and the master to enter the room. They did so, hand in hand, with Emmett behind them, and Regan's eyes caught the hand-clasp.

"Last chance, master," she said, with a friendly sort of grin. "You might as well come with us; you're not going to get out of here with this lot. The master doesn't, you know; you'll only stop them in the end."

"I'm not going anywhere with you," the master said, his chin lifting. "I'd rather meet the end of the story with my bride by my side."

"Suit yourself," Regan said, with a scornful laugh. She said to Mr. Oswald maliciously, "Looks like you'll have to move up again, Mr. Oswald!"

Susan saw Emmett's furrowed brow as he tried to parse out the meaning behind the words—or perhaps the meaning behind Mr. Oswald's stricken look—and asked the flushed, miserable butler, "Is that really what you want? Do you really want to be trapped forever as someone you know you're not?"

"Nobody cares what he does when he's not around us," Regan said. "Shut your mouth, Miss Susan! So long as he toes the line when he's in public, he can be as odd as he likes in the bathrooms. Come along, Mr. Oswald."

"Inside," said Mr. Oswald, physically pushing Susan into the room.

The gun barrel pressed coldly against her ribs, chilling her skin, and was then gone. The door shut behind them a moment later, and they all heard the brief silence before a key scraped in the lock, loud and laborious. It was drawn out in just as clumsy a fashion, and Regan's voice muttered indistinctly as two sets of footsteps faded away.

Susan turned back from the door and said matter-of-factly, "I wish you'd sit down, lummox. You look like you could use a rest."

"Why did you come back for me?" he said, dropping down into one of the chairs. "You had the key; why didn't you leave while you could?"

"Because you're the key to me," said Susan, feeling remarkably happy about the situation. She sat down on the arm of Emmett's chair with one foot propped on the seat as he gazed up at her with narrowed eyes, and looked around the room in some satisfaction. This, she knew, was a lull in the story, and in her experience, lulls were very useful for working things out and getting things done. At the very least, no one had a shotgun pointed at their faces any longer.

The hound, as if it agreed, coiled itself in a semi-circle, laid its chin on its paws, and huffed a sigh.

"I'm starting to think that you might have had a better chance of getting out without me," the master said ruefully, squeezing Janet's hand and then releasing it.

He turned in a circle that took in the entire room, small as it was, and then removed the glass stopper from a blood-red decanter and poured a couple of measures of brandy into two glasses. Janet took one of them in her left hand and looked down at it with glazed eyes, then back up at the master.

Susan, her eyes fixed on the two of them, saw the dawning comprehension on Janet's face, and the curiously slow shift of emotions. The master lifted the glass to his lips as Janet's fingers seemed to reach for her pendant and failed to find it; the barest breath of a moment later, that same hand swiftly slapped the glass out of the master's hand.

"Don't drink that!" she said, in a choked voice.

"Good heavens!" said Susan, at last understanding Mrs. Carmichael's dire utterances and the exact reason for the lack of Janet's necklace both at once. "You came here to kill him, didn't you? That's what you meant about making sure that no one else ever had to come here! You came to the manor with the knowledge that there was something here that could kill him and the exact know-how to use it to kill him."

"You can't bring weapons into the manor," Janet said tiredly as the master dropped down into the nearest couch, very nearly frozen, and stared up at her. She sat down on the other side of the couch, avoiding his eyes. "Whoever or whatever enters the field of the story curse is changed into a form that fits the story. If it's a weapon, it gets changed into something else altogether."

Susan swivelled a little on the arm of Emmett's chair, and he made room for her other foot to rest on the seat of the chair, meeting her eyes with one of his brows raised.

"So you thought that it was a good idea to use a weapon that was already here," she guessed.

"I've studied poisons since I was a little girl," said Janet, turning her head just slightly to meet Susan's eyes briefly. "Ever since they took my oldest sister by force when I was eight. I knew that I wouldn't be able to take a weapon in if I went—and I had a very long time to figure out the best way to do what I needed to do once it was my turn. I managed to get my pendant in, and I even managed to get some information out."

"About the poisons room?"

Janet nodded.

The master looked dazed. "What are you talking about? There's no poisons room! You really came here to kill me?"

"How could I do anything else when you'd already killed my sister and hundreds of others?" demanded Janet hotly, leaning toward him in the fierceness of her anger.

"Me?" He stared at her, astounded. "I didn't kill all of them! I didn't kill any of them!"

"Not directly," said Janet, and she seemed even more exhausted than before. "But you're the master, and just because of who you are, they die! They're bred to die, allowed to die—they're *meant* to die. Because you're the master, and you have to have a bride."

"He's not actually the cursed master," Susan said, willing to be helpful in a love affair that looked as though it might last longer than the death of the manor and its story curse. "He was the footman originally. How long ago did the previous master die?"

The master swayed in his seat and said with difficulty, "I'm...the master. I have to be the master."

"He's not—he's not the original cursed master?"

Susan wasn't sure if Emmett or Janet was watching her with more attention—Emmett with a kindling understanding, and Janet with horror and hope both vying for precedence on her face.

Janet spoke again, her voice trembling, "He has to be the master."

The master said, "I...have to be the master. There's no choice."

"Think about it," Susan said to the master, very gently and slowly. "Think about what you just said. What do you mean when you say that you didn't kill *all* of them? What do you mean, you *have* to be the master? Who told you that you had to be something you aren't?"

The master stared at her, and it was evident to Susan that he was thinking about it directly for the first time, without any substance or interference clouding his thoughts.

"The curse has been stopping you thinking about things," she said. "You should probably try to answer the question. If you think it'll help, I'll ask in another way. Either that, or the lummox can ask."

"No, it isn't—" He stopped, and wet his lips. "That is—I don't —I'm not the master. I mean, I haven't always been the master. I came here—I don't remember when I came here. It was a long time ago, and at that time, I was a wandering musician, I think. Then I was a gardener until someone died during the story. I was a footman after that until the master died."

Janet stared at him, her eyes welling up again. "The curse isn't attached to you specifically?" she asked the master. "It's attached to the manor?"

"The manor is the curse," said Emmett, as if to himself. He had settled himself back in his chair as if perfectly comfortable to be imprisoned with Susan perched on the arm of his chair. He glanced sideways at her. "Or is it the ghosts?"

"I think the ghosts have been here so long that they've more or less melted into the manor—I fancy it's the manor itself doing the damage. Well, the manor and the spirit of the first master: either he grew into it, or it grew into him, but somehow the two of them seem to have been combined into a nasty mess of anger, mistrust, and bloody murder. The manor, or the first master, or both of them together, played with his son and his son's wife until the two of them were gone. They set the stage and the players, then make the same story play out over and over again—and they don't really play fair."

"The poisons room," said Emmett, in understanding. Susan didn't look at him, but it sounded as though he was smiling. "And the temptations to do away with each other or betray each other."

"Exactly so," Susan said. "And the manor was apparently clever enough or awake enough to be able to use the same knowledge that Janet came into the manor with, to tweak the story. I rather think that's how it did a lot of things."

A lot of things was a very nice phrase behind which to hide dreams and ghosts of Emmett. Susan couldn't help glancing back down at him, and saw that he had nearly closed his eyes—and if his head hurt anything like as much as hers had hurt when she was hit on the head, she didn't blame him.

She touched the top of his head to send a trickle of her own magic wriggling through his hair as Emmett asked, "Where *is* the poisons room, by the way? I wouldn't have expected any such thing to be in the manor."

Susan couldn't help laughing, deep in her throat. Emmett heard it and it seemed to rouse him: he tipped his head back to look at her again and seemed to find pleasure in just looking at her—which, she found suddenly, was far too much to deal with.

She cleared her throat and looked away, explaining, "The poisons room—it's the master's resting room. I don't know who put the plants in there, but it wasn't him. Every one of them is poisonous, isn't it, Janet?"

Janet shrugged without energy. "All of the ones I could identify were poisonous. But it doesn't really matter, does it? I couldn't bring myself to kill him—or to let her do it when she offered. Now it's too late, and we're probably all going to die anyway."

The master, his voice thick, said, "It matters to me."

Janet didn't react when he leaned over the foot of velvet that separated them and clasped her hand, but when he said, "You were just trying to stop the curse", tears spilled over, and she looked across almost fiercely to meet his eyes.

"Stop it!" she said. "You can't just let people walk all over you! I was going to kill you!"

"Yes, but you didn't," he said, and lifted the hand that was still reddened from her slap earlier to display it. "And you could have let Mrs. Carmichael do it and kept your hands clean, but you didn't."

"How are we supposed to get the Perfect Result now?" asked Janet, briefly meeting the master's eyes and then looking away again. "I won't—I won't try to kill anyone again. But even if Mrs. Carmichael and the others don't try to kill us today, how long do you think we'll survive now that the manor knows we know what's going on?"

"The manor can only bother us according to its own rules," Susan said, though she was aware that the manor had much the same attitude toward rules as she did. "All we have to do is get the key back again and move on to the next door. We've already been through two—the third one should do the trick, shouldn't it?"

Janet, of whom she had asked the question, nodded. "That's what they teach us as little girls. Everything is in threes in the castle on the hill if you live long enough. Red, green, and blue. I knew there would be three doors."

The master looked at her in horror. "You learned about this as a child? They teach it to you in school?"

"Where else are we supposed to learn the things we'll need if we want to try and survive?" she asked simply. Of Susan and Emmett, she asked, "Should we try the windows, do you think?"

"I'm more inclined to try the door again," Susan said, feeling her pockets for the lockpicks that she usually had stowed in the deeper, hidden pocket.

Emmett said briefly, "We're not going out the windows," just as her fingers closed about something big and familiar and metallic.

"Dear me," said Susan, drawing the manor key from her pocket and gazing at it in fascination. The butler must have slipped it into her pocket while she was pressing the barrel of the gun into her ribs. "It seems as though Mr. Oswald has made a decision after all!"

Emmett leaned forward, laughing, and rose. "Underestimating your charms again, stripling?"

"I very much doubt I have any charms that would appeal to Mr. Oswald," said Susan, springing to her feet. "Better, lummox?"

"I'll do," he said. "We'd best be moving as quickly as possible. I feel the place disintegrating around us."

Susan could feel it; she didn't doubt that Janet and the master, who each followed them to the door with alacrity, could feel it, too. The manor was falling apart, with a single thread still leading onward and outward, and there would never be a better or safer opportunity to get out.

She slid the key into the lock and it fitted without a single noise, making her chuckle again as it turned soundlessly. "Goodness," she said to Emmett, who was at her shoulder. "I should have known when I heard the other key scraping like that in the lock. Off we go —whoops! Maybe not!"

The open door, so close an escape, had been barred by two very tall, green-clad obstructions.

"Found you," said Footman One, with satisfaction.

"How delightful!" said Susan, and hit him in the face.

Both of the footmen stumbled back as if she'd hit them both together, Footman One clutching his nose, and the hound thrust itself into the hall, barking. Neither of the footmen made another move forward, their eyes moving warily from Susan to the hound.

"Came to help," said Footman Two reproachfully, at length. "You shouldn't hit us."

Emmett, who had pushed through Janet and the master to square up beside Susan, looked down at her enquiringly. "Is this something you know about, too?"

"Good heavens, no!" said Susan. Of the footmen, she asked, "Are you saying you want to escape as well?"

"Get in, get out, and do it quickly," said Footman One. "That's what we wanted to do."

"Yes, but *why*?" Janet asked. "What under the suns is going on?"

"No idea!" said Susan happily. "But the manor is doing something very unravel-y around us, so I really think it's a good idea to find the door we need and get out while we can."

"All right, but if they try to lock us up again—"

"If they try to lock us up again, I'll hit them both," said Emmett, interrupting Janet. "Which way do we need to go?"

"The tight, coiled part," said Janet, her small, pointed chin setting. "It's like we're untangling a knot. I'll know the door when I see it."

The master, his eyes sharper than Susan had yet seen them, grabbed Janet's hand and said, "This way!" pulling her toward the part of the manor that, to Susan, still felt most tight and puzzlesome while the rest of reality seemed to unwind slowly around them.

She met Emmett's eyes and, as one, they followed the others with the footmen behind them, until the end of the corridor seemed to draw near and dance before them in a shimmer of movement and light.

Janet's footsteps slowed, as though by instinct, and she looked over her shoulder at the others. "Does it—does it look like *fire* down there?" she asked uncertainly.

"Heaven knows!" uttered Susan beneath her breath, and darted toward the end of the corridor with Emmett close behind.

She had barely made it to the end of the hallway when Mr. Oswald stumbled around the corner, clutching one bloody arm to her chest. Her face all sharp angles and shadowed edges that lit with firelight, she said with wild eyes, "I've set fire to it. It's all going to burn."

SEVENTEEN

"Oh, good work!" said Susan congratulatorily. "That should sort out anything that we don't take with us as we leave. Are you coming?"

"I'm not staying here," Mr. Oswald said, with an odd light of triumph to her eyes. Susan thought that it was perhaps as close of an answer as the butler could give to that question right now, and she was satisfied with it.

"We can't go this way," Emmett said, striding past them to look up and down the hallway. "We'll only be trapped in the flames. We'd better go back the way we came and hope for another door."

"Have to go that way," said Footman One, shuffling past Susan and toward the flickering end of the hallway.

Emmett exchanged an astonished look with Susan and caught at the collar of his uniform. "Not that way; it's too dangerous."

Footman One, jerkily, said, "Hall. *Stand*."

"I beg your pardon?" Susan said, forgetting everything else to stare at him.

"Hall stand," said Footman Two, striding past her and then past Footman One, who also broke free.

Together, they loped toward the flickering flames and Susan, understanding far too late, started after them only to be jerked to a stop by Emmett's large hand around her arm.

"We have to go with them," she said up at him, almost wildly. "Brennan isn't burned—but he might be soon. They're going to get him!"

Janet stared at her, her fingers curled tightly into the hound's fur on one side and clinging to the master's arm on the other. "Why would they do that? What do you mean, you have to go with them?"

"Curran and Katrina!" uttered Emmett, and took off at a run after the footmen.

"Get each other out safely!" Susan told Janet and the master sharply, pressing the key back into Janet's hands. "Leave the door open for us."

Then she, too, hurled herself into the cinder-and-magic-edged hallway and after the others.

The smoke sank into her nose, her clothes, her hair, as she ran. And as they ran, the gardeners in the lead, the staircase to the attic began to appear from the smoke ahead of them at the end of a hallway to which it had no business being attached. Susan grinned a savage grin and pushed herself harder, though the smoke clogged her lungs as well. The footmen were too much a part of the manor —still so much more a part of the manor than being the Katrina and Curran that Susan knew—that the manor itself couldn't help but allow them into the areas they needed to be.

It couldn't do anything about the way that footsteps thundered behind her, either—two people at least, but Susan rather thought there were three—and she wasn't at all surprised to find that the door at the top of the smoky succession of staircases was a blue one, brighter than it ought to be in the half-light and shifting red of flames that licked at the staircase below them. Janet pushed through all of them to shove the key into the lock of the door, and as she did so, it seemed as if the entire manor separated from itself and expanded in clear, separate threads.

She tumbled into the attic and immediately threaded her way through the piles of furniture and trunks that filled the room, aware of the others doing the same around her but focused on her own search. Brennan was here—he *had* to be. He was the reason they had found the last door at all; they had all given up something to look for him, and for most of the present company, that something was the likelihood of being able to escape. As much as it had tried to force the results it expected, the manor, it would seem, was fair in the way it accepted the unexpected result.

She didn't see Brennan, but her hand alighted on something smooth and familiar as she caught herself on the corner of a trunk that had ripped through a dust cover, and a voice said creakily, "Thought...you'd get here sooner...old thing."

Susan, nearly weeping with relief, shouted into the roar of fire and the discombobulation of the manor unravelling around them, "He's *here*!"

The footmen were there at once: they didn't hesitate, but lifted the hall stand that was Brennan and made off with him—not toward the door again but toward the broken balcony that Susan had already plummeted from. The floor smoked and sank and snapped beneath their feet, but they strode on without regarding anything but the opening, and then they were gone.

"It's the way out!" shouted Janet, her hand gripping the master's. "I don't think there's much time before the floor collapses; we need to go now!"

Mr. Oswald didn't hesitate; she threw herself from the balcony as the hound danced on scrabbling, shifting paws, waiting for the bride and the master to escape. Emmett's hand closed around Susan's as the master and the bride followed Mr. Oswald, and the hound launched itself into the smoky unknown, but Susan still hesitated. There was something else—something she kept forgetting.

Her eyes fell on the tumbled, messy top of one of the trunks, and she saw firelight playing on carved, dusty, wooden horses. Five horses. Susan sprang for them with a wild laugh and began stuffing them into her pockets one by one as the floorboards moved warningly beneath her.

Emmett was there in a moment, scooping up the last three

horses in one hand and seizing Susan's hand in the other; he tugged her toward the final door, but she could hear someone screaming in rage, or fear, she wasn't sure which. As she hesitated, flames burst through the blue door and into the room, consuming the far end of the room.

"Come back!" said those flames, with the voice and very nearly the face of Mrs. Carmichael. "*You're ruining everything!*"

Susan hesitated once more, for the barest moment, her hand in Emmett's insistent one. Mrs. Carmichael and Regan had done and allowed dreadful things, but they were as much prisoners of the manor as she and Emmett had been—perhaps more.

"You can't save them," Emmett said in her ear; then he picked her up bodily and threw both of them into the madness of fire, freefall, and uncertainty.

The manor screamed, and Mrs. Carmichael screamed, and the entire world came apart at the seams as they fell. Then Susan hit grass with the dubious padding of a heavily muscled horselord beneath her and tumbled into a roll, rather more effectively protected by the arms around her from too much damage.

The world stopped turning and the hound stopped howling; Susan found herself breathless and motionless with her head on Emmett's chest, staring up at a sky that was real and clear and had three suns in it that were easily visible. Horses moved nearby in a solid, familiar sort of way that had Susan gasping with relief, and someone sobbed on her right while someone else coughed as though they had tried to use their voice in a way that wasn't quite familiar anymore.

"Got your voice back, Miryum?" she asked, and turned her head to see that the spot that had been full of hound was now full of Miryum, still coughing.

"Just," she said shortly, and coughed once again. Beyond her, the master sobbed with his head clasped to Janet's chest and her arms around him, and she added with a swift look at them, "Seems like it'll take a while to get used to. I'll go see to the horses."

Susan flopped down again to rest against Emmett's chest, feeling as though she wasn't quite ready for the harshness of reality yet. Since Emmett didn't seem to feel the need to move either, they lay as they were and watched the last of the embers dance in the air until the other horselords regained the use of their bodies and Miryum returned with the horses, whole and seemingly unharmed.

It was too much not to expect Emmett to get up and check on Juniper, and Susan was already sitting up when he stirred and rolled to his feet to murmur into Juniper's mane and pat his chestnut neck. Miryum, having found the horses and checked on them, immediately formed a commlink with her well-polished belt buckle, leaving Susan to think that she really ought to do the same to let Belle know she was safe, after all.

Rather too tired for the effort of finding something reflective, she looked around at the others instead. Mr. Oswald sat by herself, arms around her knees, shivering. She was having the same kind of reaction as the master—but without having anyone to do for her what Janet was doing for the master, it would seem.

Susan searched through the pack she shared with Emmett to find a light cloak and one of the packages of dried, sweetened plums that she usually carried, carefully manoeuvring around Emmett to do so. She tossed both items to Mr. Oswald, who caught them as though she had expected them to be pelted at her and gazed down at them for some time without using them, tears in her eyes.

"The one is warmer on, and the other is sweeter in," Susan advised her, and, looking around at the assembled, disordered horselords, said fondly, "It's good to have everyone back again, isn't it?"

"Tongue," said Brennan, gazing up at the sky. "Got one again."

"Good for you, Brenners," she said.

"All very well and good, old thing, but how was I talking in there without a tongue?"

Miryum ended her commlink for what seemed like the single purpose of staring at him. "Is *that* what you're most curious about?"

"You were a dog," he pointed out. "Had a tongue. Didn't talk. There I was, without a tongue, and I was still talking. Got to admit, it's strange."

"It's not strange at all," Susan said. "I very much doubt whether anything, curse or person, would be able to stop you from talking by the simple expedient of removing your tongue. As for Miryum, well, she managed to express herself pretty well. I should have guessed exactly who you were."

"We were otherwise occupied," said Emmett, looking at her meditatively.

Susan found that she couldn't meet that gaze. Somewhat at random, she asked Miryum, "What did they have to say? When you commlinked?"

"We've been gone a month without contact," she said. "The papers are all still here, so we'd probably better think about moving on as soon as we can. The horses seem to have been kept in some sort of stasis, by the looks of it. They're all well."

"Shall we go to the town first?" asked Emmett. There was a speculative sort of tone to his voice, and Susan doubted as much as he seemed to that anyone would want to do so.

"I'm not going," said Janet. She coloured a little as everyone's eyes fell on her, but put her chin up. "I know it's not up to me, but if you're all going there, I'll move on with Jasper to the next town. There's nothing there for me except excommunication or a trial, anyway."

The master, at the sound of his own name, lifted a head of what was now very ginger hair, and said somewhat hoarsely, "I'll go where you go."

"Of course you will," she said, and the fierce tone was back to her voice. The master smiled a little blindly, and she added, "They wouldn't let you in, anyway."

That, thought Susan, was painting it rather mildly. She was quite certain that the master would be dead within a few minutes of entering the town below the hill. Even if the town didn't collapse at the loss of the magic that had fed down from the manor, there were probably enough women who would share Janet's previous desire to do away with the man they thought had killed so many other women over the years. From their vantage point, Susan was quite sure that she could already see smoke in various places around the town—a decent amount of manor-connected furniture was probably burning right about now. That was another mess better avoided.

She asked the butler, "What are you going to do, Mr. Oswald?"

The woman turned her eyes away from the mound of ruins, her eyes bright with that fire that still burned somewhere within her, and said, "My name is Florence. That's what it was before I came here, and now that I'm going, I'd like it again. I'll come as far as the next town with you; after that, I don't know."

Susan would have liked to have asked if the others had different names—had the manor hid away the names of Helfer and Regan, and even Mrs. Carmichael, and simply slotted them into the parts of Helfer, Regan, and Carmichael as they fit?—but the horselords were already on the move to prepare their horses. There would be time to go over what had happened and find out where everything now fitted in the slightly different world they had emerged into.

"I don't fancy being run out of town," Emmett said. "Or killed. I'm for the next town and finding somewhere out of the way to bunk down."

"Next town," said Curran and Katrina in concert, and glanced at each other somewhat ruefully.

"Not going anywhere that I'll have to be in danger of my life again," said Brennan. "Had enough of danger while you two long-legged bottle-bobbers were carting me around the manor. Might as well make for the next town and call m'mother to let her and the girls know I'm safe."

"Don't worry, Brenners," Susan said. "I won't let anyone else turn you into a hall stand, and I'll make sure Emmett approves of any and all towns we enter."

"That'll be the day," he said gloomily, and Susan couldn't help laughing.

Some things might now be subtly out of place and not quite right, but Brennan's gloominess was as familiar as it was comforting.

. . .

Freedom from the manor gave Susan a clearer mind to think. The journey on to the next-closest town, where they might have a chance to contact Glause and family again without worrying about being caught by any possible pursuers, also gave her the time to think, sheltered as she was from Emmett's attention by his broad back.

Given such time, it occurred to Susan—at some stage between swinging herself into the saddle behind Emmett and dismounting after a good five hours' slow riding to keep pace with the walkers—that rather than obliterating her heart-squeezing feelings, the destruction of the manor had had absolutely no effect on them at all. If anything, they seemed to have become more solid and difficult to avoid—though perhaps the difficulty lay in the fact that she spent the entirety of that time with the solid warmth of Emmett in front of her.

She was perturbed enough with her discovery to help the horselords unsaddle and brush down the horses in complete silence, and when they sat down to eat and drink that night, she carefully avoided her usual place next to Emmett. She hadn't considered that this would put her under his thoughtful, considering gaze from across the table, and while the others ate and drank and laughed with Janet and Jasper—rejoicing, no doubt, in the return of their human bodies and abilities—Susan found herself mumchance and worried. At some stage, she would have to excuse herself to Emmett for the ways in which she'd shamelessly used him during their time in the manor. Feeling as she did, she doubted her ability to be able to do so without giving away her true feelings.

At some stage in that far-too-long and far-too-hot night, Susan found Janet sliding into the seat next to her, which Brennan had vacated not more than a few moments ago. She was thankful for it —Emmett had risen just as soon as Brennan left his chair, and she had been suddenly, dreadfully afraid that he was going to sit there instead.

"I'm sorry that things got so...confusing in there," Janet said, with a shy kind of honesty that Susan was beginning to suspect was her chief weapon. "I think I must have figured out that it was the manor that was cursed instead of the master himself just a little while after you did, and I couldn't think how to tell you without saying too much. All I could do was play games and try to make sure I wasn't misunderstanding you."

"Oh well, I fancy I'll have to say the same back," Susan said, just as frankly. "I knew I had to play the part of the Jealous Maid, but when you started to play back to me with the Jealous Mistress, I was never quite sure whether it was real or not. By the by: the night before Brennan disappeared, you were talking things out with him, weren't you?"

Janet looked down into her cup. "Yes. I always had the dilution syrup in the suite, but I'd been looking for the poisons room, and I finally figured out how I was going to get it that night."

"Yes, he told me not to drink anything without letting the hound at it first," said Susan, a bubble of laughter rising in her chest in spite of her heaviness. "I found your dilution syrup, but I'm afraid it didn't occur to me that it was a medium for dispensing poison to anyone but yourself—or to connect it with your pomander!—until you stopped Jasper from drinking whatever it was that Mrs. Carmichael left."

Janet drew in a deep breath that shook a little. "I thought for too long before I did it, even then. Sometimes I think that the manor was right to expect the worst of me."

"I find that you often get what you expect," Susan said. "I wouldn't be too hard on yourself—you did think he'd killed your sister, and you didn't kill him, after all!"

"I'm glad I didn't," she said, her eyes on Jasper, who gazed back at his bride with an adoration that made Susan's mouth twist a little in rue.

The master and the bride had got their happy ending, whether within the confines of real life or the story. They had given up enough to appease the story and had got it back tenfold. Susan was inclined to think that she had given up something that she would never have a chance to get back.

"Then you must have been the one who dosed the master— Jasper—with lilly-pilly," she said, looking away. "I thought it was Mrs. Carmichael, but that was the night you got what you needed."

Janet laughed as if she couldn't help it. "I was so angry! He'd given me the key and told me that I should get out as quickly as I could without even trying to save himself. That night, even after he'd already given me the key, he trustingly drank whatever I gave him!"

"I can see how that would be irritating," Susan said, and this time, her smile was genuine.

"Mrs. Carmichael came to me this morning—or whatever time it was before you found me in the breakfast room. She seemed to know exactly what I had planned, and she said that if I wouldn't do it, she would. She said I'd gotten soft, and asked me whether or not I really cared about being free and freeing everyone. I already had the poison by then, of course, but I couldn't bring myself to use it. Somehow, I couldn't bring myself to throw it away, either. Now that I know that Jasper wasn't the master—"

Janet stopped and shivered, and Susan felt a certain coldness creep over her own skin.

"It was a setup from start to finish," she said. "Even if you'd killed him, it would have just picked someone else to be master and started all over again, and of course you would have died for betraying him. The whole thing was terrifyingly clever—although, I think the most frightening thing was how mindless it was! All those rules and regulations, and all the possibilities that were accounted for, and there wasn't more than a mess of ghosts and maliciousness and far too much magic!"

"That's why I can't be sorry that Mrs. Carmichael is dead," said Janet. She said it defiantly, but looked down again despite that. "They all—we all had the same choice. And I know that the manor was pushing us the way it was, but we all chose to do what we chose to do."

"Yes," said Susan, rather hollowly. "We all chose to do what we chose to do."

She waited until Janet and Jasper began to talk of retiring for the night, then slipped away during the good-natured ribbing that ensued, feeling slightly flushed from wine and the warmth of the night. Her room was hot and sticky, however, and Susan felt scarcely less hot and sticky. She climbed out her window while the others were still talking and drinking in the next room, and dangled herself over the edge of the roof to drop into the garden below, through which she had already seen a pleasant creek.

Emmett was waiting for her when she climbed softly back onto the roof, cool and refreshed and still a little bit damp, to sneak back into her window. She saw his huge form by moonlight, propped up against the outer wall of her room with his arms resting on his knees.

Susan regretfully gave up her first idea, which was to bid him a breezy good night and climb swiftly back into the safety of her stuffy room, and instead sat down beside him, resolved to have the thing over and done with. Emmett must certainly have noticed that she had been withdrawn and uncommunicative throughout the day.

"Ah," he said, as she sat down. "So you are going to talk to me again. I wondered if you'd just go back in."

"There's no fun in that," Susan said, with the faintest of rueful laughs. "What do you want of me?"

"I don't like being ignored," he said. "And I'm uncomfortable."

"Don't worry, lummox," she said, with a pinch of sickness at her heart. "You're free again. I'm not going to claim your hand in marriage to restore your reputation in the eyes of the world."

Emmett coughed, or laughed, she wasn't sure which. "Aren't you? What if I run into danger with a runaway bride again?"

"Then you'll be free to either accept or decline her advances as you choose, without a story curse muddying the waters for you, I suppose," said Susan.

Emmett's hand closed reflexively and relaxed again, and Susan would have liked to have thought that it was frustration in his voice when he asked, "Are you saying that everything that happened in the manor was the curse? The feelings, the kisses?"

Susan took in a breath and let it out rather more quickly than intended. Emmett was being far blunter than she had expected of him, and she couldn't be anything other than honest in return.

"No," she said. "Well, not for me, at any rate. The manor must have picked up something from me that made it spin the story in that way when everything began, and I'm afraid you got caught up in it because of me. There's no need for you to worry about it. They're my own feelings, and I'll sort them out."

There was a silence that went on for a little bit too long to allow Susan to avoid looking at Emmett. When she did look at him—a quick glance sideways when she couldn't bear it another moment—his head was down, and he was looking at his hands.

She knew that look: he was considering what he was going to say, trying to find the best way to put the words in order.

It hurt to breathe, but it would hurt more to talk. Susan said anyway, "We're outside now, after all. You don't have to—you don't need to worry about my feelings. I'll get rid of them somewhere."

A quick breath escaped Emmett; he turned his head and said, "Horselords don't share their horses."

"You—what?" Susan said, bewildered. "Yes, you do! We've been burdening poor Juniper for the last few years!"

Emmett straightened and turned until he was facing her properly, then said with deliberation, "Horselords don't share their horses with anyone but a life partner. At the time, I would have throttled Brennan for trying to say it, but—"

"So that's what he was trying to say," Susan said, dazed and almost at random. Her chest no longer hurt, but it was just as hard to breathe as it had been before.

"I've been in love with you for years," he added, with a brief, private sort of smile. "It looked like there was nothing I could do about it without frightening you off, and I thought I'd rather keep going on as we were than risk losing you."

"As though I could have left you!" said Susan indignantly. "I don't think I've ever considered life without you from the moment I met you. I'll have you know, lummox, I've been desperately trying to stifle my feelings in that dreadful place for the last week because I didn't want to take advantage of you!"

"I told you," said Emmett, lifting her far hand and passing it between his own as if he was seeing it for the first time, "that I wouldn't be so easily nose-led around the manor. You said that the manor picked up on feelings—why do you think I had such trouble with dreams before you did? I was following dreams that I thought were you down the hallway like a fool from the first night we were there."

"If they were anything like my dreams of you, I'm surprised they got you out of bed at all," said Susan frankly.

She would have continued, but as she spoke, Emmett took the hand he already held and cupped it against his cheek, drawing her closer in the movement. In fact, with the palm of her hand against his roughened cheek, her water-cooled fingers soaking in the warmth of his skin and the breath caught in her throat, Susan found she couldn't speak at all.

She wasn't required to do so: Emmett leaned toward her, wrapping his free arm around her waist as she shifted forward to meet him, and kissed her. Susan let go of thoughts and dreams and returned the kiss with all of the enthusiasm that had been squashed by guilt when she was still within the manor.

When they had settled back against the sun-warmed wall, Emmett's arm unfamiliarly yet comfortably around her shoulder, there was time for companionable silence and a slow but growing grasp of delightful reality.

Susan smiled out into the darkening night; Emmett played with her fingers.

He said, as if to himself, "As soon as I knew you were having dreams of me, I was certain you'd come into the manor with feelings of your own—I just didn't know if you'd realised it."

"I suppose," said Susan, with a very slight stiffness to her voice, "that's why you allowed Janet to cling to you and kiss your cheek."

Emmett's cheeks had reddened slightly when she threw a look up at him. He said, "Ah. That's something I'm not proud of."

"Good heavens!" said Susan, pulling away very slightly in amazement. "You were doing it to make me jealous!"

"The bride—Janet—already seemed to have a good grasp on what needed to be done to keep the manor happy, without saying too much aloud," said Emmett, his arm tightening around her. "It might have been the manor making me do it, but at least part of the reason I did it was because I wanted to know for sure that it meant something to you."

"Two birds with one stone, in fact," said Susan, nodding. It wasn't as if she hadn't done the same thing herself when she kissed Emmett in the breakfast room. "Lummox, you'll remember that I told you how I rebuffed a very sleepy master from using my shoulder as a pillow for your sake."

Emmett, who had laid his head on that shoulder a moment before, silently tilted his head and kissed her on the neck.

"Oh well," she said, catching her breath. "Just as long as you know it. Lummox, I don't think we can reasonably sit here all night and swap kisses; there's rather a lot to be done tomorrow, and I don't think any of us have slept properly in the entire week or month we were in the manor."

"I don't care much about tomorrow's work," said Emmett, nudging another kiss into her neck, this time closer to her jaw.

"Perfectly understandable," allowed Susan, "but Curran and Katrina are grinning at us from the window one over, and I'm pretty sure that Brenners is staring disapprovingly from above, so—Emmett! I won't be kissed in mixed company! You'll corrupt Brennan's pure young mind!"

ACKNOWLEDGMENTS

With many thanks to Dory Hulburt, Sue Snow, Peirce Baehr, Tiny Ladybug, Midnight_Moonlight, and Sarah Taleweaver, who each provided names for our players!